Darkness is Coming

by SM SMITH

Camelot Publishing

Copyright © 2020 SM Smith

ISBN: 979-8-675-06450-2

Dedicated to Heidi, Alex, Sabrina and Garrett

AUTHOR'S NOTE

Darkness is Coming is a work of fiction. Names, characters, places, events, and incidents either are the product of the author's imagination or are used fictitiously. Any resemblance to actual persons living or dead, commercial entities, schools, professional sports teams, events or locales is entirely coincidental.

PART ONE

"There's a darkness on the edge of town…"

Bruce Springsteen
Darkness on the Edge of Town

CHAPTER 1

Priscilla Cabot gagged down her vomit. Her jeans and underwear were soaked; the tang of urine overwhelmed her nostrils. Suffocating under a coarse burlap hood, her hands and ankles bound, she lay helpless on the back bench of the van. A coarse exchange in Arabic rambled up front. The word "bitch" didn't need any translation. She drifted off again.

The van slowed, waking her as it detoured off the main road, jolting her body with each bump. Rough, masculine hands yanked her to a sitting position and untied her. Her legs wobbled as she stepped outside. She fell on the scree, scraping a knee, a brew of phlegm, puke and blood erupting from her lips.

What will John say when he learns that I've been kidnapped? Her husband was president of Credit Lafayette, one of the largest banks in the world. He still loved her, would pay any ransom to bring her home safely. They would rescue John Junior too, their only child, gone missing on a post college graduation tour of Europe. Clinging to those tenets like flotsam in a stormy sea, she fought for her sanity.

The hands lifted her hood and held a canteen in front of her lips. She swiped her frosted blond hair from her eyes and nodded, too eagerly. The tepid water sloshed down her throat, spilling over her chin onto her stockinged feet.

Priscilla looked up into two masked faces, trying to remember their features, but the meeting outside the café in Istanbul, her son's last known address, was a blur now. Both men were medium height, wiry, strong. The one who had hit her wore a camo jacket, and was now pointing an automatic rifle at her; the other sported a black and white Real Madrid jersey with a knife holstered at his ankle.

She quickly surveyed the landscape, barren and deserted. The van blocked her view of the highway, but no headlights zoomed by. A blanket of stars still carpeted the night sky.

"Money? Dollars? You want money?" Priscilla rubbed her thumb and index fingers together in the universal sign for cash. No response from either of her captors.

"My husband is rich. He'll pay. Just don't hurt me."

"We know," soccer man replied, reaching back into the van and handing her a pair of orange sweatpants. He glanced at her soiled jeans and pointed to a scrawny bush by the roadside.

Priscilla clasped the sweats, searching for somewhere private. No luck and no sympathy either. She turned into the darkness and swept aside a branch. Both men kept her in full view. *Fuck them.* Peeling off her jeans and underwear, she squatted to pee, her stream crackling against the rocks and dirt. She pulled on the pants, cinching the waist cord to hold them up on her sculpted hips, and stepped forward.

Soccer man bound her wrists, a bit looser this time, and pointed to the van. She bet they were headed south for Gaziantep and then the Syrian border. She recalled videos on YouTube. ISIS hostages all wore orange too. The realization stabbed deep into her abdomen. *Breathe. Breathe. John will work out a deal. He's good at that.*

Soccer man got behind the wheel, while his buddy placed the burlap hood back on her head and guided her into a prone position on the back bench. The van slowed as another vehicle sped past. Her captors exchanged terse words.

Seconds passed. Another unintelligible exchange in Arabic. The van pulled into the left lane, picking up speed and passing the slower vehicle. The chassis groaned, but soccer man kept his foot on the gas.

The sounds of another vehicle on the right. Or was it the car that they had just passed? No, definitely a second car. Camo man shouted, panic now clear in his voice. A burst from an automatic weapon. Glass shattering. Bullets ripped into the van, pummeling his body. The van slowed, swerved, accelerated, then slowed again. Priscilla rolled herself onto the floor and brought her knees into a fetal position. Another round of gunfire.

The van crashed, buckled and came to a complete stop. Priscilla rocketed forward, wedging between the captain's chairs in the middle row, wind exploding from her lungs. Unknown voices shouted outside. Something blunt battered open the door. Fresh air washed over her. Boots tramped through the wreckage. A trace of floral body wash mingled with the stench of sweat, gunpowder and gasoline.

"Yo, Mrs. Cabot, how y'all doing?" a female voice with a Texas twang called out.

***

"Goodnight stars; Goodnight air; Goodnight noises everywhere."

Gangly tall with curly, chocolate brown hair, a freckled, button nose, and a bronzed complexion reflecting her mother's deep roots in the hills of Judea, Mayar Tabak closed *Goodnight Moon* and smiled at the twenty-odd tiny faces hinging on her every word. Their caretakers, ringing the perimeter of the cramped reading room at the Morningside Heights branch of the New York Public Library on West 113th Street, led a brief round of applause. A scowling, pony-tailed mom in lavender Lulu Lemon tights tapped her silver Rolex signaling for her daughter, preoccupied with the search for a treasure buried deep in her left nostril, to come to her.

A senior at the School of Engineering at Columbia University, just a few blocks north on Broadway, Mayar had volunteered to read to the toddlers for thirty minutes every other week since spring of her freshman year. She stuffed four large picture books into her backpack and slipped her right arm into the sleeve of her winter coat.

"Great job, Mayar," a deep baritone rumbled from the back of the room. A jovial black man with a beach ball body waddled forward. His son, Spiderman action figure in hand, followed a half step behind.

"Thanks, Mr. Montgomery."

"Jerome wishes that you would be the reader every day."

"So do I, but studying gets in the way."

"You still planning to take the Con Ed test after graduation, aren't you? It's a great place to start your career."

"Yes, sir. Thanks for all your help. That manual that you lent me really explained the grid." Mayar adjusted the coat on her shoulders and tugged the zipper to half-mast.

"Now, don't go shouting about that. I really wasn't supposed to give it to anyone."

"But you're not working there anymore, right?"

"No. I got an offer that I couldn't refuse, as they say. I started January 1 at JP Morgan - assistant vice president in their IT department."

"Wow. Congratulations."

"Well, we've got to be going. Tasha's got dinner on the stove. Say good-bye to Ms. Tabak now, Jerome." His son dutifully waved Spiderman in recognition.

Mayar tucked the folds of her beige hijab under her chin and secured the hood of her jacket over it as she approached the glass doors leading to the street. A February wind whipped an empty McDonald's bag down Broadway. Striding briskly, head slumped, her mind drifted to a photo that sat in a place of honor on the desk in her dorm room. Snapped last year in front of the Dome of the Rock on the Temple Mount in Jerusalem, one of the holiest sites in the Muslim world, it featured Ahmed, her half-brother, five years her senior, holding the hand of Fatima, an elfin girl in a dandelion yellow sundress about the same age as her rapt listeners this afternoon. *Where were the libraries for Fatima and other young girls in the Muslim world? Where were their schools?*

Lost in reverie, she almost missed the text. Ahmed lived in Haifa, but traveled frequently around the Middle East. They communicated now almost exclusively on Telegram, an encrypted messaging app.

Her phone, stashed in the back pocket of her jeans, burped again in the sequence that she had set up to alert her of his encrypted missives.

Mayar ducked into a bodega, removing a glove to read the disappointing news. Twice. Before the message self-destructed. *Inshallah. We will find another way.*

CHAPTER 2

"My life savings are gone. Just vanished into thin air." Sitting in a once pink armchair in the front parlor of a gracefully aging brownstone on Greene Avenue in Brooklyn's Bedford-Stuyvesant neighborhood, Elvira King shifted her cane to her left hand and adjusted the shawl around her shoulders. "Now, I'll have to sell this house. It's been in my family for almost a century," she added, her lilting voice cracking mid-sentence.

"We're here to help. Or try to, at least," Taryn Booker, 26-year-old cybersecurity manager at Brightify's New York City office, replied. Brightify was the world's largest social media company, providing a platform for almost two billion people around the world to illuminate the photos, timelines, likes and dislikes of their lives. "We don't get many handwritten letters these days."

"How long have you had a Brightify account? Does anyone else know your password? Do you keep it written down anywhere?" Rhonda Freed, her associate, machine-gunned the questions like a true New Yorker. The two young women sat on the sofa opposite Mrs. King, a battle-scarred coffee table nestled between them. Rhonda halted her interrogation to sip her tea.

"I'm not really sure," Elvira began, visibly struggling to collect her thoughts. "My daughter, Betsy, she's a nurse in South Carolina, bought me a computer and taught me how to use Brightify two years ago after my Wendell passed. She wanted me to stay in touch with her and the kids. I have three beautiful granddaughters." She pointed to the array of framed photos positioned on the table.

Taryn picked up a photo and admired the young girls. "Did you click on any of the ads on Brightify?"

"No. Betsy warned me not to. She showed me just where I could click." Elvira refilled Rhonda's cup. "Pretty fussy about it actually."

"Never?" Taryn asked, brushing an errant strand of her honey-red hair from her eyes.

"Well, almost never." Elvira straightened in her chair and sighed. "One time, there was an ad – it flashed – for Xeljanz. That's for my arthritis. Rheumatoid arthritis." She flexed the fingers of her right hand. "Couldn't do that before Xeljanz," she added, resting her hands in her lap. "Only problem is it costs over $2,000 a month."

"Wow. What about Medicare?" Rhonda asked. She looked out the bay window at a school bus passing by.

"Xeljanz is pretty new, so insurance won't pay the whole cost," Elvira responded. "This advertisement promised a 50% discount. With the first month free. If I had a Brightify account."

"Tough to pass up that deal," Taryn said.

"I knew it sounded too good to be true, but I had to check it out."

"So what did you do after you clicked on the ad?" Rhonda asked.

"I don't remember exactly. I typed in my Brightify password, but then I never saw anything more about buying my Xeljanz. Just a page with all these headlines about prescription drugs I never heard of."

"In English?" Rhonda again.

"Yes, although I did think one or two of the words were spelled funny. But then again, I never won any spelling bees," Elvira chuckled.

"Did you do anything else?" Taryn's turn now.

"No. Just went to bed and forgot about it."

"The drug site that you logged into was a trap. It installed a keystroke logging app on your computer," Taryn explained.

"A what?" Elvira asked.

"An application that secretly records all your keystrokes and sends them off to the bad guys. It slows your computer down a little, but you probably didn't even notice," Rhonda chipped in.

"So, that's how they got the password to my bank account. I check it every Sunday night."

"That's exactly right," Rhonda continued. "What happened next?"

"On Monday afternoon, I went to Key Food down the street but they rejected my debit card. Couldn't be, I said. I had just checked my balance the night before. But when I called my bank, Credit Lafayette, the branch manager came on the phone and said the account was empty."

"The bad guys worked fast," Taryn noted. "How much did you lose?"

"Twenty-seven thousand and sixty-three dollars," Elvira said, eyes forward, no emotion visible. She reached onto the coffee table and handed Taryn her bank statement. "It's a copy. You can keep it as proof, if you need it."

"That's a lot of money," Taryn said, folding the sheet into quarters and tucking it into her backpack.

"All I had, I get my social security. And I rent out the top two floors here. Had to refinance though, twice, to get them cleaned up." Elvira dropped her gaze to the floor. "It's hard to make ends meet most months."

"We can help you with some groceries," Rhonda offered, reaching for her purse.

"Now don't you be foolish. My church sisters will see me through."

"What did the police say?" Taryn asked.

"Two young men from the FBI came by. Said they'd try their best to get my money back, but they couldn't be too optimistic. I was the victim of a criminal gang located somewhere in Russia."

"You weren't the only victim," Taryn sympathized.

"Are you ladies hackers too?"

"No, not really. We're computer scientists, I guess," Rhonda replied.

"Mrs. King, we're going to look into your case. And we're going to do our best to make sure that those ads don't appear on Brightify ever again," Taryn declared, standing. "But we can't promise much more than that right now, unfortunately."

Out in the street, the two Brightifiers bundled up against the February chill. The temperature must have dipped ten degrees since the pale, winter sun had slid below the horizon.

"You headed back to the office?" Rhonda asked, her petite frame swamped by a knee-length Canada Goose parka. She knotted a navy cashmere scarf around her neck as Taryn, a full head taller, nodded.

"Look, we've waved the flag for Brightify. And Mrs. King really appreciated our visit. But you know we really can't do anything to help her, right?" Rhonda continued, pulling out her phone and tapping the Uber app. She lived about ten minutes away in Williamsburg, a much trendier section of Brooklyn.

"I just can't give up -- at least not yet," Taryn replied, shivering as she zipped up her black Mammul shell over her puff down hoodie. *Might as well be back home in Colorado. At least it snows there.*

"Don't drive yourself nuts, OK? I'll call you later." Rhonda flagged down a Prius that appeared to be hop-scotching along Greene Avenue.

"Got it," Taryn winked and headed for the subway back to Manhattan.

***

The ride back to her office, a desk in a bullpen in a converted industrial plant on the fringe of the meat-packing district, was too short for Taryn to formulate much of a plan. By moving in downtown ten years ago, Brightify was the first of the Silicon Valley tech giants to make a splash in the Big Apple, a move that ignited the growth of its advertising revenue and transformed the company into a money-making machine.

Brightify had recruited Taryn straight out of Cornell University's School of Engineering where she had graduated near the top of her class in computer science. The opportunity to work on the leading edge of technology and social media, combined with the six-figure salary, had proved irresistible. She fast-tracked through a rotation in product management, market research, and infrastructure development before the company asked her to head east and manage its cybersecurity activities in New York last year.

The button-down culture in New York, however, contrasted sharply with the free-wheeling style of the West Coast. The promotion last month of Marco Micolo, a salesman, to the top spot in the city was a clear statement of who ran the show here. Taryn had only met with her new boss twice. She doubted that he would know a block of code if it hit him on the head.

Taryn marched along the perimeter of the football field sized, open plan floor, a maze of low slung partitions delineating the boundaries of various departments and working groups. Exposed pipes and HVAC tubing crisscrossed the ceiling. She passed a punching bag, a smoothie bar, and a treadmill. An admin whizzed by on a motorized scooter. Business appeared to be bustling along as usual tonight.

Her three-person team was always easy to find: the Colorado state flag flew over their corral. Their primary goal was to defend the Brightify platform against the click fraud, trolls, fake news and hack attacks that might dissuade corporate advertisers from spending their dollars. The letter from an individual like Elvira King was a rarity, only reaching Taryn's in-box because of its connection to Big Pharma.

Karim James was at his desk, muscled neck taut, fingers waltzing over the keyboard, headphones nesting over his ears. Born in Harlem to a single mom, Karim had worked his way up through the prestigious Prep for Prep program. Football and programming, hacking to be precise, were his prime avocations. The former propelled Karim to a full ride at Yale, while the latter earned him his job at Brightify. Taryn tapped his shoulder; he turned and grunted a greeting before returning to the task at hand.

She passed Rhonda's empty space in route to the espresso machine. Rhonda Freed, a product of an exclusive Upper East Side, all-girls education since kindergarten, had won the New York state spelling bee in grammar school and was valedictorian of her class at Penn.

All this Ivy League talent is getting its collective butt kicked by a gang of Russian thugs. But not for long. Taryn returned to her workstation, steaming mug of cappuccino in hand. She speed-dialed James Mangano, her primary contact at the FBI. They met six months earlier at an FBI-sponsored cybersecurity seminar and had worked together on two previous intrusions at Brightify.

"Hey beautiful, what can I do for you tonight?" he answered. Single, street smart and Hollywood-hot – tall with wavy dark hair and classic aquiline features - Jimmy would have met every criterion on Taryn's Tinder profile, had she ever admitted to posting one. Only her personal prohibition against mixing business and pleasure kept her hands out of his pants.

"We visited Elvira King this afternoon. She said that she had spoken with two FBI agents. I'm guessing you were one of them."

"True that," he replied.

"I want to help her," Taryn said, running her tongue over her lips to savor the cinnamon flaked steamed milk.

"So do we. But there's not much more we can do. The cyber signature spells Russia - loud and clear."

"You're sure it's not local gangbangers that downloaded some Russian malware?"

"Yeah, we're sure. They cracked the SHA-1 digital certificate hash.

That takes at least six figures worth of brute force compute power. And we traced them back to a server lair in Novgorod, outside of Moscow. That's the territory of CyberBanda – a loose collective of hackers with ties to the FSB. Somebody's probably freelancing here, but we wouldn't be surprised if the gang does contract work for the Kremlin too."

"So, that's it?' Taryn drained the last of the cappuccino. Russia, Ukraine, Eastern Europe - that part of the world was all the same to her. Gray, faceless, and unrelenting. She envisioned an army of storm troopers sitting at their computers in a windowless room, puffing cigarettes as they launched poisoned emails into the ether.

"For now, yes. Look, you know hacking into foreign countries is barely a criminal offense over there. We have zero chance of an arrest, let alone a conviction."

"It's not even worth pursuing a search warrant to continue the investigation?"

"Nope. We've got other fish to fry. You should move on too. You're just banging your head against a brick wall."

"Can you give me anything to go on?"

"CyberBanda's leader goes by the handle of Viktor, but good luck in finding any more information on him."

Taryn fiddled with her keyboard, calling up a search engine. "OK, thanks," she added absentmindedly. Karim flashed thumbs-up as he left the office.

"It's almost eight. Let's have a beer," Jimmy asked.

"Thanks, but I've still got too much to do here."

"Tell me you're not going to work on this case."

"I'm not sure. I can be a blockhead sometimes." The vision of Elvira King's drooping shoulders and grimace of despair would not fade away.

"Bring me something with boots on the ground here in New York and I'll jump right on it."

"I'll remember that. Thanks." She said a quick good-bye.

Like the Kings, Taryn's family had lived in one home for her entire life, a two story, A-frame cabin just inside the main entrance of the six hundred acre IPO Ranch in Carbondale, just outside of Aspen. Her parents had managed the IPO for its owner, Bill Gunn, a private equity guy, since her dad's discharge from the army in 1991. Although Taryn was only twelve at the time, she recognized the fear on her parents' faces when they learned that the ranch might be sold because of Gunn's over-leveraged stock market positions. Fortunately, the market had rallied and the Booker family had stayed put.

Elvira King was not going to lose her family home if Taryn could help it. She dug out an old laptop from her bottom drawer. Scrubbed clean of any personal data and connected only to the "guest" Wi-Fi, it was her go-to weapon in cyberbattles. First things first, though, her stomach growled for dinner.

Bingos Pizza had delivered to her apartment last month. A great deal too. And they'd deliver right to the Brightify lobby.

After clicking in her order for a Hawaiian-style pie and Caesar salad, Taryn switched to the Tor browser to access the dark web. It would bounce her requests to servers all over the world, obfuscating her actions to all but the most sophisticated eyes.

She searched not for Viktor, but for the Fancy Bear malware that the Russians had used to attack the Democratic National Committee. Hackers were always looking to boost their street cred, and sharing the tools of their trade was a prime publicity vehicle. Taryn figured that if CyberBanda had ties to the Russian military, the gang might not be expecting an attack from that source. She also downloaded CryptoWall, a ransomware Trojan that might help Elvira get her money back.

Two hours later, her arsenal was complete and her pizza was history. Even though she was a cybersecurity professional, the ease of the entire download process was surprising. *How are the good guys ever going to win?*

All Taryn needed now was to bait the trap. She created a dummy Brightify account, buried her malware package under a timeline of photos and files, and began to Google search for information on Xeljanz and other arthritis drugs to attract CyberBanda's attention.

At three AM, determined to finish before her eyelids yielded, Taryn refueled with black coffee. The deserted floor had the spectral aura of a cemetery at night. It was a losing battle. Her head lolled before settling face down on her desk. A grizzly lumbered across her dreamscape, dipping its paw into a pot of honey.

CHAPTER 3

"Hey, wake up. Did you pull an all-nighter?" A familiar staccato penetrated the fog of Taryn's sleep. The aroma of hot coffee wafted from a Starbucks cup floating somewhere over her head.

Groggy, Taryn blinked and looked around, gaining her bearings. "Yeah, must have. Didn't mean to." She stretched her arms, noticed Rhonda sniff and recoil. "Grungy huh? What time is it?"

"Seven thirty," Rhonda replied.

"What are you doing here?" Taryn asked.

"I felt guilty about calling it quits yesterday afternoon, so I thought I'd get an early start today." Rhonda hung up her parka and sat down. "Bigger question though, is what are you doing here?" She tapped her keyboard to log in to the Brightify employee portal. "Better yet, don't tell me."

"OK." Taryn looked at her own screen, searching for a flashing Xeljanz ad or any other sign that an intruder had visited her dummy Brightify account. "Nothing doing here anyway."

"The smarter hacking gangs, like CyberBanda, sometimes wait and watch an account to make sure it's active," Rhonda noted without looking Taryn's way.

"You've done some homework."

"I re-read the FBI report last night. Shoot me over the name of your fake friend and I'll post to the account today. While you go home and shower."

"Thanks," Taryn replied, standing, shaking the last cobwebs from her brain. "Phew." Her armpits were worse than grungy.

***

Taryn returned to the office at four - rested, clean-clothed and deodorized. Rhonda and Karim were sleuthing away at their desks.

Taryn checked the newsfeed on her honeypot page from the laptop. It was now fleshed out with likes, comments, and tags. Rhonda had cleverly photoshopped herself into a snapshot. Unfortunately, CyberBanda still had not shown up.

Disappointed, Taryn shifted her attention to the backlog of work that had piled up. She closed the laptop and slid it to the corner of her desk, forcing herself to stay focused for the next two hours. Karim left early to meet his mom for dinner. They chatted briefly on his way out. Finally, the temptation proved irresistible. Taryn flipped the laptop back open.

"Bingo," she muttered, bouncing to attention in her chair. A Xeljanz ad flashed on the screen. She immediately clicked, followed the link to CyberBanda's phony Brightify logon page, and then entered the username and password for her false account. Within sixty seconds, Taryn's anti-virus tool signaled that malware had wormed its way into her system.

"Perfect." The bear had nibbled on the bait. A little more and she could snap the trap. Knowing that her keystrokes were being captured, she clicked around the web for several minutes, filling out a form for a free AARP newsletter and registering for a pottery class. When the malware delivered her information back to CyberBanda, it would deliver her own attack payload as well.

Noticing the activity, Rhonda wandered over to Taryn's desk. "Anything?" she asked.

"We're in the get-acquainted stage now," Taryn replied and provided a brief update on her progress.

"How long you think until our attack bot reports back in?"

"Hours, days, weeks, maybe never. If the Russians are as smart as everyone says, they'll destroy it and we'll never hear from them again."

"That would definitely suck," Rhonda said.

"Why don't you go home. You've been here all day. We'll check again in the morning."

"I've got just as little social life as you do. Let's grab a beer and come back later."

"Deal," Taryn replied, spinning her chair to fist bump her partner in crime.

***

"Unbelievable. Fucking unbelievable." Taryn could barely contain her excitement when they returned to the office an hour later. The screen of her laptop was loaded with files that her attack bot must have copied from the CyberBanda servers. She scrolled through several pages with Rhonda looking over her shoulder.

"Better than sex," Rhonda shared her enthusiasm. "Now what?"

"My favorite post-coital question," Taryn quipped, then pointed to her screen and turned serious again. "I'm not really sure. There's a ton of stuff here and it's all in Cyrillic."

"Karim minored in Russian, didn't he? But, who cares, you made your point. CyberBanda knows it's been hacked, right?"

"I think so, but we'll know for sure in forty-eight hours."

"What's going to happen in forty-eight hours?"

"I programmed my attack bot to put a ransomware lock on the CyberBanda server after it downloaded the files. The only way that CyberBanda can access them again is to pay up."

"Let me guess, twenty-seven thousand and sixty-three dollars?"

"Payable directly to Elvira King's bank account. In US dollars." Taryn held her bottle up for a toast.

"Brilliant. Fucking brilliant." Rhonda clinked in celebration.

"We need to tell our new boss. And Jimmy Mangano at the FBI too."

"Why tell anybody? At least not yet. Micolo could care less about the Russians. They don't affect his bottom line."

"Maybe you're right. It's too late to call anyone now anyway," Taryn replied, closing her laptop.

"Time to go home." Rhonda swilled the last of her beer, wiped the dribble off her chin with the back of her hand and tossed the bottle in the recycling bin.

CHAPTER 4

Taryn tossed all night, Cyrillic characters spinning around her brain like kids on a merry-go-round. Finally, at seven, she braked the carousel and climbed out of bed. She would talk to Micolo as soon as she got to the office. Mangano could wait. No boots on the ground here.

After fussing in her closet for a good ten minutes, she settled on khakis and a prim powder blue button down for her big meeting. No hacker-ware – jeans and tees - but no need to overdress today either. Micolo's guard would go up if he saw one of his techies too well-scrubbed.

Coffee and a yogurt in hand, she sat down in front of her home computer, a gaming grade rig that consumed virtually all her desk space. The apartment, a one bedroom plus deck on the third floor of a restored, pre-war brownstone on Bank Street in the West Village, was her pride and joy. Expensive, particularly for a walk-up without a doorman, but a great location within easy walking distance of Brightify.

Burnished hardwood floors, working fireplace, oriental rug, white sofa and loveseat filled Taryn's living room which flowed into a cozy alcove for her home office. Two windows, trimmed with thick muslin curtains, looked out onto the narrow tree-lined street. It was a world away from the isolated caretaker's house on the ranch in Colorado where she grew up.

Taryn scanned her inbox. Full, as usual. She dashed off a quick reply to a cybersecurity colleague in the Chicago office, skimmed an update on a systems development project in San Francisco, and deleted a handful of reminders from personnel. A message header from Con

Edison, the company that delivered electricity to the city – including her apartment - caught her attention. It seemed to be asking her to logon and confirm her credentials. Another phishing scam, she probably received at least one of these lures every day. She stashed it without reply.

Running late now, Taryn hopped into a taxi for a ten-minute ride to work. As head of the office, Micolo was the only executive who merited a full-scale, glass-walled suite. She hoped to catch him before his first appointment, but his office was still dark when she got off the elevator.

Taryn was pleased to see that her team was already going full speed. She pulled the attack laptop from her drawer, nudged Rhonda and pointed to Karim, lost in his computer and his music. Might as well put the Russian expert to work.

Rhonda playfully massaged Karim's neck to get his attention. He wore a powder blue Yale hoodie over cargo shorts, the macho uniform of choice for hard-core techies this winter. "Yo, big guy," Rhonda said when Karim finally removed his headphones.

Taryn scrolled through the voluminous listings that she had hijacked from CyberBanda servers the night before. Files, folders, apps, docs, executables, emails – probably layered in some hierarchy and password protected. "I need you to make some sense of this for me."

"What do you want to know?"

"All I want for now is a summary of what's here." Taryn paused, scanning the listings again. "But, don't go opening any files yet, OK," she added.

"Where'd you get this stuff?" Karim asked.

"Not your concern." *I want to protect your deniability.*

Rhonda arched her brows, but said nothing. She fiddled with the buttons on her cardigan.

"OK, boss lady. I'll get to work," Karim replied.

Taryn returned to her desk and logged onto the Brightify portal. Response seemed really slow this morning. She wanted to kick the machine, but then noticed a handful of colleagues milling outside of the cybersecurity corral, waiting for her attention.

"What's up?" Taryn asked.

She was assailed with a cacophony of voices:

"We wanted to check on system performance."

"The help desk is overrun with complaints."

"I heard that Brightify was hit with a DDOS attack. A big-time DDOS attack. Like a million devices in the botnet."

"It might take down the whole city."

"Whoa, I'm cybersecurity, not network operations. I'm sure the network ops center in San Jose is on it already," Taryn soothed. A botnet was a collection of internet-connected devices, including computers, phones, and even thermostats, that were harnessed together like robots by a master controller. In a Distributed Denial of Service (DDOS) attack, the controller would command the botnet to overwhelm a target website with traffic, potentially bringing it to a crashing halt.

Again, replies waterfalled from the group:

"A botnet this large could only be run by a big-time player."

"Or a nation-state."

"Like China. Or Russia. Someone's who's really pissed off."

"Why Brightify?"

Shit. Fuck. Shit. Taryn peered down the long corridor to Micolo's office. The light was on. "Let me get back to you guys," she answered, as she burst through the group and arrowed towards the corner office.

Wearing a navy blazer, pink shirt and honey bow tie, Micolo was talking with a junior salesman, also suited up, although in a less blinding array of colors. They had obviously just come from a client breakfast, learning of the botnet attack as soon they reached the office.

Micolo dismissed his subordinate and closed the door. He ushered Taryn to sit down on one of the two Scandinavian teak chairs positioned in front of his glass table-topped desk.

"Clients are lighting up the phone lines already. Please tell me that Brightify is not going to crash."

"Our NOC team out west is the best. They've been hit by DDOS attacks before. I bet they'll have a status report posted any minute."

"That's not too comforting," Micolo replied, shooting his gold cufflinks as he steepled his hands on his desktop. "Our advertisers will not pay for a social media network that no one can access."

"I'm sure by now our guys will have identified the sources of the attack and diverted the message traffic. Then they'll bring as much server capacity online as necessary to restore operations to an acceptable level. We'll go to the cloud vendors if we have to. But I can't tell you how long that will take." Taryn fidgeted in her seat. It was going to get worse.

"If you're not here with an answer, then why did you come in?"

"I might be the cause of the problem." She explained her efforts to hack the Russians and get Elvira King's money back, leaving Rhonda's assistance out of the conversation.

"So, you launched a cyberattack against a Russian gang, possibly affiliated with the Russian government, on your own? Without the FBI? Without a warrant?" Micolo's voice steadily rose.

"Yes, sir. I screwed up. But, I joined Brightify to make a difference in the world, not sit on the sidelines like a tackling dummy," Taryn replied.

"You broke the law. You're not on the sidelines – you're out of bounds." Micolo paused. Taryn prayed he was looking for a bright side.

"How much did you recover for Ms. King?" Micolo asked.

"She lost $27,063, but I don't know if she got any of it back yet."

"Do you have any idea how much this little botnet attack is going to cost Brightify to fix?"

"A lot more than that, sir."

"Plus, the goodwill of our customers and advertisers."

"Like I said, I screwed up and I take complete responsibility."

"That's admirable," Micolo said, standing. He twirled to stare out the window, tracking an airplane on the horizon before turning back to Taryn. "Let's give it a few more hours. We don't have much choice anyway. Maybe this attack had nothing to do with you."

He rested his hand on Taryn's shoulder as he steered her towards the door. "No sense airing our dirty laundry in public unless we have to. In the meantime, I'll call our legal department and let them know about our conversation."

"Thank you."

"Go home and wait for my call. Don't talk to anyone else. Maybe we can keep this all in-house."

Taryn shuffled back to her team. *Is Micolo going to go to bat for me, or throw me under the bus?*

Unaware of Taryn's meeting with Micolo, Rhonda exploded out of her seat, barely containing her glee. "Elvira King just called. She said that all her money returned to her account. Credit Lafayette said it must have been an accounting error, but she said it was a miracle."

"What did you say?" Taryn asked.

"Praise God. Hallelujah."

"Right answer."

"I guess CyberBanda really wanted its files back," Rhonda said.

"I think I know why," Karim piped up, holding three pages of print-outs, folded in half. "You said not to open any files, but you didn't say I couldn't open the folders." He handed the package to Taryn and watched while she unfolded it. "This folder was nested three deep. I had to crack a password to get there." He pointed to a set of names circled in red on the top sheet. "The folder contained forty files. I don't think the names need any translation."

"Wow," Taryn said, skimming the key page. She passed it to Rhonda.

"No shit," Karim replied. "What do you think is in the files?"

"CyberBanda hacked these guys?" Rhonda broke in, almost shouting, but Taryn cut her off with a karate chop signal and reclaimed the print-out.

"This list stays with us for now." Taryn ordered, re-folding the pages and tucking them into the back pocket of her khakis. "These files could just contain a bunch of news clippings for all we know." She stuffed the attack laptop into her backpack and reached for her coat. "Or they could be decoys, or booby-traps."

"Where're you going?" Rhonda asked.

"Home," Taryn replied, providing a summary of her conversation with Micolo. "I'm the only one who reached into the Russian servers. I'm taking full responsibility," she added.

"Bullshit. We're all in this together," Rhonda confirmed.

Karim nodded, then checked a message flashing on his computer screen. "Our NOC has the DDOS under control. Brightify performance should be back to normal in the next hour."

"I have a feeling the fireworks are just starting," Rhonda said.

***

Taryn lit the kindling in her fireplace on Bank Street, watching the two logs catch, crackle and flame. *That could be my career — up in smoke — if I don't make the right move now.*

She dialed a familiar number in Ithaca, NY and wandered towards the windows as the phone rang. A light snow had begun to fall, dusting the treetops in white powder. The snow transformed her streetscape into a scene from an impressionist painting – for about 24 hours max. Then blacks, grays and yellows increasingly stained the canvas.

"Hello," a matronly voice answered.

"Hi, Dr. Bierman. It's Taryn Booker."

"Taryn, it's wonderful to hear your voice again. It's been too long." Even after twenty-five years in upstate New York, Hayden Bierman's voice had never lost its melodic, Southern cadence. The eldest daughter of a prominent Charleston rabbi, she came to Cornell to teach labor history and fell in love with a fiery Russian immigrant who taught computer science.

"I know. I keep meaning to drive up but work always seems to get in the way."

"You're calling for Lev, I presume?"

"Yes, is he home?" After acing Professor Lev Bierman's courses in her freshman and sophomore years, Taryn had been invited to join a coterie of top students who assisted the professor both with his mundane teaching requirements and his special projects. She had fond memories of winter evenings in Ithaca, sipping port in front of the hearth in their rambling Tudor home on Cayuga Heights.

"No, I'm sorry to say that he is out of town. Again. He will be so disappointed to have missed your call."

"Can you please ask him to call me as soon as possible? It's urgent." Rumors had always swirled around the Cornell campus that the professor donned a superhero cape at night to serve as a senior cyber advisor, private jet waiting to whisk him around the world at a moment's notice. Taryn could confirm several of his accomplishments on the FBI's National Cyber Investigative Joint Task Force, if she wanted to spend the rest of her life behind bars.

"Why, of course. You take care now. And come see us."

Taryn walked into the kitchen, her laptop beckoning from the table. She ignored it, heating up a can of soup on the stove and microwaving a leftover breast of chicken for lunch. After cleaning up, she withdrew the laptop and cradled it in both hands. *What's in those files? What's the harm in peeking?*

The buzz of her mobile saved her from a decision. No caller ID.

"This is Taryn."

"Ms. Booker, always a pleasure to hear your voice."

"Professor Bierman?" She had no trouble identifying the guttural cadence.

"Yes, yes. Returning your call."

"Thank you. I need your advice."

"I saw that Brightify got into a little scrape today. With a nasty gang of my former countrymen, if my sources are correct." Born in Moscow, the Professor taught Applied Mathematics at Leningrad State University, since renamed St. Petersburg State, for ten years until he emigrated to America in 1998.

"That's right. But there's more to the story." Taryn provided the details of the past two days.

"An admirable goal on your part, but rather like sticking your fingers into a beehive. One has to wonder if the prize is worth the pain."

"That about sums it up."

"I'm going to text you a number. Can you take a photo of the list of names and send it to me?"

"On the way," Taryn replied, switching her phone to her left hand to snap the picture. "I recognize most of them, but I'm not really a Politico junkie." Taryn paced the apartment while the Professor reviewed the list.

"Quite an impressive club – congressmen, senators, governors, the mayor of New York, a smattering of CEOs. Even two prominent members of the Russian Federation Council."

"So CyberBanda's gathering political dirt?"

"The Russians are experts at *kompromat*," Bierman declared.

"They certainly helped our President get elected in 2016."

"Now, I believe Moscow may be searching for ammunition to keep him there in 2020."

"That's a pretty sinister interpretation."

"Typical of a liberal, left-leaning professor at a major East Coast university."

"If the shoe fits…," Taryn chuckled.

"You jest, young Ms. Booker. But I crossed paths with Mr. Putin when he was a senior advisor in the St. Petersburg mayor's office, promoting business opportunities for his cronies. He is a devious man. When Yeltsin promoted him to run the FSB, I knew it was time for me to find a new home."

"What if *these* files are just a bunch of news clippings?"

"Highly doubtful, but there is only one way to find out."

"So, I can dig in?"

"Fire away."

Taryn sat at her desk. "I'll start with the Governor of Colorado. He visited the ranch once to meet with the big boss. I saddled up his horse."

"I'm waiting," Bierman replied.

"Tax returns…an email exchange with a well-known oilman in the state…his two kids' report cards…a physician's report after his wife's visit to an alcohol rehab clinic – that was always in the rumor mill."

"Nothing explosive here, but CyberBanda is clearly trolling. Illegally, I might add."

"No surprise. Should I check a few more names?" Taryn asked.

"No. I think that would put you in an even more compromising position."

"I'm already compromised. It's hard to be half pregnant." She paced into the kitchen and back through the living room.

"There is nothing you could do with the information anyway. At least nothing that would help your cause. Let me run your situation by one of my contacts in Washington."

"OK. I'll sit tight."

"That's the best plan. Given the DDOS attack today, I think we can safely assume that CyberBanda has traced your hack to Brightify but not necessarily to you personally. Otherwise, you would have heard from them directly."

"But they know *someone* at Brightify now has access to their files. That might prompt the gang to act sooner rather than later to try to flush me out," she said.

"True, true. I'm out of the country now, but I'll get back to you within twenty-four hours. Hopefully, your analysis will not prove prescient.".

CHAPTER 5

The next morning, Mayor Bernard Rosen, flanked by two aides, strode up the broad steps and past the Greek columns that served as sentries for the grand entrance of New York's City Hall. Completed in 1812, the renaissance-style palace was originally New York's tallest building, designed to provide stature and elegance to the mercantile capital of a fledgling nation.

He stopped under the balustrade and turned, forcing his entourage to brake quickly. Newly elected last November, he still thrilled at the view of his city from this vantage point: the well-fortified plaza anchoring a leafy park, pedestrians bustling around its borders, the skyscrapers of Wall Street lurking down Broadway.

Or, maybe Bernie liked this spot because he felt tall here, a giant almost. At five feet seven, there were not many places where he felt larger than life. Born in Brooklyn, educated at City College and Columbia law, a career civil servant, New York had always been his home.

Rosen entered the marbled lobby, silently saluting the bronze statue of George Washington that greeted him. His gaze lingered on the sweeping stairway leading to the second floor of the grand rotunda, where Abraham Lincoln's body had lain in state after his assassination, and then up again towards the rosette-tiled domed ceiling. The upper floors were typically reserved for ceremonial events.

"Good morning, Loretta," Rosen said to the senior officer of the security detail guarding his working sanctum, a wing just off the lobby on the main floor.

"Morning, sir."

His executive assistant, Katherine Whitworth, a regal woman who had served the two previous mayors, sat at her post in the vestibule outside his private office. Highly capable, she added a white shoe veneer to a blue-collar administration. "Briefing papers are on your desk, sir. You have meetings at ten and eleven. No plans for lunch today."

Rosen nodded, skipping the pleasantries, anxious to get the day started. It was the people's turn now, the mantra that guided his team, cementing his bond to an electorate weary of a city government that had tilted towards the wealthy and powerful for too long. Education, housing and recreation for the masses would be the pillars of his first term. Only forty-eight, he dared to dream of a lengthy tenure in this office.

Before he could settle, Serena Thomas, his chief of staff, a normally affable African-American with unruly curls spiraling in every direction, appeared at his doorway. As Rosen's top deputy for the past ten years, she was the only staffer with walk-in access. Her tortured expression signaled a situation that required immediate attention.

"Please tell me this report is fake news," she croaked, lifting the remote off the conference table and switching the channel on the television imbedded in the far wall from CNN to Fox News.

SEX TAPE SURFACES
MAYOR ROSEN IN MOSCOW THREESOME

The headline scrolled across the bottom of the screen, while two commentators discussed the details. DC Leaks, a website allegedly involved with the Russian hack during the presidential campaign, had just published several photos, not suitable for viewing by all, the commentators warned. The site also threatened to release a full video.

After a five second pause, ostensibly to allow viewers to usher the young or prudish out of the room, a still image filled the screen: Bernie Rosen, or someone with an extremely close resemblance, wearing only his boxers, sandwiched between two buxom, Slavic beauties, nipples and pubic regions airbrushed to meet broadcast standards.

The mayor gagged, slumping into the chair behind his desk, transfixed. "It's not fake," he croaked. One night, almost two years ago, too much vodka, too far from home. *I was front-runner to be the next mayor of the greatest city on earth. I felt like I could leap tall buildings in a single bound.* He had never told his wife, Jacqueline, or anyone else.

With no word from the women, fellow attendees at an international conference on urban planning, since the incident, Bernie prayed the evening was buried for good. The women said they were from Novgorod, he remembered, joking that it was just south of Gomorrah. He realized, too late, that they had tried to warn him. *The day of reckoning had come at last.*

Another photo rotated onto the screen, all participants now unclothed, then a third and a fourth, Bernie's face clearly recognizable in each one. The camera must have been in the wall at the head of the bed. It was all a set-up. *But why? And why now?*

His wife, his sons, his office, his city — Rosen's brain careened out of control. He couldn't focus on what the commentators were saying. Dry-heaving, he reached for the trash bin.

"Mayor Rosen, Bernie, are you OK?" Serena rushed to his side, reaching for his elbow to provide support. He could see Ms. Whitworth discretely close the door, a concerned frown on her normally stoic face.

"Yes, I think so." Rosen straightened, inhaled deeply, three times. He pointed to the television. "Please turn it off."

Serena plodded across the room to do his bidding, returning at the same funeral pace to sit in the leather armchair across his desk. "We're going to have to comment. Soon."

"I need to talk to Jackie first." They had been married for twenty-four years. Good years. Faithful years. Rosen speed-dialed from his desk phone. First, the private line at Gracie Mansion. No answer. Then Jackie's mobile. Her recorded greeting asked him to leave a message.

"We can deny it all. Claim the photos were Photoshopped," Serena offered. "We can sue DC Leaks and Fox."

"Someone will dig up hotel records or my expense reports. Or interview the bartender. Or the doorman. I was housing commissioner at the time. The trip was legitimate city business."

A sharp knock on the door. Ms. Whitworth opened it. "Your wife is here."

"I'll leave you two alone," Serena said, rising. "But we need to have a statement by noon at the latest." With a sympathetic nod, she acknowledged the First Lady, no make-up but dressed in gray wool slacks and a cowl neck sweater, as they passed.

Shorter than her husband, and rounder, Jackie Rosen maintained her composure until the door clicked.

"Was that you?" she pointed to the dark television monitor. He nodded robotically.

"*Putz!* How could you do this to us? All of us?" The agony now clearly visible on her face.

Bernie stood, reached for his wife's hand. "I'm sorry."

She yanked her fingers from his grasp. "I'd rather pet one of those cockroaches in our old apartment...." She turned away, tears trickling down her cheeks.

"I made a mistake. An enormous mistake. But it was just once. I swear. I never met those women before that night or heard from them afterwards."

"Until today."

"I'll get down on my knees and apologize if that helps."

"What do the whores want? Didn't they reach out? Send a blackmail note, or something?"

"No, nothing. It's been almost two years."

"The TV claimed that a source at Brightify discovered the photos first. Did you post them, or text them, like some pervert?" Jackie staggered, then sat down.

"No, no, no. I never saw the photos before today. I didn't even know they existed."

"I wish I could believe you." She reached into her purse, fumbling with a packet of Kleenex.

"Please, it's the truth. I'd do anything to erase that night. Anything." He stood, hands at his sides, helpless.

"Then how did Brightify get them?"

"I don't know. I hadn't thought about it." He offered his handkerchief, but Jackie swiped it away. He watched it parachute to the hardwood floor.

"What are you going to say to the press? To the people? To your sons?" she beseeched.

Bernie sighed, sat down again behind his desk, head slumping into his hands. His fingers forged crevasses through his pompadour, gelled rigidly into place every morning like a glacial ice cap.

"I'm going to tell the truth," he replied, staring up at the ceiling, hair askew. The statement, now out in the open, eased the weight of guilt. He dropped his gaze to lock in on Jackie. "But I'm going to need your help. Please."

***

The Fox report of the DC Leaks dirt mesmerized the entire floor at Brightify, the drone of the newscast overwhelming the normal hum of activity. The cybersecurity team gathered around Taryn's desk to watch.

"That's bullshit! Why would anyone at Brightify leak those photos?" Karim screeched as the last photo faded from the television screen. "How would anyone here even find them?

"Who would have believed that little mensch had it in him? A threesome, no less," Rhonda asked rhetorically.

Taryn ignored the banter, concentrating on Fox's comments regarding Brightify, a ripple of nausea roiling her stomach. This was much worse than she had imagined yesterday.

"Wait a second. Rosen's name was on that list, wasn't it? Karim said, lowering his voice.

"Do you think CyberBanda's targeting Mayor Rosen, or us?" Taryn mused out loud. *Or me?*

"Us, as in Brightify? Or us as in us?" Rhonda asked, sweeping her palm around the bullpen.

Taryn's mobile buzzed before she could answer. No caller ID. "I've got to take this," she said to her team, stepping out into the corridor. "This is Taryn," she answered the phone.

"Ms. Booker, I am afraid to say that your analysis has proved correct. CyberBanda couldn't restrain itself any longer."

"Professor Bierman. Wait a sec. I need to find a private place to talk." Taryn stepped into a vacant conference room, closing the door. "OK, better now."

"I believe that the Russians felt they could kill, or rather tarnish, two birds with one stone."

"The mayor and me?" Taryn did not appreciate the professor's first choice of verb.

"The mayor and Brightify," he clarified. "Since his days as housing commissioner, Bernard Rosen has been a thorn in the President's side. CyberBanda probably set up the sting with blackmail in mind, but decided to make an example of the Mayor instead."

Taryn sat on the edge of the conference table while the professor continued. "Brightify is a bastion of free speech. It amplifies the voice of the masses, often in opposition to those in power. And the chief executive of your company, I believe, has personally spoken out against Russia of late."

"Now, Brightify looks as tawdry as a tabloid," she said.

"CyberBanda's goal exactly."

"But CyberBanda's a criminal gang. They care about money, not politics."

"In Russia, there is little separation between the two. I fear our nation may be headed in the same direction," the professor said.

"You don't seriously believe that the White House is behind the release of these photos?"

"No, most definitely not. But I do fear that one hand may be washing the other."

"I'll save the analogies for later. What do I do now?" Taryn asked, twisting so that her back faced the glass wall of the conference room. And no one passing by in the corridor could read the desperation in her words.

"We are all voyeurs at heart, so those lurid photographs will occupy the public's attention for a little while," Professor Bierman replied.

"And then?"

"The public will want to know how they materialized. How they ended up on DC Leaks. Were privacy laws violated?"

"That may not bode well for me."

"But you did not leak them. You did not even know they existed. And you voluntarily reported your activities to your superior."

"I'm not sure if my boss will defend me." Taryn replayed her conversation with Micolo in her mind.

"But I most certainly will."

***

Refusing to wear sunglasses, Jackie Rosen squinted into the late afternoon glare, waiting for Bernie to advance to the podium on the top step outside City Hall. A sea of microphone-sprouting reporters roiled on the plaza beneath them, threatening to surge upward and spill into the venerable building. She knew now how her Jewish ancestors must have felt, huddled in the public squares of medieval Europe, waiting to be burned at the stake.

Bernie reached for her hand, trying to interlock their fingers in a public display of solidarity, but she balled them into a fist, forcing his retreat. Instead, Jackie fussed with the waistband on her charcoal suit. She had returned home mid-day to dress appropriately. *What's appropriate attire for the betrayed political wife to wear onstage anyway?* Her hairdresser had tried to tame her frizzy curls, but they appeared to have a mind of her own, framing her face in somber hoops of gray.

She stole a furtive glance at her two sons, rushed home from college in Binghamton, standing tall in matching Navy blazers on Bernie's far side. She was standing here on this stage for them, for their legacy, not for her cheating husband. *How could he do it? How could he keep it inside for so long? How did she miss it?* She wanted to smack him, scream at him, make him pay dearly for the public embarrassment they must all now endure. But that would come at home, later.

Wearing a navy pinstripe suit and a subdued maroon tie, Mayor Bernard Rosen stepped up onto the footstool that his chief of staff had discreetly placed behind the podium. He cleared his throat, sipped from a glass of water, and peeked down at the media howling for his hide.

"My dear wife, Jacqueline, and my sons, David and Robert," Bernie paused to shuffle his papers while the camera panned over his family. "First and foremost, I am here today to apologize to you and ask for your forgiveness so that we can begin to rebuild our life together."

The horn of a fire truck clanged in the distance. A protestor with a homemade sign, proclaiming 'three is too many for me', tried to climb over a barrier, but was restrained by the police.

"While in Moscow two years ago attending a planning seminar," Bernie continued, "I had a sexual liaison with two women. It happened one time, and one time only. I had no idea that the liaison was being filmed, and certainly never authorized the release of any photographs. I have never received any communication from the women, or anyone representing them. The incident has not in any way affected my ability to fulfill my duties as mayor, nor do I expect that it will have any impact going forward. Adultery, while defiling of both my family and my religion, is not a crime.

"I want to emphasize my deepest contrition for my actions two years ago, and repeat my apology to my wife, my family and my constituents. I breached your trust and I pray that I may earn your forgiveness."

Bernie took a half step back, almost stumbling off his makeshift platform, and let the crowd absorb his words. Then he seized the podium with both hands. "But, I also believe that we may be witness to a serious violation of the fourth amendment of the Constitution of the United States of America. As a citizen, I will utilize all remedies to defend my right to privacy. As mayor, I will ask the District Attorney to initiate an investigation immediately to protect that right for all of us. Thank you and God Bless."

Jackie watched the crowd disperse. No questions were allowed. She reached for her sons, pulling them close. They trailed Bernie back into City Hall. The apology was from his heart; it was the right approach.

But the final part of the speech was a calculated risk. Bernie had followed the advice of his media consultant. Distract and attack. Create a scapegoat. Become the victim. The mayor had won election handily. Give his supporters a bone to chew on. Bernie had asked her approval of the strategy, and she had given it – as long as he admitted his transgression first.

How would the people react? She, and the boys, had done their part. They would have to put their heads down and weather the storm. The consultant said it would blow over within a week. Her marriage, her entire life, was on the rocks, but she would not let either disintegrate without a fight.

***

Taryn watched the Mayor's press conference at her desk. Brightify was a vulnerable target constantly under attack by governments and activists around the world because of its potential to disseminate fake, misleading or illegally obtained news. The mayor's play for victimhood might find a modicum of support.

She tried to shift her attention back to work with little success. Rhonda and Karim gave up early and left, but she wasn't ready to go home yet. At 8PM, her phone rang, Micolo's name flashing on the Caller ID.

"Taryn, I need you to come to my office. Now, please."

Dead girl walking. Micolo's door was closed. Taryn knocked.

"Come in."

She lifted her head and forged forward. Micolo sat at his desk, collar undone, tie loose. Two women, suited up in business attire that barely concealed their holstered pistols, turned to look at her.

"We're detectives with the NYPD. We need to ask you some questions," announced the shorter woman, stout with dimpled, cherubic cheeks.

"I know that you didn't leak anything," Micolo said, shaking his head. "But, Brightify is going to have to suspend you until the investigation is complete. It's only temporary and with full pay."

"Wow. Double-teamed," Taryn replied, maintaining her posture. She faced the detectives. "I've got my attorney lined up. He's waiting for my call. I'll answer your questions when he gets here," she added. *Thank you, Professor Bierman.*

"Your lawyer can meet us at the station then," the detective said, sending a quick text before ushering Taryn towards the door.

"I'm sorry, Taryn. Orders came straight from the top," Micolo's last gasp.

The two cops flanked her as they marched to the elevators. The few Brightifiers still around were tethered to their screens and didn't bother to look up. Unfortunately, the paparazzi were waiting in the street. The shots of Taryn, ducking to enter the squad car, accompanied the front page headlines the next morning.

CHAPTER 6

Mayar checked her watch. Time for prayer. She rolled out a simple rug on the floor of her dorm room and faced east towards Mecca. "Allahu Akbar," she chanted with her hands raised, then kneeled on the rug to complete the ritual.

The photo of Ahmed and Fatima loomed over her. Fatima's mother, Suze, had taught both Ahmed and Mayar the Quran at their mosque in Brooklyn until she had traveled to Gaza several summers ago. Suze quickly fell in love with an al Qaeda fighter and decided to stay. Not surprisingly, the story did not have a happy ending. An Israeli artillery bombardment killed the couple shortly after Fatima was born.

Luckily, a sympathetic family in the West Bank offered to take in the baby. Ahmed provided financial assistance while Mayar provided long distance affection, not realizing how strongly she would grow attached to a child she had never met. In hindsight, Mayar realized that she threw her energies into her blossoming relationship with Fatima to compensate for her own fractured family.

Mayar's mother, Haani, emigrated to the United States twenty-three years ago with her then four-year-old son, Ahmed, after her first husband had died of a heart attack. They settled in the middle-class Sunset Park section of Brooklyn where Haani married Faakhir Tabak, a prosperous Oriental rug merchant. Mayar was born a year later.

The Tabak family thrived until the planes crashed into the Twin Towers. Overnight, the neighborhood grew hostile towards Muslims. In 2004, Faakhir left for a purchasing trip to the Middle East and never returned. Six months later, he reached out to Haani from Baghdad where he had united with a long-lost brother. Soon afterwards, Haani learned that Faakhir had been killed in a shootout with American occupation troops

Mayar forced her distractions aside and focused on her laptop, open to a diagram of the electrical circuitry of her dorm. Compensating for his own lack of computing skills, Ahmed had provided a virtual introduction to Viktor, a Russian, a graduate of the Voronezh Military Engineering Institute outside Moscow, the world-renowned incubator of hacking talent. Over the past three years, he had skilled Mayar in the black arts during late night online tutorials.

With Viktor's help, Mayar cracked Columbia's building management system, designing a program that could alter the flow of electricity. She lived in a campus apartment with three other seniors. Each girl had her own room, but they shared a common living area, small kitchen and bathroom. Mayar pulled a blue sweatshirt over her jeans and fiddled with her hijab in the mirror. Locks of unruly hair always seemed to escape.

She knocked on the door across the hall.

"Yeah? Who is it?" A female voice twanged.

"Mayar."

"What do you want?" Amy Blaustein sneered as she opened the door.

As warm and friendly as ever. "Can I borrow your blow dryer? Mine's broken."

"I'm using it now. You can have it in fifteen minutes."

"No problem. I'll check with Sarah and Kathleen."

Amy flicked her door shut. Mayar returned to her room, but left her door open. *Right on schedule.* Amy always showered after dinner, blow-drying her hair in her room. Time to give the Jewish princess a jolt.

Mayar unplugged her laptop from the wall socket, tapped on the keyboard and counted to five. Nothing. One more tap.

"Shit! What the fuck!" Amy flung open her door and screamed.

Mayar shuffled back into the hall. Sarah raced down the corridor. Mayar peered inside Amy's room and saw a wisp of smoke. "Need help?" she called.

"No. I think things are under control now." Amy held up her hair dryer. "It just blew up on me."

"You sure the flames are out?" Sarah shouted, returning with the red fire extinguisher canister in hand, elbowing past Mayar.

Mayar stepped back into her room with a smile, closing the door this time. *Success!* Of course, this was just a trial run - child's play really. She and Viktor had a zillion hours of coding work ahead to complete their malware and situate it properly.

But, she was ahead of herself. Before their malware could do its dirty deeds, she had to penetrate the Con Edison grid. To breach the network, she needed access credentials. To gain these credentials, she needed to send personalized emails to Con Ed employees, luring them to reply to a spear-phishing trap. The math was simple: the more lures that she tossed and the more attractive they appeared, the greater her chances of success. To reach this scale, she must hire outside help. And outside help cost money. *Inshallah,* Ahmed would not fail again.

CHAPTER 7

Unaccustomed to an hour of down time, let alone two weeks, Taryn struggled to keep her mind and body in shape while on suspension from Brightify. Once the DA's office completed questioning her, she had little reason to stay in New York, so she had flown back to her family home in Carbondale, just outside of Aspen.

With no fresh powder overnight, the basement firing range at the Roaring Forks Gun Club was packed by 9AM, the air crackling with cordite. Wearing a flannel shirt, jeans and knee-high leather boots, Taryn found an open tunnel and unpacked her shooting case. Her father, Mark, who had stormed into Iraq with his Army regiment in 1991, taught both his daughters to handle guns before their middle school years. Family shooting excursions, deer hunting in the fall and target competitions every spring and summer, were staples of their youth.

Taryn donned protective glasses and electronic earmuffs before snapping a magazine into the grip of the Glock 17L. Setting her feet and steadying the pistol with both hands, she aimed at the target twenty-five feet away. She exhaled slowly, waiting for the last breath of air to exit her lips, before firing. Again and again and again. Taryn emptied the magazine, her bullet holes forming a tight circle at the core of the target, her satisfaction growing with every shot. A new target; a new magazine, same result.

Shooting usually cleared her head, but her world had turned upside down. The government investigations of DC Leaks, Brightify and Taryn Booker were still underway without any regular SportsCenter-

37

like reports on their progress. Her lawyer warned that she could face criminal charges for her hack of CyberBanda, although he thought that scenario was highly unlikely.

But unlikely did not mean impossible. Taryn remembered flying home from San Francisco to accompany her mom, Anne, to the hospital for her first CT scans. The oncologist had said that the chances of the tumor spreading were slim. Sadly, the doctor was wrong. Mom passed away a year later.

Unfortunately, the lack of official news left the door wide open to speculation. Ignoring her better instincts, Taryn checked the Twitter feed for #JailTaryn. Set up by an anonymous source with the handle of JusticeJoe, it featured a daily dose of tweets cajoling the US government to enforce its own anti-hacking laws. Today, JusticeJoe predicted a lengthy jail term for Taryn and re-tweeted a link to a tabloid article detailing the sexual predators in women's prisons. Several other tweeters piled on with misogynistic insults of female programmers, while another added to the noxious stew by fantasizing about the sexual allure of natural redheads. Taryn stuffed her phone into her back pocket in disgust. If her dad ever saw....

Professor Bierman had warned Taryn to avoid any response, volunteering to quarterback her defense himself. He lined up behind-the-scenes support in Washington and guided her friends in their more visible efforts on the ground in New York. Rhonda filmed a video of Elvira King that went viral on YouTube, while Karim established the #FreeTarynBooker hashtag and organized an army of tweeters to counter JusticeJoe. Although Brightify was in legal limbo too, Marco Micolo looked the other way at his cybersecurity staffers' activities, lending at least tacit support to Taryn's cause.

Thinking about even the slim possibility of jail skyrocketed Taryn's anxiety level back to code red. With the rest of the morning to kill, she drove over to the gym. It was half full, but she didn't register any familiar faces. Anonymity was just fine, especially after the media attention in New York.

Taryn changed out her shooting clothes in the locker room. "Shut Up and Dance" blared from the speakers. Ten days of snowboarding had hardened her thighs and calves, but she wanted to get in some upper body work too. After sets on the bench press, followed by lats and curls, dark stains of sweat pooled under both arms of her orange and blue Denver Broncos jersey. Her hair dripped as if she had stepped out of the Amazon rain forest.

Before Taryn could towel dry, her newly acquired ringtone, Blake Shelton's "Lonely Tonight" rumbled from her gym bag. The phone almost slipped from her fingers, but she caught it just in time to answer.

"Hey, Jimmy. What's up?"

"Just calling to check in," the FBI agent replied. "Hope you're not letting JusticeJoe and his Russian pals jerk your chain."

"I kept away most of the week but I couldn't help peeking again this morning."

"Bad idea." Jimmy had obviously already read the latest tweets.

"Yep," Taryn said. "I bet they're mostly bozos from CyberBanda, but they still get under my skin sometimes."

"That's the beauty of the first amendment. Everyone's entitled to his opinion. Even if they work for the Russian government."

"The government? Not CyberBanda?" she asked.

"Moscow has an entire department devoted to cyberpropaganda. The trolls work twelve hour shifts and have to post at least a hundred comments every day. Our analysts think they're behind almost all the JusticeJoe stuff."

"We fight those sock puppets every day at Brightify, but I didn't realize the Russian government would stoop that low to support a gang of crooks."

"All's fair in love and war, I guess. Anyway, I thought you could use some good news today."

"I'm all ears." Taryn perked up.

"I can't say too much, but I reached out to a law school buddy in the Manhattan prosecutor's office."

"And?"

"Odds are …they're going to drop the case. Against you, at least. Nobody's wants to prosecute you for hacking the Russians. You're like a cyber Robin Hood."

"Robin Hood? I like the sound of that," Taryn chuckled. *Fuck you, JusticeJoe.* "But when will I get official word the investigation's closed?"

"I'm not sure. Some investigations just fade away without an official announcement. Especially if there's a political angle. And, the city may still be trying to wrangle a settlement out of Brightify and DC Leaks."

"Good luck with that." Taryn replied, as she sidled over to a quiet corner of the gym. She sat down on a vacant exercise bike, finally getting a chance to wipe the moisture from her face. "Still hard to believe our Mayor Rosen was banging two bimbos in Moscow."

"Crazy world, huh?" Jim laughed. "Remember, we're still in the market for hot tips on any cybercriminals in New York."

"Yeah, I know. You're ready to jump on them," Taryn teased, pedaling aimlessly on the bike.

***

Back home, showered and snug in red sweatpants and hoodie, Taryn glanced out the window: the sun, low in the vast Colorado sky, peeked through breaking clouds. A doe and two fawns skittered into the forest. She pivoted away from the rustic panorama, slapping her palm on the sill in frustration at her enforced idleness.

With only her collie, Prince, for company, she began to prep a roasted chicken for dinner in the kitchen of the two story, A-frame cabin just inside the main entrance of the six hundred acre IPO Ranch. Her family had managed the IPO for its owner, a wealthy venture capitalist, since dad's discharge from the army. Dad was "Mr. Outside," while Mom, a computer science major herself back in the day, had handled the ranch's books, as well as the oversight of the academic lives of her two daughters.

Once the chicken was in the oven, Taryn dawdled on her laptop beside the fireplace in the great room. Prince curled at her feet. She searched the Times, the New York Post and the Daily News, for any coverage of the Rosen sex scandal, but there was nothing. In fact, none of the major city papers had run an article since the third day after Rosen's speech at City Hall. The mayor appeared to have survived the storm.

Not surprisingly, Taryn's Brightify email flow had dwindled steadily since her suspension. Only one message this afternoon, a correspondence from a Con Edison employee, William Murdoch, a supervisor in a data center in New Jersey, confirming that he had clicked the link and changed the password on his Brightify social media account, as Taryn had requested.

I would never have sent this guy a notification to change his password. Taryn checked her "sent" folder to be sure. Nothing there. She thought about verifying Murdoch's credentials to see if they were valid, but then remembered her lawyer's admonition to avoid anyone else's data. For a long time.

Taryn filed away Murdoch's message, closing her laptop with a shaky hand. She stomped out to the woodshed and carried back an armful of logs, Jimmy Mangano's earlier request fermenting in the back of her mind. Reopening her laptop, she forwarded the Murdoch email to him with a brief explanation. The FBI could do the digging for her.

Before she could square up the woodpile, a horn honked outside. A van had just pulled up to the gate, another one following right behind. Both sported logos from Vail TV stations. Prince raced to the window, barking furiously at the intruders.

Taryn watched a reporter, a twentysomething guy, too well-coiffed to be a Carbondale local, amble up the driveway, a camera-toting tech in his wake. The doorbell chimed, but Dad beat her to the door.

"I didn't know you were home," she whispered.

"I'll take care of this. You're supposed to stay under the radar," Mark said, waving her back. "Can I help you?" he asked, opening the door.

"Is Taryn Booker here? We're looking for a comment on the news out of New York. Brightify has agreed to contribute a million dollars to a fund for computers for the city's middle schools. In return, the city will drop its investigation," the reporter said, brandishing a microphone like a sword. "Any quote from Taryn?"

"My daughter's not here. Please leave us alone."

"We'll just wait then – if you don't mind."

"I do mind, but the road out there is public property. Just stay off the ranch and out of my driveway," Mark answered, closing the door before the reporter could fire off any more questions.

"Temperature's supposed to drop below zero tonight," he said, walking past Taryn and into the great room. He added a fresh log to the fire. "Let's see how badly they want a story."

"Thanks," Taryn said, hugging her father as news settled in. "I never thought this mess would follow me home."

"This settlement's good for you, isn't it?" Mark asked, sitting down on the overstuffed hunter green sofa.

"Yes, super. A million dollars is petty cash for Brightify. And it doesn't look like the company admitted any wrongdoing. But I still need to close the loop with my lawyer and my boss."

"What's all the commotion outside?" Constance asked as she burst through the door from the garage, her blond hair still showing the dampening effects of a day packed underneath a snowboard helmet. "It's like opening night at the rodeo."

Mark flicked his head towards Taryn. "Your sister can explain."

Taryn hopped up and grabbed a Stella from the fridge, returning to the great room to give a quick synopsis of the day's events.

"Sounds juicy," Constance concluded. "I better go and clean up. Just in case anyone wants to take my picture too."

"Who would want your picture?" Taryn cracked. "But I'll go upstairs with you. I've got to make some calls. Then I need to pack."

"You're going back to New York?" Dad deadpanned as he drew a blanket, its plaid faded by years of snuggling, over his knees. Prince jumped up on the sofa, but Dad steered him back down to the floor.

"Yeah." Taryn finished off her beer. "It's time to return to the real world."

"You still have your gun in your apartment?" he probed as he reached for a handful of pretzels. "There's a lot of crazy people in the city. And they know your name."

Maybe Dad knew more about the denizens of the social media netherworld than she thought. "Two pistols, dad. Licensed, locked, and loaded."

"A girl always needs to carry extra protection, right?" Constance teased, eliciting a stern glance from her big sister.

CHAPTER 8

Taryn and her dad stomped across the snow covered yard to the stables in the soft dawn light. Constance had chosen to sleep in, promising to rise in time to drive Taryn to the airport for her flight to New York. A wrangler waited in the corral, a statuesque chestnut mare tethered to her wrist.

"Morning, Ms. Taryn. Morning, sir," she said as she gently brushed the mane of her charge. "Granny was a little restless last night, so I thought I'd bring her out to wait for you."

Granny, aptly named after Taryn's grandmother, a feisty, frontier woman who had raised Mark and his two younger brothers single-handedly, had been her ride since high school. Taryn whispered soothingly in her horse's ear as she reached for an apple in her pack.

"Don't spoil her now," the wrangler warned.

Mark emerged from the stables astride a coal black stallion while Taryn climbed into the saddle. She held the reins with her left hand and ran her right over the stock of the Winchester rifle scabbarded by her side.

"There was a cougar sighting up in the hills last week," Dad explained as he took the lead. The pair ambled for a mile along the gravel road, plowed the day before, that bisected the ranch before veering right along a less-traveled path. The horses knew the way, climbing confidently in the knee-deep snow through the majestic pines and spindly aspens of the Rocky Mountain foothills. They were headed to Gold's Ridge, the highest point on the ranch, and a long-time favorite Booker family picnic spot.

As they broke the tree line onto a gently sloping meadow, Taryn coaxed Granny into a trot.

"Careful, Taryn," her father called.

"We've got it under control," she replied, as both rider and horse seemed to relish the acceleration. Granny whinnied, straining to take her speed up another notch, but Taryn reined her back. Mark followed, three lengths behind.

In ten minutes, they reached the apex of the ridge, circling to appreciate the grandeur of the Roaring Fork Valley and the surrounding white-capped peaks.

"Never gets old," Taryn said, reaching into her saddlebag for another apple for Granny.

"Do you really want to go back to work for that company?" Dad asked. "They were pretty close to tossing you off the wagon."

"Brightify's changed, sure. It's more corporate now, but I still love my job."

"What about your new boss?" Dad sipped from his canteen, searching his daughter's face for a reaction.

"Micolo? I haven't figured him out yet. One minute he acts like an asshole; the next I think he might be on my side. I'm meeting with him tonight at the office soon as I land." Taryn's long-winded reply left a trail of smoke in the frigid, high country air.

"I guess it would be tough to walk away from all that money."

"It would. But money isn't my top priority. You know that. There's a thrill to working for the biggest and best company on the Internet." Granny tossed her head, anxious to get moving again.

"The Army's got a great cyber program now, you know," dad said, tightening his grip on the reins to make sure his mount knew they weren't going anywhere yet. "We've all got to do our part to make America great again."

"C'mon dad. If I'm not cut out for the corporate world, how would I do in the Army?" Taryn asked, purposely avoiding the more delicate discussion. "I'll do my part, but in my own way."

"OK, I'll leave it be. It's too beautiful up here to talk politics anyway," he paused, nudging his horse closer to Taryn. "But you come home again soon. I miss you."

"Love you too, daddy," Taryn said, gently spurring Granny to begin the descent back to the ranch. She tugged the reins at regular intervals, communicating clearly that there would be no trotting on the downhill slope.

A snarl emanated from the woods as they approached. Granny reared back, bucking her front legs high into the air. Taryn slammed her heels into the stirrups, barely maintaining her balance. "Whoa, girl," she commanded, slowly bringing her charge under control, while scouring the tree line for the source of alarm.

A tawny cougar, maybe eight feet long, emerged, growling again. Muscles tensed, fully prepared to defend his turf, the predator pulled up thirty yards short of Granny.

Taryn ripped the long gun from its scabbard, clamping her knees to the saddle. The horse calmed, defiantly standing her ground, as Taryn sighted at the cougar's chest. One more step and she'd have to pull the trigger. Dad sidled up to her right, his rifle at the ready. She wouldn't need a second gun.

The cougar snarled once more, but didn't advance, content to stare menacingly at his nemesis. The stand-off lasted ten seconds before the cougar tossed his head and crashed back through the forest. Taryn relaxed and lowered her rifle.

"That cat's as ornery as you," dad commented.

"Not quite," she replied.

***

The adrenaline surge from the cougar encounter didn't wear off until Taryn had checked in for her flight, bustled through security and slumped into a seat in the waiting area by the gate. With forty-five minutes till boarding, she started to nod off, but Blake Shelton's syrupy ringtone snapped her upright.

"Congratulations. I just got off the phone with the assistant prosecutor. The city is dropping the investigation of you. Just like I expected," her lawyer announced.

"Fantastic. I can't believe it's all over."

"The federal government actually jumped in at the last minute, citing national security concerns. They wanted you to sign a gag order, prohibiting you from ever releasing the other names on the list of CyberBanda files."

"What did you tell them?" Taryn popped a mint into her mouth.

"I told them where to shove the gag order. The horses have already left the barn. And you've been harassed enough."

"Thanks."

"Professor Bierman thinks the request came straight from the White House. No one there wants to acknowledge that the Russians might still be tossing stink bombs into our politics."

"The professor might be running low on friends in Washington."

"You know the old fart. He always lands on his feet."

With the weight of the investigation off her shoulders, Taryn slept for the entire flight.

***

"Come on in, Taryn. Welcome back," Marco Micolo beckoned before she even knocked on his half-open door. "Close it and sit down. I wasn't expecting you before eight."

"My flight landed fifteen minutes early," Taryn replied as she followed orders, settling into the chair in front of her boss's desk. She had rushed back to her apartment, changing into a fresh-from-the-cleaners' shirt and denim vest.

"How are you?" Micolo asked, loosening his Hermes tie, chartreuse with a montage of polo players.

"Much better now that the investigation's over."

"The DA was just trying to blow smoke up our ass. He didn't have much of a case."

"My ass, to be precise." Taryn shifted in her seat.

"Yes, yes. I can understand how you feel that way. But you had tremendous support here at Brightify. We weren't going to let you down."

"I wasn't always sure of that."

"Remember, the company was under investigation too. Our lawyers wouldn't allow any unsupervised communication."

"OK, thanks for the explanation. I'd like to get back to work now," Taryn started to stand. "I've got some catching up to do. I set up a staff meeting for first thing tomorrow morning."

"Slow down," Micolo said, rising himself. He pivoted, opening the half-sized refrigerator discretely situated in the cabinet behind his desk, emerging with a split of Veuve Cliquot and two crystal glasses. "A little victory celebration is in order first, I think."

"Really?" Taryn's shoulders snapped back as if Micolo had applied an electrical shock. She was even more surprised when he stepped around to deliver her glass and pour the champagne.

"Cheers," he said, sitting on the edge of his desk, tasting the bubbly, looking down on her. "You've become quite the celebrity, you know."

"I wouldn't go that far." Taryn replied, placing her glass on the desk, unsipped.

"That video of Elvira King caused a big-time commotion. Her bank, Credit Lafayette, is one of Brightify's larger advertisers. John Cabot, Credit Lafayette's president, called our president directly. Said he'd be proud to offer you a job anytime."

"Wow. I'm flattered. But I'm pretty happy here."

Micolo swirled the champagne and took another sip. "I'm pleased to hear that, but there's going to be some changes at Brightify. I'm re-organizing cybersecurity in New York to report into our IT department, rather than directly to me."

"So I'll have a new boss?" Taryn fingered the stem of her glass.

"Yes, a good man. He's worked in IT for twenty-two years."

"Sounds like a demotion to me." *And you want me to celebrate?*

"That's not the way I see it," Micolo said, standing. "Look, I'm not a computer guy. I got hung out to dry here too. I need a more seasoned IT executive to supervise things, that's all."

"I screwed up going after CyberBanda, I know it. But I've had time to reflect and I've learned from it."

"Taryn, you're a maverick at heart. You always will be. The corporate world may not be the best place for you."

"I never thought I'd hear that from anyone here at Brightify."

"I do have your best interests at heart. You've been under a lot of stress. I want you to take a few days off and consider your career options. Then come back to Brightify, if that's what you think is best."

"Do I have a choice?"

"Perhaps we can have a drink, or dinner? To talk about your future." Micolo sipped his champagne again, peering over the rim of the glass to measure her response.

"Wow. Thanks." Taryn replied, standing up. "I think I'm going to go home. I've had a long day."

"Of course, of course." Micolo reached for her elbow, letting his hand linger until Taryn stepped away. "No rush. I'll be here."

Did Micolo just hit on me? Taryn waited until the elevator reached the deserted lobby before clenching her fists and silently mouthing a huge scream. She needed to get the tension out of her system - even if the security guard at the front desk looked at her like she was crazy.

CHAPTER 9

Did I win or lose? Taryn woke up the next morning still unsure. The more relevant question, however, was *What do I do next?* The short answer was stay away from Micolo. She had no interest in pursuing that relationship any further. As far as career alternatives, she was free from the cloud of the investigation and could go anywhere. Maybe Brightify was still the best option, but she was beginning to feel like a cowgirl trapped at a debutante cotillion.

Taryn conference-called Rhonda and Karim, providing a summary of her conversation with Micolo. They agreed to meet for dinner that evening.

Next, she dialed a familiar office number in Ithaca. She owed Professor Bierman a giant thank-you. He was traveling, so she left a message, stressing that her call was not urgent.

She refilled her coffee cup and returned to her desk. Sunlight reflected off the cars parked on Bank Street, but she could tell by the school kids at the bus stop, wrapped up like Eskimos, that its promise of warmth was an illusion. Snug in red sweats, a security blanket from her days at Cornell, she had no intention of leaving her nest this morning anyway.

Linked In, hacker blogs, corporate bulletin boards, job posting sites. For the next three hours, Taryn scanned the web to get current on the employment opportunities for cybersecurity professionals. She thought about reaching out to John Cabot at Credit Lafayette, but the prospect of working at a big bank didn't seem any more appealing than staying at Brightify.

Although she worked in the cyber field every day, she had been safely ensconced in the Brightify bubble for four years now, shielded from the noise of the marketplace. Executive recruiters, headhunters, had called on occasion, but they were usually trolling for dissatisfied Brightify employees and she cut their pitches off early. *Have I fallen into that category now?*

If she was going to leave Brightify, she wanted to join a young, dynamic company. Taryn dug through her desk drawer – cable bills, restaurant receipts, an invitation to a friend's wedding – for a business card. Alexa Kurtz was the managing partner of Klinger and Kurtz, a venture capital firm. VC's were always looking to stock their portfolio companies, usually start-ups or early stage, with the best and the brightest. *Would she remember me?*

A phone call seemed old-fashioned, but Taryn was feeling lucky. Ms. Kurtz's assistant put her right through.

"Alexa, thanks for taking my call." Taryn forced herself to slow down. "When we met at the Black Hat conference in Vegas last summer, you mentioned a company in your portfolio that you thought might be a good fit for me."

"Yes, Lightning Strike. They're still looking for a senior analyst in threat intelligence. It's a high-profile position at the leading edge of cybersecurity. Not an easy slot to fill."

"Well, I might be interested now." Taryn clicked on the company's website.

"Fantastic. When I saw your name in the papers, I was hoping that Brightify's loss would be our gain."

"Thanks for the vote of confidence. I see Lightning Strike's based in Tel Aviv."

"The founder was a lieutenant colonel in the Israeli army. Is that, I mean Israel, a problem for you?" Alexa asked.

"Not at all." Israel was a hotbed of cybersecurity activity. Professor Bierman often noted that he'd be a millionaire by now if he had made the *Aliyah* there instead of emigrating to America. "In fact, a stretch out of the country might be just what I'm looking for," Taryn added.

"To be honest, the job is in the New York office, but you would be spending a good chunk of time in Tel Aviv. That's where most of the techs are. Almost everyone's alumni of Unit 8200, Israel's top cyber organization. Checkpoint and Palo Alto Networks were started by 8200 alums, you know. And Lightning Strike has clients around the world, so you would need to travel regularly," Alexa said.

Taryn paced through her living room. "The founder's a woman?" she asked, trying not to sound too interested.

"Yes, Shahar Ram," Alexa laughed. "The Israeli army is an equal opportunity employer."

"I'd like to meet her." So much for restraint.

"Of course, but why don't you start out with Montel Rice. He's in New York. We just hired him to run our US business."

"OK. Sounds great."

"I'll ask him to call you to set up an appointment as soon as possible."

"I look forward to his call. Thank you." Taryn signed off. *Music to my ears.*

Taryn's excitement was short-lived. Another Con Edison email had infiltrated her in-box. Something was definitely up and she was likely in the middle of it. Taryn called Jimmy Mangano to see if he had made any progress on the previous Con Ed emails, but he was out of the office. She tossed her phone on the desk in frustration and headed for the shower.

CHAPTER 10

"What a fucking week!" Dennis Walecka moaned as he opened the refrigerator and grabbed a can of Bud. Six foot two, blond locks curling over cinder block shoulders bursting out of a red and black Bingos Pizza polo, he was proud of the fact that no one could ever peg him as a hacker at first glance. "I spent six fucking months delivering pizza to penetrate that fucking Bingos system, now the FBI is crawling up our ass, pinging our servers like they're playing fucking pinball. We should have had another couple of months at least before anyone noticed we were inside the network."

"Fuck the FBI. Their queries will die somewhere in Romania. They'll never track anything here," Brian Valentine snickered, taking off his tortoise shell glasses and wiping them with his handkerchief. Short, apple cheeked and pencil thin, dressed in khakis and a powder blue button-down, Brian was just a pocket protector away from a role in The Big Bang Theory. He was as bland as vanilla ice cream until he sat down at his computer.

The partners had met at a General Assembly class on network security. Despite their physical disparities, they quickly bonded over a common interest in breaking into systems, not protecting them. Their two-bedroom apartment/home office was on the ground floor of a weathered six story brick building on East 19th Street in Flatbush, a downtrodden block largely populated by recent arrivals from south of the border.

Brian watched two brown-skinned toughs saunter by, sipping from bottles thinly camouflaged by paper bags. He meandered over to his workspace, the left half of a nicked-up Formica picnic table scavenged from a garage sale, and plopped down on a wobbling folding chair. "You think we should lay low for a while?" he asked.

"Why push our luck," Dennis replied, settling on his side of the table and firing up his computer. "I read in Wired that The Hacking Team sold its toolkit to the FBI."

"The Hacking Team? The company from Italy? They're the guys that helped the North Koreans and the Chinese crack down on dissident citizens, right?"

"That's the one. Their clients can track GPS locations, log keystrokes, and even listen in to conversations from the computers that they're targeting."

"The FBI must be getting pissed at guys like us kicking their butts all the time," Brian replied with a triumphant smile. He reached into a McDonald's bag and emerged with a handful of golden french fries. "We got like ten thousand credit cards already from the Bingos site. We can start selling them on the Dark Web forum. That'll pay the rent."

"Since I'm not delivering any more pizza, I'll have some time to put back into that Con Edison deal now." Dennis plucked a few fries, washing them down with another gulp of beer. "I thought you were fucking crazy putting the hours in digging through all the Bingos names, but that Taryn Booker account turned out to be a gold mine."

"Good thing for us Booker likes pizza," Brian replied.

"Ten of her Con Ed contacts actually replied to my phishing emails." Dennis pantomimed reeling in a big catch. "What fucking morons."

"You gonna throw out a few more lines?"

"Not for a while. A couple of the replies got through my filter, so Booker's probably seen them by now."

"I wouldn't worry about that. I bet Booker's got other things on her mind the past few weeks. The DA cracked down on her pretty hard for messing with the Russians."

"I read that Brightify settled, so I bet she's back at work now. I think I'm just going to flesh out the Con Ed profiles that I snagged and stay away from Ms. Booker," Dennis said, bravely tipping his rickety chair back on two legs.

"Really? You're going to stay away from Ms. Booker?" Brian chuckled pointing to his screen. "Check this little clip out then tell me you're going to stay away."

"You little pervert. Did you tap Booker's webcam?" Dennis asked, rolling his eyes as he piloted his chair back to solid ground.

"Why not? She wanted a cheap pizza. Nothing in life is free, right?"

"All right, asshole, let's see what you've got." Dennis rose and shuffled over.

"I caught her this afternoon. She must have left her phone by her computer and had to run out of the shower to answer it. Dripping wet and naked as the day she was born. Great tits, huh?" Brian beamed.

"Major league," Dennis whistled in admiration. "And you were going to keep them to yourself? A little video to jerk off to?" He pantomimed another hand gesture.

"Fuck you. I'm not showing you anything else."

"You got more? Like an ass fuck or a blow job?"

"I tried, man, but Booker lives like a fucking nun."

"Enough bullshit. We need to get down to business," Dennis said as he returned to his own workspace. "I'm shooting you over five of the Con Ed names. See what you can find out about them."

"Who's paying us for this?" Brian asked, scarfing down the last of the fries. He crumpled up the paper bag and three point tossed it into the wastebasket.

"Some guy named Sully. He private messaged Pizza Boy on Dark Web last week." Dennis stretched his shoulders and started typing.

"You probably should shut down your Pizza Boy handle with the FBI busting our chops now."

"Good point. I'll bag it as soon as we're done with Sully. I don't want to spook him."

"What does Sully want the profiles for?"

"Fuck knows – probably wants to scam the meters," Dennis replied without looking up.

CHAPTER 11

Taryn's dinner plans with Rhonda and Karim downsized to a quick salad at Chelsea Market across the street from the office. The reorganization had blindsided them as much as it had Taryn. They both had to get back to work. They were all friends, good friends, and would remain so; but this was business. They would talk again in a few days.

Taryn hailed a cab to head downtown. Before the taxi traveled two blocks, her phone rattled with a text from Jimmy Mangano.

> **J: Got some info on your Con Ed emails**
> **T: Great**
> **J: Call me for details**
> **T: Are you still at the office?**
> **J: Yep. Want to stop by?**
> **T: On my way**

Special Agent Mangano was at his desk, white shirt collar unbuttoned, tie askew, nose pressed to his computer screen when Taryn arrived. A shark grey Armani jacket draped over his chair.

"Hi, Jimmy," Taryn called, registering the pleasant surprise on his face as he turned. Her bruised ego welcomed the attention. "Working solo today?" she asked, nodding towards the empty desk across from Jim's.

"Lou's at a seminar on encryption technology this week. Unfortunately, the bad guys are using it much more effectively these days." A father of two young children, Lou Totti had been Jim's partner since Jim had finished his training at Quantico four years ago.

Taryn folded her jacket in her lap as she sat down in the empty chair in front of Jim's desk. With as few f-bombs as possible, she summarized her conversation with Micolo, leaving out his dinner proposition. She also hinted at her willingness to consider a fresh start somewhere else.

"I could send one of my goombah buddies from high school over to break Micolo's knees," Jim suggested. He had grown up in Canarsie, a blue-collar neighborhood in Brooklyn, predominantly Italian and Irish, living at home while attending City College, followed by Brooklyn Law.

"As the song goes, cowgirls don't cry. But I need to get to the bottom of this Con Ed mess - even if I don't stay at Brightify."

"All set. Take a look," Jim replied, pointing to his screen. "We found the Upatre malware embedded in all your emails."

"That's the downloader, right?" She pushed her chair to Jim's side of the desk

"Yep, Upatre injects the Dyre Trojan horse into the machine of anyone who opens the email. Dyre then lies in wait and captures the credentials of any system that the victim logs onto."

"Con Ed's anti-virus shield should have caught the malware," Taryn commented.

"Probably. But some companies skimp on their subscription payments so they may not have the latest virus signatures in their database. And the best virus designers manage to stay one step ahead of the anti-virus shields anyway. It's a giant game of cat and mouse."

"The Dyre designers are supposed to be the best."

"You can tell by the way their code buries into the rootkit of the target machine," Jim said, tapping on his keyboard to bring up another block of code. "It can take control of the entire computer. Hard drive, keyboard, microphone, webcam, everything."

"Have you tried to trace the emails back to their source?" Taryn asked.

Jim nodded, clicking on a chart. "We traced the attacks back to a server lair, but the black hats are running on a bullet proof network that they probably rented from a spammer in Eastern Europe. It's a dead end."

"But we're not quitting," Jim continued. "We're going to set up a honeypot to see if we can attract the attackers. Our techs have some new toys with the firepower to penetrate the botnet and blow it up."

"Cool. Any other leads?"

"Not really. There's a boatload of hackers out there. We don't think any of them accessed your account, but you can look."

Taryn wheeled closer for a better view of the screen. They spent the next two hours analyzing cyber scams, attack vectors, and malware designs.

Trojans, honeypots, penetration, firepower. The musky traces of Jim's cologne stoked a fire Taryn thought had smoldered months ago. She caught herself peeking at Jim's silhouette as he tapped on his keyboard. He was good-looking. If she got the job at Lightning Strike, they wouldn't be working together any more. And she might be in Israel, or traveling much of the time. Maybe it's time to cross the Rubicon.

The office had emptied out. Completely. They'd have to sweep a few papers off his desktop. And the photo of his family too. But, the opportunity to do it in an FBI field office did have a certain allure. She slid lower in her chair, uncrossing her legs, right foot tapping the floor. *Let's see if he makes the first move.*

"Shit!" Taryn bolted upright, snapping out of her fantasy, pointing to the screen. "These pizza delivery hacks at Bingos. I order from them all the time."

"Did you ever open their emails or reply to them?"

"No. I mean hardly ever," she said sheepishly. "Once I was really hungry and it looked like a great deal…" Taryn faded out as she contemplated all the files stored on the computer in her apartment. She knew that 90% of all hacks started out with spear-phishing emails, like the one that she had probably opened.

"You OK?" Jim asked. "You look like you just saw a flying pig."

"I better go home and check my computer." The prospect of her bare ass on Jim's desktop didn't look quite so exciting now.

"Stay calm. Your computer's probably fine," he comforted, patting her hand. "You've had a rough day and nothing's going to change tonight anyway. I'll talk to the agents on the case in the morning." Jim turtled his chair back from the desk and checked his watch. "Why don't you join me and Marcy for dinner? Her sister is in town and we're going to grab some sushi in Nolita."

"Marcy?" *That came out of nowhere. Jim never mentioned a girlfriend by name before.*

"Marcy Peluso. She's a model. I've been seeing her for a couple of months now."

"A Brooklyn girl?" *Boy, was I headed in the wrong direction.*

"Yeah, but from Park Slope," he replied.

"Thanks for the invite, but I've already eaten," she blurted, giving Jim a quick goodbye hug before he could protest.

***

Taryn race-walked home, taking the final flight of steps in her building two at a time. She plonked down at her desk without even bothering to remove her coat; her fingers flew across the keyboard. After the session with Jim, she knew exactly what to look for. She found the first fragments of offending code in twenty minutes. No need to look any further. Taryn smacked the side of the monitor and yanked out the power plug in disgust. This computer was destined for the trash.

Now what? How do I explain it? I was just ordering a pizza but I made an amateur mistake. People will forget I hacked the Russians. Now, I'll just be the cybersecurity chick who got hacked herself. Was I targeted directly? Is CyberBanda after me? Or was it just bad luck? I need answers. Otherwise, I'll be taking the hit. Again.

CHAPTER 12

Allah smiles upon us. Ahmed had deposited just enough funds into Mayar's operational account to keep their plan on schedule. She never questioned the source of Ahmed's income. They were both soldiers, fighting for a just cause in their own way.

With money tight, Mayar haggled online over the price of the Con Ed profiles as if she was hawking rugs in her father's bazaar. Ahmed had suggested that she use "Sajida," a nomme de guerre in honor of the female suicide bomber executed by the Jordanians as her online handle, but she had disagreed. It was too blatantly Arabic. Americans, even the ones with criminal inclinations, might stay away. "Sully", short for "sultan" at least in her mind, was much less threatening.

Pizza Boy wanted two thousand dollars for a complete identification package. He must be smoking strong weed. She messengered him an offer for five hundred and tried to turn her attention back to her schoolwork.

While Mayar and Ahmed redoubled their religious intensity after their father's desertion, Haani slipped away from Islam. Tension in the Tabak household ratcheted steadily higher, ultimately driving Ahmed to Palestine and Mayar to move in with the family of a girlfriend from the mosque. Mother and daughter rarely spoke anymore. Just as well. Ahmed warned that their mother now posed a security risk.

Pizza Boy's response finally arrived. Mayar accepted his compromise - one thousand dollars, payable in Bitcoin to preserve anonymity on both sides of the transaction.

She sent a Telegram apprising Ahmed of her progress. Ahmed answered immediately: **Allahu Akbar**. She sent another message asking for news of Fatima. Did she go to school? Was she learning to read? Yes, and yes, but no details. *Typical male. I will ask Ahmed to arrange for Fatima to join me in Raqqa after my work here in New York is complete.*

***

Sitting in a cafe on the boardwalk in Tel Aviv, Ahmed Hazboun shut down the Telegram app and stuffed his mobile back into his pocket. On his twenty-first birthday, he had traveled to Dubai to connect with his step-father's brother who suggested that Ahmed could best serve the cause by utilizing his Hazboun roots to return to Israel and settle there.

The Sunni organization outside Iraq was thin at the time, enabling Ahmed to rise steadily from foot soldier to lieutenant to captain. While still commanding a corps of fighters anxious to take the battle to the enemy, he now faced the additional challenge of raising money - both for Raqqa and for his baby sister's special project.

The payments to Pizza Boy were just a small component of the costs of her operation. The big dollars went to Viktor and his gang of Russian cyber-thieves. They were not tutoring his half-sister, and protecting her identity, for free.

Much more expensive though, was the extensive research that the Russians were performing to unravel the complexities of the electrical grid and design a cyberweapon to attack it. While Mayar could locate the neglected door in the Con Ed castle, she could not build the heavy weaponry necessary to bring the walls down.

Ahmed's mobile beeped with a Telegram message.

V: You're late
A: You will have your money soon
V: We can renegotiate our terms
A: I will pay you
V: Of course

Fucking infidels. One thing to hire the Russians for their technical expertise, but another to become their lackeys.

Ahmed sipped a coffee and scanned the evening throng. Linen blazers, rakish hats, stiletto heels, bare mid-riffs, and bouncing breasts shuttled by. Surprising to most Westerners, Tel Aviv was a party town. With a robust gay community and a smorgasbord of clubs, bistros, and cafes, it was a jewel on the Middle East playboy circuit. He fingered the dime bag of smack buried deep in his pocket and checked his watch. The pathetic whore was late.

John Cabot Jr. - wealthy parents, an Ivy League diploma, and a nose for blow - fit perfectly into this scene. Ahmed had, in fact, recruited the wayward boy and invested heavily in grooming him, but JJ had mysteriously disappeared last summer. Ahmed needed him back – or, more precisely, needed his mother back. He didn't like sticking his camel's nose down the same well so quickly, but he had few alternatives.

When Priscilla Cabot traveled to Istanbul to trace her missing son's trail, his operatives lured her into a trap. Her ransom would have solved his financial needs. Unfortunately, John Cabot's enormous influence spurred the Turkish police to cooperate with American special forces and rescue Priscilla in route to Raqqa. He lost two of his top men in the shoot-out. But she was the prize, worthy of another try.

"Hey. Sorry, I'm late," Fiona Peterson mumbled as she shuffled to his table. Spectral thin and sallow, she brushed strands of blond hair from her face, revealing the high cheekbones and emerald eyes of a once beautiful woman now sunk into disrepair.

"Do you have the photo?" Ahmed sneered, stroking his pencil-thin mustache. His squat, fire hydrant physique, gym-hardened biceps and swarthy complexion completed a menacing package.

"Yeah, yeah. Right here." After wiping her dripping nose with the back of her hand, Fiona reached into the back pocket of her threadbare jeans to produce her phone.

"Perfect," he replied, careful not to touch the phone as he leaned over to view the shot that a passerby had snapped last summer of Fiona and JJ, smiling and tan with the beach and Mediterranean Sea in the background. Hard to believe that the woman in the lime sarong was the same person that was sitting at his table now.

"What's the date on the photo?" Ahmed demanded.

"Date? How am I supposed to remember the fucking date?" Fiona sniveled, her hands fluttering.

"Give the phone to me." He didn't have any choice now. Ahmed accessed iPhoto, confirming that the photo was snapped on August 20th. He thought about changing it to yesterday, but realized that the move might not stand up to scrutiny and could cast doubt on the photo's authenticity.

Ahmed had trolled social media for months for signs of JJ without any luck. *If Priscilla Cabot had any more recent photographs of her son, she never would have traveled to Istanbul to search for him.* He handed the phone back to Fiona and cleaned his hands with a paper napkin. "You can post it now."

"You got something for me?" Fiona picked up the napkin and honked viscous fluids from both nostrils into it.

"Right here," Ahmed tapped his pocket. "But I want to see the posts first."

Fiona's fingers tap-danced like a drunken sailor across her screen. "Brightify, Twitter, Snapchat and Instagram." She looked up at Ahmed as if he held a sack of gold.

Ahmed scanned each post before slipping the plastic bag to Fiona under the table.

Fiona snatched it and stuffed it into her purse. "There'll be more, right?"

He nodded. "Much more. If Mrs. Cabot comes to visit."

CHAPTER 13

The private elevator whisked Priscilla Cabot to the top floor of Credit Lafayette's headquarters on Park Avenue. She breezed into the reception area wearing navy slacks, a taupe silk blouse, and a gray Chanel blazer. A poppy orange Hermes bag dangled from her wrist; a matching ribbon held back her flawless ponytail. *JJ escaped from Turkey. He might still be alive!*

She had wanted to share the good news with her husband last night, but he had stayed in the city. And didn't pick up his phone. Not for the first time, sadly.

"Mrs. Cabot. What a wonderful surprise," Betty Linkton, John's prim executive assistant said as she ushered Priscilla through the entrance foyer, decorated with plush Persian carpets and dark woods. "I trust that you are surviving our dreadful weather. Mr. Cabot is in a meeting right now, but I'll let him know that you're here." She pointed Priscilla to a maroon leather sofa. "Coffee?"

"No thank you. Please tell John that I do not plan to wait long."

Four minutes later, John's doors opened and two smartly dressed millennials marched out. They both nodded deferentially, but did not slow. Priscilla didn't recognize the mop-haired young man, but she had a strong hunch about the identity of the leggy Latina in the scarlet pumps. *She's not John's first fling, and, undoubtedly, won't be the last.*

"Pris, you're looking radiant this afternoon," John complimented as he stepped across the foyer to kiss her cheek. "Let's talk inside."

He led the way through the polished oak doors that opened into the opulent corner office befitting the second-in-command of an international bank. The inner sanctuary had a sailing motif featuring teak furniture, an oil painting of a whaler tossing on a foaming sea, and Baccarat vases blooming with freshly cut flowers. Views of a snow-dappled Central Park in the fading afternoon light beckoned from a wall of windows. He guided her to a captain's chair and sat down opposite her.

Priscilla picked up a gilt framed photo of the Cabot family cruising on a chartered yacht in the Bahamas that rested on the glass tabletop. "JJ looks so happy here."

"He was twelve years old."

"Don't you have any more recent photos?" she asked, looking around the office.

"I have another meeting in ten minutes," John said, checking his watch. "What brings you into the city?"

"Our son may have surfaced," Priscilla declared, digging into her purse for her phone, holding it tightly to her chest. "I found this photo on Brightify. Last night." She wanted her words to stab at her husband's heart. "The girl, her name's Fiona, went to Yale with JJ. I think she came to a Christmas party at our house once."

"I had an important dinner meeting last night," John mumbled, reaching for his wife's phone. The image of his son, smiling and healthy, visibly shocked him. "Where was the photo taken? When?"

"In Tel Aviv. I'm not sure when. The point is, it was just posted yesterday." Priscilla fumbled in her purse again, but this time she pulled out a pack of Newports and lit up.

"You can't do that here," John said.

Priscilla inhaled deeply and blew a ring of smoke towards her husband. "The Turkish police had a record of JJ's entry so how did he leave the country without anyone noticing?" she asked.

"I don't really care how JJ left Turkey. This Tel Aviv photo is great news," John continued.

"Because JJ left Istanbul?"

"Yes, he was alive and he traveled to Israel." John paused, exaggerating a cough. "Not Syria."

"Why would he go to Syria?"

"Read the papers, dear. The FBI catches disaffected young people every day trying to join the Islamic State. They're going to start their lives over and build a better world. And Turkey is right next door to Syria. The police told us that Istanbul is full of ISIS recruiters."

"JJ? Our son?? Join ISIS? You're crazy."

"He had problems. Who knows what was going on in his head?"

"Did he ever talk to you? About his problems?" Priscilla asked, pointing her cigarette at John. Noticing it was almost down to the filter, she looked around for an ashtray. John shook his head sadly, strode over to the credenza and returned with a coffee mug, emblazoned with Credit Lafayette's seal.

She stuffed the stub into the cup. "JJ is not a jihadist. It doesn't pay well enough. God knows, he always needed money." She reached into her purse for another smoke. "And we always gave it to him."

"Don't," John commanded. Priscilla snapped her purse shut.

"Let's face it. JJ had a drug habit," he continued.

"I don't believe that JJ was an addict. He was more likely a businessman. Just like his father."

"I'm not sure that's a compliment."

"It's not," she said.

John picked the soiled cup up off the table and walked into his private bathroom. Priscilla could hear the sink run for a brief second. Then, her husband returned. "What do you want to do?" he asked.

"Call this girl Fiona. Maybe she's in touch with JJ. Maybe they're shacking up together right now."

"That can't hurt. And after that?"

"I'll go to Israel if I have to," Priscilla snarled.

"You can't be serious. Not after what happened in Turkey. I can't save you again."

"No, you're clearly too busy for that," Priscilla retorted, purposely gazing towards the door of her husband's office.

"Look, our son is twenty-three. We've searched the earth for him. We met with the State Department, the NYPD, the FBI. We hired a private investigator. There's no ransom note. No warrant for his arrest either, as far as we know. No body, thank god. And now we have this photo."

"You're saying I should just sit tight?" It was Priscilla's turn to stand.

"JJ doesn't want us to find him right now. Maybe with good reason."

Priscilla straightened her scarf. "Maybe you don't want to find him. It might not be convenient. It might create bad publicity. But, I'm his mother and I'm not going back to Palm Beach to play golf!"

John hushed her, signaling with both hands to calm down. "Pris, you've survived a horrible ordeal. A traumatic experience. You've got to understand the after-effects. What did that Turkish captain tell you?"

"He warned me that ISIS is always on the look-out for wealthy foreigners to kidnap. Particularly women traveling alone," she recounted robotically. "But Israel is safe. You can come with me."

"You know I can't leave right now," he said, pointing to the stack of papers on his desk.

"Then don't come home either," she hissed. "I'll find someone else to accompany me." Priscilla slammed the door shut on her way out.

CHAPTER 14

"Cyberattacks are insidious. They're relentless, invisible, faceless. We can't see the enemy's uniform or the color of his skin," Montel Rice snapped, brown eyes flaring with determination. Caramel skin softened his chiseled features into a boyishly handsome portrait. Only a crown of tightly trimmed salt and pepper hair hinted at his age and military experience. Taryn sat at attention across a slab of varnished oak supported by two roughhewn sawhorses that served as Montel's conference table.

Lightning Strike's sprawling loft on West 22nd Street reflected the breakneck pace of the company's growth. Programmers and their detritus were crammed in everywhere. Many worked at communal tables, headphones glued to their ears. Two giant screens displayed maps, one of the United States, and one of Europe, Asia and Africa, with flashing red, yellow and green lights highlighting various states of cyber-stress. Al Jazeera footage rolled on a television monitor. The corner workspace, surrounded by a barricade of mouse gray fabric-covered partitions, was the only sign of Montel's stature.

"They assault our clients' networks in so many ways," he went on, launching his limber, six-foot frame gracefully from his seat to the whiteboard to diagram several attack vectors. A burgundy knit tie dangled from his neck. He had grown up in the Pacific Northwest, initially cultivating his computer skills at the University of Washington. Upon graduation, Montel enlisted in the Army, qualifying for the elite Ranger regiment, before eventually joining Cyber Command for what turned out to be a ten-year tour.

"They only need to find one gateway that's not secured," Taryn added. She had chatted with Professor Bierman over the weekend. Not surprisingly, he thought an entrepreneurial Israeli company, like Lightning Strike, would be a good fit for her. Now she had to sell herself to Montel.

"That's right." Montel tapped a marker on the board for emphasis. "Servers, laptops, tablets, phones, even watches are connected now. Our customers have hundreds of thousands of ports to defend. And the black hats have unlimited time and unlimited compute power. They *will* break in eventually."

"We utilized a multi-layered defense approach at Brightify," Taryn said.

"Almost every sophisticated business does that now. It may slow down the hackers for a few weeks, but it doesn't stop them. That's where Lightning Strike comes in. We set up decoy servers that trap the attacks after they penetrate the perimeter. Then we assess their cyber signatures, determine their source, and assess the potential damage they can cause. After we've completed our analysis, we strike – if our clients give the order."

"Are you concerned about ISIS?" Taryn asked, pointing in the direction of the television screen outside Montel's cubicle.

"Russia, China, Iran and North Korea are our clients' top nation-state priorities, roughly in that order. But we're concerned about everyone. Even common criminals here in America are getting more cyber savvy every day." Montel turned away from the board and marched over to the conference table. "As for ISIS, they're extremely active on social media, but we don't see much of them in the trenches. At least not yet."

"The United States needs to divert funds from conventional weaponry to cyber. We need to upgrade our penetration tools, payloads, facial recognition and analytics – just to get started." Taryn said.

"Damn straight. It's like Pearl Harbor in 1941. The prime assets of our country are docked in the harbor, barely defended, vulnerable to attack."

"And that wall we're building on the Mexican border won't help us much either."

"Hell, no. The Kremlin must be laughing its ass off. We're spending all that money, all that time and energy, to stop a few field hands from entering our country while the real enemy crawls across the fiber optic cables at the bottom of the ocean without detection."

"I guess that's why the world needs Lightning Strike." Taryn pushed back in her seat.

"And that's why Lightning Strike needs you. Your hack of the Russians was brilliant. And you had the balls, pardon my language, to pull it off."

"Thanks," she chuckled. *Balls have never been my problem.* "I'm interested in the job."

"Fantastic," Montel said, walking towards his cubicle's exit, ushering Taryn to follow. "Let me walk you over to Penelope Spencer's desk. She runs Research here in New York. You'd be working for her."

"Excuse me," Taryn said, rising. "I'm not going to leave Brightify to get buried on the org chart here."

Before Montel could respond, one of the techs - cargo pants, scruffy goatee, thick glasses - burst in. "Yo, Montel. The chief security officer at Wells Fargo's on the line. And he's pissed off," he huffed, ignoring Taryn.

"I better take this," Montel sighed, returning to his desk, shoulders sagging. "Sit, sit." He motioned for Taryn to stay.

"Yes, Charlie, we've got all our oars in the water. We've isolated the malware but we haven't been able to reverse engineer the code yet. Our staff in Tel Aviv is looking at it too."

Taryn's interest was piqued.

"OK, I know your C-suite is nervous," he paused, listening to the Wells Fargo exec. "And I know that your Lightning Strike contract is up next month. I'll get back to you as soon as we know something. Bye."

"Mind if I look?" she asked.

Montel hesitated, obviously weighing his options. "Sure." He projected a block of code onto the white board. Taryn stood and walked over to get a closer look, studying for several minutes.

"I'm going to bet this is coming out of Novgorod," she said, tracing two lines of commands. "CyberBanda used the same exploit technique to hack the ad servers at the Big Pharma websites - effective but not particularly elegant. Here's an open source patch that might help."

She scribbled on a pad lying on the conference table, ripped off the top sheet and handed it to Montel. "And I would send a warning to this email address. Tell CyberBanda - if they don't behave - you'll inform the Kremlin that they've been hacking Federation Council accounts. I wrote down two names so they know you're not playing games."

Montel raised his eyebrows, but dutifully typed in Taryn's suggestions. Within thirty seconds, a reply to his email appeared. *"Krasny Pizda.* My Russian's not too good," he chuckled. "But I think you struck a nerve."

"Red Cunt. Sounds like one of the old JusticeJoe tweeters," Taryn said as she stepped behind Montel to read his screen. "Those boys in Novgorod are sore losers."

Montel shook his head in disbelief. "You saved my ass. Maybe I can make a change in your job description."

"I'm listening," she replied, sitting back down across the desk from Montel.

Montel tapped his pencil several times. "What about becoming Lightning Strike's free safety, if you will, surveying the field and jumping into our high priority projects?" he asked. "Reporting directly to me."

Much better. "I've got a few questions." Taryn said.

"Shoot," Montel replied, easing back behind her desk.

"I understand that you just joined Lightning Strike a few months ago. What brought you here?"

"Fair question. I could tell you about the great technology, and the stock options, but the truth is - I needed a change of scenery. My boys are off in college now," he said, pointing to a framed family photo. "And, my wife, Carol, left me two years ago," he added.

"I'm sorry. I didn't mean to get personal," Taryn said, shifting uncomfortably in her seat. *The last thing I need is another boss on the prowl.*

"That's fine. It was a long time coming. A military wife has a tough life. I thought about retiring, playing some golf, traveling. But, I just turned forty-seven and I still have a lot of cyber-asses to kick," Montel chuckled. "I met Shahar Ram, Lightning Strike's founder, last winter at a conference in Europe. She convinced me to come on board - start a new life in a new city."

OK, that sounds reasonable.

"Who are Lightning Strike's top clients?" Taryn asked, consciously steering the conversation back to business.

"We serve eighty percent of the Fortune 500, plus forty-two

national governments around the world. We're just starting to get local governments and municipal agencies too."

"Con Edison?" Taryn inquired.

"Yes. They have a subscription to our cyber-signature assessment service, but never bought any of our other products. Why?"

"Nothing really. I had some odd activity from Con Ed people on my Brightify email account over the past few months."

"Con Ed pumps electricity to all New York City, so you'd think they would have a pretty sophisticated cyber defense."

"But they don't?"

"Not yet at least," Montel, replied, shaking his head. "For a long time, Con Ed was like a major league team with a minor-league budget. But they're making progress. The federal government is pushing everyone on the grid to bump up their cybersecurity spend."

She drummed her fingers on the table. "I'd like to work on Con Ed right out of the gate."

"Sure." Montel smiled. "We'd love you to come on board at Lightning Strike as soon as possible." He lifted a green pendaflex file on his desk, withdrew a sheet of paper, and ripped it in half. "That was your old offer," he said, stuffing it in the trash. He wrote down a new set of figures and handed the page to Taryn. "Here's our new offer – salary, bonus and stock."

Now it was her turn to smile. Less of a pay cut than she expected and the options could more than make up for the difference. "This works," she tucked the offer into her purse. "I'll give my notice at Brightify tomorrow."

CHAPTER 15

Mayar Tabak slapped down the screen of her laptop computer. "Allahu Akbar," she muttered under her breath, trying to maintain calm. The Con Edison network had flummoxed her again. She wanted to turn the lights off in New York City, not crawl record by record through some arcane information system trying to locate the account of a manager with global access. The system was so patched together and disorganized that it was easy to get lost. *Maybe that was Con Ed's cyberdefense strategy?* Viktor, the Russian, told her that it might take a year. How did hackers stay sane?

She stood and paced, wearing a tread in the already threadbare rug in her dorm room. A steady drizzle pinged the windowpane, better rain than snow, perhaps a sign that spring was approaching. A potpourri of brightly colored umbrellas scampered across the main quad: her fellow students hustling to the library, the dining hall, the gym. *Do they care about anything besides their own narrow, selfish lives?* She had a country to build.

Mayar checked her Con Ed list one more time.

Wilmer Santiago - cleaning services manager

Beth Soler - assistant benefits manager

Kate Austin - librarian

Gerard Herschkowitz - billing

Nick Lozano - dispatcher

The five sets of credentials that she had purchased from Pizza Boy all belonged to low level bureaucrats. She had logged in, explored their portal pages, checked out accessible files and apps, and logged out. Soler's account had led her to a database of employees in Queens, but she needed a second password to open it. Viktor might be able to crack that later. Santiago had access to an equipment closet, but it contained mops and brooms, not servers or switches. Mayar yawned. She had been up all night - first with her schoolwork, then with her hacking. She needed a drink.

She slipped a rain slicker over her faded Columbia sweatshirt, hood up to cover her hair, and headed downstairs. Joining the parade of students on the quad, Mayar headed out the main gate and crossed Broadway where a packed Starbuck's beckoned. The line at the counter snaked almost all the way back to the front door. Lost in her own quest, she ignored the idle chatter that enveloped her.

With chai tea and blueberry muffin in hand at last, Mayar searched for a table. Her hall mates, Amy and Sarah, and two other students that she vaguely recognized boisterously commanded the middle of the room. She steered clear, veering off into a corner. A couple at a table near the window appeared to be sweeping up their crumbs, so she shuffled in that direction, but two youngsters, freshmen obviously, beat her there. Sighing in frustration, she turned to leave. The drizzle outside had escalated into a downpour. She put her cup down on the corner of the counter to zip up.

"Mayar? Do you want to join us?" Amy called out, pointing to a now vacant chair sandwiched into the middle of their ring of cheer.

Mayar looked around one last time. There were no other options. "Yes. Thank you," she replied. Rolling her eyes, Sarah scraped her chair a few inches to the right to allow Mayar entry.

"This is Heather Sands. And this is Allison Gold." Amy made the introductions. "We all went to high school together."

"How nice," Mayar said, gingerly sipping her tea.

"We were talking about the geek that did the interviewing for Goldman today. I don't think he smiled once. Did you meet with him?"

"No."

"What are you planning to do after graduation?" Sarah interjected.

"Me?" Mayar asked, putting down her cup. "I'm not sure. Something in energy conservation, I hope."

"Mayar's a computer whiz. She belongs in *CSI: Cyber*," Amy teased, causing Mayar to duck her head in embarrassment.

"Allison's an intern in the mayor's office," Sarah interjected, pointing to her friend, a buxom girl with boyishly flipped hair.

"Working hard to become a full-time politico," Amy smirked as Allison's cheeks bloomed crimson. Mayar intently studied her cup of tea.

"Energy conservation? Mayar, that sounds interesting," Allison changed the subject. "The mayor's planning a big new recycling center on Staten Island. Our office is also meeting with Con Ed to plan for the annual summer surge. The city had three brown-outs during last year's heat wave."

"Really?" Mayar perked up.

"Nobody wants to risk a full-scale blackout."

"The grid? That's my specialty. I'd love to talk to you sometime," Mayar said tentatively. Her phone vibrated in her pocket. She snatched a quick look - a Telegram message from her brother. "Sorry, but I have to go," she declared, standing.

"Call me," Allison said, reaching into her purse for a business card from City Hall.

"As friendly as ever," Sarah commented as soon as Mayar was out of earshot.

Mayar stepped into the ladies' room and locked the door. Ahmed was not supposed to contact her today.

Another victory! More will follow! Her brother's message included a link to an article in the *Jerusalem Post*, reporting on an attack on a bus just outside the Old City. A lone Palestinian had killed two Israelis with a knife before the police shot him. *A patriot! But a fool too.*

She sat down on the toilet seat. How to tell her brother and his soldiers that these efforts were as futile as a mosquito nipping an elephant in the ass? How many mosquitos would it take to get the elephant's attention? How many to induce it to change direction? *But boys like their toys. Knives, guns, bombs - they are all the same. My plan is different.*

Alhamdulillah, she messaged back. Let Ahmed bask in his triumph. Maybe the victory will spur him to find a way to deposit the funds she needed in her offshore account. She watched for sixty seconds until the messages destructed.

The storm had not relented but Mayar couldn't wait. She dashed across Broadway, through the quad and up to her dorm room. The rain waterfalled down from her hair onto the keyboard of her laptop as she logged onto the dark forum. She left a private message for Pizza

Boy: ten grand if he could gain access to the second level of the network. And twenty-five if he could get an administrator's ID. That should get his attention.

CHAPTER 16

Dennis Walecka and Brian Valentine climbed up the stairs from the subway platform, exiting onto Broadway. The Saturday morning sunlight snapped them awake after the hour ride from Brooklyn. Dennis pulled a black Brooklyn Nets ski cap down over his ears to ward off the chill breeze, while Brian adjusted his glasses and re-read the address from the clipboard that he carried in his gloved hands.

The men spun around twice to get their bearings before heading east on 94th Street towards Central Park West. They skirted around a growling pit bull dragging along its paunchy handler. A couple sporting matching green headbands with the Spartan logo of Michigan State pushed a double-wide stroller packed with blankets and babies. Tracking the house numbers on the apartment buildings and bodegas, they reconnoitered past their destination, a nickel gray multi-family brownstone on a narrow block lined with leafless trees. They stopped at the light on Columbus Avenue and circled back.

"You ready?" Brian asked.

"Yeah," Dennis answered, cautiously sweeping his vision back and forth along the street. "Are you sure this is the right guy and the right address?"

"Mr. George Andropolis has been a VP at Con Ed for the past ten years. I confirmed his bio on LinkedIn. He replied to our phishing emails from Brightify so we got his social, his address and his employee number. When I hacked into his desktop, I found the password to his phone. If we get his phone, I bet we either find his Con Ed passwords, or enough personal information to figure them out ourselves."

"OK, OK."

"Stop acting like a pussy. There's twenty-five large on the line," Brian goaded his partner.

"Fuck you. I'll get the guy's phone."

"Take that hat off. Look professional. I'd do this myself but you're a much better talker than me. I'll be on lookout," Brian said, stepping back towards the line of parked cars. "You got the business cards?"

Dennis scrunched his lips as he unzipped his coat to reveal a fire engine red Verizon button down. He patted the chest pocket. "Right here."

"And the new phone?"

Dennis nodded. "I got it. Are you sure we got the right carrier?"

"I called Verizon last night to report a telephone problem. They confirmed that Andropolis is a customer."

Dennis reached out for a good luck fist bump, then strode purposefully up the stoop of the brownstone. He stabbed the button on the intercom and waited.

"Who is it?" a tinny voice replied as if beaming in from another planet.

"Verizon. Here about your phone."

"What phone?"

"212-531-2587. That's your number, right?"

"Yeah. But I didn't call Verizon."

"Your phone's been hacked. We can see it at our operations center. Didn't you see the email?" Dennis paused a second then added, "I've got a new one for you. No charge."

"A new iPhone?"

"Yeah, the latest model. Hey, It's cold out here. Mind if I come upstairs?"

The buzzer shrilled. Dennis pushed open the lobby door and stepped inside.

"On the second floor," Andropolis called, poking his head around the top of the staircase. Wire thin, he was wearing a forest green polo and khaki slacks.

"Here you go, man," Dennis said, offering a handshake with his right hand while conspicuously displaying the box with the new phone in his left. "I just need your old phone."

Andropolis pulled an iPhone 5 from his pocket. "How do I know this is for real?"

"Here, call my office," Dennis replied, handing over a business card. He peered into the apartment while Andropolis tapped in the number and spoke to Brian for several seconds. A mammoth TV console, at least ten years old, dominated the drearily furnished living room. *Either Andropolis is really frugal or Con Ed doesn't pay shit.*

"What about my contacts and other stuff?" Andropolis asked immediately after he disconnected with Brian.

"I can help you with that. It'll only take five minutes."

Andropolis swapped phones. He ripped open the box and removed the new device, rolling it over in his fingers. "My son has one of these. He lives in Queens."

"Best phone on the market. When it's running on the best network, of course," Dennis replied reciting Verizon's advertising tag line while tapping away on Andropolis' old phone

"Thanks, man." Andropolis offered after checking his updated contact list. "Have a great day."

"You get it?" Brian called when he saw Dennis bounding down the stoop.

"What do you think, asshole?"

"Let's get back to Brooklyn," Brian said, fist-bumping his partner again. "We've got to open up this phone and crack Andropolis' passwords. I'm sure the old fart is not using anything too complicated." They turned towards the subway.

"Show me the money!" Dennis shouted as they pranced down the street.

CHAPTER 17

Allison Gold scrutinized herself one last time in the ladies' room mirror, adjusting the simple pearl earrings and smoothing her charcoal slacks down over her hips. She was taking a risk, appearing unannounced at the Mayor's office, but she calculated it was her best, and probably last, opportunity to show off both her work and commitment to the cause before the big decision.

She looked at her watch. Only three thirty - the staff meeting was not scheduled to start until four. Perfect. She lifted her leather portfolio off the countertop and strode out the door. Ms. Whitworth did not look up as Allison approached.

"Excuse me," Allison said, shuffling her feet as she waited for a reply.

"Yes?" Whitworth asked.

"Can I get a few minutes with him? It's about the Pier 40 project."

"Can't it wait until the meeting?"

"Not really. He asked me for some information about the community group that's fighting his proposal to sell air rights. It's pretty important."

"He's been tied up all afternoon," Whitworth sighed. "But, I'll check." She stood, knocked on the Mayor's door, and entered, closing it behind her.

Two minutes later, Whitworth emerged. "He's still engaged. He may free up before four but he's not sure. You can wait out here if you like."

Allison tried to hide her disappointment, but a sagging smile betrayed her emotions. She had pulled an all-nighter working on this presentation. Taking a seat on the burgundy sofa, she started tapping away on her iPad to make sure that Whitworth saw her earnest intentions.

All the semester internships would be expiring in several weeks. Only two of the six interns would be hired for full-time positions at City Hall. Allison intended to be one of the winners.

She was re-reading an interview with a community board member, when Mayor Rosen's voice boomed from deep within his den, "Allison, come on in." She bubbled up like a boiling teapot.

Seated behind his massive oak desk, collar undone, lavender tie at an obtuse angle, shirt sleeves rolled up, Mayor Rosen set the postcard picture of the energetic, but over-worked, public official. His hair, flawlessly coiffed like a well-manicured lawn, was the only incongruity in the scene.

"I know that you're really busy, but I thought that you'd want to see this before the meeting," Allison said, striding confidently across the office. She set her iPad on his desk, paging quickly to her presentation, spinning the screen to face the mayor.

"Here are the metrics from my survey of the community board and the leadership of several other stakeholders in the Pier 40 complex," she announced leaning over the iPad to point.

"Hmm. There's definitely support here. If we sell the air rights, then we can use the funds to repair the pier before it sinks into the Hudson and keep the recreational facilities available to the public. Ben Olinmeister thinks we can get forty million."

"Forty million dollars? That's incredible," Allison gushed.

"Thanks, but Ben and his staff in the development office did the heavy lifting."

"Ben's counting on you to close the deal though. We worked together on this presentation," Allison explained, bouncing up to smile at the mayor. "Let me show you the key details," she added.

"Excellent," the mayor commented, leaning in to emphasize his enthusiasm, when she finished. "I'm liberal, and proud of it. But, I'm not anti-business, or anti-wealth, like the press always writes."

"We won't be bullied by billionaires who want to turn the city into their private playpen," Allison stood as she recited the mayor's campaign slogan.

"The staff is waiting in the conference room," Whitworth

interrupted, standing in the doorway.

"We're on our way," Rosen announced, standing up. He quickly reached for his suit jacket, tailored to add definition to his otherwise slack physique. "After you," he said as he ushered Allison out.

Allison walked a step ahead of the mayor, but slowed so they would enter the conference room together, parleying about her presentation. The optic had the desired effect, she noted, as several heads turned. Even Merriweather Gardner, her primary rival, flashed a look before re-engaging in conversation with Beverley Crock, community relations director and ardent opponent of any high-end development.

Willowy tall with a thick braid of cinnamon hair tumbling below her shoulders, Merry was foxy in every sense of the word. A graduate of the University of Virginia, she affected the doe eyed innocence and slow drawl of a Southern belle, surefire winners among the hard-boiled New York men that surrounded her. *If she says 'y'all' one more time, I'm going to puke.*

Stealing away at a staff social last Wednesday, Allison and Merry had handicapped the internship field. Julio Gonzalez was a lock among the three men, by far the smartest and hardest working. And a minority, they both acknowledged without actually saying it out loud. Chardelle Robinson, an African-American, was the third woman in the hunt. Capable, but not in their league. If Thomas picked Julio, then she would likely be free to select the second full-timer based solely on merit. Serena Thomas, the mayor's chief of staff, would make the ultimate decision, but Allison hoped the mayor to speak up on her behalf

"May the best girl win," Merry had proclaimed, offering a toast with a shot of Jack Daniels. *Bullshit.*

Thomas chaired the staff meeting, standing up front by the white board, while the mayor sat at the far end of the conference table. Crock led off with Merry manning the laptop projecting their slides to the room.

Crock highlighted the community's fear of increased traffic, the environmental impact, the overload to local schools and services, the disruption from construction, and the lack of any new jobs for residents. Allison scribbled several notes on points that she wanted to rebut. Merry incorporated two videos of emotional interviews with long-time residents at the end of the presentation. *Clever - wish I had thought of that.*

"Well done," the mayor complimented. "But, I don't see anything new here. Without the money from the real estate deal, the engineering studies predict the pier will just fall into the river one day." He turned towards his chief of business development. "Ben, what do your people have to say?"

Olinmeister pushed back his chair and stood. Wearing a navy Joseph Abboud suit that spotlighted his athletic frame, Ben Olinmeister looked more like a hedge fund tycoon than a civil servant. Only thirty-five, he had risen rapidly because of his fundraising skills and personal relationships with the young, hip generation of the city's business elite, particularly in the high tech and finance sectors.

In her peripheral vision, Allison noticed Merry lift a red pen off the table and languorously slide it back and forth between her lips. Olinmeister coughed twice and sipped from a bottle of mineral water. She fingered the start key on their presentation, ready to sink the opposition.

"Beverley's raised some important issues. The environment is a hot button with my people today. Maybe we should commission another study here. It will only take a few months."

What the fuck?

"Really?" Mayor Rosen asked, not bothering to hide his surprise. "We've covered the environmental issues before. Why should we retreat now?"

"Well, Beverley and her team have added a new slant here. I want to review the ramifications," Ben replied.

"OK then. This meeting's adjourned. Ben, come down to my office." The mayor ordered as he marched out. Olinmeister stuffed his paperwork back into his briefcase and chased after him.

"Nice job, ladies," Serena Thomas complimented as she followed them out.

Beverley and Merry exchanged victory smiles as they helped clean up. Allison seethed as she closed her laptop. Julio wandered over. "Want to go out for a beer?" She shook her head at first, then changed her mind. "Sure, I need a drink," she replied.

"Want to join us?" Julio asked Merry.

"No thanks. I still have work to do." Merry patted her laptop affectionately. "Y'all have fun."

Asshole.

***

After two Cosmos with Julio, Allison stomped back to work. The damp, evening chill, the last vestiges of winter, had settled downtown. She was thirty yards away from the security booth on the plaza fronting City Hall when she saw Ben Olinmeister on the way out, chatting with Merry Gardner. *That bitch!* Allison pulled the hood from her quilted down jacket over her head and tucked between two parked cars, pretending to scan the street for a cab

Allison followed as Merry and Ben headed west along Chambers Street, uncoupled but heads tilted together in animated conversation. Merry's long ponytail, flouncing from the back of a Wahoo's baseball cap, appeared to tickle her ass. They swung north on Greenwich, Merry looped her arm inside Ben's elbow. He disentangled and appeared to stop, but Merry kept moving, quickening her gait. After a moment's hesitation, Ben skipped to catch up. Allison ducked into Dunkin Donuts, popping out a few seconds later to see Merry tug Ben into an alley between two buildings. Still bolstered by the Cosmos, Allison couldn't resist walking by, head down but eyes swiveling towards the lovers, now lost in a tongue-sucking embrace in the dark.

Holy shit! What would Rosen say? What about Ben's wife? Allison recalled a leggy brunette at the office holiday party back in December. Pregnant with their second child. *What a douchebag - fairytaling down the street like a besotted teen.* But Ben's infidelity was not her problem. It was who he was fucking, or, more likely, who was fucking him that threatened her.

Allison reversed course, heading back along Chambers Street. She hopped down the steps to the uptown subway, a plan brewing to initiate a strategic partnership of her own.

***

Mayar Tabak didn't hear the knock. With headphones clamped over her ears, Amy Winehouse lamenting in the background, she was immersed in her homework, diagramming the electrical circuitry of a to-be-constructed skyscraper. She looked up when she saw the door

83

to her room open a crack. Reflexively, she snapped her laptop shut.

"Who is it?" she called out as the opening widened. It was Amy's friend from Starbuck's, Allison. She said something, but Mayar couldn't hear. Volume down. Much better.

"Hi," Mayar replied uncertainly, standing, headphones now ringing her neck, her eyes conveying the unspoken question.

"I need a favor," Allison answered without any more prompting.

"How can I help you?"

Allison detailed her predicament at City Hall, emphasizing her civic and moral duty, not her selfish interests.

"You want to spy on your co-workers?" Mayar asked when Allison concluded.

"That sounds so crass."

"But you want to check on their texts, emails and instant messages?"

Allison nodded. "Social media too. Brightify, Instagram, Snapchat."

"WhatsApp?"

"Sure."

Mayar reached into her desk drawer and pulled out a slim silver zip drive. She plugged it into a slot on the side of her laptop, sat down and began typing. Allison watched Mayar's fingers fly over the keyboard.

"You're going to need a RAT," Mayar deadpanned as she worked.

"A what?"

"A Remote Access Trojan. A stealthy rodent that creeps around a computer network gathering cheese, and delivering it to you every night," she replied, removing the zip drive and petting it gently. "This one's called Blackshades. Just plug the zip drive into your friend Merry's computer for thirty seconds."

"That's all?" Allison asked, a smile spreading across her face as she fondled the slender device with her thumb and forefinger.

"Just make sure that you destroy the drive when you're finished."

"Wow. Thanks. I owe you." Allison replied, stuffing the drive into her coat pocket. "You're into the grid stuff, right?"

Mayar swallowed hard, but nodded.

"Well, if I meet any of the bigwigs at Con Ed, I'll check to see if they have any internships available."

"That would be very helpful."

"See you around," Allison said, waving half-heartedly. "Stop by City Hall sometime. I'll give you a personal tour," she tossed over her shoulder as she exited.

Beaming, Mayar walked over to her dresser and picked up the picture of Fatima, lightly tracing the outline of her daughter's face with her index finger.

CHAPTER 18

"Can I come in, sir?" Taryn asked, rapping on the partition surrounding Montel Rice's office space.

"Sure. I've been meaning to stop by and say good-bye," Montel beamed, waving Taryn forward. "You're heading to Tel Aviv tomorrow night, right?"

"Yes, sir. I'm really looking forward to the trip."

"Fantastic. You've been at Lightning Strike for what, a month now? Everyone treating you well?" he asked.

"All good, sir."

"Lose the sir, please. You're not in the Army. Neither am I," Montel said with a smile. "What's on your mind?"

Taryn walked over to the whiteboard and picked up a black marker. "I think that Con Ed might be under attack."

"Under attack? That's a pretty aggressive claim." Montel stood, circled his desk and leaned against its far side, arms folded across his chest.

"OK - under attack might be a little strong, but I think that I have concrete evidence that hackers have penetrated the system." Taryn wrote three names on the board in block letters:

AUSTIN
SANTIAGO
SOLER

"Remember, in my interview, I mentioned some suspicious email activity on my Brightify account?" When Montel nodded, Taryn continued. "A friend of mine did me a favor. She rummaged through my deleted email bins and recovered a handful of names. Con Ed employees who replied to messages that I never sent."

"Go on," Montel asked, arms now hanging loosely at his side.

"ClickSecurity let me demo their user behavior analytics for a month, so I was able to establish baselines and scan for outliers and unusual activities."

"What do you mean by unusual?"

"Logons at odd times, like between 1 and 4 AM. Or database queries that the system rejected - repeatedly. Or, frequent requests for new passwords. The typical tactics hackers might use to scout a system."

"Honest people get lost too."

"I know," Taryn replied. She tapped the names on the board. "But what are the odds that these three showed up on all the lists?"

Montel frowned. "So, you think a hacker spoofed your Brightify account to target Con Ed employees, and is now using that information to attack the Con Ed system? Have you contacted Con Ed yet?"

Taryn nodded wearily. "Hackers attack their system every day. Usually a disgruntled customer trying to change their bill. Their endpoint security is solid, not foolproof, but good enough to catch the amateurs. Net, they're not too concerned. At least not yet."

"But, what about the pros, particularly the ones who might attack the grid? They're the ones that Lightning Strike's worried about."

"The truth is even the pros would have a really hard time getting into the grid. All the systems are automated and managed from highly secure, remote locations. The physical security at the control centers and on the streets is impressive. And the grid control systems are totally disconnected from the administrative and billing systems. Air-gapped. There's no way for a hacker to jump from one network to the other."

"But...?" Montel ruminated as he ambled over to the window behind his desk.

"But I believe that something's up," Taryn replied.

Montel strode back across the room, stopping only a few feet from Taryn. She could smell the coriander in his cologne. "What's your plan?" he asked.

"I have one more name," Taryn wrote GEORGE ANDROPOLIS on the board. "He's a VP. A big fish. But I think that his credentials have been compromised, too. I want your permission to set a trap."

"Whoa, slow down, cowboy. I trust your intuition but I want our techs to look at that virus signature. Compare it to the ones in our databases to see if it has the marks of any of the big-time players. And our lawyers need to sign off too."

"How long will that take?"

"A few days at most, but you can start the ball rolling tonight. Someone is on the desk in Tel Aviv 24/7."

"I'll put together an info package and send it over. I also think that we should alert Mr. Andropolis, so he can start changing his passwords immediately," she said.

"I served overseas with Joe Leary, Con Ed's Chief Security Officer. I'll give him a call first. But nothing else for now. Agreed?" Montel replied, offering a handshake.

"Understood, sir."

***

After shipping off the Con Ed details to Lightning Strike's Israeli office, Taryn headed to the gym, counting on an endorphin draining workout to throttle down from work. She would be flying the red-eye tomorrow evening and needed to sleep well tonight. Her phone buzzed on the walk home. Tel Aviv already? No, a text from Jimmy Mangano.

J: Still at the office?
T: Nope. Walking home from the gym. Where r u?
J: Still at work. Got a lead on the pizza guy.
T: Fantastic
J: We should talk.
T: Leaving for Israel tomorrow night. Call me in the AM?
J: What about a beer now?
T: Need to shower.
J: Not for me.
T: Meet me at the White Horse in 30 min.

***

The White Horse was an old-school, West Village pub dating back to the nineteenth century as a writer's nook. Freshly showered, Taryn was standing at the end of the bar, halfway through a Stella, when Jim entered in business attire sans tie, his lean, disheveled look attracting attention. A frizzy blonde, left hand pinned by a weighty diamond, peered around her beloved as he passed.

Unlocking her Pandora's box of erotic fantasies, Taryn summoned the almost forgotten image of a spirited coupling on a bare desk in a dark, deserted FBI office. *Was Jim off-limits tonight because they would be working together again? Was Marcy still in the picture?* Sensing the answers to both questions were yes, she quaffed her beer in a silent toast to reality, even if it sucked sometimes.

Jim kissed her cheek, lingering for a beat longer than friendly, before disengaging to order a Goose Island IPA. He pointed towards a just vacated booth in the corner. "A Chelsea Morning," vintage Joni Mitchell, played in the background. "You look zonked," he said.

"A little dumpling-eyed, but I'm OK." Taryn led the way, waiting for Jim to settle before shifting to business. "What's up with the pizza guy?"

"I spoke to the agents handling the Bingos breach. The company thought it had to be an inside job. They scoured their employee records and came up with a handful of possibilities. Our guys winnowed the list down to this guy - Dennis Walecka. No prior criminal record," Jim said, pulling out two photos from his jacket pocket. "Here's his employee ID."

"Nice tat," she jibed, pointing to the fire-breathing dragon on Walecka's right bicep. "Why him?"

"He started as a delivery man for Bingos about six months ago. After he got booted out of ASA in Brooklyn for hacking their system. Of course, the school never reported the crime for fear of spooking the student body. Happens all the time."

"How did Walecka penetrate the Bingos firewall?"

"He had an affair with his supervisor, a thirty-five-year-old single mom. She had entry level access and Walecka took it from there. We were able to trace most of his actions emanating from her account."

"Why did she come forward now?" Taryn swallowed the last of her Stella.

"Walecka dumped her last week. A few hours after he quit Bingos."

"Sounds like his timing coincides with the FBI stepping up its investigation."

"Yep. Our techs also got some insight into Walecka's cyber signature. Pretty vanilla actually. He was using an off-the-shelf malware stack."

"Just like my Con Ed hack," Taryn bolted upright.

"There's certainly a coincidence, but we haven't confirmed they're identical yet," Jim calmed her.

"When are you going to arrest Walecka?"

"We have to find him first. The address and bank accounts that Walecka listed are cold."

Taryn searched for a waiter to bring another round. "Doesn't sound too promising then."

"Every cop on the street will have this photo. And we listed Walecka's cyber profile at Proofpoint, Kaspersky, Lightning Strike and a couple of other threat intelligence databases."

"Do you have any of the IP addresses that Walecka uses as home base?"

"We're tracing them now, but that could take some time. Meanwhile, we hope he tries to hit another big shop in the city. They'll recognize Walecka's signature, shunt him off to a sandbox, and call us in."

"Sounds like a plan then." Taryn scanned the crowded bar again, standing, finally giving up on their waiter. "I need another round. You?"

Jim shook his head, sipping his half-finished beer. His gaze followed Taryn's blue jean clad butt as she returned to the bar, thinking briefly about what almost was, or what might have been. He had moved on, but he would be lying to himself if he said it was completely without regret.

His phone buzzed. While Taryn was chatting with the bartender, he surreptitiously checked Snapchat. A selfie from Marcy. As expected, she was waiting for him at the apartment that she shared with a friend on First Avenue. Her lush dusky hair fell well below her shoulders framing a freckled nose, toothy smile and pouting lips. Demure in her plaid PJs, buttons fastened right up to her neck, chest thrust forward, she flirted naturally with the camera.

Another buzz. Another photo with a more compelling message this time.

M: Coming soon??

Marcy's PJs were now off. Only a strategically placed Pooh Bear kept this image from an X rating. Jim slapped his phone back into his suit pocket.

"A toast to the capture of Dennis Walecka!" Taryn announced, placing two shot glasses on the table.

Jim laughed, raising his palm in a vain attempt to slow his friend down. Taryn had only one mode – direct, head-on assault. She was passionate and brave and, no question, on the fast-track to somewhere. He would have to watch out for her, or she could get hurt.

"I'll pass. I should go. Marcy's waiting up," Jim said, raising his beer bottle instead. "Have a great week in Israel. Safe travels," he offered.

"To safe travels," Taryn replied, knocking down the first tequila in a single swallow.

Jim lingered for five more minutes, anxiousness apparent, before giving Taryn a bon voyage hug and heading for the door.

Taryn was not accustomed to being left alone at a bar. *No sense wasting a drink.* She sipped Jim's untouched shot while surveying the handful of revelers congregating at the bar.

A football player type, sinewy shoulders busting out of a supposed-to-be-loose-fitting V-neck, caught her eye. He winked and ordered another two shots of Patron. Clearly paying attention, she thought approvingly. As he sidled over, Taryn envisioned a wide receiver, fast feet and soft hands. *Is it the body or the booze or the opportunity for a last-night-in-town fling?*

Football guy placed a shot down in front of Taryn, daring her to down it. She looked up - peach fuzz, freckles, and two puss-popping zits on his nose - and shook her head. It was too late and he was too young. She reached for a twenty-dollar bill to cover the drinks and headed for the exit.

CHAPTER 19

Dennis Walecka strolled along Church Avenue in the heart of Flatbush savoring the spring sunshine, unusually early for the last days of March. He sipped from his mega-sized black coffee taking in the pedestrian bustle surrounding the subway station and the array of discount stores, groceries, and fast food joints that flanked it. He noticed few white faces on the street. The low-income neighborhood was all he could afford - right now at least.

The aroma of grilled chicken and Caribbean spices wafted from the Checkers Diner, reminding Dennis that he had hardly eaten for the past forty-eight hours. He and Brian had pulled a hackathon, only stepping away from their computers to piss out the Red Bull that kept them going. The phone that they had snatched from George Andropolis, the Con Ed VP, had opened a gold mine, the real deal, not the low-level stuff that they had gleaned from the other accounts that they had sent over to Sully.

Their quest had started slowly, but, sometime yesterday, Andropolis' credentials started opening doors. Brian smiled for once when he saw the files coming across their screens. They were going to take a few hours off, then go back in and scrub the data. Sully had sent them a wish list. If they could fulfill it, he might be able to afford his own place downtown in a few weeks.

What is Sully going to do with all the Con Ed shit he seems willing to pay so much for? Brian thought Sully was the leader of a hacker team planning a data breach like they had read about at Target and Home Depot. Con Ed serviced over three million customers in the city. That data was extremely valuable.

Dennis wasn't so sure. Buried in Sully's list were requests for information on switches, network architecture, power stations and maintenance facilities. He didn't think any of those requests had a purely financial motivation. *Is Sully planning a hit on the electrical grid? Maybe he's Chinese or Russian? Who the fuck cares if he pays cash?*

The staccato rap beat of his ringtone interrupted Dennis' reverie. "Yo!" he boomed before crashing down to reality when he saw the caller ID, his homeboy on the NYPD.

"Hey dog."

"What up?"

"You, man. I'm staring at your ugly mug on my iPad right now. You're at the head of the FBI's 'most wanted' parade."

"Fuck!"

"You got it. Lay low, my boy."

"I owe you, man."

"Damn straight. Later."

Dennis pulled the Nets cap from his pocket and tugged it down over his ears. *Sully is going to have to up the ante.*

***

"Ya kalb!" Mayar swore under her breath when she read Pizza Boy's demand on her laptop later that night. The immoral dog had raised his price by fifty percent. He claimed to have obtained high level access credentials but was being pressured by the police. *Why would the police pressure him? Could it lead to me?* She messaged back that she needed to see proof of the quality of the materials before she would pay anything for them.

Mayar stepped away from her computer to plug in her hot pot. A cup of tea would calm her nerves while she waited for a reply. *I must be strong if I want to build the caliphate.* The icon flashed indicating another encrypted message from Pizza Boy. It contained a link and password to a file storage locker on the dark web.

Praise Allah! Pizza Boy had uncovered several treasures that dovetailed perfectly with her research. A schema of the Sherman Creek station in northern Manhattan included critical information on the transformers and switchgear. Con Ed buys its power from generating sources, like the Robert Moses Niagara Falls plant upstate. The power is delivered to the city over high voltage, long distance lines. Large transformers at stations like Sherman Creek step down the voltage so that the power can then be distributed to local substations which in turn feed electricity to residential and commercial customers across a grid of underground and overhead cables. Switching gear manages this electrical flow with the capability to break the circuit when necessary. Because of the danger of electrocution and fire from the high voltage lines, Con Ed's power stations were built like impenetrable fortresses. *Pizza Boy may have just uncovered an open door.*

Mayar wanted a second opinion on the data trove. She sent a Telegram message to Viktor including the link to the files. Mayar checked the time - midnight here. She knew that Viktor was located somewhere in Eastern Europe and kept a nocturnal schedule, so he might be asleep for several more hours. *Waiting again. The hardest part.* She tried to turn her attention to her studies, but fell asleep over her laptop.

The beep of the message indicator woke her at three. Viktor must be up early. She fumbled with the keys in her eagerness.

V: Very good stuff
M: Worth the price?
V: Maybe. Much work still ahead
M: I am prepared
V: Many have tried already
How does he know?
M: I will succeed
V: We can help
We?
M: Allah will guide me
V: You will need our help too
M: Of course
V: Ahmed must raise more money
M: Yes
V: It will be dangerous
M: My brother is not afraid

Mayar signed off. She would have to string Pizza Boy along until Ahmed came up with more funds. In the meantime, she would see what pearls her little RAT had pried from Allison and her friend's computers in the mayor's office.

***

"I'm at the airport. Just wanted to check in, sir." Taryn scanned the overhead monitor. Her El Al flight would begin boarding in ten minutes.

"I thought that we agreed on no more 'sirs'? My name is Montel."

"Sorry, sir. Any progress on Con Edison?"

"Maybe. The phishing malware used at Con Ed looks identical to the malware the FBI just circulated at Bingo's. Off-the-shelf. Not tremendously sophisticated. But, that doesn't necessarily prove that the same guy did both attacks."

"Fair enough. But they both look like lone wolf strikes?" Taryn asked.

"We can't be sure yet, but we don't see any signs that anyone's working for a foreign government."

"That's good news, I guess. What did Con Ed have to say about it?"

"I called my army buddy, Leary, their CSO, directly."

"And?'

"He's got more important threats to worry about than off-the-shelf hackers. The Con Ed grid is resilient and fully redundant. Even if an attack knocked out one node, which he thinks is highly unlikely, they could reroute electricity a thousand different ways."

"That's it?" she asked, kicking her wheeled suitcase with the heel of her gray suede boot.

"No, there's more. Leary does not want any extra attention that might stir up a hornet's nest with the public. The last thing this city needs is a panic attack."

"What about Andropolis' passwords?"

"Leary is going to have lunch with him next week. Andropolis is a senior guy, so Leary doesn't want to embarrass him. If Andropolis agrees, Leary will have his cyber team review his logs to see if there's been any suspicious activity."

"So where does that leave us?"

"Taryn, relax. Go to Israel, learn our products, meet our people."

Her exhale of exasperation was loud enough for her boss to hear.

"And have a little fun, too. It's a great country," he added.
"Yes, Montel."

CHAPTER 20

Taryn's head felt like it had survived the spin cycle of a washing machine by the time she reached the baggage claim at Ben Gurion International Airport. Despite Montel's advice, she had tossed in her narrow seat for the entire flight, unable to shake the image of Dennis Walecka. She had little doubt that he had hacked her credentials, albeit randomly, to burrow into the Con Ed system, even if the Con Ed people themselves seemed unconcerned about the breach.

Israeli border security appeared extra vigilant this morning, so it had taken forty-five minutes to clear the passport control line. All she wanted to do now was crash at her hotel for a few hours. Montel's assistant had said there would be a car waiting. She scanned the crowd. Several livery drivers were lined up, but none had a sign with her name on it. Exasperated, she checked her itinerary for a phone number to call.

"Ms. Booker?"

Taryn whirled to face a soldier, automatic pistol holstered at his hip, about her height with wind-whipped olive skin, bushy dark hair, and the supple musculature of a ballet dancer. Thick brows guarded soft blue eyes that probed through and around her, flickering across every detail of their surroundings. At least she thought he was a soldier. He wore a camo jumpsuit, red beret secured over his left shoulder, but his uniform lacked any identifying patches, ribbons, or insignia.

"That's me," she replied.

"I'm Eli Stern. I'll be taking you over to Lightning Strike this morning." He took command of her suitcase and pointed to the exit.

"Today's Saturday, the Sabbath. I thought that…"

"Shahar would like to see you immediately."

"Let's go," she replied, sweeping her wayward hair off her forehead as she followed his raffish silhouette out into the sunlight. *Should have cleaned up a little more.*

The ride from the airport was only an hour in light traffic. Taryn could smell the Mediterranean as she stepped out of the sedan in front of the high-tech office complex on Arieh Shenker Street in Herzliya, a northern suburb of Tel Aviv. Although situated at the heart of Israel's Silicon Wadi entrepreneurial zone, the street exhibited all the exuberance of a ghost town this morning. She strode into the glass-walled lobby, found Lightning Strike on the building directory, and pushed the button for the elevator. No service on the Sabbath. She trudged up the steps to the fourth floor.

With a knee-length strawberry kaftan barely camouflaging her heft, Shahar Ram waited in the vestibule. "A nice walk, eh? Welcome to Israel," she announced, enveloping Taryn in a hug. Sparkling, emerald eyes highlighted her otherwise plain, pumpkin shaped face. "Lev Bierman said that you were one of his brightest pupils."

"Do you know the professor well?"

"Cyber spooks generally travel in the same circles."

Shahar led Taryn back through a labyrinth of cubicles, largely deserted but neat, the exact opposite of the New York office. "Lightning Strike's really just an extension of the work that we started at the Unit," she explained when they entered her office. The azure sea, framed by a picture window, seemed to stretch all the way to France.

Taryn knew that "the unit" was Unit 8200 of the Israeli Defense Force Intelligence Corps, arguably the world's most technologically innovative and aggressive cyber lab. It maintained a massive listening post in the Negev desert that monitored all forms of communications in the Middle East, and elsewhere, with much less constitutional restraint than its equivalent, the National Security Administration, faced in the United States. Although never officially confirmed, the Unit's greatest triumph may have been in 2010 with the planting of the Stuxnet malware in the centrifuges of Iran's nuclear complex, effectively delaying its progress for several years.

"My country is under cyberattack every day," Shahar continued. "So we had to develop the means to evaluate, prioritize and defeat our enemies. I founded Lightning Strike to commercialize this technology and sell it to our friends outside of Israel."

"These friends, as you call them, are helping defend Israel too - at least indirectly," Taryn commented.

"That's true. Cybercrime is expensive, but the costs are ultimately manageable. Cyberterror, on the other hand, might be the greatest threat facing the democracies of our world. We must cooperate and share intelligence if we're going to thwart it." Shahar pointed to a chair at the chrome-framed, glass conference table beside her desk.

"Easier said than done," Taryn said as she sat down.

"I read your report on Con Edison. That's why I asked you to come into the office right away." Pleased, especially after Montel's discouraging feedback, Taryn leaned forward, eager to hear where Shahar was headed.

"As you can imagine, we have a high degree of interest in communications emanating from Raqqa." Shahar projected a slide on the sixty-inch screen on the far wall. "ISIS's cyber efforts have largely focused on recruitment and encouragement so far." Shahar flipped through several ISIS campaigns. "Social media, Twitter, videos. Calls to arms. Gruesome images seem to attract young people unfortunately. But they haven't posed a serious threat to Israel, or to our clients and friends."

Shahar paused for a sip of water from the bottle on her desk. "In the last few weeks, though, my colleagues at the Unit have come across several messages that are potentially more disturbing. It appears that someone in ISIS command has developed an interest in SCADA technology," she continued.

"SCADA?" Taryn asked, reaching into her bag for a pen to take notes.

"Systems Control and Data Acquisition. Smart machines. They can run factories, airplanes, railroads, electrical grids."

"Like Con Edison?"

"Exactly. Very sophisticated technology that requires a high level of expertise to program. It would require a team of skilled hackers to mess with it. Well above ISIS' capabilities today. At least that's what we thought."

"But something's changed?" Taryn swiveled her chair away from the screen.

"Possibly. We recently learned that Viktor, a well-known nomme de guerre in the black hat community, now has ties to Raqqa. His CyberBanda gang has launched several successful attacks on democratic governments, most recently in the Ukraine, among other projects."

"I've had the dubious pleasure of CyberBanda's acquaintance."

"On occasion, ISIS will employ locals to do their dirty work," Shahar continued. "...particularly when they can't plant their own operatives on the ground."

"Dennis Walecka?" Taryn asked incredulously. "He's a jihadist?"

"Probably just a mercenary. Your report indicated that he appears to be infiltrating a network that's outside his normal sphere of operations."

"So, you put one plus one plus one together and get...?"

"A possible cyberattack on the New York City electrical grid. I stress 'possible.' This may all add up to nothing, of course."

"But if you're right, who's paying Walecka? Who's really in charge?" Taryn asked, now standing up.

"Billion dollar questions. Hopefully you can help us find the answers." Shahar closed her laptop. "I'd like you to spend the next few days with our people here. You need a crash course on SCADA devices and ways to attack and defend them. It's a different world than the social media systems you've been working on in the States."

"I'm ready," she replied, stifling a yawn.

"I forgot. You're still on New York time. We've booked you into the Dan Accadia by the beach. Why don't you go back there and get some rest? Eli will pick you up at 8 tomorrow morning."

"I'm fine. We can start now."

"We've had enough work for the Sabbath already. We'll put in a full day tomorrow."

***

Taryn was burrowed deep underneath her comforter at the Dan when a buzzer blasted somewhere in her room. She heaved to her side, dragging her brain slowly back to consciousness, and reached for her phone on the nightstand. Karim James.

"Hey," she garbled.

"Sorry to wake you."

"How could you tell?"

"I was hoping you could help me out."

"Sure." Taryn realized that she might have sounded less than enthusiastic. "What do you need?" she added with a little more zest.

"Priscilla Cabot, my college roommate's mother, called thirty minutes ago. She asked me to accompany her to a meeting. In Tel Aviv."

"I'm pretty sure I'm already here," Taryn cracked, sitting up to looking around her hotel room.

"My thought exactly."

"I'm only half awake but I'm betting there's more to this request."

"Good bet. Mrs. Cabot can give you all the details herself, but here's the background." Karim inhaled deeply before continuing. "I was really close to their son, JJ, for my first two years at Yale. Spent time at their home in Greenwich; even went skiing with them in Vail on February break. Pretty amazing trip. But then we split, or rather I split, the summer after sophomore year. JJ drugged out, dropped off the football team, began to run with a bad crowd. Rumor had it that his folks used some pull to get him out of a bust in New Haven for dealing coke. He took a year off, did some serious rehab, and then returned to Yale."

"Sounds like a happy ending." Taryn walked over to her window, opening the curtains to see the beach, but it was still dark out.

"Not quite. JJ left for Europe the day after the graduation ceremony. He posted photos regularly on Brightify until late August. The last one was from Istanbul. Then he completely dropped out of touch. Until last month."

"When he called his mother?"

"Nope. Another friend from Yale, Fiona Peterson, posted a photo of the two of them in Tel Aviv."

"After six months of nothing, this photo surfaces. Then what?"

"Mrs. Cabot waited for a call, a text, another post from JJ – but nothing for the whole month of March."

"So now Mrs. Cabot wants to come to Israel and visit with Fiona?"

"Yep. She's a tough woman, the kind who won't take no for an answer. But, there's even more."

"I'm listening," Taryn sat back down on her bed.

"Turns out Mrs. Cabot went to Istanbul in early February to track down JJ..." Karim paused again "...and got kidnapped by some ISIS thugs." He filled Taryn in on the details.

"Shit."

"Luckily, she got rescued before they crossed the border into Syria."

"And she wants to come back for more?" Taryn asked incredulously.

"That's what I said. But she's a mother. And JJ's her only child. She'd do anything to find him."

Taryn stayed silent for a few seconds. "What about her husband? Isn't she married to John Cabot, the president of Credit Lafayette?"

"Yep."

"I've never met Mr. Cabot, but Micolo said he called to put in a good word for me after that Elvira King video." Taryn opened her laptop and logged into the hotel wi-fi. "And he's not coming to Tel Aviv?"

"Nope."

"That says a lot right there."

"Agreed. But John Cabot's a high-profile guy with multiple agendas. I'm not saying he's given up on his son, but I think he's wary of any public blowback from JJ's actions."

Taryn googled John Cabot, scrutinizing his photo. She thought about her own father. He would search to the ends of the earth if she ever went missing.

"I know this is a huge ask. But, Israel's a safe spot. And the Cabot's were like my second family for a while at least," Karim persisted. "And Fiona's a friend too. The three of you could meet in a restaurant or somewhere out in the open. You could bring someone from Lightning Strike if you wanted."

"I'd like to help the Cabots, but something doesn't feel right." Taryn searched for a news story about Priscilla Cabot's kidnapping and rescue, but found nothing. "Why don't you send me that photo of JJ and Fiona? I'll run it by an old friend and make sure he thinks the meeting's cool."

"On the way."

CHAPTER 21

"You're looking much more vibrant today," Eli commented when Taryn settled in his back seat on Sunday morning. She was wearing khakis with a maroon tee and a distressed leather blazer, her hair tied back in a ponytail.

"That obvious, huh?" Although she had barely slept much after the call from Karim last night, Taryn too was surprised at how rejuvenated she felt.

"It's my job to notice," Eli replied. A snug navy polo rippled over his abs as he steered through the clutter of traffic surrounding the hotel entrance.

"Are you in the military?"

"Officially retired as of three years ago, but still in the reserves."

"You're pretty young for retirement."

"Thirty-six, but thank you."

They drove along the coastal road in silence for a few minutes. Taryn noticed more activity on the streets, especially for early on a Sunday morning.

"Today is a work day for most of us," Eli said, as if reading her mind.

Six day workweeks, great education system, military training for everyone. No wonder the Israeli economy is booming. "Do you work for Lightning Strike?"

"For Shahar, primarily. We want to make sure our best people are protected. In case the cyber war ever turns into a real war."

"I thought Israel was safe."

"It is - most of the time. But we must always be vigilant."

"And prepared," Taryn noted, her eyes flashing to the pistol on Eli's hip.

Her ringtone interrupted their conversation.

"That photograph that you sent over a few hours ago?" Professor Bierman asked haltingly. Although the Caller ID was blank, Taryn had no trouble identifying his gruff voice.

"Yes, sir."

"Your friend, young Mr. Cabot, has been on our radar for some time, unfortunately."

"That's not a good sign."

"When Mr. Cabot visited Israel last summer, he got involved with a nefarious crowd. Drug dealers and terrorists."

"Why didn't the Israelis arrest him?" Her question jolted Eli like a cattle prod. He cranked his head to flash a puzzled glance in the rear-view mirror.

"Israel is a democracy. They don't just go around arresting people. Besides, they wanted to see who else turned up."

"So, what happened to JJ?"

"I am embarrassed to say that John Cabot Jr. just dropped out of sight. Per the timestamp on the JPEG file, the photo was taken last August, about the time we lost track of him."

"JJ's mother plans to come to Tel Aviv to meet with Fiona, the girl in the photo. Mrs. Cabot would like me to accompany her to the meeting." Taryn crossed her legs and glanced out the window at the sea.

"Mrs. Cabot's last excursion in search of her son detoured badly."

"Yes. I'm aware of that. But, I take it that the FBI would have an interest in learning as much as possible about JJ's whereabouts."

"The Israelis as well."

"Then I'll accept Mrs. Cabot's invitation."

Bierman acknowledged his appreciation and signed off. Taryn texted Karim to let him know the meeting was on. He could send her contact information to Mrs. Cabot in the morning.

"We're here," Eli announced, guiding the car to a stop.

***

"We're going to visit our threat evaluation lab on the third floor today," Shahar said, leading the way down the stairs. "You'll need this to enter," she added, handing Taryn a lanyard with her photo ID to wear around her neck.

After displaying their badges to the security guard in the third-floor lobby, they sallied past a warren of partitioned office spaces occupied by earnest young programmers, heads down at their keyboards. The second security stop required validation of their fingerprints by an electronic reader. Another bevy of programmers, slightly more gray hair this time, greeted them. A retina scan was required for passage through the third security checkpoint.

"We're in," Shahar announced at last, pointing proudly to a windowless situation room: five giant screens on the wall; five technicians - three men, two women - hunched over monitors. She gave a brief greeting to the team, then continued "This is the Red Room. All the computers here are air-gapped; no network connection to the outside. No DVDs or zip drives allowed inside. We want complete separation from the internet and all other systems at Lightning Strike." After Taryn nodded her understanding, Shahar led them to a vacant workstation and rolled up her sleeves. "Miriam, can you get us started, please?"

"Yes, Ms. Ram," a puckish girl, no more than eighteen years-old, with long, straight hair bounded to the front of the room.

"Miriam just joined us a few months ago after she completed her two years of required military service with the Unit," Shahar explained. "She's a graduate of Magshimim, a government sponsored program for high school students from underprivileged areas who have demonstrated exceptional skill in computer science. Miriam's become our wonder child on virus design."

"Ms. Ram asked me to give you a brief tutorial on SCADA viruses," the young lady began, blushing, as she aimed a laser pointer at one of the monitors displaying a wall of programming code. "Like all malware, SCADAs have two basic components - a delivery vehicle and a payload. The big differences are the target and the layers of complexity. Most commercial viruses, like the Upatre one that Mr. Walecka utilized in his pizza scam, indiscriminately attack every machine that they encounter. They have a minimal level of encryption and generally don't do much to evade an up-to-date anti-virus scanner. Also, Microsoft, Apple, and Android regularly patch their operating systems to shut down known attack vulnerabilities."

Basic stuff, but Taryn nevertheless was impressed with the poise of the young data scientist. She scribbled a note about the code that Miriam displayed and nodded for her to continue.

Miriam clicked to a new screen. "SCADA viruses, on the other hand, are highly targeted attackers. This one, for example, is vectored only at Siemens industrial controllers. It will scan every machine it lands on but will only install itself on Siemens gear." Pointing to clusters of code circled in red, she added, "It utilizes multiple levels of encryption and four different zero days in the Siemens operating system to make sure it gets inside."

"Four zero days? Someone spent a lot of time and money going after Siemens," Taryn interjected. The 'zero' referred to the number of days that the software developer, Siemens in this case, would have had to fix the bug. Like a secret passage into a fortified castle, 'zero day bugs' could be extremely valuable because no one, except the discoverer, knew about them. The FBI had supposedly paid over a million dollars for a zero day that would unlock an iPhone belonging to a suspected terrorist.

"Exactly. This package buries deep into the memory of the Siemens controller to avoid detection. Once in place, it evaluates roughly four hundred variables specific to the environment. When a designated event occurs, the embedded virus will come to life and take control of the machines."

"How did the designers deliver the virus?" Taryn asked.

"Great question," Shahar cut in. She joined Miriam up by the monitor. "Unfortunately, the answer is classified."

I bet she's talking about Stuxnet - the virus that the Israelis planted to screw up Iran's nuclear program. Holy shit, that must be the code on the board.

"An agent, a human agent, just popped a zip drive into a Siemens controller somewhere?" Taryn wondered aloud. *An agent undercover in Iran no doubt.*

"We need to get to work," Shahar ignored Taryn's question and retreated to her seat. "I want you to become familiar with the attack vectors and the holes in the controller architecture that they exploited."

The three women spent the rest of the day analyzing the Stuxnet code line by line, until Taryn finally emerged from the Red Room at seven-thirty. She was surprised to see Eli waiting in the car downstairs.

"Back to the hotel?" he asked when she opened the door.

"Yeah, I'm beat. I'm surprised you're still around."

"Shahar wants me to look after you. You're our prized recruit, you know."

"I'm flattered, but I don't think I need a babysitter," Taryn snapped as she climbed in.

"I wouldn't call it that."

"You're right. I'm sorry. It's been a long day." She settled into the backseat and stared blankly out the window, trying to unwind. No luck. She reached for her phone and speed-dialed Jim, reaching him on the second ring.

"Hey, just wanted to check in."

"Great timing. I was just going to call you," Jim replied. "Walecka posed as a Verizon rep to con a senior Con Ed guy out of his phone. We finally got a positive ID."

Taryn snapped upright. "George Andropolis, I bet."

"Yeah, how did you know?"

Montel's message to Leary obviously stirred the pot. "His name came up in my research at Lightning Strike. I thought his credentials were compromised," she replied.

"Well, you were right. Andropolis had access to all kinds of personnel and billing records. Con Ed is going through them right now. Could be a big data breach. Every company experiences them now, unfortunately."

"That's all?"

"What do you mean?"

"What about field operations? The electrical grid?"

"Andropolis didn't have access to the grid. Just the admin stuff. At least that's what he claimed."

"What's the next step?" she asked.

"Con Ed will notify its customers as soon as they can determine the scope of the breach. And we're circulating Walecka's photo again. We've got him tied to both Bingos and Con Ed now."

"OK, thanks."

"Look, I know you've been thinking the theft of your Brightify credentials might be a lead-up to something much bigger, but it looks like both jobs were pretty routine hacks – all too common these days. I just hope we caught in time to prevent any major damage."

Taryn exhaled in frustration. First Montel, now Jim - both downplaying her gut feel that something big was up at Con Ed. Only Shahar appeared to be in her corner. She wasn't going to quit but she couldn't be a sore loser either.

"You're right. Congratulations - it could be two big wins for you."

"Look, we're going to nail Walecka soon. The pressure's on, and he's bound to make a mistake."

"You can take Marcy out to celebrate."

"I'd like you to meet her sometime. She's…"

"Hey, I've got to go. Keep me up." Taryn disconnected, immediately regretting her bitterness. *Jim's a good guy. He deserves to settle down. If that's what he wants.*

She tried to fit Stuxnet into the puzzle. The virus was tremendously complex, developed by a nation-state that had devoted millions of dollars and thousands of hours of programming talent to it. If anyone was trying to attack Con Ed, they would need a similar cyberweapon. Russia? China? Iran? They each had the resources but knew that the US would retaliate in kind for any cyberstrike. North Korea? The government in Pyongyang was reckless enough to try anything, but they seemed to be spending their big bucks on nuclear weapons these days.

ISIS? Nothing to lose, but no one thought they had the talent or the money for this kind of job. *Could they have a silent partner in CyberBanda? Pretty far-fetched.* Maybe Jim was right. Just another hack. Like he said - all too common these days.

"Bad news?" Eli asked, breaking the silence.

"Not really." She sighed and turned back to the window, surveying the landscape of the well-to-do Tel Aviv suburb. Neatly groomed lawns, gated entrances, sleek high rises, shopping malls and office parks whizzed by. It really did look like Silicon Valley. *But what if Jim is wrong? And Walecka is a pawn in a much bigger game? The FBI will find out for sure when they locate him.*

"How did you get into hacking?"

"Excuse me?" Taryn replied, still lost in Walecka-land. "Hacking? I prefer to think of myself as a cybersecurity analyst."

"Whatever," Eli chuckled. "How did you get started?"

"My mom majored in computer science. I grew up on a ranch in Colorado - didn't have many friends nearby - so I had a lot of time to spend online. I found that I liked to code. It's creative. It's analytical. It's precise. Hacking just ratchets the adrenaline up a notch."

"Your scuffle with the Russians sounded pretty exciting."

"I guess I got a little carried away there. But, that's my dad's genes

– he's ex-military – doesn't tolerate getting pushed around." A modest grin creased Taryn's face, as she acknowledged Eli's low-key compliment. "What about you? Where are you from?"

"I grew up in Kedumin. It's a settlement in the hills of the West Bank. A beautiful spot."

"Aren't the settlements dangerous places to live?"

"Unfortunately, yes," Eli replied. He glanced skyward and bit his lower lip. "Too dangerous sometimes."

"You lost someone you loved?" she asked, leaning forward.

"Yes, my wife and son. They were victims of a suicide attack - almost ten years ago now."

"Oh my god. I'm so sorry," Taryn said. Her current professional drama immediately plummeted in significance. She settled into the quiet safety of the car and left Eli to his memories for the remainder of the ride.

***

A message from Priscilla Cabot awaited Taryn back at the hotel. Exhausted, she washed up and slipped into her PJs before returning the call.

"Thank you so much," Priscilla gushed before Taryn could even say hello. "I hate to ask your help, but, John, my husband, won't come to Israel with me. He thinks I'm crazy. Thinks our son will turn up whenever he's ready. But I don't buy that. I'm JJ's mother and I'm going to do everything in my power to find him."

"Karim filled me in on your experience in Turkey, so we need to agree to some conditions." Taryn paced back and forth in her room.

"Anything you want."

"The meeting with Fiona needs to be outside in a public place. And I want to have a friend with me. For security."

"I don't want to scare Fiona away. She's the only link I have left to JJ." The desperation was obvious in Priscilla's quavering voice.

"OK, my friend doesn't have to meet Fiona, but he has to be close by. That's the only way I can help you, Mrs. Cabot."

"I understand," Priscilla replied, toughening up, pausing to consider her next step. "I'll reach out to Fiona right now. If she's amenable, I can fly over tomorrow night and arrive in Tel Aviv on Tuesday morning."

"I'm going to be in meetings that run pretty late that night," Taryn replied, sitting down at the desk and jotting down a note on a hotel stationery pad. "Can you set our rendezvous up for Wednesday night?"

"Of course. You don't know how much I appreciate your help."

CHAPTER 22

Mayar knew she would be late for her morning lecture, but she didn't care. She skipped into the shower and dressed quickly. She was going to see Fatima today. Ahmed had set up a Skype call. He would be on the line too. It had been weeks since she had visited with Fatima, even longer since she had actually seen her half-brother.

"Hello, my darling," she cooed in Arabic as soon as the little girl's dimpled cheeks appeared on screen. Wearing a white smock, Fatima was sitting on Ahmed's lap, holding a faded pink blanket in her hands.

"Go ahead," Ahmed whispered, careful to keep his face out of the picture.

"I miss you," Fatima replied in halting English. Mayar splayed her fingertips against the image of her daughter's face and gently stroked her hair. She wanted to burst through the screen and wrap her in her arms. They spoke in Arabic for ten minutes. She liked to eat grapes. It rained yesterday. She wanted a cuddly dinosaur, like Barney. Say goodbye now, Ahmed nudged.

"Good-bye, mommy."

"Good-bye, my sweet. I will see you soon - in Raqqa," Mayar said, wiping a tear from her eye. It was the first time that Fatima had called her "mommy" – as if the little girl knew Mayar's plans to adopt her as soon as they reached their new home. Leathery female hands lifted Fatima from her half-brother's lap.

"Does she have enough to eat?" Mayar asked.

"Yes, *Alhamdulillah*. The women make sure of it. They know her mother is a fighter."

"And you? Are you well?"

"As well as can be. Business is difficult, but..."

"Shh. Not on this call."

"I will send you a message shortly. By the usual channel. Fi Amaan Allah." Ahmed concluded before the screen went dark.

Mayar sat at her desk immobile for five minutes, surveying her cramped dorm room. HP laptop, Jambox speaker, textbooks, refrigerator, Wi-Fi, electricity 24/7 - she was so much luckier than her sisters in the Middle East. But I would give it all up for them. I am a soldier, fighting for Fatima and thousands of other young girls. They deserve a better life - in their own homeland. Free from Israeli soldiers in the streets and American missiles falling from the sky. ISIS isn't perfect, but it has succeeded in carving out a nation where all others have failed. I will do my part to ensure its success.

The Telegram icon blinked on her screen. Ahmed. Allah will guide me.

A: I have good news
M: Yes?
A: The rich American has returned in search of her son
M: Go on
A: I have arranged for an infidel whore to bring her to me
M: Why will she come?
A: For news
M: Is her son in Raqqa?
A: No. The coward ran away. He probably died in an alley with a needle in his arm
M: But the mother does not know that
A: Correct. Or she would not be here
M: Her husband will pay dearly for her return?
A: Yes.
M: You failed the last time she was in your grasp
A: We will not fail again
M: Insha'Allah

Pizza Boy pressured her almost every day now for money, whining that the police were hunting him with increasing intensity. He would need to leave New York City shortly. Mayar clicked on her keyboard to check the balance on the operational account that her brother provided. As she suspected, he had not deposited any new funds this week.

Even if Ahmed succeeded in kidnapping Priscilla Cabot, it could take weeks, or longer, to collect the ransom. She would have to figure out a way to stall Pizza Boy. And if Ahmed fails again? Her mother, and her wealthy third husband, had reached out several times over the years, offering to help with her tuition, but she had not returned their messages. Viktor had also indicated that he could help with money. Both options, unfortunately, came with strings attached. I will find a way. Allah will guide me.

CHAPTER 23

"Fancy seeing you again," Taryn joked as she opened the car door outside Lightning Strike's office building on Wednesday night. Four straight days and nights in the Red Room with Shahar and her techs had battered her brain and body like a cage fight with Ronda Rousey. The conversations with Eli on the drives back and forth to the hotel each day had become a welcome respite, so welcoming that she found herself now sitting up front in the passenger seat.

"At your service," Eli replied. "We have plans tonight?"

"Yes. Thanks for coming along."

"Not babysitting, am I?" Eli winked.

"I really was a bitch that first night."

"The term did cross my mind."

"Well, your assistance tonight would be most appreciated." she said, surprised at her sense of relief.

"Where to?"

"First, back to my hotel to change. After that, I'm not sure. All I know is that I'm meeting Mrs. Cabot at The Carlton. She said that we could catch a cab there to meet her son's friend Fiona."

"OK then, you have a driver for the entire evening. No need for a taxi."

With a pistol in a shoulder holster under his blazer. Hopefully that won't be necessary.

Taryn sprinted up to her room, returning in twenty minutes wearing all black - jeans, tee, boots, and a Helmut Lang cardigan.

"You clean up well," Eli remarked, as Taryn settled in next to him.

114

"Very New York, but maybe a little goth for Tel Aviv."

"Suits the occasion, I guess," Taryn replied. Her hours at work had distracted her, but anxiety over the upcoming meeting had swept down like an avalanche.

"What brings Mrs. Cabot to Israel?" Eli asked as he drove south along the coastal Ayalon Highway into Tel Aviv. In the light evening traffic, the drive to Priscilla's hotel located on the marina would only take twenty minutes.

"Her son," Taryn replied.

"Does he live here?"

"No. Priscilla thinks that he got lost here. She hasn't heard from him in nine months so she's trying to trace his travels."

"No communication at all?" Eli's military antennae were activated.

"No."

"That's not good."

"I know." Taryn looked out the window, taking in both the sea and the signage for the Dov Airport which handled domestic flights. JJ could be anywhere in the world - if he was still alive.

"Is Tel Aviv her first stop?"

"No. She traveled to Istanbul in February. It didn't go well." Taryn relayed what she knew about Priscilla's kidnapping and rescue, realizing that she should have told Eli this information sooner.

Eli veered into the right lane and slowed down. "And who are you meeting tonight? I'd like to request a background check. Just to be safe."

"Fiona Peterson. She went to Yale with Mrs. Cabot's son."

They traveled in silence for the next ten minutes, crossing the Yarkon River, the unofficial border of central Tel Aviv. The barren, white masts of the sailboats docked at the marina loomed like sentries in the night.

Priscilla was pacing in front of the hotel, smoking a cigarette. She wore tailored, hunter green slacks and a short chocolate colored leather jacket with a matching Hermes bag in her grip. She tossed her cigarette butt to the pavement and reached into her bag for another as the car approached.

The Carlton's uniformed valet opened the door for Taryn as they pulled up. "I'll only be a second," she said as she swung her legs out.

Before she could stand, Eli reached for her shoulder. "Relax, I'm here. I'll look after you."

Taryn nodded and stepped to the curb.

"Mrs. Cabot?" she called. "Are you ready?"

Startled, Priscilla dropped her just lit cigarette, nervously grinding it out with her toe. She strode towards Taryn, extending her hand. "Thank you, again, for coming tonight."

"It's really no problem at all. My associate from Lightning Strike, Eli Stern, will drive us if you don't mind. He knows the city well," Taryn replied, pointing the way to Eli, who had just stepped around the car to open the rear door. He had buttoned his jacket, hiding the bulge from his gun.

"Where're we going? Eli asked, as Taryn followed Priscilla into the back.

Priscilla waited for Eli to return to the driver's seat. She fumbled in her purse for a note. "Hoodna," she read. "It's on Abarbanel Street."

"That's a popular bar in Florentin. There's a lively street scene in the neighborhood," Eli replied approvingly. "It's only about fifteen minutes from here," he said, shifting into drive. Once they were safely away from the clutter of the hotel entrance, he cast a quick glance in the rear-view mirror at Taryn.

"What else can you tell me about Fiona Peterson?" Taryn asked, picking up Eli's cue.

"Not much. I understand that she's quite the party girl, but that's not a surprise. My son is no angel himself."

Taryn assessed her companion in silence for the next ten minutes. Was Priscilla incredibly brave or incredibly foolish? Or both? Taryn remembered sitting by her mother's bedside in the final days watching helplessly as she wasted away. *Would I have traveled anywhere in the world if I thought there was even a sliver of hope of finding a miracle cure?* She refused to even accept that mom was gone until they wheeled her corpse out into the hall. How could Priscilla *not* try to find her son? No matter what the cost.

"The gem of the Middle East," Eli announced proudly, as the lights of the Tel Aviv skyline came into full view - modern office skyscrapers, terraced residential towers, luxury hotels on the boardwalk.

"Honestly, it's much more than I expected. It doesn't look..." Priscilla's voice trailed off.

"Jewish?" Eli finished her sentence.

"I was going to say 'biblical'," she snapped.

"Touché," Eli laughed. "I guess I'm a little too sensitive. You're thinking of Jerusalem. Its roots go back three thousand years."

"I'm going to stay a few extra days to tour Jerusalem and Bethlehem," Taryn chipped in.

"You should have an escort in Bethlehem. It's in the West Bank under the control of the Palestinian Authority, not the Israeli government. We've had some incidents in the area lately," Eli replied.

"I'll take that into consideration." *Is that an offer?*

"Almost there," Eli announced five minutes later as he turned onto Abarbanel.

Florentin had the gritty look and feel of New York's East Village, an industrial zone gentrifying into hipster heaven. Corrugated roofed warehouses and storefronts mixed with low rise apartment blocks. Although only 9PM, the street was clustered with Tel Avivians out for a good time. Several cafes overflowed into the sidewalk A motorbike buzzed by, nosing in front of them. Eli stopped as the biker waited for a silver Smart car to pull away from the curb, opening a spot.

The aroma of meat roasting on a vertical spit in a street stall reminded Taryn that she had skipped dinner. "Smells delicious."

"That's shawarma. A local delicacy. Do you want to try it?" Eli asked.

Priscilla checked her watch. "Go ahead. I've eaten, but we're a few minutes early."

"I'll order for you. Hoodna's just down the block," Eli announced gallantly, double-parking and escorting Taryn and Priscilla out onto the street. She watched Eli instruct the swarthy chef who carefully shaved off slices of lamb, wrapped them into a pita with cucumbers, tomatoes, onions, and tabbouleh, and liberally sprayed the mixture with an orange chili sauce. He handed the gyro to Taryn along with a bottle of water. "Enjoy."

Taryn ate greedily, leaning over to ensure that the hot sauce dripped onto the sidewalk, not her sweater. The spices almost brought tears to her eyes but she wouldn't let them slow her down. She caught Eli watching her, but he quickly returned his glance to the traffic on the street. Priscilla sipped from a bottle of water and lit up another cigarette.

"Much better," Taryn announced, tossing the remnants of her dinner in a trash can and wiping her lips with a strip of paper towel.

"Let's go then," Eli said.

"I think we'll be alright on our own now," Priscilla replied.

"It looks like there are some open tables outside," Taryn added. *Where Eli can keep an eye on us.*

Eli nodded his approval. "I'll stay with the car. I think that I can hear the band from here anyway."

Priscilla led the way to the periphery of Hoodna, scanning the jeans clad revelers lounging outside for Fiona. Without saying a word, she marched inside. Taryn had little choice but to follow. They stopped briefly in the bar where a crowd had gathered to watch a Champions League football match, Arsenal vs Barcelona, on the large screen television. Patrons lounged on an array of furniture straight out of a second-hand thrift store. The gaping jaw of a saber tooth tiger stared at them from a spray painting on the wall. Still no Fiona.

Priscilla spun around, locating an entranceway leading deeper into the establishment. Taryn reached for her elbow, but Priscilla was already gone. *Where's Eli?*

The back room had the aura of a cave, dark and low-ceilinged. Priscilla foraged around the scattered tables, searching for a familiar face in the dim light.

"Hello Fiona," she said at last. A wraith wedged into a low-slung seat raised her hand in recognition.

"That's me," Fiona replied, her tremulous voice barely audible. She wore ripped jeans and a faded, long-sleeve Yale tee with sweat stains seeping down from both armpits. Her hair fell limply to her shoulders, framing a gaunt, troubled face.

Priscilla sat down next to Fiona. "How are you?" she asked.

"Surviving. Barely, I guess."

Taryn walked over to the bar, lingered for a few minutes to let Priscilla break the ice with Fiona, and then returned with three glasses of water. Priscilla made a brief introduction and motioned for her to sit down.

"Fiona was just filling me in on the last time she remembers seeing JJ. Please continue," Priscilla said, clasping Fiona's hand.

"It was on the beach last summer. August. He was with some friends from England, I think."

"What did you all do?"

"Partied. For a few days."

"Then?"

"They left."

"Do you know where they went?"

Fiona shook her head. "No. JJ just said they had to move fast."

"Was he in trouble with the police?" Priscilla took a sip of water. When Fiona wiped her runny nose with her sleeve, Taryn noted the needle tracks on her wrist.

"I don't think so," Fiona replied at last. "Look, you said you would be able to help me out - with some money. I'm a little short right now."

"Of course," Priscilla reached into her purse and counted out five fifty dollar bills.

Fiona's languid eyes flashed awake at the sight of the cash. She grabbed the fifties before they could disappear, stuffing them into the rear pocket of her jeans. "Thanks. This will help."

"Do you need some food? We could stock some groceries for you," Priscilla offered, tilting her head towards Taryn.

Taryn winced. *This girl needs more than orange juice and a salad.*

"I'll be OK." Fiona sniffled again. "JJ did say something about checking out Croatia. He thought he could crew on a boat to get there. Asked me to go too."

"Dubrovnik? The islands? This is the first time I've heard anything about Croatia," Priscilla asked, her tone perking up at this new sliver of information.

"Hvar, I think," Fiona replied, shrugging. "Then he just disappeared. I haven't heard from him since."

"Hvar's a big party island. Some friends went on a bike trip..." Taryn offered.

"Why didn't you go with him?" Priscilla interrupted.

"I don't know. Probably should have. Any place would have been better than here."

"Did JJ mention the name of a boat? Or a captain?" Priscilla resumed the questioning.

"No, but I've got a friend, Ahmed. JJ did some work for him. He might be able to help."

"Do you know Ahmed's last name?" Taryn asked.

"Hazboun," Fiona muttered, looking around the room as if someone might be watching her.

"What kind of work did JJ do?" Priscilla rolled on, signaling to Taryn to let her take the lead.

"You should talk to Ahmed yourself." Fiona brushed back her stringy hair, then paused for a second, biting her lower lip. "He might want a little ..."

"Money's no problem," Priscilla replied, opening her purse. "Where's your friend?"

Taryn's stomach started to grumble.

"He's in Ramallah. We might be able to meet him tonight. If I can reach him." Fiona fumbled in a pocket, finally retrieving her phone.

"Mrs. Cabot, I don't think..." Taryn interjected, but Priscilla held up a hand. "Let's see what Ahmed says. Maybe he can come here." Priscilla handed two more bills to Fiona, "Go ahead, give him a call."

A wave of pain rippled through Taryn's loins. She doubled over, waiting for it to subside. "I need to use the ladies room. I'll be right back," she announced, stumbling up, keeping a palm on the table for balance.

When Taryn returned, Priscilla and Fiona were gone. She scanned frantically around the room. A fire door in the back was ajar. She pushed it open, stepped into the side street, and checked both directions. *Shit!* She dialed Eli: "Meet me out front. They ran away."

***

Eli circled the Florentin neighborhood twice, but no luck. "You said Fiona's friend lived in Ramallah?" he asked.

"That's what it sounded like," Taryn replied.

"Any idea about location?"

Taryn shook her head. Eli stopped at a red light. "Ramallah is designated an Area A in the West Bank under control of the Palestinian Authority. Israeli citizens are legally prohibited from entering the city, but Priscilla and Fiona, as foreign tourists, can visit. They're going to have to go through Israeli checkpoints to get there though. I'll text the border patrol a photo of Mrs. Cabot that I snapped in the street."

Taryn continued to scan the streets as they drove. "Did you get a name on Fiona's friend?" Eli asked.

"Ahmed," she replied. "Ahmed Hazboun."

Eli's head jerked, sending the car swerving to the right. "Ahmed Hazboun? Ahmed Hazboun? He's a very bad actor."

"How do you know Hazboun?"

120

Rather than respond, Eli commanded his phone to dial and began talking rapidly in Hebrew over the speakerphone. The female voice on the other hand replied in the same language.

"I served in the West Bank," he replied to Taryn after his phone conversation concluded.

"But I thought you said that the West Bank was under control of the Palestinian Authority, not the Israeli Defense Force?"

"It is," Eli answered, keeping his eyes straight ahead as he accelerated onto the highway. "I was in Duvdevan, a special forces unit. We infiltrated militant groups in the West Bank and brought the terrorists to justice."

"You were undercover?"

"Yes, *mista'arvim*, Arab dress. I spent a great deal of time tracking the Palestinian underworld. Hazboun was on our radar, but we were never able to pin him down."

"That sounds extremely dangerous."

"The risks were manageable. For me at least. Unfortunately, my wife and son paid the price."

"They were killed in revenge?"

"We'll never know for sure."

They drove on in silence for the next twenty minutes. Taryn studied Eli's face: clean shaven, chiseled features, lively intelligent eyes, olive skin. With a little deeper tan, and maybe some facial hair, he could easily pass for a Palestinian. *What kind of man volunteers to fight behind enemy lines? What kind of man comes back out?*

The security wall that surrounds the West Bank loomed as their car approached the Maccabim checkpoint. The Israelis had begun construction of a West Bank border fence in 2002 in response to repeated suicide bombings emanating from the region. The barrier now encompassed over three hundred miles of concrete, electrified wire, trenches, and patrol roads.

While the barrier did dramatically improve the safety of Israeli citizens, Taryn could easily understand the anger it provoked on the other side. She tried to imagine growing up behind a wall with outside travel, work and trade severely restricted. On the other hand, what would it be like to live every day in fear of a terrorist walking down main street in a suicide vest?

There must be a better way - for both sides. But Jews, pagans, Arabs, Muslims, crusaders, and Saracens have all fought for this holy land for thousands of years. Why should anything change now?

Eli lowered his window to speak with the green bereted border patrolman, again in Hebrew. As they rolled through the gate, he turned to Taryn. "He warned us to stay alert. There's a gang with firebombs and stones on the loose."

"Are there any police out there?"

"We have every inch of the road under video surveillance, and the Palestinian Authority police will intervene too, but it's almost impossible to stop the kids from slipping in and out of their towns, particularly at night."

"What about Priscilla and Fiona?" Taryn asked, feeling much better about Eli's pistol.

"Border patrol said they went through about fifteen minutes ahead of us in a car with Israeli plates."

"Why didn't the border patrol stop them?"

"We want Hazboun." Eli accelerated sharply, gunning the engine, pinning Taryn in her seat.

"So you're going to use Priscilla as bait? That's exactly what Karim said the Turks did to her," she snapped, pointing a finger at Eli's face.

"I'm not surprised," Eli said, without taking his eyes off the road.

"But you're going to do the same thing? Risk *her* life? Again?" Taryn's voice rose in anger.

"We've got a car following her. Remember, Priscilla Cabot has been warned many times. She's chosen to play a dangerous game," Eli replied evenly.

"It's her son. Did she really have a choice?" Taryn sunk back, her stridency dissipating as she realized how personal that question really was.

Eli didn't flinch. "No," he said.

Eli's telephone buzzed before Taryn could say any more. A male voice this time, but again in Hebrew. She could see Eli tense, then give a command, and hang up. He accelerated again. She gripped her armrest, checking the speedometer as the car hurtled past 180 kilometers per hour.

"What's happening?" Taryn asked.

"They went through the Qalandia checkpoint but bypassed the turn for Ramallah on the other side."

"Where are they going?"

"They're driving north on Highway 60 now, so my guess is

somewhere else in the West Bank."

Taryn could see the signage for Qalandia as they approached. It was a massive checkpoint, the concrete wall soaring twenty-five feet high. Traffic appeared to flow easily into the West Bank, but Eli pulled over to chat with a patrolwoman. Taryn glanced up at the sentry tower peering over the wall like a periscope. The barrel of a rifle peeked out of a sniper's nest at its summit.

"This looks like a scene out of one of those noir spy movies…Checkpoint Charlie and the Berlin Wall," she commented when Eli closed the window.

"We're at ground zero now," he replied as they wheeled through the control point into the West Bank.

"Don't the Palestinians feel like they're living in a giant prison?"

"We're just trying to keep the bad guys out of Israel."

"Looks like you're keeping everyone out of Israel," she muttered, gazing at the line of cars waiting to enter the country. Eli only glared in reply. He accelerated into the rotary that spun them out onto Route 60. Taryn stared silently out the window, the lights of Ramallah fading in the distance. Another phone call broke the silence. Taryn waited impatiently for a translation.

"They pulled into the town of Jifna. Looks like they're having a coffee. Our follow team can't stick around any longer."

"Maybe it's all kosher then?" Taryn joked, hoping to ease the tension.

Eli offered her a smile and rolled his eyes. "Not likely with Hazboun, but we'll see. We'll be there shortly."

Eli glided past the dimly lit cafe. Priscilla and Ahmed were sitting outside on the terrace. Alone. Fiona and the mystery driver had vanished.

He parked across the road, fifty yards away from the cafe. A lone streetlamp cast an eerie glow on a village that appeared at the crossroads of modern times and antiquity. The dome of a mosque surfaced in its center, while a church steeple pointed towards a bright crescent moon. Brick apartment blocks battled sandstone dwellings for frontage on the main road. An alleyway meandered into the darkness.

"Almost too good to be true," Eli muttered as he adjusted his shoulder holster. Taryn unbuckled and opened the door, but Eli held up his hand. He opened the glove compartment and removed a

Glock.

"I understand that you know how to use this," he said, racking back the slide to chamber a bullet.

Taryn nodded, wrapping her hand around the pistol's grip as she pointed the barrel upward and tested the trigger guard with her index finger.

"Please put the weapon in your purse. We're on our own now," he said.

CHAPTER 24

Jifna was eerily silent. Taryn could see pricks of light, scattered like decorations on a Christmas tree, in the hills in the distance. The night air here was noticeably cooler than Tel Aviv. She buttoned her sweater, but Eli allowed his jacket to blow open in the breeze. She checked her bag to make sure it was unlatched before slinging it over her shoulder.

On the terrace, Ahmed reached across the table to refill Priscilla's cup. Taryn and Eli approached on the opposite side of the street. They walked close together on the uneven sidewalk, following a low stone wall in the semi-darkness. Eli paused at a rusted gate, peering through the pickets into a vacant courtyard before waving Taryn onward. He raised his hand to stop behind a battered blue pickup parked haphazardly against the curb. Shielded by the truck's cab, they watched the conversation on the terrace. Priscilla appeared calm as Ahmed talked into his mobile. Eli tilted his head back, while signaling to Taryn to remain silent.

She followed Eli's glance away from the cafe, but saw nothing in the darkness. Eli turned and kneeled, unholstering his weapon. At last, she heard an engine rumble to a stop down the street behind them. Taryn could discern the shape of another pick-up truck, headlights obviously out. Feet smacked the asphalt. Eli yanked Taryn's elbow, dragging her down beside him.

Hands clapped. A rhythmic chant swelled. Taryn picked up the word, 'Allah,' several times, 'Palestine' and 'Israel' too, but the rest was in Arabic. It grew steadily louder as the gang marched down the street towards them. Taryn counted ten silhouettes.

"Free Palestine. Death to Israel. Praise Allah," Eli whispered in translation. "So much for our quiet night in the West Bank."

Before she could reply, headlights barreled down the road from the other direction. Brakes screeched, as a desert-crusted minivan pulled up in front of the cafe blocking any view of the terrace. The doors to the van gaped open. Four youths jumped to the pavement brandishing AK-47s. Red and white checked kufiyahs concealed their faces.

A rock flew over their heads, smashing harmlessly into the stone wall. A second one crashed the windshield of the pickup in front of them. The chanting gained urgency. Taryn could sense the blood lust in the angry voices.

"We've been ambushed," Eli declared calmly, swiveling his head between the two teams of attackers. Taryn dropped her purse in the dust and reached for her pistol. Eli tapped several times on his phone, then stuffed it into his back pocket.

"The real fighters are the ones by the van. I'll take them. You get to Priscilla," he ordered. When Taryn nodded her understanding, Eli rolled into the street firing. A masked gunner collapsed, blood spurting from his neck. A second returned fire, while the other two split to take cover on either side of the van. Eli utilized the darkness to scurry to the far side of the road. Taryn heard a cry of agony behind him. Friendly fire must have struck one of the marchers in their rear. She could hear the rest disperse.

Taryn took two strides and dove over the stone wall, rolling her shoulder to absorb the landing. She crawled behind the wall until she guessed that she was even with the van. Puffs of gunfire exploded in the street. She peeked over the wall. A flurry of bullets ripped through the van. She searched for the Palestinian shooters, but they were out of sight. A muzzle flared from underneath a table on the terrace. Another from the far side of the van. Eli was pinned down.

A shriek pierced the cacophony of the battle. The fourth Palestinian, an elephantine, bearded man, had tossed Priscilla over his shoulder like a load of laundry, a burlap sack knotted over her head. Ahmed led the way into the alley that ran alongside the cafe. Taryn aimed her pistol, but didn't have a clear shot. She flopped over the wall, praying that the shooters would stay focused on Eli. At their next burst, she sprinted after Priscilla.

In typical medieval fashion, the alley curved gradually upward into a maze of streets that fed into the town square. Gates were down; doors were locked; windows were shuttered. A tired streetlamp cast a dim glow up ahead. Taryn slipped on the well-worn sandstone. *Richard the Lionheart might have crusaded through here a thousand years ago.* She regained her footing, clinging to the shadows as she stalked Priscilla and her captors.

Encountering a fork in the alley, Ahmed stopped and reconnoitered. Elephant man waited for instructions, Priscilla's limp form barely reaching halfway down his back. Taryn ducked behind a cracked earthen bench. A car horn honked twice in the distance. Reacting to the cue, Ahmed pointed to the left.

Taryn had to act now. She kneeled and steadied her forearms on the bench, gripping her Glock with both hands. *Stay calm. Just like hunting deer.* She breathed deeply, slowing her heart rate, and aimed at his right knee. The pistol jumped as the blast rattled the narrow confines. Elephant man screamed as the bullet shredded his thigh. He crumpled to his side, sending Priscilla rolling off his shoulder into a pile of trash.

Elephant man roared in anger, unsheathing a knife from his belt. Its blade glistened in the moonlight as he grabbed Priscilla's leg. Taryn fired again, her bullets perforating elephant man's chest, the knife clanking on the stones. *First time I've ever killed a man.*

Ahmed dove for cover, coiling up next to Priscilla, the fallen knife now in his grasp. He slashed at Priscilla's hood and ripped it off. Grabbing a handful of her blond hair, he pulled hard, yanking Priscilla up to her knees and then to a standing position, careful to keep her body between himself and Taryn. Priscilla screamed, her eyes plastered open in fear. Blood trickled from a wound in her scalp. *Her head must have hit the pavement when she fell.* Taryn had no shot now.

Ahmed began to drag Priscilla towards the fork in the alley, his right arm hammer-locked around her neck. The horn blared again. And again. Ahmed turned towards the sound, loosening his grip. An atavistic wail emanated from deep inside Priscilla as she chomped down on Ahmed's forearm, her teeth sinking into his flesh. Now, it was his turn to scream in agony as Priscilla spun away from his body.

Taryn squeezed off three shots in quick succession. Ahmed's head exploded like a Halloween pumpkin.

Taryn raced to Priscilla's side, stepping around Ahmed's decapitated body. Priscilla lay folded into a fetal position, eyes glazed, staring into space. Her hair was ragged and thickly matted with crusted blood.

"JJ's dead. JJ's dead. My son is dead," she mumbled.

Taryn hugged her tightly. "We'll worry about JJ later. Let's get you somewhere safe first," she whispered. She rocked the grief-stricken mother in her arms.

Another shot rang out from the dark. *Eli?* A bullet ricocheted off the wall behind her. *What the fuck?* The second bullet pierced Taryn's right shoulder, splattering a scarlet spray onto Priscilla's face. Taryn dove to her left, rolling along the ground. Another volley of gunfire. Bullets skipped off the stones. Priscilla's body bounced like a basketball.

"No!" Taryn screamed, trying to grip her pistol with her one good arm. A muzzle flashed behind her. A mass landed with a thud deep in the alley up ahead.

A motorcycle engine roared, its lone headlight blinding. Taryn shakily aimed her pistol at the light. "Taryn, it's me," Eli yelled. He jumped off the bike, tucking his weapon into his belt. He kneeled at her side, holding her.

"You're hit," Eli said as fingers found her bloody shoulder. Taryn nodded. "Must have been a sniper in the shadows," she replied.

"He won't be shooting anyone else," Eli said, as he scanned the carnage.

"Priscilla?" Taryn beseeched.

"She's dead," he replied. "We have to get out of here now or we'll be next."

Eli cradled Taryn, gently lifting her off the ground, carrying her towards the bike. The numerals of its license plate were green, signaling Palestinian registration. "Where did you…" she started to ask, but then noticed a bright scarlet stain smeared across the seat.

Eli wiped away the fresh blood with his sleeve and seated her. He peeled back Taryn's sweater to examine her wound. "The bullet passed clean through. You'll be OK, but we have to get you to a hospital." He stuffed his handkerchief under Taryn's shirt to staunch the bleeding. Eli climbed onto the bike, wrapping Taryn's arms around his waist. "It's going to hurt, but you have to hold on." Taryn nodded again, grimacing as the bike thundered forward.

She clamped the seat with her knees and rested her head against Eli's back as he gunned the motorcycle towards Ramallah. The klaxons of Palestinian Authority police cars filled the night, but Eli never slowed. Pain knifed through her shoulder at every bump. At last, the towers of the Qalandiya checkpoint emerged from the darkness. An Israeli ambulance welcomed them on the other side.

CHAPTER 25

"Ms. Booker, as always, a true delight to see you," Lev Bierman intoned, a colorful bouquet of flowers in hand. With unkempt silver hair, a seersucker suit, and red, white and blue bow tie, Bierman resembled a living caricature of the Russian émigré turned Southern gentleman.

Taryn beamed, sitting as upright as she could manage in bed, right arm suspended in a sling, shoulder heavily bandaged, throbbing like it was the bass drum in a marching band. "Professor, what a nice surprise." She wiggled the fingers of her right hand in an attempt at a wave. "You shouldn't have."

"It's been too long. But, I envisioned that we would meet high above Lake Cayuga, rather than a hospital room in Jerusalem," Bierman chided as he approached Taryn's bed, laying the flowers flat on the nightstand.

"Well, Brightify was growing a bit confining, so I thought a change of scenery was in order."

"Scenery, yes. I thought you needed a change as well. But I did not expect you to swap your computer for a pistol." The professor reached out and patted her good hand. "How are you feeling?"

"A little beat up. A little shaken up. I've never shot a man before."

"It is quite a sobering experience, I'm sure. But the world will not miss Ahmed Hazboun."

"Is that why you're here in Israel?" Taryn readjusted her sling.

"That's part of the reason, yes. I'm also here at the invitation of the Israelis who suspect there might be a link now between

130

CyberBanda and Daesh."

"Shahar hinted at that. But the Russians and ISIS? Aren't the Russians the ones who bombed Raqqa last year?"

"An astute observation. But priorities change. Alliances shift. Officially or unofficially. As you well know, my specialty is the money trail. So, I am here to start my search at the source."

"With Ahmed Hazboun, JJ Cabot and Fiona Peterson?"

Bierman paced over to the window, as if searching for his next words. After a few seconds, he set his jaw and sat down next to Taryn. "As I mentioned on the phone, John Cabot Jr. veered badly off course. The young man had a penchant for cocaine and heroin. He fell under the spell of Hazboun, a commander for the Islamic State in the Sinai. Among other deeds, Hazboun peddled drugs around the Med to raise hard cash for the cause."

"JJ's dead, isn't he? Priscilla Cabot told me before she was killed," Taryn's voice trailed off.

Bierman nodded grimly. "The information that you gleaned last night concerning Cabot's nautical departure from Tel Aviv was the final piece of the puzzle. We just confirmed the remains of a previously unidentified body that washed up on the coast of Corfu with dental records provided by his father."

"And Fiona?"

"She's in custody in Israel and will hopefully choose to tell us whatever she knows about Mr. Hazboun's activities." Bierman reached for the pitcher of water resting on the nightstand. He filled a paper cup and handed it to Taryn, then poured another for himself.

"There's more, isn't there?" she asked.

"Mr. Cabot made a video renouncing America and declaring his allegiance to Raqqa. We have a copy."

"I'm sure JJ was strung out when he did that," Taryn declared.

"Probably so, but it doesn't matter. It's still treason."

"But, did JJ do anything else besides talk?"

"We believe that Hazboun measured young Mr. Cabot for a suicide vest. It would have been a recruitment bonanza to have an American blow himself up in Israel."

"But JJ tried to escape. That should count in his favor."

Bierman sipped his water slowly. "It does, but that's not much help to him now," he added.

"Mr. Cabot must be devastated."

"Yes, he is. Given his position at Credit Lafayette, we've offered to keep the details of family's demise classified. The publicity would not benefit anyone – except the Islamic State."

"Will that fly?" Taryn winced as she twisted her hips to get more comfortable.

"I believe that Mr. Cabot will choose to mourn his wife and son in private."

"Priscilla Cabot was a good woman - and a good mother," Taryn said, holding back her tears.

"I am quite certain she was," Bierman replied, standing to leave. "But we are at war. More good people will die before it's over."

"Where's her body?"

"In route to New York. The official story will be a shootout between Israeli special forces and Hamas fighters trying to kidnap an American tourist. The Israelis will take a beating for operating in the West Bank, but it will blow over in time, as it always does. Your name will remain out of the newspapers as if you were never there." Taryn closed her eyes, calculating the implications of Bierman's last words.

"Ms. Booker, anonymity is your best protection against anyone who might wish to avenge Mr. Hazboun's demise. Please do not toss it away lightly."

"I understand, Professor," Taryn replied, her eyelids slowly growing heavy with exhaustion.

"And try to refrain from assuming a position in the front lines again. For your own safety," the professor said, but he was warning Sleeping Beauty. He swept a lock of hair off the forehead of his prize pupil. "I'll let you get some rest."

***

As soon as she awoke, Taryn cradled her phone tight against her ear.

"Hi, Dad," she said. "Glad I caught you at home."

"Taryn. I'm glad you called. We're all worried about you. We read about that American woman who got killed in the West Bank."

"I'm fine, Dad. Just a crazy week. Working day and night."

"Do you feel safe?"

"Of course, I'm in Jerusalem now. There's a huge wall and battalions of Israeli police between here and Jifna."

"Jifna? Was that where the shooting was? We didn't see many details in the papers here."

"Tight security, I guess."

"OK. Well, you take good care of yourself."

"I love you, Dad. Say hi to Constance."

***

Elephant man rose, blood dripping from his riddled torso. The moonlight glinted off the blade of his knife. Ahmed trailed a step behind, Priscilla's blond scalp in his hands. "Allahu Akbar. Allahu Akbar," they chanted. She could see the whites of their eyes as they approached.

The buzz of the telephone jolted Taryn awake. She sat up, shook her head, surfacing from her nightmare. *No regrets. Those bastards got what they deserved.*

The blue sky outside the window had melted into twilight. The phone by her bedside rang again. Jim Mangano.

"Hey," she answered, still groggy.

"How are you?"

"Sore," she replied, gently massaging her shoulder.

"Could have been a lot worse from what I heard."

"Yeah, I got lucky."

"Hope you've had a chance to rest today."

"I wish. Professor Bierman stopped by with some news. Then two officers from the Israeli police force visited for a chat."

"I know you can't say much more."

"Officially, I wasn't even there."

"Well, I just wanted to let you know that I was thinking about you."

"Thanks. I'm glad you called." Taryn sipped from a cup of water. "Any progress on Walecka?"

"No. He's doing a good job staying underground."

"Too bad. My boss at Lightning Strike thinks he could be part of something bigger after all. I'll fill you in when I get back to New York next week."

"I want to hear everything you've got." A long pause before Jim continued. "But I have some news too. Good news."

"Shoot."

"Marcy and I are engaged."

"Wow. Congratulations. I wish you guys all the happiness in the

133

world." Marcy's a lucky girl, Taryn thought, looking around her empty hospital room.

***

Taryn had just stabbed the last cucumber slice in the salad on her dinner tray when Eli knocked. He wore neatly pressed jeans and a powder blue button down, open at the neck.

"Shalom," he greeted as he stepped into the room with a mischievous smile and a brown paper grocery bag in his hand.

"Shalom," she replied, wiping her lips with a napkin. "You clean up pretty good yourself."

"The doctors tell me that you're doing well. And your police interrogators confirmed that your account of last night corroborated mine."

"So where does that leave me?" Taryn rearranged the front of her hospital gown with her good hand.

"Free to go whenever you're feeling up to it."

"Fantastic. Tomorrow hopefully."

"And then?" Eli asked as he sat in the chair next to her bed.

"Then back home. Back to work."

"Will you stay in Israel for the weekend? I'd like to show you my country. It's beautiful, and full of surprises - like you," he asked, placing his hand over hers.

Taryn's eyes widened, devouring Eli's face, his features softer now, the warrior home from the battlefield. "I'd like that very much," she replied, intertwining her fingers with his, pleasantly surprised at the lightness of his touch. "But on my next visit. I need to get back to New York as soon as possible."

"Is there someone else?"

"No," Taryn shook her head. "Definitely not."

Eli grinned as he reached into the paper bag and pulled out two bottles of Goldstar. "Then we need to toast," he said, popping open a beer and handing it to Taryn.

"To Israel?" she offered.

"L'chaim," Eli countered.

"Yes. L'chaim. To life."

PART TWO

"I've seen the lights go out on Broadway,
I've watched the mighty skyline fall."

Billy Joel
Miami 2017

CHAPTER 26

"Can I come in?" Serena Thomas asked, standing at the transom of the Mayor's office.

"Of course, of course. What's on your agenda this morning?" Rosen asked as he closed the file he'd been reading.

"I hate to bother you, but this came across my desk last night," She placed an official looking report with the FBI seal on his desk. "I thought you'd want to see it."

"OK," he replied, scanning the title, but not picking up the document.

"It was in my regular security briefing package. I wasn't even going to bother you with it, but the report concerns CyberBanda."

"Assholes," Rosen muttered, just loud enough for his chief of staff to hear. Except for an occasional joke on late night TV or a snicker behind his back at a fund-raiser, the "Moscow Ménage", as the press had labeled it, had died down weeks ago. Thankfully, his PR flack had been right, for once. "What do they want now?" he asked, fearing the answer.

"Nothing. Like I said, I think this is just noise," Thomas replied.

"But…?" Rosen rolled his right hand for her to continue.

"But, a college professor, Lev Bierman up at Cornell, filed this report. He consults for the FBI, and possibly others, on cybersecurity. Evidently, he was in the Middle East a week ago, and believes that he might have uncovered a financial link between CyberBanda and ISIS. He stressed this is real early stage work, requiring more investigation. Much more."

"Why do I care?"

"Because Bierman, with some help from the Israelis, also believes that CyberBanda and/or ISIS might be scouting out the New York City electrical grid for a possible cyberattack."

"Might be scouting…what does that mean?"

Thomas shrugged. "Well, I did a little scouting myself. Bierman has the reputation in Washington of being outside the mainstream. Some people say far outside. Sees foreign cyberspooks in every closet. He even got his hand slapped for being part of the intelligence cabal that vastly over-rated the Iraqis WMD capabilities prior to the Gulf War." She paused before plunging ahead with the rest of her story. "It gets even better though. Bierman's top student at Cornell was Taryn Booker. And they're still close. He was supposedly masterminding her defense during the city's investigation of the Brightify leak."

Rosen arched his brow as he calculated the meaning of Thomas' information.

"And guess what Ms. Booker is doing now?" Thomas continued, not waiting for a reply. "She left Brightify to join Lightning Strike, an Israeli cybersecurity firm. And she conveniently happened to be in Israel at the same time as the professor."

"I have nothing against Booker personally," Rosen said. *She was a convenient scapegoat.* "But are you saying that she and her professor are concocting some story for revenge? That sounds really crazy, right?"

"No. But I do think that Booker might be looking for ways to restore her reputation. Maybe there's a consulting contract in it for her new firm and the professor. Both good reasons to create a Russian conspiracy theory. Who knows?"

"What do you suggest we do?"

"Nothing at all. The professor's report says this work is still early stage. Let him do the digging. There's absolutely nothing here that requires your immediate action."

"OK. I've got a black-out planning meeting coming up on my schedule anyway. We can use that session to do a little investigation of our own. Make sure our grid is well-protected."

"Perfect. I'll write a memo to the file to say that we've discussed the situation and you've initiated appropriate action."

"Where are we with that blackout review meeting?" Mayor Rosen screeched over the intercom before his chief of staff had even exited his office.

The last thing that I need is a disaster like a blackout, regardless of the cause, rocking the city during my first summer on the job. And. if there was an "event" outside our control, then I need a plan to keep the city running. In writing. No mayor ever got credit for keeping the lights on, or the subways rolling, or the garbage collected, but, boy, if essential services ever failed…

"My, we are cheerful this morning," Katherine Whitworth replied. "The meeting is confirmed for April 26th, two weeks from today. Allison's been working on the attendance list. I'll ask her to come down."

Within three minutes, Allison appeared, brandishing a backpack full of paperwork. She handed the summary page to the mayor.

"Looks like we'll have a full house," he commented, scanning the list.

"Con Ed, FEMA, DHS, FERC, NERC, New York State ISO, Coast Guard, Border Patrol, Nuclear Detection Office, Health Affairs, FBI, NYPD, Fire Department, Sanitation," Allison rattled off the names. "A woman from the NSA. And our own people on housing, health and welfare. I tried to cover all the bases."

"What a clusterfuck," he mumbled, still looking down at the single-spaced page. "How am I going to get this gang to formulate an emergency plan for the city? I bet they couldn't even agree on the lunch menu."

"I'm sure you'll find a way, sir. Anything else?" she asked.

"Another subject. Pier 40. Our project seems to have stalled. Have you and Ben been schmoozing with any new developers interested in the air rights deal?"

"Not really," Allison replied, a Mona Lisa smile creasing her lips. "Ben seems to be focused elsewhere."

"I got that impression as well," The mayor abruptly swiveled his chair to signify the end of the interview. He tapped on his intercom, "Ask Ben to come in, please."

***

The sight of Gracie Mansion, the official residence of the Mayor of New York, always perked Bernie up after a long day downtown at City Hall. Archibald Gracie, a Scottish merchant, had built the original mansion in 1799 as his country escape, overlooking a meandering bend in the East River five miles north of Wall Street, the center of the city at that time. An unpretentious, Federal style structure, the mansion hosted a meeting of Alexander Hamilton and the New York Federalists in 1801 to raise $10,000 to launch the *New York Evening Post*. It also served as an ice cream parlor and restroom facility for almost thirty years at the turn of the twentieth century. Mayor Fiorello LaGuardia took up residence in 1942, initiating the mansion's current role.

I came this close to losing it all. He handed his trench coat to the butler, slipped into the library and poured a scotch. Bernie needed fifteen minutes to gather his thoughts before dinner with Jackie. She had fulfilled her promise, standing by him. Her motherly, no-nonsense New Yorker mien had clearly helped his cause; but the ordeal had taken its toll. Some nights, Jackie was her old self – warm, humorous, insightful; other times, she could be truculent and withdrawn.

Bernie gazed at the river as he sipped the last of his cocktail, listening to his wife's footsteps trundling down the stairs. The Moscow memories he had secretly savored as confirmation of his masculinity now made him gag in disgust; but, he had had two years to make his peace. Jackie too would need time to heal.

"How was your day?" she asked

"Difficult," Bernie replied, deciding to pass on a second scotch. He recounted his meetings with Allison Gold and Ben Olinmeister. Pier 40 was supposed to have been his administration's first signature accomplishment, much needed after that brouhaha with Brightify. Now he would need to find a replacement - something flashy that the media could chew on.

Ben tried to blame the delay on the community activists downtown who had filed a lawsuit to sabotage the air rights deal, but Bernie lit into him. Something in his underling's meek acceptance of the delay tactics, normal for most city projects, had set him off. Bernie wanted winners on his team, or at least players who wouldn't take defeat lying down.

"Do you think Ben is lobbying for a new job in the private sector? It's only been three months but...," he added.

"Maybe Ben's got something else on his mind. Or someone else," Jackie interjected.

Bernie arched his brows. "Allison? I don't think she's interested in..."

"What about the *shiksa* with the long red hair? I saw her huddling with Ben at our last fund-raiser. Looked a little too cozy to me."

"Merry? Now that would explain things a bit," Bernie mused.

"A wife and two little ones at home. Ben should be ashamed of himself."

"I'll ask around. See if Serena or Katherine have noticed any wandering eyes. I'm not going to let a cheating husband bring down my administration."

Bernie reached for his wife's hand, but she pulled back. *Definitely not the time to discuss CyberBanda or Taryn Booker.*

***

At 6:45, Jackie rolled over, the other side of the bed empty and cold, her husband still banished to the guest room. She tugged the down comforter over her goose bumped shoulders and buried her head underneath a well-feathered pillow. Their honeymoon in Paris, the weekend in the Catskills the first time her folks had taken the boys, inauguration night in Gracie Mansion … all those memories tarnished now.

A threesome? My Bernie? She couldn't let go. *But, did one night negate twenty-four years of marriage?*

Bernie was still a good man. And a good father. Their sons had pleaded with her to forgive him. In the end, that's why she had stayed. And defended him – at least in public, weathering the media inferno, scarred but victorious. Brightify had paid a million dollars to the city's schools. That Booker woman had been run out of town. Now it was time for the Rosen's to move forward. To accomplish what they had dreamed about when Bernie first decided to run for mayor.

Jackie sat up, feet searching for slippers while she peered out the bedroom windows, dawn streaking over the river. She was ready to step out of Bernie's shadow and take ownership of her role as First Lady. Appraising her full figure in the bathroom mirror, she would start by reserving a seat at Soul Cycle for a spin class at nine. *A little less of me would set a better example.*

Knotting the belt on her bathrobe, Jackie walked down the hall. Always the optimist, Bernie left the guest room door open each night. He was awake, sitting up in bed reading the *Times*.

"Good morning dear," he said, folding the paper as soon as she appeared. He scooted over to make room for her to sit on the bed.

"Busy day," she replied, standing. "I've got appointments till noon and a job interview at two."

"A job interview?" Bernie practically bolted upright.

"For a position suitable for the First Lady," she clarified.

"That's wonderful. I can make a few calls."

"Don't. I'll surprise you."

CHAPTER 27

The call from her mother hit Mayar like a sucker-punch to the stomach. Ahmed was dead. Killed in a shootout with the Israelis. Haani sounded more relieved than grieved. At least he didn't slaughter any innocent civilians. The conversation was short. No false promises to get together soon.

Mayar gave herself one day to mourn before steeling herself to move forward alone with her mission. The knock on her dorm room door that afternoon was long overdue.

"Who is it?" she asked, imagining the Gestapo or the KGB on the other side.

"Special Agent James Mangano, Federal Bureau of Investigation."

They're here at last. She straightened several textbooks on her desk and adjusted her black headscarf. Ahmed and Fatima smiled at her from the Dome of the Rock. *Allah forgive me!* She had forgotten about the photo resting atop her dresser.

"One second, please," she called out, burying the personal treasure in a drawer piled haphazardly with underwear. *I must act like a soldier now. Give them nothing.*

"Come in, please. How can I help you?"

"This is my partner, Special Agent Lou Totti. We're sorry to bother you at this difficult time, but we need to ask you a few questions."

"I understand. I don't have much room for you to sit here, but…" Mayar said, stepping back towards her bed.

"No problem. We're used to being on our feet. Our condolences about your brother," Agent Mangano replied.

"My half-brother," she corrected.

"Yes, your half-brother. When was the last time you saw him?"

"Five years ago - before I started here at Columbia. I don't believe he's returned to the United States since then." Mayar sat down on the edge of her bed and crossed her legs.

"What are you studying?" Agent Mangano glanced briefly at the books that she had purposely left out on her desk.

"Electrical engineering and computer science." *I've got nothing to hide. The FBI could easily find this information out from my school records anyway.*

"When was the last time you spoke with Ahmed?"

"He called on my birthday last year," she replied, pleased to change the subject away from her school work.

"Can you tell us his phone number, please?" Agent Totti interjected. Mayar made a show of retrieving her mobile from the purse by her side and reciting the number.

"Did you email regularly? Chat online? Skype?" Agent Mangano again.

"No. We weren't particularly close."

"Are you aware of the details surrounding your half-brother's death?"

"Only that he was shot by the Israelis."

"Are you aware that your half-brother was involved with the Islamic State?"

"No," she replied, purposely widening her eyes in surprise. "We didn't discuss politics."

The agents tossed several more softball questions at her before indicating that the interview was over.

"That's it?" Mayar asked, her eyes flicking to her laptop before she could rivet them back to Agent Mangano.

"Yes, for now at least. Were you expecting more?"

"I wasn't sure. Muslims aren't too popular in America right now," she replied, smoothing down her headscarf.

"You haven't committed any crime and you're not under investigation. This is a free country. We're just trying to touch all the bases," Agent Mangano replied soothingly.

When the agents left, Mayar closed the door and counted silently to twenty-five. When she could contain herself no longer, she dug into her drawer and clutched the photograph of Ahmed and little Fatima to her chest. "With Allah's help, I will not fail you," she vowed.

***

"I bet there's something on her computer that she didn't want us to see," Jim announced on the 8PM video call. Taryn, sitting in her cubicle in New York, and Bierman, up in Ithaca, were on the other ends of the line. Both had returned from Tel Aviv eight days earlier. The professor's report linking ISIS and CyberBanda and Con Ed, while highly speculative, had given him the opportunity to stay on the case.

"I'm not sure where you get that. Tabak seemed pretty calm and collected for the whole interview," Lou disagreed. "Let's not start chasing ghosts in the attic."

"She's majoring in Comp Sci and EE, right? What's the topic of her thesis?" Taryn asked.

"Don't know, but we can find out," Jim said.

"It might not be important, but can't hurt to know." Taryn followed up. *Shahar had hinted that ISIS might employ outside contractors for work in foreign lands. Bierman was tracking Ahmed Hazboun. A link from Russia to Raqqa to Mayar Tabak to Dennis Walecka – the boots on the ground in NYC – was not such a wild hypothesis anymore.*

"A wiretap of Ms. Tabak would be extremely helpful," Bierman commented, a tinge of wishful thinking in his voice.

"Not a chance. What would I tell the judge, she might have flinched?" Jim replied.

"I don't see any grounds for a warrant either," Lou said. "What are the odds an ISIS commander confided secret plans with his baby half-sister living a world away?"

"Unless she was part of the plan," Taryn chipped in.

"A sleeper? A distinct, and potentially dangerous, possibility," Bierman contributed.

"We can try to classify Mayar Tabak as a 'person of interest', but we won't be able to do much more. Despite your suspicions, Professor, we have absolutely no evidence that her brother was planning anything at all here in the States. And the courts would not look too kindly on the United States government spying on a grieving family without extremely good reason. The NSA is in enough hot water already," Jim said.

"You're probably right, Mr. Mangano. A sparring session with our government's lawyers is about as sublime as a swim in an alligator infested lake, as my dear wife would say. I will pursue my investigatory work from afar," Bierman said.

"Unfortunately, the gators are after you again, Professor," Lou said, holding up a poster showing a grainy photo of Bierman with Arabic writing underneath. "Our boys intercepted this Daesh communication. It went out last week to their affiliates around the world. I'll email it over."

Bierman examined the page for several seconds. "It looks like Mr. Abu Bakr al-Baghdadi, the supreme leader of the Islamic State, has issued a fatwa calling for my assassination in retaliation for the murder of Ahmed Hazboun."

"But you had nothing to do with…" Taryn's voice trailed off as she remembered her anonymous role in the event.

"It's not the first time that a terrorist organization has threatened to remove me from our fair planet. I'm proud to say Saddam Hussein issued my first death warrant in 2002."

"I would recommend a security detail. For the next few weeks at least," Jim piped in.

"Professor, listen to Jim, even if it's just for Hayden's sake," Taryn pleaded. "Ahmed Hazboun's friends are extremely nasty people. Some extra protection can't hurt until we see if things blow over."

"Your concerns are most appreciated, but we've been down this road before," Bierman continued, pushing his chair away from his desk. "Although it is the first time that someone has promised a reward of one thousand virgins in paradise for my demise," he chuckled.

Taryn ended her evening with a three mile run along the well-lit path tracing the Hudson River shoreline, ending up back at her apartment. Before she could peel off her sweats, her phone buzzed. A text from Eli: **Miss you**. It was early morning in Tel Aviv. She smiled, recalling their intertwined fingers that last night at the hospital in Jerusalem, pleased that he was thinking of her at the start of his day.

CHAPTER 28

Mayar slammed her palm down on the desk, spilling her morning tea over a corner of the diagram of the Sherman Creek power station. She grabbed a napkin to pat the document dry before the stain could spread.

The Pizza Boy information had crashed her into a dead-end. She had spent the entire week tracing an administrative chain and had succeeded in gaining executive privileges. But her victory was hollow. She had learned how much the manager of Sherman Creek had saved in his 401-K, but she couldn't find one entry point for the controllers that managed the power transformers housed at the site. Without that access, her plan was doomed.

Frustrated, she shut her laptop and searched for a headscarf and jacket. She would be late to class if she didn't hurry. Rushing out, Mayar tripped over a box lying on her threshold. Simply wrapped in brown paper secured by a plaited string like the one the bakery used to tie boxes of fresh cookies, it must have been leaning against her door. There was no name or return address. No markings at all. She looked up and down the hallway, but it was deserted and every door appeared closed. The aroma of fresh-brewed coffee wafted from Amy's room. She picked up the box and shook it. Nothing. She stepped back inside, placing it on her bed, and stared. *Leave it and go to class. Maybe it was left by mistake.* But her curiosity won out. She ripped off the wrapping and opened the cover. *Class will have to wait.*

The black flag of the Islamic State lay folded neatly inside. Instantly, she felt as though every ounce of oxygen had been sucked from her room. Mayar gasped and stepped back. *Who knows about my plans? Why send the flag? Why now? Is this a trap?* Rushing to her window, she drew the shade down until it touched the sill. She ran her index finger lightly over the black cloth, but withdrew again. Her door was unlocked. She latched the bolt before returning to the package.

Her body palpitated as she unfurled the flag, smoothing it over her bed. Mayar knew its message by heart. The banner read "There is no God but Allah. Mohammed is the messenger of Allah." The script in the white circle at the flag's center, resembling the prophet's seal, repeated the edict.

A white envelope lay at the bottom of the box. She removed it gingerly, turning it over several times in her hand, before breaking the seal. A photo of Fatima! My little angel! On the back of the photograph, scribbled in English, was the command: Meet me at Tom's Diner at noon. *I am not alone after all.*

Mayar refolded the flag and scoured her room for a safe place to hide it. Finally, she lifted her mattress and tucked the flag underneath. The snapshot of her adopted daughter went into her purse.

***

Only three blocks down Broadway from the main entrance to Columbia's campus, Tom's was the quintessential college diner, made famous by its appearances on the Seinfeld television show. Mayar was not a regular, but she had eaten its greasy food on several previous occasions. She arrived a few minutes before noon, still an early hour by college standards. Not surprisingly, diners were sparse - three seated at the counter, several others scattered at tables and booths. No familiar faces. *A relief, but who am I meeting?*

An overstuffed behemoth with an unruly beard, wearing a black knit kulfi cap, dishdashi robe and combat jacket, appeared behind her at the door. She waited for a look of recognition, but only received an icy glare in return. *Should I expect a hug?* She stepped towards him, but then heard her name called softly from the middle booth.

"Mayar. Please join me here," a gnarled man about her own age with a sun-starved complexion, thick glasses, scruffy goatee and wisp of a mustache, unfurled from his seat to welcome her. Wearing jeans and collared denim shirt, topped by a Mets baseball cap, he looked the part of a fellow student. He placed his *New York Times* down and ushered her into the seat across the table. His mobile rested in front of him.

"My name is Nimr. I'm honored to meet you."

"Hello," she replied. "I didn't know who to look for."

"Yes, well, I have no desire to broadcast my allegiances," he commented, casting a dismissive glance at the wanna-be jihadi who had trailed her into the diner. "Would you like something to eat? Some tea, maybe?" he continued.

"Tea would be fine."

Nimr signaled for the waitress, ordering a pot of tea and a cheddar cheese omelet with buttered rye toast. "I'm hungry," he explained as Mayar fidgeted in her seat, her fingers steepled together on the table top.

When the waitress departed, Nimr reached across the table to clasp Mayar's hands. "I grieve for your brother, as you do. But, we must carry on with our mission. Do you agree?" She nodded, swallowing hard.

"Your brother spoke highly of you. I can see that he was correct in his assessment. He indicated that your work, your bravery, has tremendous potential to benefit our state. I am here to assist."

"What can you do?"

Nimr paused as the waitress arrived with their tea. The diner was rapidly filling with the lunch crowd, the noise level starting to swell. "I'm afraid that my computer skills are limited to streaming on YouTube…"

"So you know?"

"Yes, your brother briefed his commander, who, in turn, briefed his. Your support reaches all the way to the top of our organization."

"In Raqqa?"

Nimr's eyes widened, as he motioned for Mayar to hush. "We will deliver whatever assets you need," he declared. Nimr shifted his attention to his breakfast which arrived fortuitously after Mayar's last question.

"Several days ago, I received two visitors," Mayar said as Nimr swept a slice of his omelet onto a piece of toast.

"Yes, I know. But they appear satisfied by your interview. No one has been following you," he said, tapping his mobile. "I received the all clear message before you arrived."

"You have…"

"Only a handful, but men who are steeled to the task." Nimr reached into his backpack on the floor and withdrew a bright blue and orange scarf, sporting the Mets logo. He handed it across the table to Mayar. "You should proceed with your work. If you need me, wear this," he commanded. "We will meet here at noon the next day. Just like today."

"Someone will be watching me?"

"Protecting you," Nimr corrected.

"I have been working with an associate located outside of the country. My brother introduced us."

"Yes, Viktor. We are acquainted. And there is an American as well?"

"He goes by an alias, Pizza Boy. I don't know his real name."

"I don't like to involve an infidel."

"He's only in it for money."

"Then we will see that he gets what he needs. As long as he remains useful."

Mayar looked around, but no one was paying them any attention. "I should be going," she said.

"One more thing," Nimr replied, reaching into his pack again. He handed her a thin paperback with its title, *Blaze of Truth*, prominently displayed in Arabic. "Words to inspire you from our leading poetess, Ahlam al Nasr."

"Dreams of Victory," Mayar noted, translating the author's name.

"Sleep well, Sajida," Nimr said, as he slipped away from the table.

CHAPTER 29

Shake the throne of the cross,
and extinguish the fire of the Zoroastrians
Strike down every adversity,
and go reap those heads.

The next morning, Mayar sat at her desk reading *Blaze of Truth*. Ahlam al Nasr, the author, was the pseudonym for a young Kuwaiti woman who had left her home to join the revolution. *A soulmate.*

Next, she scanned a headline on the *Times'* homepage highlighting community opposition to a rumored forty-million-dollar payment from a real estate developer to the city simply for air rights to build a skyscraper. *If New Yorkers would pay that much money for a view of the Statue of Liberty, how much would they pay to turn their lights back on?*

Ahmed had promised that their fledgling Islamic State would use the ransom money to build schools, libraries, houses and hospitals. She would become a champion for Islamic women, as valuable as any of the fighters in the Syrian Desert. She only wished that he could be alive to see their victory. But, he would surely be watching in Paradise.

Mayar closed her eyes, imagining New York City in darkness, the infidels cowering in their high-rise apartments, their ransom payment building schools, roads and hospitals in her new country. How much should they ask for? Millions, at least. Billions? She would have to discuss it with Nimr, her commander now. He had called her Sajida, a martyr's name. She was a soldier of the Islamic State. *Inshallah*, she would soon wear the niqab and show the world that she was a true patriot.

Her computer beeped. Viktor had set up an encrypted chat session on Telegram. She rose and knotted her robe around her waist. Time to go to work.

M: Was the information about the Sherman Creek facility helpful?

V: Yes. It confirmed the manufacturer and model of the smart switches in the substation.

M: How is the creation of the malware progressing?

V: Outstanding. We are adapting the Stuxnet code from the Israelis. Ha! We should be ready to launch our attack this summer as planned.

M: Praise Allah. How will you attack?

V: Our virus will change the voltage regulator setting on each switch from automatic to manual at a designated time. The switches will then overload the transformers with power and melt them down.

M: Won't the system controllers recognize the change in the switch settings?

V: We have designed the virus to mask the change by sending out reports that all is normal.

M: Are you sure it will all work?

V: Of course not. But it will not even have the opportunity to work unless you are successful at breaching the system's defenses. We need a point of vulnerability to insert our payload.

M: I understand. But I am having difficulty right now.

V: You must succeed. And quickly. We have identified four zero day defects in the switch software architecture to ensure that our weapon strikes home. But they could become useless at any moment. Our arsenal of zero days is now bare. We have invested all our resources in you.

Who's we?

M: I will not fail

V: You have met with Nimr?

M: Yes

V: Nimr is a good man, but he will not accept failure - especially by a woman. He will replace you.

M: Replace me?
V: Yes.
M: I will not fail

A stab of desperation tore at her stomach, but Mayar willed it away. She was not going to be replaced, or worse, now that she had met with Nimr and could identify him. Although she no longer had her brother to protect and support her, she was a soldier, she reminded herself, and was going to act like one. *Take responsibility into your own hands. Do not rely on anyone else.* She would go out and inspect several targets herself. Find a way inside, so that she could plant Viktor's virus with a thumb drive.

She hated to search on Google again, but she did not have any other option. Two Con Ed substations were on the Upper West Side. The one on Amsterdam Avenue was just a short walk away. She lingered over the search page for a second before clicking on another entry entitled: Metcalf Station.

In 2013, a team of unidentified snipers attacked the PG&E utility substation located in a remote area outside of San Jose, California, damaging 17 transformers. Investigators, reviewing surveillance camera videos, identified flashlight signals and multiple muzzle blasts. They discovered cairns of rocks surrounding the site that riflemen had used to mark shooting positions as well as empty shell casings, all wiped clean of fingerprints. The damage took months to repair. No one had ever been arrested. The chairman of the Federal Energy Regulatory Commission called it "the most significant incident of domestic terrorism involving the grid that has ever occurred." *So far. Wait until the infidels suffer the damage that my team will inflict.*

Mayar looked out her window at the quad below, bustling with students. *Where is Nimr's man? Is the FBI watching me too?* She didn't like the idea of being followed - by anyone. *How can I evade them? What would a real spy do?* Recalling a book review in the *Times*, she opened a new tab on the browser on her computer, clicking to the Amazon website. *Palace of Treason*, a novel by Jason Matthews, CIA field operative for thirty-three years, promised to deliver a detailed account of actual tradecraft in the streets of a hostile country - and lots of sex. She downloaded the title, heated a pot of tea, and lit a sandalwood candle, infusing a sensual fragrance to her room. Loosening her robe, she sat down to read.

When she got up to stretch, night had fallen. The novel had delivered on all counts. Allah would not approve of the licentious activities triggered by the tensions of espionage. She swiped the syrupy fingers of her right hand against the soft terry of her robe. They had wandered beneath her waistband - twice. *Maybe a husband would be useful after all. A handsome fighter, perhaps. In Syria. After my jihad is complete.*

Starving, she poked around in the small refrigerator under her desk for a yogurt and fruit. A bag of pita chips rounded out her dinner. After cleaning up, she was ready to apply the other techniques expounded in the book. She printed out a map of the neighborhood, dug into her drawer for a red sharpie, and plotted her SDR, surveillance detection route, for the next day.

CHAPTER 30

Donal Brogan, the eldest of the four brothers, was the first to arrive. He wrapped his knuckles three times for luck on the base of the Christopher Columbus statue that anchored the circular, pedestrian plaza at Columbus Circle. Set like an island in the middle of a busy intersection in midtown Manhattan, the plaza itself was surrounded by splashing fountains and well-fortified shrubbery with three distinct, entry portals. Accordingly, it was an easy spot for his clan to reach but difficult for anyone to follow unnoticed, particularly at 9AM on a Sunday morning.

Donal had entered the States five months ago on a tourist visa to scout out new business opportunities. Unfortunately, pickings were slim. The Brogans were a family of warriors going back several generations. Their father, an IRA bomb maker, had died in Maze prison but not before teaching his four sons the arts of battle. With peace prevailing in Ireland for years now, the Brogans had turned to the export market as soldiers for hire.

His brothers had flown into the States the day before, arriving on separate flights at separate airports. Tim, the youngest at twenty years old, entered the plaza first, strolling slowly through the Eighth Avenue entrance. Donal checked to make sure that no one was trailing before removing his Yankees cap. Noting the all clear signal, Tim walked by without a flinch of recognition. No more than a minute later, Gerard entered from Central Park South, and promptly exited downtown. Michael followed two minutes after that. Donal waited and watched for another five minutes before leaving himself.

The last car of the uptown C train was the next checkpoint. Exiting the plaza, Donal waited at the traffic light behind a gaggle of Japanese tourists snapping photos, then walked a block downtown to West 58th Street where he descended the escalator into the New York City subway system. The C was a local, lumbering up the residential and lightly populated Central Park West, and therefore rarely crowded, certainly never at this hour. On the other hand, it ran infrequently, leaving the four brothers to pretend to ignore each other for the fourteen-minute wait.

Again, Donal performed surveillance duty. A leggy brunette in platform heels, headphones clamped onto both ears, separated Tim and Gerard, while a street musician set up his keyboard a few feet away from Michael. The smell of soot and urine lingered in the stale underground air. When the subway arrived at last, the Brogans boarded in pairs by separate doors. The brunette, still enraptured with her music, was the only other passenger. The brothers congregated silently between the support poles in the middle of the car as the train lurched forward.

Two stops later, convinced that they were still free from prying eyes, Donal exited the train and marched to the rear of the platform. His brothers followed, forming a tight semi-circle around him, partially shielded by an overflowing dumpster.

Donal pulled the flyer with Professor Bierman's picture from the back pocket of his jeans and handed it to Michael. "A new job order from a former customer," he said, tapping his foot and looking towards the station entrance. "Our cut-out in London forwarded it to me last week."

"My Arabic's is a wee bit rusty, but it looks like our old friends want us to eliminate Professor Lev Bierman," Michael said.

Gerard leaned over Michael's shoulder to look for himself. "A thousand virgins in Paradise...quite a rich prize."

"What the fuck are we going to do with a thousand virgins?" Tim asked. "That bullshit's for the towel-heads in the Middle East, not me."

"A thousand virgins is code for a million dollars - payable to our account in Namibia," Donal explained, taking back the flyer. "When you get a little older, and wiser, I'll teach you the financial side of the business," he teased.

"Bierman's a big-name cyber guy. An ex-Russian actually. Writes the occasional newspaper column blasting the Kremlin," Gerard said.

He had flown in the day before, as did Tim and Michael, each on separate flights.

"Sounds like he doing more than writing these days." Michael chipped in.

"And the fatwa bullshit gives Moscow a layer of deniability, doesn't it?" Tim asked.

"Smart lad." Donal said.

"And we add another layer." Gerard again.

"Only if we fuck up," Donal cautioned. *In which case, we'll likely be dead.*

After peering up the tracks to check for an approaching train, Tim asked, "Will Bierman have a security detail?"

"That's why we're all here," Donal replied, as a mom with toddler in tow approached, eying them warily before about-facing and retreating towards the station entrance. "We strike as soon as possible. Our friends from the old sod will deliver our tools."

Donal clapped as a subway train rumbled into the station. "Gerard, you and Tim will accept the package. I'll send you instructions shortly. Now, be gone."

He had set up separate safe apartments, scattered around the city, for his brothers. Gerard and Michael departed at 81st Street; Tim at 86th. Donal stayed onboard until 125th, where he went up the stairs and then down to the other side of the station to catch the express back to his own home in Brooklyn.

***

"Go reap those heads." The line resonated in Mayar's brain as she stepped out of her dorm at noon, wearing a pink headscarf and matching sweater with a backpack slung across her shoulder. The sun had broken through a low ceiling of gray clouds, adding a surprising warmth to the spring day. A few students scuttled about, but the campus would likely loll until noon at least.

She noted a stubby man with an olive complexion and pencil mustache slouched against the corner of her building, smoking. A freckled redhead with a bandanna tied around his neck sat on a bench reading the *Times*. Two women in baggy Columbia blue sweats were stretching for a run. One had a mole on her right cheek, while the other had a purple streak dyed into her fashionable bob. She had to train herself to remember faces, and look for repeaters along her route.

Mayar strolled down College Walk, the main pedestrian thoroughfare, and turned towards Low Library. A tall African American, hair braided into cornrows, followed. Mayar ascended the steps to the main entrance, but then swung around abruptly as if she had forgotten something. The basketball player brushed by her. From the heights, she scanned the quad but didn't see anyone out of place. In fact, Mayar hardly saw anyone at all. She returned to College Walk and exited campus onto Broadway.

She descended into the subway just outside the main gate, and waited for the downtown 1 local train. Only three other passengers were on the platform, none familiar. Just as the train rumbled into the station, Freckles loped down the stairs, a Yankees cap replacing the bandanna. Head down, he entered the same subway car as she did. *Not whom I expected. Unless he's FBI.* Shivering at the thought, she pretended to read a Seamless ad above her head before taking a seat at the far end of the car. At the 96th Street stop, the express train waited across the platform. She counted to three, then bolted out of her seat, jostling another passenger as she switched trains. Freckles also made the transition, squeezing between the doors of the express as they closed.

Mayar rode the express for two stops, exiting at Times Square. The giant hi-def billboards blared their wares; the Naked Cowboy strummed his guitar; Elmo and Mickey Mouse pranced for the tourists. Eyes forward, she bulled her way uptown through the gawkers clogging the street. Ducking into Bubba Gump's Shrimp restaurant, she removed her scarf and sweater, swapping them for the replacements, a much less conspicuous black and gray, that she had carried in her pack. She left the restaurant in the middle of a swarm of other customers, blending quickly into the crowd on the street.

After crossing the snarled intersection of Broadway and Seventh Avenues, Mayar backtracked to the Times Square subway station, this time taking the express uptown. *No sign of Freckles.* She switched again at 96th Street to the local and got off two stops later at 110th Street. She waited on the platform for five full minutes, watching all the other passengers spin through the turnstiles and climb the stairs to the street. She was alone. *No one on my tail. Black, the CIA call it.* Time to case her first substation.

As imposing as Fort Knox, the three story, polished granite building squatted on Amsterdam Avenue, consuming the entire block from

109th St. to 110th St. Its sheer face was devoid of a single window. The unmarked entrance was a fortified steel door large enough to accommodate a small truck or van. Mayar reasoned that the design was the only way that a high voltage power station could safely reside in a residential neighborhood.

She crossed the street to a bistro, ordered a tea and baguette, and sat in the window watching. Nothing. *The substation is unmanned.* So obvious, but she hadn't really thought about it before. Maintenance personnel had to enter at least occasionally, perhaps Nimr could recruit someone with credentials, but otherwise there was no way to get inside and insert Victor's virus into the network. A Metcalf Station style armed attack would be futile too.

But the machines inside the substation needed to communicate with their controllers outside. Con Ed had invested in superfast fiber optic wiring at least a decade ago to handle the most critical parts of the load, but she bet that some data was sent over a wireless network as well. There was probably a secure smartphone app that the administrators used to monitor operations.

Data in motion was highly vulnerable. The New York City electrical grid had been operational since the late nineteenth century. While it had been modified and enhanced many times, the last big overhaul occurred just after Hurricane Sandy in 2012, there had to be some older, weaker links somewhere. The older the hardware, the less rigorous encryption it could support and the easier it would be to crack.

She remembered reading about one of the big retail credit card data heists. The hackers had intercepted wireless communications between the cash registers in the stores and the servers back at corporate headquarters. Hackers at a recent convention had bragged that they could break into airplanes, trains and traffic lights.

Mayar paid the bill and headed out into the street. She wanted to check out one more substation just to be sure. She walked along 110th Street towards the park, but then turned and doubled back after crossing Columbus Avenue. She stopped twice, ostensibly checking her phone, while scanning the pedestrians behind her. No one trying to duck out of sight. Comfortable that she was still black, Mayar strolled to Central Park West and boarded the C train downtown.

Although its facade was softened by a swath of teal colored panels, the substation on West End Avenue looked similar to the one uptown

- squat, sheer, and unassailable. Mayar did not need to stay long. She had already formulated her plan.

CHAPTER 31

Mayar awoke at dawn on Monday, immediately contacting Viktor to set up another stealth chat session. Reaching underneath her mattress, she stroked the Islamic State flag before performing her morning prayers. She showered, dressed and sipped a cup of tea while waiting for Viktor's response. The deadline for her thesis presentation was only three weeks away. Graduation loomed as well. *Do they really matter anymore?* The beep from her computer saved her from answering the question.

M: We can break into the substations by intercepting their wireless transmissions.

V: That might work.

M: Can you get me a device to try?

V: Yes. The HackRF Jawbreaker would be perfect. It can fit in your purse, hack into a broad spectrum of frequencies and download communications to your laptop. We can crack the encryption and reverse engineer the code over here.

M: Praise Allah!

V: I will set up the interceptor and ship it to you

M: Send two. There are many substations to cover.

V: You must move quickly

M: We are still on schedule

V: We may need to accelerate

M: ??

V: The Americans have been warned

M: ??
V: A report has been filed with the FBI
M: Where? By whom?
V: You do not need to know the details

Viktor hacked the FBI. Impressive. They texted for another five minutes about the Jawbreaker, its software defined radio technology, and the success that another hacker recently had breaking into the control system of a moving car. Viktor added a few tips about using the Jawbreaker out on the street. Mayar didn't notice the black envelope slipped under her door until she signed off.

***

Nimr waited on the Broadway median, sitting alone on the pockmarked bench at the 113th Street intersection. The shrubbery on the narrow strip that divided the four lanes of traffic added a welcome green touch to the gray palette of the boulevard. A bus lumbered by on the uptown side, while two taxis raced for a passenger heading downtown. Mayar sat, tucking her curls underneath her scarf. Nimr turned to her, but then waited as a class of preschoolers, linked together as if they were alpinists scaling Everest, trundled by, a teacher at both ends of the rope.

"Did you enjoy your jaunt around the city yesterday?" he asked at last.

"Excuse me?" Mayar stammered.

"You know what I'm talking about. Foolish woman, you have a mission to accomplish and you are playing Mission Impossible on the street."

"I was doing reconnaissance for our project and wanted to make sure that I wasn't being followed," she asserted, maintaining her bravado.

"You cased a Con Ed substation on Amsterdam and one on West End. If we can track you, don't you think the FBI can as well. There are closed circuit television cameras all over the city."

"I'm sorry."

"There is no room for apologies any more. Mistakes will get you arrested now, or worse." Nimr swiveled to survey the street around them. "You've increased the risk of exposure for me and my team as well."

Mayar drooped her shoulders, but remained silent. Nimr reached into his pocket, fumbling for something, his eyes boring through her. After an interminable second, he withdrew an object wrapped in wax paper, slowly opened it, and took a bite of a poppy seed roll. A trace of butter, or maybe hummus, dripped from his upper lip.

"Good, you are learning to listen," Nimr said, wiping his mouth with a paper napkin. "Now, did you acquire any useful information from your excursion?"

Mayar recounted her conversation with Viktor and their plan for the Jawbreaker. Nimr stood, crumbled the wax paper into a small ball and tossed it into the trash. He returned to the bench, sitting closer to her this time. A volley of car horns erupted. Nimr retreated slightly, a look of exasperation crossing his face. She smelled paprika on his breath when he leaned into her face.

"A good plan, but I do not want you navigating the city streets any more. Go to class, the library, wherever you need to be on campus, but keep your head down."

"Who will operate the interceptors?"

"Your American friend, the pizza man? Can he help?"

"For a fee, yes. But he has his own issues with the police as well. He may not want to be on the street."

"Then you must explain to him that he has no choice. He's in too deep already."

Nimr did not wait for her reply. He slipped into the next cluster of pedestrians crossing Broadway and disappeared.

***

"Bro, check this out," Dennis Walecka called across the living room of their apartment.

"I'm busy, man," Brian replied, keeping his eyes locked on his computer monitor. "I've got my own shit to deal with. Money-making shit." His fingers flew across the keyboard.

"That's what I'm talking about asshole, real money. Come here."

Exasperated, Brian made his way over. "OK, show me what you got. It better be good."

"My man, Sully, wants me to stroll around the city with a wi-fi interceptor tucked into my pocket. Says he'll pay a hundred bucks an hour for my time."

"A wi-fi what?"

"A device that plucks radio signals out of the air. Hackers all over the world are using them now."

"Where does he want you to stroll?" Brian asked.

"Said he'll tell me when he's all set up."

"I bet he wants you to scout around some Con Ed sites," Brian grumbled as he cut loose a booming fart.

"That's cold, man." Dennis shook his head as wheeled away from his partner. He walked over to the window and shoved it open halfway. "No more shit. We've got rent due next week."

"Remember we talked about the Con Ed systems being air-gapped - the electrical controls totally separate from the administrative stuff?" Brian asked.

"Yeah." Dennis sniffed the air twice before returning to his workspace.

"Well, it sounds to me like your buddy wants you to help him jump that gap. That's serious shit. Means he wants to mess with the electrical grid."

"Who gives a flying fuck. He's our only money making opportunity right now," Dennis said.

"I give a fuck. What if Sully is a fucking terrorist? You want to be the one to blow up your own city?"

"Fuck New York City. The fucking cops are looking for me every day."

Brian sat down on the edge of Dennis' desk. "Use your head, man," he said, pointing at his temple. "What if Sully is really Homeland Security trolling on the internet for dickheads like us? They do that all the time, you know. We could spend the rest of our lives in jail."

"You think Sully could be setting us up?"

"Who knows. You ever meet him?"

"No," Dennis replied, tilting back his chair on a forty-five-degree angle. "But, I think Mr. Sully is going to have to show his face if he wants us to do any more of his dirty work."

"Us?" Brian turned away again. "Speak for yourself. I'm out of this gig."

CHAPTER 32

"All set," Jim Mangano declared as he checked the Glock in his shoulder holster. Standing in front of his desk, he smoothed the lapels of his suit and loosened his tie. He would look like a thousand other Wall Street executives heading home after a hard day on the trading floor.

"Then we're ready to roll," Lou Totti replied, zipping his black, bureau-issued windbreaker. "It's been months since we've been out in the wild actually looking for bad guys."

"Nervous?" Jim asked.

"No. Just bug-eyed. Too much time on the computer."

"Well, tonight could just turn out to be a wild goose chase." He stared at the four Interpol photos pinned to his cubicle, committing the subtleties of each face to memory.

"But your source said..."

"Gerard Brogan's in town. He's meeting a handful of the Real IRA men tonight at the Irish Hunger Memorial." Jim reached for his overcoat. "Something's up."

"The Real IRA are bad dudes. My aunt's from Portrush. She thinks they're 'fooking' murderers. Still won't accept the Peace Accords that stopped all the killings," Lou said. "But only one Brogan? Don't they usually travel in a pack?"

"The smart money would be on a Brogan family gathering, but right now, all we have is a tip about one of them. I've requested DHS to scan their facial database of recent arrivals for the other three, but Border Patrol is swamped with deportations so it will take a few days."

"Let's see what we see." Lou slung his pack over his shoulder and pointed towards the elevator bank. "After you, Big Jim."

The sun was in its last throes of the day, casting a spotlight on the Hudson River through a peephole in a wall of leaden clouds. The two FBI agents walked downtown for several blocks, then headed west on Chambers Street, crossing the traffic clogged West Street to enter the residential enclave of Battery Park City.

"Nice digs," Lou commented, scanning the row of luxury apartment buildings soaring above Teardrop Park and the river esplanade.

"Great views," Jim noted, soaking in the neighborhood with the appraising eye of a potential tenant.

"You guys decide where you're going to live after the wedding?"

"Not yet. Marcy's not too keen on moving back to Brooklyn."

"No surprise there. What bride really wants to move into her new husband's old bachelor pad?"

"I'm not giving up that easy, but I have a sinking feeling I'll be outvoted."

Lou shifted his load to his other shoulder. "Maybe that engagement ring will change Marcy's mind. Kendra showed me the photos on Facebook. It had to cost you a fortune."

"She's worth every penny."

"Spoken like a true husband to be. Hey, we're looking forward to coming to the engagement party next week."

"Marcy's sister's been planning it. Should be fun." Jim stopped in front of the North End Grill. "We should split up here. I'll take the east entrance. You circle around to the river side of the memorial."

"We're just taking pictures, right?"

"If you spot any of the Brogans, call me. Don't try to be a hero."

The Irish Hunger Memorial Garden is planted on a half-acre platform that cants gently up towards the Hudson. Encompassing wild native grasses and a roofless nineteenth century stone cottage that was brought over from County Mayo, the tract commemorates the million and half men, women and children who perished in the famine from 1846-50.

The sun's dying flare illuminated the memorial as Jim entered at street level. The trail, highlighted with beach ball sized stones from all thirty-two counties in Ireland, quickly forked. The right branch headed into the cottage where three men lounged against a roughhewn wall, their faces obscured by the shadows. On the far end of the cottage, a passageway, lined with illuminated bands of text highlighting the story of the great hunger, ran under the garden and back out to the street. *Lou should be positioned there. In the tunnel.*

Jim veered left, the trail snaking upward to the summit, two stories above the plaza. A lone figure paced back and forth at the peak. *A look-out?* Jim climbed slowly, a tourist taking in this hallowed land. He would only have one furtive, downward glance to identify the loiterers in the cottage without arousing their suspicion.

A cigarette lighter flickered below. He picked out a face - the handlebar mustache of the city's Real IRA leader. *At least we're in the right place.* The lighter flickered again. And again. It was met by a single flash from inside the passage.

He texted Lou.

J: BINGO
L: EYES ON
J: HOW MANY?
L: 1
J: STAY PUT

Jim hesitated, wanting to confirm the identity of the mystery man inside the tunnel. He didn't have to wait long. Tim Brogan, wearing a dark pea coat, stepped forward. He had grown his hair out to shoulder length, but couldn't disguise the telltale crescent scar on his right cheek. Tim shook hands with each of the three other men. The tallest, curly hair and a Viking beard, swung a backpack down from his shoulder and handed it to Tim, receiving a nod of thanks in return.

The soft gray blanket of twilight had settled quickly over the garden. Jim shifted to get a better view, sending a loose pebble skittering down the trail. The rustle caused the congregation in the cottage to stir.

"Coppers!" A bellow from above.

"FBI! Freeze!" Jim ordered as he reached for his pistol and settled into a marksman's stance.

"Shit!"

"Fuck!"

"Cocksucker!"

A frenzy of movement below. Jim tracked Tim heading back

towards the passage, the cottage chimney blocking his angle for a shot. Footsteps thudded from above. He swung his gun around. Too late.

The watchman dropped his shoulder and bowled into him like a fullback leading a power sweep. Jim cartwheeled downhill as his assailant rolled to his feet.

"Gerard? You OK? Gerard?"

"Timmy, move your ass! Now!" Gerard ordered, brandishing a Colt 45 revolver, sighting on the FBI agent's tumbling body.

Recovering to his knees, Jim scrambled for his Glock in the dirt. Gerard Brogan fired once, missing, a spray of scree peppering the slope. Jim squeezed off two shots both ripping through Gerard's chest. The IRA gunman collapsed in a bloody heap.

Jim counted three shapes, silhouettes in the moonlight, sprinting into the passageway towards Lou. "Lou! Coming at you! Lou!"

He strode purposefully down the path, eyes flashing from side to side. *Where were the other three Brogans?*

"All good here, boss." Lou's voice echoed from the passage. "But, no sign of any Brogan."

Relieved at his partner's safety, Jim explored the cottage, whipping his pistol into every corner. Spotting an alcove on the far side of the chimney, he pasted his body against the wall for protection. "Tim Brogan! FBI! Game's over!" he shouted. No reply. Jim waited, no need to rush. The IRA man was trapped. Still no sound. Crouching low, finger on the trigger, he inched forward into the alcove.

Empty, except for a field mouse scurrying across the dirt floor. He entered the passageway. Pistol drawn, Lou had two of the Real IRA thugs lined up against the wall, their arms and feet spread wide. "Help is on the way," his partner called out, his free hand mimicking a phone call. Jim spun around. One more check outside. *Tim Brogan couldn't have just disappeared into thin air.*

Jim eyed the chimney, incandescent in the moonlight, as he stepped out from cover. A handful of gravel crackled against the left corner of the wall, drawing his attention. Suddenly, a shadow, spreading its wings like a giant bat, loomed in front of him.

"You fucking, murdering bastard!" the shadow hissed.

The short hairs on Jim's neck bristled as he realized his mistake. *Tim Brogan must have shimmied over the wall of the roofless cottage. And found his brother's dead body.*

Jim pivoted, ducking, a vain attempt to avoid the weighty stone hurtling towards him. It plonked his skull and shoulder. Sinking to his knees, he heard the snap of bone and the clang of his pistol on the floor. Blood, his blood, trickled into the dirt. Footsteps faded away into the gloaming. An ambulance siren wailed, speeding towards him.

CHAPTER 33

Taryn trudged through the lobby of NYU Medical Center at ten the next morning. Jim was still in the OR. Emergency brain surgery. His parents, sister, and Marcy were there. Lou had urged Taryn to stay home, promising to contact her the moment there was news, but she couldn't wait any longer.

The information desk pointed her towards the elevators to the surgical waiting room. Two nurses, coming off duty, chatted animatedly as they passed by. An obviously new father, a blue "It's a Boy!" balloon bobbing from his hand, unable to contain his toothy grin, shared the ride up. She exited first, scanning the signs, stepping left, realizing she was headed the wrong way, spinning around.

The corridors seemed to grow dimmer and narrower as she approached the critical care unit. A doctor in green scrubs, head down checking a chart, bustled towards her. A nurse at the main station looked up from her screen as she approached.

"Jim Mangano?" Taryn asked.

"Agent Mangano's family is in there," she replied, pointing the way, lips locked in a poker face. Not a good sign.

A uniformed NYC cop, standing at attention at the door to the lounge, shifted aside to let Taryn enter. Jim's parents, still youthful, sat holding hands, alone on a row of tangerine upholstered chairs. Rosemarie, his older sister, dozed on the bench behind them, rosary beads clasped in her hands. An athletic brunette paced by the far window. Two other men in suits, FBI agents Taryn guessed, talked quietly in the corner. No sign of Lou.

Taryn hesitated for a second, then approached the young woman. "Marcy?"

Marcy looked up, a wan smile flickered. She wore faded jeans, boots and a Mets' sweatshirt, Jim's favorite team. A Rorschach worthy coffee stain crept down from her neck. "Taryn, thanks for coming," she said, running her fingers through her wayward hair. "I'm a mess."

Taryn reached out and hugged her. "I wanted to be here with all of you."

"I know." Tears welled in her eyes, red and raw from the all-night vigil. "He's still in surgery. The doctor said she's not sure if ..."

"He's going to make it," Taryn said, wrapping her arms tightly around Marcy's shoulders.

"We've been praying all night." Marcy reached for the silver crucifix looped around her neck, the halo diamond of her engagement ring amplifying the fluorescent light overhead.

"Me too."

Lou stepped into the room, a steaming cup of coffee in hand. He nodded towards Taryn, still comforting Marcy, and joined his fellow agents.

All heads spun towards the door when Dr. Rodriguez entered. Netting still covered her bobby-pinned hair, a surgical mask dangled below her chin. She asked Jim's parents, sister and Marcy to join her outside in the hall.

Taryn looked skyward. Submarine gray clouds hung low over the East River and the Queens skyline. A steady drizzle beat against the window. "Please god..." she silently exhorted. Lou shuffled over to embrace her. They held each other tightly for several seconds.

Gripping the elbow of her future sister-in-law, Marcy wobbled back into the waiting room, tears streaking down her cheeks.

"My Jimmy made it," she garbled.

***

Sipping from a paper cup, Dr. Rodriguez returned to the lounge after the immediate family had left for the recovery room. "Agent Totti?" she asked, searching the unfamiliar faces.

"Yes, Doctor."

"You're his partner?"

"Yep. Her too." Lou stepped forward, nudging Taryn alongside.

171

"As you well know, Agent Mangano took several nasty blows to his head. The first from the stone that was, um, dropped on him, the second when he hit the ground."

"But, he's OK?"

"He survived the surgery, and is resting now. He has a grade three concussion; his skull has multiple fractures and his collarbone is broken. Fortunately, his brain appears intact and all vital signs are stable. But he won't regain consciousness for a while. We'll know a little more then."

"Best case?" Taryn asked, biting her lip.

"The best case is that Agent Mangano has a giant headache for several months, and is gradually able to regain all motor, aural and cognitive functions," Dr. Rodriguez replied. "But, he's not out of the woods yet. Not even close. The next few hours, the next few days, are critical."

"Thank you." *No point asking about the worst case.*

"When can we see him?" Lou inquired.

"We're going to keep Agent Mangano in the ICU for observation, so I recommend that only his immediate family visit for the next twenty-four hours at least. Even their time with him will be limited."

"Understood," he replied, squeezing Taryn's hand.

"Any other questions?"

Both Taryn and Lou shook their heads. After the doctor left, Lou stepped over to other two agents, waiting anxiously in the corner. Taryn returned to her perch by the window. The rain had stopped and a pale streak of sunlight broke through the parting clouds.

"Let's go for a walk. I need some fresh air," Lou said, returning from his pow-wow.

They walked silently, heads bowed, through the corridor and down the elevator. The cavernous lobby was well-windowed, but packed with anxiety. *Every family has its own troubles.* Taryn zipped her maroon shell, pulling a Mets cap from its pocket. Jim had given it to her at the end of last season. *He will live to see them in the World Series again.* She knew it.

Lou slammed his palm against a parking meter as soon as they reached First Avenue. "Brogan ambushed Jim. He wanted payback."

"For his brother?"

"Yep. Jim shot Gerard at the Hunger Memorial. A third brother, Michael, is still loose, probably here in the city. DHS got back to me a few hours ago, confirming a facial match with an arrival at Newark on Saturday. Under a false passport, of course."

"There's a fourth Brogan too, isn't there?"

"Donal, the oldest. DHS searched back a month and couldn't find a match, so he could be anywhere in the world. But I bet he's in our fair city too."

"Any update on Tim Brogan?" she asked, shivering as a gust blew in off the East River.

"Street surveillance cameras tracked him leaving the scene but we lost him. Don't worry, he won't get far. Every cop in the city is looking for him, and we have alerts at all the bridges, airports, train stations, you name it."

Taryn kicked at a cigarette butt lying in the street. "What about the two jokers that you captured, the Real IRA guys?"

"They'll never talk - even if we waterboarded them for the next week - which we won't do. Forget I even said that."

"Forgotten. But we have their phones, their emails, their messaging apps, right?"

"Yeah. We got a warrant last night to search everything, and tap any device that we need to."

"But, I have a hunch that Tim Brogan's not going to surface that easily."

"No. The Brogans are pros. They know how to disappear when they have to."

"The real question is why are they in town at all?" Taryn asked, jamming both hands into her jacket pockets.

CHAPTER 34

Tim Brogan peeked with his right eye, his head buried in *Sports Illustrated*, waiting for a computer in the public library on Houston Street to open. *Come on, Grandma, let's finish - now.* Last night, after the ambush at the Hunger Memorial, he had stayed in mission mode, utilizing his pre-planned escape route to avoid the cops' camera network and deposit the backpack with the supplies in his apartment in Alphabet City, just a few blocks from here.

Grandma was packing up at last, closing her purse, buttoning her frayed wool coat. A Goth chick - blond, butch, black cargo pants, black tee, braless - stepped towards the open seat, but he cut her off with a glare that froze her tiny tits. She tossed her nose in the air as if the silver ring embedded in it was tied to a puppeteer's string.

He should have stayed in his apartment, but he needed to know. Sitting down in front of the computer, his hair now pony-tailed, face obscured by the hood of his Kelly green Celtics sweatshirt, he typed in a news search. His photo was posted on the homepage of the *Times*, but there was still no official update on FBI Agent James Mangano. *I hit him square in the head. The bastard who killed Gerard should be dead.* Tim rubbed his lower back, still sore from ripping that boulder out of the ground.

After setting the timer on his phone, Tim opened a new window on the screen. He would only stay online for ten minutes, even here in the anonymity of the library. *Brightify never fails. The cops aren't the only ones who use social media.* Sure enough, Mangano's fiancé had just posted an update. He was still alive - barely, if he read correctly between the lines. *Guess the engagement party is off. Maybe nature will take its course and I won't have to come back for him.*

Professor Lev Bierman's home page was also a bubbling fount of information. His class schedule, travel plans, speaking engagements, even his homework assignments, were all posted in plain sight. Tim checked Google Maps and logged off. Only eight minutes.

He exited the library, keeping his head down. Two cops on the corner of Avenue C were tied up with a traffic accident. A white Suburban had rear-ended a Smart car. Not a pretty sight. A tow truck and two more police cruisers were in line behind the wreck. *Plenty of cops in the neighborhood this morning.* An ambulance screeched around the corner.

Tim walked the two short blocks to his apartment, a third-floor walk-up studio, at a calm, steady pace, keeping one eye on a pair of patrolwomen across the street. They checked an iPad and entered the lobby of a freshly scrubbed tenement building, now converted into upscale condos. Clearly, they were looking for someone. *Guess who?*

His room was sparsely furnished, two windows with a view of an alleyway providing the only natural light. Three empty cans of Bud on the Formica table, jeans tossed on a folding chair, a wet towel hanging on a hook over the sink, and a framed photo of the four Brogan boys taken ten years ago on a football pitch outside of Belfast were his only contributions to the decor. The Murphy bed was open and unmade, a battered dresser next to it. Opening the drawers one at a time, he tossed the handful of clothes that he brought on the trip into a duffel. He lingered over the memento of his brothers, searching their faces for clues to a story that he sensed might be approaching its conclusion. *Where are Donal and Michael now?*

How did I get trapped in this hellhole, black and gray, concrete and asphalt, so far from home? County Down was all earthy greens and browns - rolling hills, gorse, dunes, coastline, forests and fields. The Brogans had never been much good at farming, or anything else except fighting. Fortunately, the world still needed soldiers and the job paid well. He had gone underground once before to evade capture. He knew how to keep moving.

Tim texted the emergency number, not sure who was on the other end, but doubting it was family. Any direct link would multiply the risk for them all. Donal and Michael would find him when it was safe.

The backpack that Connor O'Reilly had handed off the night before lay under the table, away from any sunlight that might trickle through the windows. He tossed his green sweatshirt on the bed, replacing it with a bland gray one with a Nike swoosh on the chest. He pulled the hood up and donned dark wraparound sunglasses. Time to go to work. *The Brogans always get their man.*

With the pack secure on one shoulder and his duffel hanging loosely from the other, Tim clambered down the stairs. Too late, he saw his startled neighbor, Mr. Sanders, whiskered face lost behind a brown paper bag full of groceries, shuffling upward. Two oranges, a half dozen eggs, three cans of Pabst, and a six pack of hot dogs scattered over the landing. An egg splattered in the corner, its yolk leaking from the cracked shell.

"Shit! I'm sorry," Tim apologized, his accent more Brooklyn than Belfast. He had a gift for languages that enabled him to suppress his natural brogue better than any of his brothers.

"You look like you're in a hurry son," Sanders replied, before leaning his cane against the wall and bending over to pick up the ingredients for his dinner. "I'll clean this up in a jiffy."

"Yes, sir, I am." Tim checked his watch. Only one minute to his rendezvous. Nevertheless, he dropped his duffel on the floor, pulling his hood tight over his head, and began helping the elderly black man.

"Why thank you kindly."

"Let me get the door for you," Tim lifted Mr. Sanders' keys from his grip and unlocked his apartment door. "There you go," he said, ushering his neighbor inside.

When Tim reached the front stoop, his ride, a once-white van, its paint now pinged and pebbled, was waiting. Unfortunately, the two cops had made their way to his side of the street. He watched as they approached the building next door. Only a few minutes till they knocked on his door. He swung the pack down to his waist, feeling for the comforting grip of the pistol. *Not now.*

He pivoted around and headed back inside, leaving his duffel at the front door. He started up the steps, taking two at a time, his hood falling to his shoulders.

Wearing a checkered robe over threadbare slacks, Mr. Sanders was standing with broom and dustpan on the second-floor landing. The door to his apartment was ajar. "Forget something?" he asked, a corkscrewed expression as he stared at Tim's face.

"No, er, I mean yes. My throat's a bit dry." Tim dropped his head as if he was searching for a lost penny. "Can I ask you for a glass of water?"

"No problem at all. Don't get many visitors these days anyways. What did you say your name was?"

"Thank you," Tim replied, as he stepped into the room. The studio apartment had the same layout as his own, but Sanders had warmed it up with paintings and pillows. A yellowing photo of a young couple stood framed on the counter.

"The good lord took my wife ten years ago," Sanders commented, brushing past Tim to reach for the photo. "Haven't I seen you on TV…"

Tim looped his elbow around Sander's neck and torqued violently, snapping his cervical spine like a pretzel stick. Sanders' eyes bulged. Spittle leaked down his chin. One last gasp escaped his lips before he dangled limply in Tim's arms. Tim lifted the featherweight body and laid it in the single bed, covering Sanders' torso with a blanket. Sanders looked as if he was taking a nap. "Sorry old man," Tim whispered. *I need a head start.*

Tim hoisted the studio's lone arm chair, upholstered in mouse gray, with both hands and left the apartment, carefully closing the door. He carried the chair out the front door, obscuring his face, and down the steps, grabbing his duffel on the way. *Just another tenant in transit.*

The van was waiting with its engine running. As he waddled into the street, he noticed the cops coming back outside, maybe twenty-five yards away. The blond one was tapping notes into her tablet.

Before he could reach the van's doors, they swung open. The interior was dark but he had no trouble recognizing the welcoming smile. He slid the chair inside and climbed in beside it.

"Timmy, my boy. I thought you could use some assistance," Michael said, extending an arm to wrap his brother in a bear hug.

As soon as the doors clicked shut, the van pulled away. There were no seats or windows in the back, just some loose crates resting on a tarp covering the hard floor. Tim leaned back against the van wall and drank in his brother's presence.

"New York's a little too hot right now," he said.

"And getting hotter every minute, by the look of all the coppers on the street." Michael opened a red cooler and handed his brother a bottle of Guinness.

"To Gerard," they toasted, bouncing as the van accelerated onto the FDR Drive.

"Where's Donal?" Tim asked.

"Fuck knows. He'll want to lay low until the heat dies down," Michael declared, taking a lengthy gulp of his dark beer. "But I'm like you. I want to get the job done and go home."

They sat in silence as the van proceeded uptown and out of the city, the spires of the George Washington Bridge receding through the rear windows of the van. The thick-necked driver never said a word, or even turned to look at his passengers. He steered carefully through the light traffic, keeping his speed right at the limit.

About forty-five minutes later, they rolled to a stop in a deserted corner of the parking lot at the Sloatsburg rest area on the New York State Thruway. At the far end of the lot, the golden arches of McDonald's beckoned weary travelers.

"I've got to piss," Tim said.

"Not here. Too crowded."

A gray Chevy Malibu pulled into the next spot. The driver, burly and bald wearing a black trench, climbed out, leaving the door open and the car running. He stepped into the passenger seat of the van without turning his head.

"Our chariot has arrived," Michael said, taking the wheel of the Malibu.

Tim strode around to the passenger side and buckled in. "We have a contract to complete."

CHAPTER 35

"Are they ready for me?" Bernie Rosen asked, taking a last sip of his morning coffee as he rose from his desk.

"Yes, sir. Standing room only. I had to turn the AC up and double our order of bottled water," Serena Thomas replied, waiting at the door to the mayor's office.

"Every department has to cover their ass when it comes to blackouts." Rosen stepped over to his closet and slipped on his suit jacket, a bespoke Zegna pinstripe, brand new. The mayor checked his hair, moussed in place as usual. "How do I look?"

Thomas just smiled. "Let's get going."

"Any more from our friend Professor Bierman?" he asked before leaving the office.

"Not a peep. But, remember, sir, we've called this meeting to discuss black-out planning, not cybersecurity."

Rosen trailed Thomas through the swirl of aides, deputies, and officials in the conference room, shaking hands, nodding to a few old friends. She deposited him in his seat at the head of the long gleaming oak table. The chatter in the room barely subsided. Thomas waited another second, then waved an arm and almost shouted, "The mayor is ready to begin. Mr. Murphy, you're leading off this morning."

The room gradually quieted as Tom Murphy, a tall, silver haired patrician with ruddy, bulldog jowls, stood. He buttoned his jacket and opened the presentation booklet lying on the table. "You all have a copy of this, but I just want to touch on a few salient facts," he began. "As a senior vice president at Con Edison, I am extremely proud of our service to New York. We deliver electricity to more than three million customers through a network of 94,000 miles of underground cables, the world's largest underground system by the way, and 34,000 miles of cables above ground. Now, remember, Con Ed does not generate electricity any more. We purchase it from our good friends around the state, and around the country." The NYISO representative, a bony, Pinocchio nosed woman, raised her hand modestly at the recognition, while Murphy continued. "Generator plants, like Robert Moses Niagara, produce the electricity. It travels long distance over eleven thousand miles of backbone 345 kilovolt lines. Our sixty-one area substations tap it down first to 138, then 13.8, and finally our eighty thousand local transformers take the final step to deliver 120-volt power to homes and businesses. Diagrams of the grid are all in my presentation."

"Talk to me about peak demand - like we might get this summer," Rosen cut in.

"Of course. All-time demand peaked on Friday, July 19, 2013 at 2PM at 13.2 megawatts. A normal day in the spring or fall might run about half that. Now, I know that the Farmer's Almanac is forecasting another scorching summer this year, so we're preparing for the worst case."

"What does that mean?" Rosen asked.

"Redundancy and resiliency. Con Edison has more than fifty independent suppliers of energy. We've invested over a billion dollars in the past five years fortifying our plant and upgrading its infrastructure. You know that the city's electrical system dates to the late nineteenth century. We're proud of that history but we're even more proud of our service record. Con Ed has installed hundreds of smart switches bringing our grid in line with modern technology. We've also set up demand response relationships with power suppliers outside of our region. Now, if we have a failure, even a major one, we can re-route power to our customers from many other sources." Murphy checked his notes, and continued. "Con Ed averted 65,000 outage situations last year. We're confident that we will serve the city well again this summer."

"Thank you. I can rest much easier now. But shit happens, pardon my language, right? Like in 2003 when the whole city went black." Rosen opened a folder with background information that Allison Gold had prepared. She and Merry were pancaked against the wall to his right taking notes on their iPads.

Ben Olinmeister was next to them, mooning over his hot, young squeeze. Serena had confirmed Jackie's suspicions, noting dryly that half of City Hall already knew about the affair, while the other half still thought Bloomberg was mayor. The tryst was going to jeopardize both of their careers. Serena would not be offering Merry a full-time position; and Rosen planned to ask Ben to leave City Hall by the end of the summer.

"The blackout in 2003 wasn't really our fault," Murphy explained, still standing. "It started in Ohio when one of their backbone transmission lines got overloaded and sagged into the trees. Operators rerouted power, but that overloaded other lines causing even more problems across the region. Software glitches added to the confusion. Michigan, Pennsylvania, Canada, New Jersey and New York all automatically disconnected from the grid for safety reasons. We got most of our customers back online within eight hours though. And we haven't had a system-wide shutdown like that ever since."

"You're telling me a tree branch took down most of the power on the east coast?" Rosen asked, head down, feigning interest in Murphy's presentation. "What damage could a cyber intruder do today?"

"Excuse me?" Murphy replied, sipping from a bottle of water.

The representative from the NSA, a jeans-clad, African-American woman with reading glasses perched on her nose, perked up at her seat at the far side of the conference table. "A cyberattack could knock out the grid for a long time," she stated flatly.

"We just don't think that scenario is realistic. Con Ed operates thirty-nine independent networks in Manhattan alone. We're confident our systems and our people can rectify any issues in a reasonable time frame," Murphy said, trying to escape the ambush.

"OK, but what's the plan if Con Edison can't fix things quickly? What would happen if a blackout lasted several days?" Rosen pressed.

"I thought the purpose of this meeting was to discuss the upcoming summer," Murphy's agitation obvious now.

"What if we had a cyber event this summer then? Hackers are attacking your system right now." The NSA rep was not backing down either.

"Wait a second. Do you know of an imminent threat?" Rosen interrupted. *Has she seen Bierman's report?*

"No. Just a perpetually high level of hacker interest." NSA replied.

"As I said before, Con Ed fixes problems every day to service our customers." Murphy tried to steer the conversation back to safe ground.

"But cyber is definitely different," the Federal Electricity Regulatory Council spokesman, florid-faced with a Caesarean crown of gray hair, chipped in. "Congress has proposed a bill, twice, to strengthen cyber standards in the utility industry, but the industry has lobbied against it. And stopped it cold."

"That bill was bullshit," the North American Electric Reliability Corporation rep, another graying white male, countered. "It was just a move by Washington to gain regulatory control over independent energy suppliers."

"Here, here," the NYISO representative seconded. "We've invested almost forty million in our control room to monitor the grid. It processes almost ten thousand data points per second."

"Under section 215 of the Federal Power Act, FERC has no authority over third-party suppliers or vendors," NERC piled on.

"Like Con Edison," Murphy added.

"So who's in charge of the cybersecurity of the entire grid?" the Mayor asked the room. Heads swiveled, but no one raised their hand. A cough grumbled from the back of the room. Then a giggle.

"Wait a second, I don't want you to think that we're sitting on our hands doing nothing," Murphy said. "The industry has established CRISP, the Cyber Risk Information Sharing Program, to pool our resources. And we work with the federal government agencies too."

"How many participants are in CRISP?" Rosen prodded.

"I don't know for sure. A few hundred at least."

"And how many firms are connected to the grid?" Rosen again.

"Counting manufacturers of solar panels, wind turbines, smart meters and smart thermostats?"

"Yes, everyone at the big dance."

"Several thousand." Murphy answered sheepishly.

"And each one of those thousands of suppliers represents a point of vulnerability that hackers might utilize as a gateway to take down the entire grid," the NSA rep added.

"You're blowing the threat way out of proportion. Our cybersecurity staff tells me that the time and skills, not to mention detailed knowledge of our control systems, that it would take to do real damage is enormous. Who can mount that kind of coordinated assault?" Murphy asked.

"The Chinese, the Russians, the Iranians...," NSA rep counted down.

"Look, Tom's right. This is a black-out planning meeting. It's not the time or place to get into a pissing match over our cyberdefense," Rosen interjected, standing. "But, if we had a major cyber event this summer, does every organization in the room have a disaster response plan?"

"Yes."

"Of course."

"Right here."

"That's what I hoped to hear," the Mayor said. "Now, how many of your plans foresee a city-wide blackout lasting more than a week?"

Silence settled over the room like a wet blanket. Not even a cough this time.

"That's what I was afraid of," Rosen sighed. He looked directly at the stylishly suited, brunette who had traveled down from Washington for this meeting. "And what would the Federal Emergency Management Agency recommend in that case?"

She removed her glasses and wiped them slowly before answering. "If we thought a blackout could last seven days or more, we would reluctantly have to recommend the evacuation of New York City."

***

"Evacuate the city? What a joke. Where could you even send eight million people?" Rosen stormed when he was finally able to retreat to his office, door closed, alone with Serena Thomas. "It's not going to happen on my watch."

"No sir."

"That would make Hurricane Sandy look like a summer squall."

"Yes sir."

"Here's what I want you to do," Rosen said, sitting behind his desk. He slapped a legal pad down on his blotter and began writing. "Contact everyone who was here today. Lock them in a room. I want to know what that NSA gal meant by 'a perpetually high level of hacker interest.' Find out what she thinks of Bierman's report too."

"We need to establish a task force to coordinate our cyber defense,"

Serena offered.

"And our response to an extended emergency. If we fail."

"God forbid."

"Exactly. I'll find the budget, the facilities, whatever's needed. And I want the best people on that committee," Rosen said.

"I'll schedule the kick-off meeting in the next thirty days. Any problem if I use Allison for support? She's more tech-savvy than anyone else in our shop."

"Of course. One more thing…" the Mayor drifted off for a second.

"Yes," Serena prodded.

"Find Taryn Booker. She's beaten the Russians once already. I want her on the task force."

CHAPTER 36

The young lions of Allah, clothed in camo gear, heads capped in black, some masked, some with thick, unruly beards, all with AK-47s at the ready, stormed into Mosul. Jeeps and pick-ups rolled to a stop. Terrified civilians scattered in their wake. In the background, male voices, a cappella, sung *anashid*, celebrating their love for their country and their god, and their willingness to die for them.

Mayar sat in her desk chair, eyes riveted on her laptop screen, watching the DVD that Nimr had taped into the back of the poetry book that he had given her. His note indicated that it was prepared just for her. She sipped a cup of tea and buttered a muffin as she watched.

In the next scene, the women of the Al-Khansaa brigade, swathed in black - full length burkas and niqab, only their eyes visible - patrolled the streets of Raqqa brandishing automatic rifles. The narration highlighted the brigade's role in enforcing Shariah with the power to arrest and punish other women who violated the code. *They would have stoned my mother to death.*

The clip concluded with the female soldiers leading a line of captives, chained together at the wrist, through a town square. Mayar paused the video, retrieving the ISIS flag from under her bed and resting it on her lap.

Abu Bakr al-Baghdadi, *our leader*, appeared next, his eyes radiating strength and clarity of purpose. Subtitles helped Mayar translate his message: "Islam was never a religion of peace. Islam is the religion of fighting. No one should believe that the war that we are waging is the war of the Islamic State. It is the war of all Muslims, but the Islamic State is spearheading it. It is the war of Muslims against infidels. O Muslims go to war everywhere. It is the duty of every Muslim."

Mayar's pulse raced with pride. She was part of this movement, this bold journey to defend the Muslim faith and restore the *Khalifa* to its rightful place among the nations of the world.

The video cut away to the President stumping in South Carolina during the campaign, bouffant hair in full bloom, exhorting his supporters to "bomb the shit out of these people...attack them in their homes." Snippets of interviews with faces in the crowd - male, female, young and old - echoed the anti-Muslim sentiment. Mayar gripped her butter knife tightly, imagining it was a more formidable weapon. *I will avenge the murder of my brother.*

The next scene first showed the city of Raqqa under siege, bombs falling, fires everywhere, then it shifted to a prisoner in an orange jumpsuit locked in a cage, identified as a captured Jordanian pilot. Mayar gasped as flames first licked at his feet, then consumed his body completely. Her breakfast pitched in her stomach, but she fought to keep it down. The video alternated between clips of the carnage in Raqqa and the immolation of the prisoner. At the end, the narrator, a woman, intoned "You can do to your enemy what he does to you." Mayar recognized the words of Ahlam al Nasr. The DVD concluded with a covey of olive green doves soaring aloft, heading to Paradise.

Mayar opened her dorm room door and sprinted to the bathroom. She knocked aside Amy from across the hall and banged on a locked stall door. "I'm in here," came a high-pitched reply.

She gagged, remembering the pilot's last flicker of life, then stuffed her head into a vacant sink and puked.

"You OK?" Amy asked.

She gagged again, unleashing another volley.

"You want me to call the nurse's office?"

Mayar shook her head, then rinsed her mouth and spit into the sink. She stood erect, wiping the last remnants of phlegm from her lips with a paper towel. "I'll be alright in a minute." *I'm a soldier now. Sajida is my name.*

She padded back to her room, closed the door and bolted it. Her computer lock screen displayed the black and white ISIS logo. Startled, she ejected the DVD and slid it under her mattress, along with the flag that lay sprawled over her chair. Her door had been ajar when she raced to the bathroom. *Did anyone see inside?* Mayar unlocked the door and checked the hall. Empty. *What was I expecting - a gaggle of spectators?* She would just have to wait and see.

Mayar returned to her computer and scanned Allison and Merry's messages again. The texts and photographs that the infidel whores exchanged with their lovers were immoral, but useless. A dead end. But their notes from the mayor's black-out planning meeting might be informative. She had just started to read them when Viktor appeared online.

V: We need to move up our launch date
M: Why?
V: The mayor's office will be increasing its attention on the cyberdefense of the grid
M: How do you know?
V: We have a rat in his office

My RAT. Allison's RAT. How naïve was I? Viktor had tapped my computer and used my RAT to break into the City Hall system. And dug deeper than I did. Why is he telling me now? What else did he learn?

M: I need the Jawbreaker to secure our entry point
V: It is on the way.
M: I will deploy it immediately
V: We will now target Wednesday May 16 to launch our attack. At 5PM. The start of the rush hour commute

Is Viktor now in command?

M: I will not fail you

After signing off, Mayar sent a private message to Pizza Boy, soliciting his services again, promising another hefty payment. *Viktor or Nimr? Or even my valiant Ahmed? Did it matter who was in charge? They all need me to complete the mission. And I have my own jihad to complete.*

She checked her watch. Time for a meeting with her thesis advisor. The professor advised municipalities around the globe on the implementation of smart grids. Mayar had logged many hours in his tutelage, but he would be greatly surprised to learn the true reason behind his star pupil's interest in his work.

Three hours later, Mayar swung back to her dorm. A message from Pizza Boy was waiting. The impudent ass demanded to meet Sully in person. He threatened to cut off all contact otherwise. She sent back a reply, stalling him for twenty-four hours.

Mayar didn't want to risk a meeting but she had no choice. She wrapped her bright blue and orange Mets' scarf around her neck and walked across campus to Baker Library.

CHAPTER 37

Bernie Rosen sliced his steak, New York strip of course, smiling at the blood red visible on the inside. He nodded his approval to the Gracie Mansion waiter who added baked potato and spinach to his plate. Jackie sat across from him, twice the greens but half the portion of meat on her plate. No potato either. She had lost twelve pounds in almost three weeks and looked svelte in a cinnamon Michael Kors pantsuit.

The mayor poured the wine himself, a Shaw Vineyards Reserve cab from the Finger Lakes, and toasted, "To our family." Jackie clinked her glass.

"How was your day?" he asked.

"Excellent, actually. I met with the board of the Food Bank. They've asked me to chair the gala this fall."

"Congratulations."

"The bank does great work. It feeds over a million New Yorkers, you know."

He nodded, spearing another piece of steak with his fork, while his wife continued. "But I don't want to just be a figurehead. I'm going to pitch in and get my hands dirty."

"I think it's a great idea."

Jackie nibbled on her salad. "I know what you're thinking. It will keep me busy and help our public image," she smiled mischievously. "But I'm going to surprise you."

"Actually, I was thinking about an issue that came up at City Hall the other day. You and the Food Bank might be able to help out."

"Really?" Jackie took a long sip of wine.

"If the city had a blackout that looked like it was going to last more than a few days, the federal government would want us to evacuate."

"Evacuate New York City?" Jackie coughed up a mouthful of red.

"Sounds crazy, right. But Serena reviewed some of the issues with me this morning. It could get pretty ugly after seven days."

"I'm sure. But no electricity for a week? Or longer? That's never happened before."

"I know."

"Is someone forecasting an earthquake or an asteroid strike?" Jackie laughed.

"No. A cyberstrike. We're more vulnerable than we realize." Bernie sliced up the last of the steak on his plate. "Con Ed's downplaying the threat, as you'd expect, but ..."

"So, some crazy takes out the lights in Flatbush? The rest of the city goes on living until we fix it. New Yorkers are tough people."

"The NSA was talking about the Russians or the Chinese taking down the entire city."

"Could they do that?" Jackie asked.

Bernie shrugged. "Probably."

"But, why would they do that? Wouldn't we just retaliate? Black-out Moscow or Beijing?" Jackie sipped her wine.

"Unless we couldn't trace the attack back to the source."

"What do you mean?"

"There's an FBI report, by some rogue professor, who thought that the Russians might be working jointly with ISIS on a major cyberattack of New York."

"ISIS would do the dirty work so the attack would look like some isolated terrorist plot?" Jackie asked.

"Exactly. CyberBanda, or some other Russian hacker group, would do the technical stuff."

"Do you think that CyberBanda is still mad at you? Didn't they cause enough damage to our family already?"

"I doubt this has anything to do with us personally. The implications are much, much broader than that." Bernie crossed his utensils over his plate, nodding to the waiter that he was finished.

"Like what?"

"Moscow wants to annex the entire Ukraine, for example. What better way to distract America than a cyberattack in New York?"

"While our *meshuganah* President is making America great again and threatening to pull out of NATO*?*" Jackie squared off her remaining spinach and scooped it into her mouth.

"Exactly"

"Didn't Hitler start by annexing the Sudetenland? While Roosevelt and Chamberlain and everyone else stuck their heads in the sand until it was too late?"

"I don't think we're headed for World War III, not by a long shot. Even the Professor said his analysis is still in the early stages. He could be dead wrong."

"Why wait to find out? You could launch your own cyber defense initiative. It would be considered a signature move by the new mayor. Bring in lots of press." Jackie pushed back from the table. "What's the downside?"

"Cyber's tough to spend money on because the average guy doesn't see it. It's not like putting more cops out on the street. And Con Edison is telling the world that they've got strong cyber defenses in place already. We don't want to go off half-cocked and panic people unnecessarily."

"And the city's budget is so tight. I suppose you'd have to shift dollars from another project and people would scream. On the other hand, it's your legacy. You can't just sit there and do nothing." Jackie lifted the bottle of Cab and refilled their glasses.

The butler interrupted their conversation before they could finish the wine. "Robert's on the phone. He'd like to talk to his mother."

Jackie smiled. "Our son exceeded his allowance this month, so I shut down his credit card."

"No wonder he's calling," Bernie chortled as his wife left the table. "I'd like to say hi – when you're finished with him."

***

Taryn was one of the few Lightning Strikers still at her desk at nine. She chomped on the meatball parm wedge that was dinner, washing it down with a gulp from a bottle of Stella. The invitation from City Hall that afternoon had been a huge surprise.

Montel had called her into his office so she could talk to the Mayor's chief of staff directly. Taryn assumed she was still on the Mayor's shit list, but Serena Thomas assured her that he had specifically requested her participation because of her proven investigative skills. Montel figured that Leary had somehow gotten word of Lightning Strike's probes over to City Hall, bumping Taryn upstairs and out of his hair. Either way, she didn't care. A seat at the mayor's table on a high visibility cybersecurity issue was a plum assignment.

Montel warned her about the old Chinese proverb: be careful what you wish for. And he reminded her that she had to keep up with her other responsibilities at Lightning Strike as well.

Another long night loomed ahead. Taryn glanced at a news headline crossing her screen: Blackout in Kiev. Not on her beat. She took another draught of beer and clicked on the sports feed. How were the Rockies looking this season? Pitching was always a problem at Coors Field. *Isn't Kiev the capital of the Ukraine? Didn't Shahar mention that CyberBanda had launched attacks there?*

She clicked back on the blackout story. Not much information. A short circuit in a transformer had shut down power in the Pechersk District in the city center. No word on when it would be back up again. She shot a query over to Lightning Strike's command center. It was just after 4AM in Israel, but someone was always on duty. Sure enough, the reply came back in fifteen minutes. The Ukrainian government was a client, so Lightning Strike had an inventory of all their computing gear. Their smart switches and transformers were manufactured by A&B. Model numbers were attached.

Taryn searched for the background information that Con Edison supplied for the New York City grid. Not easy to find. She wandered over to the company kitchen for some chips and another beer. She tried to call Con Ed's support desk but no one answered, so she left a voice mail. Clicking on to the A&B website, she found a white paper and documentation on the specs for their switches.

The only redeeming part about working till midnight in New York was that it was now morning in Tel Aviv. Over the past three weeks, Eli had grown accustomed to her half-coherent, late night rambles.

"Hey."

"How are you?" he replied.

"Tired."

"Go home. You need your rest." Eli was a contradiction – both a family man and a special forces operator, licensed to kill.

"I'm almost finished. Just wanted to hear a friendly voice."

"I miss you. When will I see you again?" he asked, his urgency apparent.

"Soon. I promise. But it's a mess here right now. I really need to talk to Shahar," Taryn said, providing the details on Kiev. "I need to know if there was any malware involved."

"She should be in the office in the next half hour. How is your FBI friend in the hospital? Any update on his condition?"

"I stopped by yesterday. Jim's doing much better. The doctors think he's out of danger, but they still don't know if he'll fully recover."

"Has the FBI caught Tim Brogan yet?"

"No. He seems to have disappeared."

"What about his two brothers?"

"No word on them either." Taryn stored her files and locked her desk drawer.

"Shahar's concerned about Professor Bierman. He should disappear like the Brogans."

"I'm worried about him too. But, as long as the Brogans are still in the US, the professor will be fine. He's out of the country for the next week at least."

"That's not what's on his home page."

"Bierman's home page doesn't always have the correct information," Taryn chuckled. "He's a survivor for good reason. The Brogans will be in prison before he returns."

"*B'ezrat HaShem*," Eli said. *God willing.* "Now you need to go home and crawl into bed."

"Yes, dear." *But I want to crawl into bed with you.* Taryn was certain the next time she clung to Eli, it wouldn't be on the back of a motorbike. With a bloody shoulder that felt like a chainsaw had hacked into it. Heading to the elevator, she catalogued the reasons why this romance was a bad idea. *He's too old. And too far away. And I'm not Jewish.*

Who cares? Taryn gave up the battle by the time she reached the lobby. Trudging along the slumbering streets of the West Village, her thoughts plunged down an erotic rabbit hole well before she reached her apartment.

***

"I'm not doing nothing about cybersecurity and emergency planning, you know," Bernie said as he and Jackie climbed up the stairs after their conversations with Robert. "I've already asked Serena to set up a task force to get the ball rolling." *No point mentioning the invitation to Taryn Booker now.*

"Where will she start?"

"Who? Oh, Serena and the task force. Safety comes first obviously. People were looting and rioting in the street during the blackout in 1977."

"I remember. And that only lasted one night."

"New York is a vertical city. How do we get people up and down to their apartments and their offices without electricity? How do people move around without traffic signals, subways, tunnels, or air traffic control? There would be no cell phone service or internet access. Hospitals would have to triage patients until they shut down."

"Don't they have backup generators?" Jackie asked.

"Most hospitals only have ninety-six hours of backup power. Police and fire, and many of the modern towers have some backup too, but only a few days' worth. After Hurricane Sandy, the defense department flew in extra generators but they can't cover the city indefinitely."

"How can I help?"

"You can research our food and water supplies. Does the city have any stockpiles? How long can they last? Can we create more?"

"Shit." Jackie declared as they passed the boys' rooms.

"I know. It all seems like a bad movie."

"No, I mean real shit. Sanitation. What happens when 8 million people try to flush the toilet if there's no electricity?" she went on.

"You're right. The problems keep multiplying." Bernie stopped at the entrance to the master bedroom. "Maybe we would have to move some people - the elderly, families with infants, I don't know. But I want to see if we can come up with a better plan for everyone else. I'd like you to get involved here."

"Of course, I'm a mother. This is what I do best."

Bernie reached for his wife's hand. "You're a great mother. And a wonderful wife." His hand lingered, the moment pregnant with possibility.

"What were you thinking?" Jackie broke the spell.

"Excuse me?" Bernie's hand retreated to his side.

"I'm sorry," she said, then added hurriedly, "…no, I'm not sorry. I still can't get past …your, your affair."

"I was hoping we could move on by now," Bernie replied, shoulders slumping in realization that he was fighting a losing battle – at least tonight.

"Really? Move on where? To bed?"

"That would be nice."

"One good *schtup* will make it all better, huh?"

"No. I know it won't. I'm sorry."

"You have a wife, two sons, a family, a career – and you were willing to throw it all away. For what?"

"It just happened. One minute we were in the bar, talking about the Moscow subway, the next…"

"You were all in the sack? Playing Twister?"

"Something like that. A threesome's every guy's fantasy..." Bernie straightened his posture. "I had a moment of weakness – but there was no affair. No romance." He reached for his wife again. "You're the woman that I love and always will." Jackie did not remove her hand, emboldening him. "Please give me another chance to be your husband."

"Not yet."

CHAPTER 38

Nimr waited on the Riverside Drive promenade as Mayar approached, backpack slung over her shoulder. He tilted his head signaling that she should walk with him.

Riverside Park was in bloom, a canopy of green glimmering in the afternoon sun. Daffodils sprouted at the base of the low stone wall that bordered the walking path. Down below, traffic on the West Side Highway rumbled by, largely obscured by the thick tree cover. They sidestepped a nurse and her charge, an elderly woman in a fur coat, leaning on her walker. Nimr sat on a vacant bench, patting the spot next to him. He waited as Mayar settled in, adjusting her headscarf, resting her hands in her lap.

"So?" he asked.

"Viktor set a date for the event: Wednesday May 16 at 5PM. He needs to hardcode it into the payload."

"Rush hour. Perfect. We will be ready with the ransom demand. Anything else?"

Mayar shifted nervously on the bench. She watched a squirrel scoot up the trunk of a thick oak. "Pizza Boy demanded a meeting," she said. "I believe that he is expecting to see a man."

Nimr stood and walked around the bench. Mayar had to swivel her head to follow him. He leaned over and hissed. "Then we will give him a man. I have someone who should fulfill his expectations."

"Freckles?"

Nimr laughed. "Yes. You've spotted him no doubt. His name is Graeme. Pizza Boy is expecting an Irishman, so we will give him one. Just make sure that Pizza Boy knows the meeting will be brief. For security reasons."

"I understand."

"You will contact Pizza Boy to set up the meeting and transfer the Wi-Fi interceptors to Graeme. I will brief him so that he can make the delivery to Pizza Boy. And, he will deliver this as well." Nimr withdrew a letter-sized envelope from his jacket pocket. "Give him half now as our down payment. It should ensure Pizza Boy's cooperation."

Mayar stood, ferreting into her pack for an envelope of her own. "Can you get this letter to Fatima?" she asked.

"Of course, Sajida," Nimr replied, pocketing the missive. He placed his hands on Mayar's shoulders. "Fatima will be very proud of you when she grows up. Your brother in Paradise is proud." He kissed her formally on both cheeks. "We are all proud of you. *Fi himayat Allah.*"

Mayar watched Nimr cross the street and walk towards Broadway. She shuffled uptown along the Riverside Drive promenade, the stone wall giving way to an iron picket fence. Sunlight flared over the river, but had difficulty penetrating the foliage in the park. She shivered as a light breeze blew in from the north. Nimr scared her. Even in silence, he preached death.

Death, like the execution in the video, designed to send a message to the world. The flames and screams had kept her awake all night. But, her vision was clear now. *Fear is good. It will keep me steeled to the task. My message will strike the crusaders in their own homeland. No one will ever forget Sajida!*

The letter to Fatima would explain everything. Just in case.

***

Con Ed emailed the information on their power station equipment to Taryn at noon. No surprise, it was the same A&B gear as in Kiev. *Could the Russians have sent their malware out for a local test drive?* She would do a little more digging and send an update to Serena Thomas.

The hackers they were fighting were first-rate and attacked around the clock. It would be impossible to stymie them with a nine-to-five effort. Most people thought that cybersecurity was a black art, but the vast majority of the work was drudgery, putting in the hours necessary to patch every hole in a system and track down every penetration. A little skill always helped but there was no substitute for the effort. Most industrial companies and government offices simply lacked the dollars to hire, manage, and motivate enough quality people for the job. That's why they became Lightning Strike clients.

Thinking about motivated hackers reminded Taryn about Mayar Tabak, Ahmed's half-sister. Still some loose ends there. *What's her thesis topic?*

***

Mayar checked email on the walk back to campus. A package was waiting for her at the FedEx store. She quickened her step, imagining FBI agents behind every lamppost. The clerk checked her ID, then fumbled behind the counter before locating a shirt-sized cardboard box with her name emblazoned on the front, but no return address. She hurried back to her dorm room and locked the door.

There was a knock before she could open the package.

"Yeah. Who is it?"

"Amy."

"I'm busy. Can't it wait?" The girls across the hall had not paid a social call all semester.

"Sure, I guess. I just wanted to ask you something. It's not that important."

"OK, I'm coming." Mayar stashed the package under her bed. "What's up?" She asked, standing at the open door, but not making any move to usher her neighbor inside.

Amy shifted her feet in place. "The other day, when you rushed to the bathroom…"

"Yes?"

"You left the door wide open."

"So?" Mayar held her breath.

"I saw the black flag folded on your chair."

The bottom dropped out of her stomach. "It was …an article of my faith."

"Are you still in mourning for your brother? Sarah and I don't know much about your religion, but we could take you out for a beer or a coffee or something, if you want to talk."

She swallowed hard, forcing a frown of grief. "That's very

kind. But, I'm all right now."

"Well, we just wanted to check."

Mayar closed the door and relocked it. *No more stupid mistakes.*

She unwrapped her package from Viktor with the two Jawbreakers. Each was a circuit board the size of a cassette tape with a protruding nubby antenna. She connected one to her computer with a USB cord and watched. The Jawbreaker searched for wireless data streams, like the Wi-Fi coming from the room across the hall, and began displaying its data. Within ten minutes, Mayar could eavesdrop on eight different networks running in her dorm. She disconnected the Jawbreaker and logged in to Viktor's encrypted server. She wanted to check on his progress with the virus payload.

The virus design was brilliant. It would infect every device that it encountered. If the A&B operating system was not present, the bug would simply do nothing and hibernate forever. But, if the device ran the A&B OS, the bug would immediately send a notification via an untraceable route to a sinkhole server that Viktor had established in Eastern Europe. Then it would bury deep in the rootkit of the A&B controller and sleep until May 16th at 5PM eastern daylight time. At that moment, it would awake and switch the voltage control from automatic to manual. It would also run a script camouflaging the move so that the Con Ed master controller would believe that all was normal. When the overflow of high voltage current crashed into the substation transformers, Con Ed would still be seeing green, all clear lights. As blackouts occurred, and complaints starting pouring in, Con Ed would try to re-route power, overloading more lines and causing the blackouts to cascade around the city, if not the entire country. By the time Con Ed would see what was really happening, the entire electrical grid would be in ruins.

Mayar reviewed the code one more time. Viktor's design was not typical ransomware. There was no kill switch. Once the virus was loose, it would be completely outside of their control. Even if New York paid the ransom, the entire grid might still be destroyed. *That will teach the infidels a lesson.*

Now, they just needed to inject the virus into the Con Ed network. The Jawbreakers would intercept communications between the substations and the master controller. Viktor and his team, with Mayar's help, would decrypt those communications and crack any passcodes. Viktor had built in sixteen days for these tasks, but it might not take that long. Her thesis professor had noted that many cities didn't even use passwords in the grid for fear that an operator would forget them in times of emergency.

Mayar private messaged Pizza Boy that, in recognition of his invaluable contributions, Sully would meet him at the central information booth in the main rotunda of Grand Central Station tomorrow at 6PM. A one-shot deal. The meeting would be brief. Sully would be wearing a Mets' scarf and would hand off the Jawbreaker to him.

Fifteen minutes later, Pizza Boy messaged back: what about my money?

That's better. He's back under my control. You will get paid tomorrow, Sully replied. She messaged the details of the meeting to Viktor via Telegram. He replied quickly that Graeme was ready for the hand-off from her.

Mayar wrapped one Jawbreaker in an old pink sweater and placed it in her backpack. She decided to keep the second one as a back-up. She had printed out a listing of the Con Ed substations with hand-written instructions on the back. All Pizza Boy had to do was patrol the street surrounding a substation for an hour. The Jawbreaker would do all the work, sending the captured data stream back to them via a private, encrypted VPN of its own. She counted the bills that Nimr had given her, placing half of them in another envelope and tucking it into the pack as well.

Mayar slipped the harness of her backpack over both shoulders and tied the Mets' scarf around her neck. She walked across campus and out the main gate onto Broadway. The night was warm for spring, inducing a swarm of students to abandon their study foxholes for a walk on the town. She waited for the traffic light before crossing the broad boulevard. A city bus rumbled by, heading uptown. As she stepped onto the far sidewalk, she sensed a presence in lockstep. Graeme smiled but said nothing.

Mayar entered the Starbucks and joined the queue. Graeme was three customers behind her. She ordered a chai tea and waited for the barista to prepare it. When it was ready, she found an empty spot at the counter, placing her backpack down in front of her, and sipped her tea. A minute later, Graeme shouldered in next to her.

"You're very brave," he whispered.

"You too. But why…"

"Why am I a follower of Allah?" His Boston accent emerging.

She nodded as Graeme brushed a lock of cinnamon hair from his eyes and swiveled to survey the coffee shop. His profile revealed a scar, the size and color of a strawberry, masked by the freckles on his right cheek, just below his eye.

"Not here." He reached for the pack. "I'm responsible for your safety." You should go now."

"OK. Another time," Mayar replied before slipping away.

CHAPTER 39

Grand Central Station was a zoo at rush hour. Dennis had taken the subway from Brooklyn, arriving thirty minutes early to case the spot where he would be meeting Sully. His hair was long, ponytailed under an orange Knicks cap, but he had added a mountain man beard, thick, barbed, extending down to his solar plexus, to conjure a new look.

He took up a position under the portal leading to Track 25, providing a full view of the cavernous concourse. Granite pillars supported a domed roof, decorated with an astronomical mural depicting the stars and constellations. Light flowed in through three arched, church sized windows on the east side. The main information kiosk, circular shaped with agents at several windows, sat in the center of the concourse. Travelers buzzed in for advice, then flitted away again, like bees swarming around a hive.

The business crowd was heading home, while the theater-goers were just arriving. Dennis tracked two bootylicious women tramping side-by-side across the marble floor towards the subway. Long legs, leggings and knee high boots, *I'd do either one of them.* Three guys in cheap suits with their neckties loose jostled past him, laughing and shoving, anxious to get back to the 'burbs, he bet. He watched them purchase Bud Tall Boys from the pushcart vendor positioned at the head of the track before disappearing into a waiting train. A blue Mets cap seemed to swim in a sea of pedestrians pouring down the steps from Vanderbilt Avenue, but no scarf. He kept eyes on the cap anyway, but its wearer, a teen, sliver of a mustache, overweight with baggy jeans sagging below his butt crack, never slowed.

He checked the four-faced, brass clock perched atop the information kiosk - 6:05. Sully was late. *Where the fuck is he?* Two soldiers, camo gear, body armor, and holstered pistols, patrolled the concourse. Dennis timed their route. Another five minutes passed. A cop materialized behind him, then disappeared into the bowels of the station. *How long should I wait?*

There it is! Blue and orange scarf. Young guy, tall, red backpack hanging off one shoulder, appeared to be checking departure times on the giant board across the way. The guy turned and approached the info desk. *Freckles, Sully, Sullivan, Irish - my man.* Dennis checked his palm. He had written the code word there in blue ink. Dennis approached, pretending to scan the timetables.

"Hey, you know when the next train to Poughkeepsie leaves?" he asked.

"6:32, Track 35." Graeme replied. "I'm going there myself."

They walked together towards the gate. Graeme slipped the pack off and handed it to Dennis, who gripped the strap in his right hand, assessing its weight.

"Everything you need," Graeme said.

"My money too?"

"Half now, half when the job's done."

Dennis scowled, but he'd expected as much. "What's the big picture?" he asked.

Graeme shook his head. "You've got all you need for now. Any problems, you reach out the usual way."

"That's not good enough."

"Fuck off then," Graeme replied, grabbing the handle on the pack. "I can get fifty jokers like you to do this job. It's easy money." His accent was clearly New England.

Dennis maintained his hold on the strap. "It's going to take me a week, maybe longer."

"I know. I'll be able to follow your trail." Graeme released the handle, allowing Dennis to hoist the pack onto his shoulder.

"When..." Dennis asked.

"I'll be in touch." Graeme stopped in front of a shoe shine stand. "Don't fuck up," he warned before disappearing into the crowd.

Dennis took the escalator down to the lower level, looking for the men's room. *Fuck you Sully. You couldn't find fifty jokers in all of Boston who could hack like me and Brian. You're just a working stiff like us. Not some fucking foreign terrorist. But I'll take your money.*

The bathroom stunk of shit, piss and sweat. An emaciated black man with a salt and pepper beard was bare-chested, giving himself a sponge bath at one of the sinks. *No cops though.* Dennis dropped the backpack on top of the baby-changing counter - *Who would bring a baby into this shitbox?* - and unzipped the main compartment. He reached inside, feeling the envelope stuffed with cash, quickly deciding to leave it there for now. He withdrew the pink sweater and unwrapped it, eyeing the Jawbreaker. He turned it over in his hands once, then shrugged, rewrapping it and returning it to the pack. He stuffed Sully's instruction sheet into his back pocket.

Dennis didn't get back to the apartment until just before midnight. He had canvassed two of the substations on the list, both in Brooklyn. Just walked around the block a few times with the backpack on his shoulder. Like the man said, it was easy money.

The door to Brian's bedroom was closed. *Is Brian alone or humping some babe?* He shuffled over, listening for grunts and groans. Nothing. He knocked, nothing. He knocked again.

"Fuck off." Brian called.

"Fuck you. I'm just trying to help you out. Be a friend, you know."

The door opened and Brian emerged shirtless, headphones hugging his neck, plaid boxers dangling on his scrawny hips.

"That's an ugly sight, man." Dennis exclaimed, shielding his eyes.

"I'm trying to get some sleep. Got to go to work tomorrow."

"Work? What the fuck are you working on? Except your tiny dick." Dennis laughed at his own joke.

"You can laugh all you want, but I'm getting a paycheck now. Working at SAP. Cloud operations maintenance. I've got to be in by 8."

"Maintenance is a dead-end and you know it."

"Fuck you. It's a real job. Working for an American company, not some fucking terrorist." Brian half-turned to go back to bed.

"I met Sully tonight. He's cool. I mean, he's an asshole, but he's not a fucking Arab. Just a dumb Mick from Boston," Dennis said, reaching out for Brian's elbow.

"I don't give a flying fuck if he's Tom Brady and he's got the whole New England Patriots team on his side."

"He's paying cash. Easy money. We can split it."

"What part of *no* can't you understand? Leave me out of it." Brian jerked his elbow away and slammed his bedroom door closed.

"Fuck you too. And, by the way, SAP's a German company, asshole," Dennis called after him.

CHAPTER 40

Taryn couldn't resist the temptation any longer. The orange Dunkin Donuts box, half opened on the conference table in her boss's cubicle, had tempted her all morning. She sighed in resignation as she slipped her hand under the lid and withdrew two glazed chocolate donut holes. Wheeling her chair back, she popped one into her mouth, savoring its sweetness. *Better than sex. But how would I know? It's been so long.* She sipped her coffee before devouring another. Montel paced behind her wearing out a groove in the taupe carpet, his tie already flopping loosely around his neck.

They were videoconferencing, connected to Tel Aviv via Lightning Strike's encrypted private network.

"The Ukrainians never saw it coming," Shahar's voice boomed from the screen.

"Here, look at this," Taryn said, reaching for her laptop. She searched, in vain, for a napkin, finally giving up and wiping her sticky fingers on the underside of her jeans. No clients today anyway. She punched up a page of code so that all participants could view it.

"Looks like our own baby, Stuxnet, doesn't it?" Taryn asked, moving the pointer slowly to highlight three blocks of commands. The group bantered back and forth about the code for the next hour.

When the conversation among her superiors wound down, Miriam's youthful voice piped in. "The payload is different because the malware is attacking smart switches, not nuclear centrifuges, but someone has definitely copied our delivery schema."

"Were you able to reverse engineer any of it?" Taryn queried.

"A little. The last virus signature is only two weeks old, but there are modules that were initially designed more than three years ago."

"Designed by whom?" Montel interjected, interrupting his circuit to step up to the microphone.

"We're not exactly sure," Miriam replied.

"It's the fucking Russians. Cyber Banda to be precise," Shahar broke in.

"Do you know that for sure?" Montel again.

"Absolutely, the hackers buried little Easter eggs in the code like 'Putin Rules,' 'Moscow Forever,' and my favorite, 'Good morning Unit 8200.' Cheeky bastards."

"When will the Ukrainians be able to get the switches back online?" Montel asked.

"The switches aren't the problem. It's the LPT, the Large Power Transformer. It's coils and windings are completely melted down," Taryn replied. She paused for a second. "LPT's are all custom made. Some of them are 20, 30, 40 years old, so there aren't a lot of spare parts around. And the parts that are available may not work."

"Can't the Ukrainians buy a new LPT?"

"Sure. But it might take a year to build. And it weighs half a million pounds, so it can't come in by FedEx," Taryn said pushing back from the table.

"The Ukrainians are fucked, plain and simple," Shahar concluded.

"Last question," Montel chimed in. "How did the Russians implant their virus in the Ukrainian grid?"

"The virus utilized two of the same zero day vulnerabilities that we utilized in Stuxnet," Miriam replied.

"I guessed that, but how did it access the network?" Montel persisted.

"My bet is they had an insider drop it in with a thumb drive," Shahar answered. "The Ukrainian government is littered with Kremlin sympathizers."

"They could have sent it in a spear-phishing email, or hacked into their wireless network and dropped it in over the air," Taryn added.

"We really don't know, and the truth is it doesn't really matter. Where there's a will, there's a way," Shahar replied, standing up. "I hate to end this party, but I've got another meeting." Taryn could see Miriam closing her laptop in the far corner of the screen.

"One sec. What should I tell the mayor's task force?" Taryn asked.

"When's the next meeting?" Shahar fired back.

"We haven't had a first meeting yet. The mayor's chief of staff is still trying to coordinate everyone's schedules."

"Good luck with that. Why don't you finish up your research and then we'll talk again?"

"Sounds like a plan. You all have a good night," Montel replied, reaching to shut off the video.

"Before you close the line, I've got someone here who needs to talk to Taryn," Shahar interrupted.

Montel pulled back. "No problem. I've got a client lunch in fifteen minutes. I'll leave you alone." He removed his suit jacket from its hook and left.

Taryn fiddled with the silver buckle on her belt, watching Shahar's large frame exit from view. She heard a familiar voice spar with her in Hebrew. A door closed in the background.

Eli sauntered into view in his camo jumpsuit, looking even more delectable than those glazed chocolate doughnuts. Her thighs twitched involuntarily.

"Hey," Taryn offered.

"I just got back from an airport run. Shahar thinks you're working too hard."

"Really? I didn't think the Israeli army believed in days off."

"Every soldier needs some R&R. She wanted me to check up on you."

"You're sure Shahar's not just playing matchmaker?" Taryn asked.

Eli laughed. "She's a *yenta,* but we're both really concerned."

"I'm fine. A little frayed at the edges, but that's about it."

"Your edges look pretty good to me," Eli said, sliding closer to the camera.

"You look absolutely delectable," Taryn whispered, leaning forward as if phone sex was an option. "Maybe I *am* overdue for a checkup. Can't be too careful these days. Could we schedule it for this weekend?" Her generous breasts shimmied under a pink button down.

"No," Eli replied, checking his watch.

"No?" Taryn tossed back.

"No, I don't think it's wise to wait that long. There's an El Al redeye at midnight tonight. It lands in New York at six."

"Tomorrow morning?"

"We want to get you back into fighting shape as soon as possible, don't we?"

"I'm feeling rejuvenated already."

"Can you recommend a place for me to stay?"

Taryn typed her address on Bank Street. She could see Eli checking his screen. "I can't find a hotel at that location."

"There isn't one, but I believe you'll find the accommodations satisfactory."

"And the service?"

"First class. You won't have any complaints."

***

Taryn returned to her cubicle but her concentration wobbled. She fed the code for the Kiev virus through a Windows debugger so that she could watch it waltz through its malicious payload one step at a time. She knew that the virus infected the logic controllers that managed the switches, but she needed to find out how it wormed its way inside. Since the complex virus had several thousand commands, this process could take weeks. She would need Miriam's expertise as well.

If the attack on the Kiev power station was a trial run, then New York City was in big trouble. The Kiev virus used two zero days that were already known which meant that A&B had never patched their system. She, or someone at Lightning Strike, would have to reach out to them. Tactfully, of course.

Once her team deciphered the virus code, they would also need to warn Con Edison. There was no commercially available anti-virus protection for industrial control devices. Lightning Strike would have to custom build a shield for its client. Lucrative work, she assumed.

When Taryn looked up from her desk, it was already ten o'clock. She needed to clean up her apartment before Eli arrived. And clean herself up as well. A long soak in the tub would be perfect.

CHAPTER 41

Should I make the bed?
Should I cook breakfast?
Should I wear something sexy?
Should I have a bottle of champagne on ice?
Should I jump his bones as soon as he walks in?

Waking at five, Taryn grappled with her morning agenda as she tossed in bed. When the first rays of dawn finally streaked over the rooftops at 6:15, she had decided that the answer to the first four questions definitely was no. Nothing saccharine. But the fuck-him-till-he-begged-for-mercy option worked just fine.

Taryn lolled under her comforter for another fifteen minutes, the anticipation building. At 6:30, she reached for her phone, confirming that El Al 27 had arrived on time, and then crawled back into her nest. Her operator, her fantasy man, her long-distance flirt, would soon be at the door. Her imagination wandered over the possibilities. At 6:55, her phone buzzed.

E: Be there in 10

Taryn poked her feet out to the floor and sat up. She peeled the orange Broncos tee over her head and kicked off her white sleep shorts before padding to the bathroom. She examined her bare body in the mirror, deciding to undo her ponytail and let her copper locks drape raggedly over her shoulders. A spray of jasmine perfume behind both ears, another spritz between her breasts. Satisfied, Taryn donned her thick terry robe and knotted it at the waist.

The intercom rang while she was brushing her teeth. Barefoot, she flicked on the coffee machine in the kitchen in route to the living room. The canopy of trees outside her window reflected the morning sun. The new computer on her desk, supplied and security-certified by Lightning Strike, bubbled to life as she passed, beckoning her with a list of waiting emails. *Not this morning.*

She buzzed Eli into the lobby, fiddling with a wisp of hair as she waited by her open door. His footfalls thudded double time up the steps. She bounced with nervous energy, a ski racer at the starting gate, until he appeared on the landing.

"Welcome to the Big Apple," she said, ushering him inside.

Eli leaned to kiss her, gallantly aiming for her cheek, his right arm resting on her hip. But Taryn tilted her head to meet his lips with her own and swept him into an embrace. Their first real kiss. Wet and greedy. Her hands roamed down his back from his albatross-wide shoulders to his slender, spring-loaded butt.

Eli broke off first, wheeling his suitcase into the living room, surveying his surroundings, second nature no doubt. "The Bank Street Inn," he said approvingly. His heated gaze returned, searing through her robe, firing her desire past the boiling point.

Taryn bit her lower lip, pumping up the tension one last notch before untying the sash at her waist. Her thighs quivered as she slipped the robe from her shoulders and let it slither to the floor. Naked now, she thrust her chest forward. "Let me show you the bedroom," she purred, striding past him to lead the way.

***

Propped up by her elbow, still unclothed, Taryn traced an aimless pattern on Eli's sweaty chest. He was lying on his back in her bed, the sheet covering his lower half, his eyes alert but searching the ceiling.

"You OK?" she asked.

"Yes."

"But?"

"It's been a long time."

"Deborah and Jacob, right?" Taryn dropped her hand to her own flank.

"You remembered."

"Where were you when you learned...?"

"I was on assignment. It took almost twenty-four hours for my commander to locate me."

"I can't imagine how you felt."

"I was ready to attack Hezbollah all by myself."

"But?"

"My commander pulled me out. Personally escorted me back to Kedumin. I haven't returned to active duty since."

"Do you think of them often?"

"Only every day. But I'm not here looking for sympathy. I have enough of that back home."

"It's OK. The people we've loved should always be with us. We don't *want* to forget them. Ever." Taryn let her hand return to its perch on Eli's chest.

"Have you lost someone close?" he asked.

"My mom passed away three years ago. Cancer."

"I'm sorry." Eli shifted to his side, facing her. "I hope she's not watching now," he laughed, running his fingers through her hair.

"My mom was cool - most of the time at least. That's why we were so tight."

They lingered, loosely coupled, until the urgency of the present finally overcame the ghosts of the past. Taryn's fingers dipped beneath the sheet, cupping Eli's buttocks, sliding her body towards him until they meshed. "Moving on..."

"Shahar is afraid that I've grown too hard," he whispered.

"Hard works for me."

***

"Should I pack you a lunch?" Taryn joked, as they sipped coffee in her kitchen. Showered and snug in thick grey sweats, she had decided to work from home today, leaving the Lightning Strike office to Eli on his first day in the city. He wore a Navy blazer over jeans.

"I think I can manage. Montel's taking me out."

"What are you trying to accomplish here this week anyway? In the office, I mean."

Eli fought in vain to suppress a smile. "Shahar wants a full security audit. The physical premises, our network, even the homes of our key employees."

"You got a head start there, I guess."

"Dinner tonight?"

"It will have to be late."

"I saw a grill out on your deck. I'll make us swordfish and an Israeli salad."

When Eli left, Taryn sat down at the computer, splitting her screen between the A&B manual and the virus code. Like most SCADA systems, the utility architecture consisted of remote units in the field, the smart switches, gathering and acting upon data, while reporting in over a network to a centrally located operations station. The switches ran A&B's proprietary software, while the control room ran the utility's homegrown apps on a Windows platform. The complexities of the architecture were mind-boggling. It was amazing that it actually worked so well every day.

She decided to focus first on the safety mechanisms in the Kiev system. The virus didn't create a power outage. It destroyed the voltage transformer. *What happened to the security systems that were supposed to protect the grid?*

Taryn yawned as the hours dragged on. Nine o'clock - Eli wasn't back yet. One more block of code. She would be at this for years, not months, if she didn't pick up the pace.

She would decode a virus command, trace it over to the control system, and then lose her thread in the bits and bytes of the smart switches. Or vice versa. She quickly realized that the hacking team that she was up against was first rate. They had to have worked for years to construct their virus. Shahar appeared certain that it was CyberBanda. *Who financed their efforts? Why did they attack Kiev? Where will they strike next?*

CHAPTER 42

Intimate evenings, conversation and coupling, followed grinding days of mind-numbing debugging. Eli insisted that they rest on the Sabbath, at least from work. Taryn shepherded her beau around lower Manhattan - the Statue of Liberty, Wall Street, the West Village, and the High Line. They returned to their Lightning Strike responsibilities on Sunday with Eli spending the afternoon in Bushwick evaluating the security in Montel's brownstone. Taryn continued to work from Bank Street.

Sunday night, unusually warm for May, started well enough: dining al fresco at Malaparte, a neighborhood bistro, devouring pizza, pasta, and wine; cuddling in front of the TV; languid lovemaking on the sofa; trundling off exhausted to bed. Taryn embraced the domestic bliss of the relationship, a state that she had vigorously eluded up to this point in her life.

Eli's ringtone woke them at 2AM. She reached over him, blindly searching for the offending device, her tee shirt scrunching up over her hips. With a fencer's jab, Eli snatched his phone from the nightstand, checking the caller and jumping out of bed in one motion.

"Stern."

Taryn rolled to her side, watching Eli snap to attention, naked, turning away from her as he listened to the voice in the ether.

"Yes, sir. I have my orders."

He stepped into his boxers, marched into the kitchen and fired up his laptop. Taryn rose to follow, grabbing Eli's robe from her bedroom chair.

"Here, you might be a little more comfortable," she said, tossing it to him.

"Thanks, I need to check in with my unit." He bunched the robe in his lap, but remained bare-chested.

"You're leaving." A statement, not a question.

He nodded, already absorbed.

"I'll make some coffee," she offered.

"Go to bed."

"What's up?"

"I've been recalled to active duty. I need to be at the embassy in three hours for a briefing."

"Then?"

"Then I'm on the one o'clock flight back to Tel Aviv."

"Duvdevan? Undercover again?" No answer from Eli. "You never secured my apartment, you know?"

"What?" he asked, distracted, eyes still on his screen.

"The full check - windows, doors, computers, networks. Wasn't I on your list?"

"You were on my schedule for tomorrow, actually. I guess I'll have to come back to New York," he replied, looking at her now, smiling.

"Good." She stepped behind Eli to caress his shoulder, but pivoted away when he tilted the cover of his laptop down, obviously shielding the screen from her view.

"Come back soon," she implored, turning as she reached the bedroom.

Eli just shrugged in reply, his mission gobbling his attention again.

Taryn closed the door and crawled under her comforter. *Israel is Eli's first love. Always was. Always will be.*

She didn't need to guess Eli's ultimate destination. An uprising in the West Bank, outside the Beitunia checkpoint near Ramallah, dominated the home page of the *Times* and CNN's Monday morning news. During the skirmish, a Hamas cell had kidnapped a female Israeli soldier. The terrorists demanded the release of twenty of their imprisoned fighters and five million dollars for her safe return. Israel didn't do ransoms. Its military would do whatever was necessary to get her back. Eli might be gone for a long time.

Taryn shuffled through her apartment. A half-finished bottle of wine and remnants from a wedge of Brie lay by the television. She tidied up the living room, showered and dressed, fighting the black curtain that seemed to be falling on her psyche.

Work was always her refuge, the antidote for any personal

issues. She tapped her phone to contact Lightning Strike's primary contact in Kiev. It was almost closing time there on Monday night. The conversation lasted almost an hour, a mixture of English, broken Russian, and tech talk. Taryn typed notes on her computer, checking the Ukrainian's comments with her team's findings. She sent a summary email off to Montel and Shahar, and left for the office.

Taryn was working head down in her cubicle when Montel knocked.

"You missed Eli," he said.

"Excuse me?" she replied, unsure where her boss was headed.

"He left this morning. Back to Israel. He got a call in the middle of the night."

"Oh. I guess I'll touch base with him in the next few days." She tried to maintain a poker face.

"Looks like you've made some progress." Montel held up a print-out.

"Yes, my call this morning was super helpful," Taryn replied, breathing an inaudible sigh of relief as the conversation shifted to more stable ground.

"This CyberBanda gang is top-notch, aren't they?"

"What really impresses me is the way they camouflaged the attack. They must have broken into the system several months ago and captured the logs from normal operations. It looks to me like they had screenshots taken every thousandth of a second, and then played the script back to the operators in Kiev while the system crashed."

"So the operators were like the proverbial Nero, fiddling while Rome burned?" Montel asked.

"Something like that," Taryn chuckled.

"Well, I'm glad that you stuck to your guns here. Now, when will you have enough to sit down with the Con Ed people here in New York?"

"I need a few more days. The mayor's office finally set up the first blackout task force meeting – Friday, May 19th. I was planning to present my research there. Do you want to come?"

"We should set up a preview with Con Ed before that. They're our client – we can't pull any surprises on them. Let's shoot for next Monday the 14th, at the Con Ed executive office. I want to make sure all of their top brass are there."

CHAPTER 43

After pulling an all-nighter at the office, Taryn returned to Bank Street at dawn to crash. Her head throbbed as if she had been tossed by a bucking bronco. Waking at eight, the thought of returning to Lightning Strike was about as welcome as pre-dawn ranch chores. The imagery reminded her to call home. Dad was always awake before first light. She formulated the family friendly details of Eli's visit that she would provide him, as well as the more salacious account that Constance would demand.

Before she could tap Dad's speed-dial, Taryn's phone buzzed with a text. Lou was heading to the hospital to sit with Jim. He had some information for her if she could meet him there. A perfect reason to delay her commute back to Lightning Strike.

A quick email check over her morning coffee revealed an encrypted communication from Shahar. Pursuing her concern for Professor Bierman, Shahar had requested Unit 8200 to troll its vast historical database of intercepted communications for any possible patterns in the Brogan boys' behavior that might coincide with similar pronouncements.

With the pleasant spring weather continuing, Taryn decided to bike across town. She pulled a garish blue Citi Bike from the kiosk down the street and headed over towards the Hudson. The bike path would be protected from traffic down to the tip of lower Manhattan and then back up the East Side. A circuitous route, but much safer than trying to pedal crosstown on city streets overflowing with hurried drivers.

Taryn hadn't visited Jim in over a week. His condition was

improving and Marcy was rightfully protective of her fiancé. She could sense the questions cross Marcy's mind whenever they shared space in the confining hospital room. Was Taryn a former lover, a friend, a business associate? All of the above? The demands of Lightning Strike, and Eli, had provided an easy excuse to stay away. Since Marcy had a modeling job this week, the timing of Lou's call was perfect.

Jim was sitting up, propped on pillows, when she arrived. He wore an NYPD t-shirt over his hospital gown, his right arm in a sling to promote the healing of his broken collarbone, his skull and ear heavily bandaged. Lou paced by the bedside in what Taryn had come to realize was almost a standard FBI issue gray suit. A Mets pennant adorned the wall and a photo of Marcy sat on the nightstand.

Jim smiled at Taryn in recognition; he was still re-learning to speak and could only hear with his left ear. She exchanged pleasantries with Lou for five minutes, pleased to see that Jim was following along. A nurse stopped in to check Jim's vital signs. An orderly took his lunch order.

Jim shifted, trying to stand, wincing in pain.

"I can step out," Taryn offered, but Jim shook his head. He pointed to the walker in the corner of the room and clasped his partner's elbow. "He wants to show off," Lou joked.

The trio shuffled to the nurses' station, resulting in a loud round of cheers from the team on duty, and then round-tripped to Jim's room. Lou helped him back into bed. She could see the sweat on Jim's forehead from the exertion. He leaned back on the pillows and appeared to nod off.

"You said you had some information for me?" Taryn asked.

"Yeah. Good news. Bad news." Lou replied, sitting down and opening his briefcase.

"Let's start with the bad then." Taryn leaned on the windowsill.

"Columbia won't release any information on Mayar Tabak without a warrant. Said it would be a violation of her privacy."

"Not even her thesis topic?"

"Nope. Typical Ivy League liberal approach."

"And the good news?" Taryn ignored the indirect jibe at her own alma mater.

"I got a report yesterday on a sighting of Dennis Walecka. An address in the Bronx, I think. Not his usual haunt, so I'm a little skeptical."

"What's the address?"

"You think he's up to a new scam?" Lou asked, shuffling through some files. Taryn shrugged. "Here it is. Dyckman Street," he said.

"That's in northern Manhattan, actually. Up by the Cloisters. Do you have a cross street?" Taryn asked.

"Tenth Avenue."

The Sherman Creek power station. "Are you sure?"

"Yeah, well, no. Not completely sure it's Walecka. But we are sure about the address. Does it mean anything to you?"

"Maybe."

Jim snapped awake, his eyes searching for Lou. He reached for the pad and marker by his desk and scribbled with his left hand.

"Eight? The letter B? A snowman?" Lou struggled to decipher the writing. Jim shook his head.

"Three?" Lou tried again. This time, Jim flashed both thumbs up.

"Making progress," Lou noted with satisfaction. "Three Musketeers? Three strikes? The Father, Son and Holy Ghost?" he continued as if playing charades. Jim shook his head so violently that he grimaced.

"The three living Brogans?" Taryn guessed. Jim wagged to confirm.

"The three fucking Brogans," Lou repeated.

"What's happening there? Any sightings of the thug who clocked Jim?" She looked at Lou for answers.

"No. Tim Brogan has crawled back into his hole. But every cop on the street has his mugshot now," Lou replied.

"And you're scanning the CCTV feeds every day?" Taryn asked.

"And every night."

"Then he's left the city."

"It's a big world out there unfortunately."

"What about his two brothers?"

"Nothing new. We know Michael landed in Newark, but no sightings of him since. Interpol put out a global search on Donal but no positives have come back. He could be anywhere in the world, but I'd bet my last dollar he's here with his brothers."

"Are you sure they're all still in the country?" Taryn pressed, pacing to the window and back.

"Unless they left in a box, they're here. We've got every point of exit covered," Lou replied.

"Then Professor Bierman's safe. He doesn't come home until tomorrow," she declared.

"What makes you sure he's the target?"

"Shahar, my boss in Tel Aviv, she's close to Professor Bierman too, launched a little investigation." Taryn was hesitant to reveal much about Shahar's, and Lightning Strike's, connections to the Israeli military.

"And?"

"She cross-referenced the language in the poster with communications involving other assassinations around the world over the past ten years. It seems the reference to 'virgins' has come up before."

"Not a surprise really. Those crazy jihadists all dream of going to Paradise and screwing their brains out," Lou said.

"But crazy jihadists didn't necessarily shoot a finance minister in Baku; or detonate a car bomb in Manila; or stab the mistress of an oil company executive in Aberdeen."

"Why not? That's what the papers said about that finance minister, if I remember correctly."

"True. But the Unit, I mean Shahar, also has access to data that placed one or more Brogans in the vicinity each time. And the number of virgins offered in reward was different on every hit."

"Like it was a price tag?"

Taryn nodded. "The one thousand virgins offered for Professor Bierman is top dollar. He'll be pleased to hear that." She walked over to the window, the pieces of the puzzle falling into place. "It's the perfect cover, right? Blame it all on crazy jihadists who conveniently blow themselves up and no one digs much deeper."

Jim stirred, anxious to rejoin the conversation. He rubbed his right thumb and forefinger together, coaxing his lips to mouth the words, "Who's paying?"

"Bakr al-Baghdadi, right?" Lou asked.

"You think he'd pay that much for a revenge killing?" Taryn answered with her own question. "ISIS doesn't have that kind of loose change lying around."

"Who else could it be then?"

"When I was in the hospital in Jerusalem, Bierman hinted that ISIS may have some new friends in Moscow."

"The Russians hire the Brogans for a hit on American soil?" Lou asked incredulously.

"They've rubbed out their emigres in London. Why not here?" Taryn replied.

"But how would Moscow even know about his investigation?"

"Maybe the professor's recent report to Washington circulated to the wrong hands. I used to beg him not to write reports until he had hard facts but he likes to ruffle feathers sometimes."

"When does he land?"

"Tomorrow at noon in Ithaca. Maybe it would be a good idea if we met him at the airport," Taryn said.

"Look, I'll call the FBI office in Ithaca right now and give them a head's up," Lou said, reaching into his suit jacket pocket for his phone. Taryn pulled a chair next to Jim's bed, and sat down, while Lou talked.

"Agent Richardson? This is Agent Totti from New York. I'm Jimmy Mangano's partner." He paused to listen, then added, "Jim's making progress, thanks. He appreciates your concern. And we know that your office has other investigations to pursue, but we have reason to believe that Tim Brogan, the IRA gunman, and maybe his brothers too, might be planning a visit to Professor Lev Bierman. He lands in Ithaca tomorrow."

Lou held the phone away from his ear, arching his eyebrows in disbelief. "The professor gets death threats regularly? And he can be a prickly son of a bitch to deal with? He publishes his schedule on the internet? OK, I get the picture. Well, do what you can. Thanks."

"That sounds like Professor Bierman," Taryn said, standing. "Tomorrow morning it is."

"I'll pick you up at seven," Lou volunteered.

CHAPTER 44

Tim Brogan placed his duffel carefully in the trunk of the gray Malibu, already loaded with an arsenal of automatic weapons and explosives. "I'll miss this place a bit. Reminds me of home," he said, surveying the rolling hills surrounding the small town of Vestal, just outside of Binghamton, New York. Puffy, white clouds dotted the powder blue sky. The odor of manure wafted across the fields.

"That it does, laddie. That it does," Michael replied, swiveling his head to take a last look at the dilapidated farm house, shingles weathered and worn, roof sagging like an old man's testicles. "The Airbnb advertisement highlighted 'rustic charm' and 'rural solitude.' At least it was right on one account. We haven't seen a soul out here in two weeks."

"The house served its purpose. But I didn't think that we would have to stay here this long. The fucking Professor flipped his schedule and took off out of town somewhere. Are you sure he's back today?"

"Yes. I called the Ithaca FBO and posed as one of Bierman's grad assistants. The flight ops guy confirmed that his plane is on schedule to arrive at noon."

"And we'll be there to welcome him home," Tim said as he velcroed the straps on his tactical vest. He checked the pistol grip on the AR-15 and tightened the sound suppressor at the end of the barrel. Satisfied, he laid the rifle back in the trunk and closed it gently. Stepping around towards the front of the car, he zipped up his black windbreaker and climbed into the passenger seat.

"Gerard would be proud of us," Michael added, sitting behind the wheel. He reached under the seat for his Sig Mauser. Holding the pistol vertical, he checked the magazine and switched the safety to the off position before returning it to its hiding place. "We should be at the airport in an hour," he said as he shifted the car into gear.

***

"This baby handles like a tank," Taryn laughed as she steered the whale-sized, black Suburban along Route 17 in the Catskill Mountains. They had stopped briefly at the Roscoe Diner for coffee and a pit stop with Taryn taking the wheel afterwards.

"It's got pretty good pick-up though," she added, accelerating through the town of Deposit. "What do you do with all the room in the back?"

"Kids take up a lot of space," Lou replied. "And energy."

"I wouldn't know." But Lou's comment stirred her thoughts about Eli. She couldn't even imagine having a child, let alone losing your first and only one. And your spouse. In a terrorist attack that might have come as a reprisal for your own actions. Little wonder that Eli had built a fortress around his emotions. And was so willing to jump back into the fight.

Eli's visit to New York had started out as a fling - at least in her mind. Their ages and backgrounds were oceans apart. But they had bonded more tightly than she ever imagined they would. He was a man of quiet action, a patriot. All fire, no smoke. She could relate to that.

But where is Eli now? When will he emerge from the West Bank? Would he ever be able to truly love someone again? Would his country even let him try? Taryn realized that she cared about the answers.

"We should get to Ithaca well before Bierman's flight touches down," she announced, her memory drifting to her hospital room in Jerusalem, the professor with flowers in hand, wistfully longing to rendezvous 'high above Cayuga's waters', the opening line in Cornell University's *Alma Mater*. "We can meet him at the airport."

***

The Brogan's turned off Route 13 onto Warren Road, approaching the Ithaca airport, at eleven o'clock. The atmosphere in the Malibu crackled like a locker room before the big game.

The airport landscape was flat and green, dotted with the low-rise buildings of a modern office complex and a four-story Marriott hotel. Traffic was light, not necessarily a surprise given the limited commercial flight schedule here. No planes were scheduled to land or depart until two. The sky was crystal clear, rare for Ithaca, even in May.

Michael cruised down the Research Park road passing the main passenger terminal and the East Hill Flying Club before reaching Taughannock Aviation, the hub for private air travel. A ten-foot-high chain link fence surrounded the airfield. A police car passed by in their rear-view mirror.

Pausing for just a second, Michael looped past the hangar which housed an array of small planes, ranging from single engine props to luxury jets. He headed back towards the commercial terminal, pulling into the parking area between a white BMW and a battered pick-up.

"The truck?" He asked. His brother nodded, quickly exiting the car and popping open the trunk. Tim swiveled his head to check for passers-by, none in sight, and reached for his pack. Gingerly, he removed a brick of semtex and shoved the disposable phone that would serve as the detonator into the back pocket of his jeans. Kneeling next to the rear wheel of the pick-up, he fastened the explosive to the underside of the chassis.

"Diversion is set," Tim declared as he climbed back into the Malibu.

Michael backed out of the parking space and returned to the main road. "This place is really deserted," he commented.

"Makes our job easier," Tim replied.

Michael drove the short distance to the Marriott, their designated waiting area, the lot about a quarter full. No one would think twice about cars parked there. He dialed Taughannock Aviation again, confirming that Professor Bierman's flight was on time. It was eleven-thirty.

***

As they reached the outskirts of the Cornell campus, the crescent bleachers of Schoellkopf Stadium coming into view, Taryn called the Professor's office. No answer.

"Do you want to call the airport and check on the Professor's flight?" she asked Lou.

Using his FBI credentials, Lou quickly connected. "The second caller in the past ten minutes?" he noted. "And the Professor has his own car parked at the terminal?"

Taryn stepped on the gas.

***

Tim opened the trunk, eyeing the cache of weapons. After wrapping the AR-15 in a tattered blanket, he moved the rifle to the back seat. Michael checked his pistol a final time before shoving it into his jacket pocket.

"Are you sure the plane will still have enough fuel?" Tim asked.

"It's coming up from Washington. Even if the tank is only half full, a G-5 will still get us to Caracas."

"Where there is no extradition to the US."

"It's the best we can do. Donal will have to find a way to meet us there." Tim reached back for the rifle, standing it upright between his legs in the well of the passenger seat.

"That's the plan. And Bierman will be our insurance policy," Michael said as he started the car.

"These too," Tim replied, holding up a pair of grenades.

***

The Suburban turned onto Research Park drive just as the semtex ripped apart the red pick-up. Smoke billowed from the parking lot. People streamed out of the surrounding office buildings, their mouths gaping open in disbelief and terror. Sirens wailed to the scene.

"What the fuck?" Taryn shouted.

"It's an explosion. Over there!" Lou pointed towards the main terminal on their left. "Turn here," he ordered, reaching for his pistol.

"No! Bierman's plane is landing now. Straight ahead." Taryn pointed to the sleek, white Gulfstream jet nosing down from the horizon. She accelerated past the wreckage, a wedge of charred metal lying by the curb. Two police cars, lights flashing, sped towards the blast, ignoring them.

Taryn saw the gate to Taughannock Aviation slide closed as they approached. A gray Malibu had just passed through and was now speeding across the tarmac towards the runway. She slammed down on the gas pedal, the speedometer climbing past sixty as the Suburban crashed through the steel fence.

The Gulfstream taxied to a stop, its nose facing Taryn. The door opened and a jetway dropped to the ground. Taryn could discern the silvery locks of Professor Bierman, briefcase in one hand, telephone in the other.

Brakes screeching, the Malibu slewed to a stop in front of the parked plane. Two men, ski masks covering their faces, jumped out with weapons drawn, racing to the foot of the stairs. Bierman looked up, startled.

Taryn stomped hard on the gas again, sending the Suburban barreling towards the Gulfstream. She lined up her approach - bowling for terrorists.

Intent on storming the jet, the attackers were late to recognize the threat coming from their rear. A fraction of a second before impact, one of the men spun, ripping off a volley at the Suburban. The other never flinched, spraying the Gulfstream's entrance with bullets.

Taryn saw streams of blood spurting from Bierman's torso before the Suburban's windshield shattered, glitter-bombing her with slivers of glass. She ducked towards Lou, her left-hand clinging to the steering wheel to maintain the Suburban's course. Bones snapped underneath the SUV as it pulverized the Brogan brothers, dragging them along the tarmac, the impact jarring her foot from the gas pedal. The Suburban slowed but not in time to avoid smashing into the wing of the jet. When the Suburban finally stopped, half the plane's wing lay across its hood.

Pinned in place by airbags and seatbelt, Taryn picked glass crystals from her hair and cheek, tasting her own blood as it dripped into her mouth. A brief round of gunfire flared, followed by the klaxon of a fire engine before helping hands pulled her from the wreckage.

Taryn stumbled but stayed on her feet, a paramedic guided her towards a waiting ambulance. Another responder supported Lou, his right arm dangling uselessly at his side.

The mangled bodies of the Brogan's, or what was left of them, were laid out on the tarmac. Faces ripped off, bones jutting out askew, bullet holes across their chest.

"This one tried to pull the pin on a grenade," the paramedic explained. "The cops opened fire."

"Professor Bierman?" Taryn implored.

"Hurt badly," he replied, pointing towards a team administering to a body on the ground a few feet away. The paramedic tried to examine Taryn's bleeding face, but Taryn pushed his hands away. She rushed to Bierman and kneeled by his side.

"Stay back," a second paramedic ordered, her hands soaked scarlet. "He's going to bleed out right here unless we can get him to the hospital," she added without any enthusiasm. Taryn saw two more EMS staff wheeling a stretcher towards them.

Bierman's blue eyes fluttered as he recognized Taryn. He tried to raise his head to speak. Taryn squeezed his limp fingers, leaning over so that her ear was next to his parched lips. His craggy complexion, always sallow from too much time indoors, had drained into a mouse gray shroud.

"New York. New York," Bierman wheezed, barely audible, spitting up blood. "You've got to stop it."

"I will Professor. I promise," Taryn whispered her reply. The professor sank back, his eyes staring blankly into the cloudless sky.

***

After ten stitches just below her left ear and a doctor's promise that the scar would fade, Taryn walked out of her hospital room. Agent Richardson, a rep from Homeland Security, and a detective from the Ithaca police force waited in the hall. With his right arm in a sling and his left ankle in a cast, Lou wasn't quite as mobile, but he was able to phone New York and persuade his boss to cut through the red tape and get them back to the city as soon as possible. Accordingly, their debriefing took less than an hour.

An agent from the larger Syracuse office arrived shortly thereafter to drive them home. Lou rode shotgun, crutches by his side, while Taryn sat alone in the rear.

Shahar called on Taryn's cell before they reached Roscoe. "Professor Bierman was a great man, a genius. Your country and mine will miss him."

"He and Hayden have been like family to me since my freshman year at Cornell," Taryn replied. "I wish I could have done more today."

"What could you have done? You took out two pros who were

intent to kill him. Two pros who have evaded your FBI and CIA, I might add. The world is a safer place today because of your action."

"Thank you. But I'll never shake the helpless feeling that I had holding his hand while…"

"You were with him at the end?" Shahar asked.

"Yes. He tried to tell me something about New York."

"Professor Bierman was here in Israel the past three days. He was helping us trace the money flow that finances the activities of our mutual enemies. The trail led to a broker who was part of a hawala network with its roots in the West Bank."

"Was the broker involved in the kidnapping that was all over the news this week?"

"Yes, he delivered the cash. We caught him red-handed, so he offered us new information as a trade. He said that ISIS has been moving dollars out of Raqqa and into New York over the past few months. A very unusual pattern, to say the least."

"Did he give you Mayar Tabak's name as a recipient?" Taryn asked.

"No, he would never even know who got the money. But he did reveal the location in upper Manhattan where ISIS operatives pick up cash. The FBI already has the storefront under 24/7 surveillance."

"What did you offer him in return?"

"His life."

"Sounds like Eli was involved. Are you in contact with him?"

"Not while he's… on assignment."

Taryn hesitated. "I'd like to get a message to him," she said, dropping her voice.

"No promises, but I'll see what I can do. Meanwhile, you be careful. Donal Brogan's still out there."

"Professor Bierman's dead," Taryn paused as the horrible words sunk in. "The Brogans fulfilled their contract. Donal can just collect his cash and disappear back under his rock."

"You don't know the Brogans. The million is meaningless. Donal has three reasons for revenge."

CHAPTER 45

Taryn arrived at her apartment just after midnight. The last two hours of the ride had given her time to rewind the Kiev virus in her mind over and over. As they crossed the George Washington Bridge, the disjointed strands of spaghetti code started to fall into place. She crashed until six and then attacked her computer again.

By noon, Taryn had enough confidence in her analysis to barge into Montel's office. She tossed a print-out and a thumb drive on her boss' desk. "I'm not finished yet, but I think that's the critical subset of virus commands that Con Ed has to look for."

"Are you sure?" Montel asked. "I spoke to Shahar. You're exhausted - physically and emotionally. She thinks that you need some rest."

"I'm sure. We may not have much time. The Con Ed people need to find this virus."

"You want them to scan all the software in their operations center?"

"And they'll have to run diagnostics on all their controllers and switches out in the field," she replied. "Today's Friday. If they get started this afternoon, they should be finished by our meeting on Monday."

"Work all weekend? Around the clock?" Montel mused. "Con Edison doesn't pay that well. Their people are going to be really pissed off if this is a wild goose chase."

"Yeah, well, ask them if they'd rather see their transformers go up in smoke."

***

Mayar was chained to her computer all day too, reviewing the same blocks of code as Taryn. Pizza Boy had done his job proficiently. The Jawbreaker had intercepted communications between the substations all over the city and Con Ed's central ops. Viktor and his team had decrypted the messages and prepared their payload accordingly.

Their operation was now situated as the classic 'man in the middle' approach. They could see the information flow from both sides, and add their own commands to the mix as desired. Even more important, they could camouflage their penetrations so that Con Ed would not know that it was under attack - until it was too late. Every hacker's dream.

She logged into Telegram to confirm the final details with Viktor.

M: When do we insert our program?
V: Monday May 14 at 5PM.
M: Will there be enough time for it to circulate?
V: Yes. But we want to give the infidels as little time as possible to counter it
M: The ransom?
V: Nimr is preparing the communication
M: Praise Allah

After signing off, Mayar removed the second Jawbreaker unit from its hiding place. She needed to scout locations to inject their program into the Con Ed grid. Remote sites might be best to minimize communications traffic from other sources. She checked the subway map on her phone. With only one transfer, she could visit the substations in the far reaches of Brooklyn. Mayar wrapped a patterned scarf around her head, hoisted her backpack onto her shoulder, and headed out.

***

With the search for the Kiev virus code now out of her hands, Taryn turned her attention to another part of the puzzle. *Who are CyberBanda's contacts in New York?* The gang could do the heavy hacking in Novgorod but they couldn't do everything remotely. Boots on the ground here would be necessary to scout the substations and inject the virus. Someone with motive, expertise and access. It could be anybody, but two candidates were at the head of the class.

Dennis Walecka? What was he doing up by the Sherman Creek substation? Shahar had said that ISIS would occasionally hire locals in regions where they lacked manpower, so Walecka could be in it for the money. He clearly had the hacking expertise, but did he have any contacts at Con Ed?

Mayar Tabak? She was even more of a mystery, but the fact that her brother had been an ISIS commander dangled the possibility of an ideological motive. How thick did the blood run between siblings, or half-siblings? Mayar claimed that she had been out of touch with Ahmed for years, but a deep dive into her communications history might still prove illuminating. As an engineer, she had to have a solid grounding in computer science, but that could be a long way from the skillset necessary for sophisticated hacking. The topic of her thesis could be revealing. Was she building bridges or municipal grids?

Taryn tied her hair into a ponytail and dug around in her closet for a pair of ratty jeans and an old Cornell sweatshirt. She loaded her laptop into her backpack to add authenticity to her appearance. The FBI couldn't talk to Ms. Tabak again without just cause, but there was no law prohibiting her from visiting Columbia University. She had Mayar's address from Jim's report. It was just a subway ride away.

Thirty minutes later, Taryn followed a knot of students, tipsy from happy hour, into the dorm. She knocked on Mayar's door, but no answer. Shit. The door across the hall was half-open, female laughter burbling inside. Worth a try.

"Hey," she offered, knocking and peeking inside. Two girls, both borderline plump, lounged on a red comforter, a half empty bottle of white wine and a bowl of popcorn on the table in front of them. John Legend played from a speaker by the window.

"Yeah?" the one squeezed into skinny jeans and a silvery tube top asked.

"I'm looking for Mayar Tabak."

"That's her room," Tube Top replied, pointing out the door.

"I know, but she's not home. Any idea where I could find her?"

"Nope."

"I'm Taryn Booker. I met her brother, Ahmed, in Israel a few months ago. He thought I might be able to help Mayar out this summer on a project."

"Israel? Mayar's not Jewish," the other girl answered, as she smoothed her micro-length black skirt over her thick thighs. *Could that skirt be any shorter?* Taryn struggled not to laugh.

"Her brother's dead," Tube Top added.

"I know." Taryn frowned. "But I thought Mayar might still need some help."

"Are you a computer geek too?"

Taryn swung her pack down to her hip, highlighting the outline of her computer. "A little bit, I guess. It helps pay the bills."

"Mayar's at it all the time. Amy thinks she's a hacker like Raven Ramirez in CSI: Cyber," Micro-Mini contributed, sipping her wine.

"Where did you meet her brother?" Amy asked.

"I spent last semester at Technion in Haifa and did some traveling in the West Bank on my break."

"I was in Haifa on my Birthright trip last summer. It was a blast," Micro-Mini offered, peeling a paper cup from the stack on the table and pushing it towards Taryn. "I'm Sarah, by the way. Do you want some wine?"

"Sure, thanks," Taryn replied, stepping into the room and dropping her pack to the floor. She filled the cup halfway.

"You go to Cornell?" Sarah asked. When Taryn nodded, she added, "Know anyone at AE Phi? A couple of my friends from home are sisters there."

"Sorry, I'm not a sorority girl." Taryn sipped her wine, pausing for a second before pushing ahead. "Do you know what Mayar's working on? Ahmed never gave me any details."

"Something to do with energy conservation. Electricity maybe."

"Cool. Like the grid?" Taryn asked.

"You should talk to our friend Allison Gold. She's an intern in the Mayor's office," Amy chipped in. Sarah shot her a what-the-fuck look, but Amy just shrugged and rolled on. "She's been working with Mayar on something lately."

"Do you know what happened to Ahmed?" Sarah asked, obviously trying to change the subject. "Mayar seemed pretty broken up when she got the news, but she never gave us any details."

"No, not really," Taryn replied, finishing her wine.

"What about his daughter? What's going to happen to her now?" Amy stirred the flames again.

"I didn't know Ahmed had a family," Taryn said. Amy rolled her eyes in mock indignation. *I was his killer, not his lover, bitch.*

"Mayar kept a picture of him holding a cute little girl on her desk," Sarah said. "Fatima was her name, I think."

"I should get going. I'm crashing at my aunt's in Brooklyn. Can I leave you a note for Mayar?"

"Sure," Amy replied, steadying herself, before walking over to her desk for a pen and paper.

Please reach out if you ever need help. Taryn printed neatly, adding her name and number and folded the page in half.

CHAPTER 46

Mayar returned from Brooklyn around eleven satisfied that she had scouted out at least one location suitable to imbed the virus. Her hall was quiet. No surprise on a Friday night. She retrieved the photo of Fatima from the drawer where she had hidden it before the FBI interview. *Soon, my little one. We will be together soon.* Mayar fell asleep with her daughter's angelic face floating in her dreams.

She awoke early on Saturday. *Only five days until New York goes dark!* There was little left for her to do now. Viktor would put the finishing touches on the malware package; her schoolwork held little interest. *Fi himayat Allah,* she would be in Raqqa before the end of the term.

How will I get there? Nimr would find a way to smuggle her to a city with a working airport; then a flight to Tel Aviv or Amman; a short drive to Ramallah to pick up Fatima; and finally, the last leg to her new home. She might need Viktor's help too.

Why not leave now? She was a soldier and would not desert her post. She was the only one in New York with knowledge of both the electrical grid and the attack code. Her comrades needed her in case there were any last-minute glitches. Most important, she wanted to share the celebration of her triumph with them.

The morning sun streamed across the quad, tempting Mayar to take a last tour around New York. Times Square, Wall Street, the towers of midtown - they might be forever changed after Wednesday's action. She would certainly never see them again in person. *I violated Nimr's command to stay put last night, but it had been in the line of duty.* He would have a fit, or worse, if she took off on a tourist jaunt. She had her poetry, and her Quran. A stroll in Riverside Park would be fine.

Lost in thought, Mayar was fastening the belt on her jeans when a knock on the door interrupted her reverie. Amy poked her head inside, holding a note in her hand. "A friend of your brother's stopped by last night," she said.

"Who?" Mayar asked incredulously. "You must be mistaken."

"No. She knew Ahmed from Israel. He recommended that she work with you on some project."

Mayar's stomach roiled like a choppy sea. "Project? What project?"

"Fuck if I know what you're up to. You're not exactly Miss Congeniality around here."

"Can I see that please?" Mayar tottered as she reached for the note.

"Her name was Taryn Booker. Sounded to me like she might have hooked up with your brother, you know," Amy said as she handed over the folded sheet of paper.

Mayar read the brief note several times. Taryn Booker? Taryn Booker? The name meant nothing at first, but then she remembered something. A newspaper article. Mayor Rosen's scandal. Booker had been questioned for hacking the Russians. *And she wants to help me?*

"Guess I should be going," Amy said, still dawdling at the door. "Are you OK? You look like you're going to puke again."

"Yes, yes, I'll be fine," Mayar mumbled, but she knew that her world had just taken a wrong turn. She willed herself to sit and regain her composure after Amy left. A venomous snake uncoiled inside her stomach, preparing to scale up her esophagus. She grabbed her Mets' scarf from the closet and raced out the door.

***

"Hey, this is Taryn Booker. I'm calling about a project you're working on with Mayar Tabak up at Columbia. Thought I might be able to help. Ring me back. Thanks." Taryn left a voicemail for Allison Gold. *Let's see if the fish takes the bait.*

Sitting at her kitchen table, Taryn, still in sleepwear, finished her morning coffee, dawdling over her laptop. She scanned the *New York Times* home page a final time. Coverage of the battle at the Ithaca airport was still rampant, featuring a flattering obituary of Professor Bierman and a lengthy resume of the Brogans' murderous activities around the globe. Another article speculated about Tim Brogan's escape from Manhattan, adding the strangulation of an elderly black man in Alphabet City to the bloody list. The world would not miss Gerard, Tim or Michael Brogan.

The FBI had artfully spun the incident to deflect as much attention to Special Agent Lou Totti while Taryn remained the "unidentified other occupant" of the vehicle. Lou balked at the hero's role at first, but relented when his superiors reminded him that he would also be a potential target for the last living Brogan brother. He insisted on a 24/7 bodyguard for Taryn anyway, but this time it was her turn to object. She had her pistols and her anonymity. They compromised with the city granting Taryn a license to carry a concealed weapon for personal protection, a difficult to attain "perk" usually reserved for celebrities and their protectors.

Like a typical email junkie, Taryn couldn't sign off without a quick check. All quiet on the Con Ed front. No word from Eli either. Not a surprise, but the combination of a slow workday with spring sunshine had marginally inflated her hopes.

She stepped out onto her back deck to stretch. The trees were in full bloom below, adding a splash of color to the cityscape. She laid out a pair of white jeans and a sailor-striped top on her bed and ran the shower. She was due to meet Karim and Rhonda for a long-delayed brunch in thirty minutes.

Her ringtone blared just as she finished squeezing shampoo into her hair. Never fails, she laughed silently, quickly rinsing and pushing back the shower curtain. She grabbed a towel and skipped into the bedroom, grabbing the phone off the top of her bureau on the fifth ring.

"Hey," she answered, a drop of suds in her eye obscuring the caller ID.

"This is Allison Gold, returning your call."

"Thanks for getting back to me so fast." Taryn replied snapping to attention, while clumsily trying to wrap the towel around her dripping torso with her left hand.

"No problem. But I'm not sure that I can help you."

"Your friends said that you were working on a project with Mayar Tabak."

"Which friends?"

"Amy and Sarah. I stopped by their dorm the other night, looking for Mayar but she wasn't around." Taryn gave up on the towel and let it drop to the hardwood floor.

"I don't really know what they're talking about. How do you know Mayar?"

"I don't. I met her brother in Israel a few weeks ago. He thought I might be able to help her with a computer project." Taryn was standing in a puddle now.

"What kind of project?" Allison's voice quivered as if she was afraid to hear the answer.

"The electrical grid," Taryn replied. *Might as well swing for the fences.*

"Oh, I don't know anything about that." An audible sigh of relief. "That's Mayar's gig."

"What are you working on with Mayar then? Maybe I can help." Naked, Taryn sat down on her bed. "I'm pretty good with computer stuff."

"What's your name again?"

"Taryn Booker."

"Look I've got to go. I barely know Mayar, and I don't need your help."

"Sure. No problem. You've got my number if you change your mind."

***

Graeme caught up with Mayar on Broadway, just outside the Columbia gates. He stood close to her, waiting for the light on 114th Street to turn green. Two boys, freshmen she guessed, flanked her as well, colorfully recounting their Friday night activities. She tuned them out, fixing her gaze on the signal, the name 'Taryn Booker' pounding her brain.

"Is something wrong?" Graeme asked without turning his head.

"I'm not sure," she replied. "Yes, I think so," she added, shaking her head. "I need to talk to Nimr."

Graeme scowled at the public mention of their leader's name. "Walk along Riverside Drive. We'll find you." He pivoted to his right and darted across the boulevard.

***

237

Red Farm, an upscale Chinese restaurant located in a townhouse on Hudson Street just a few blocks from Taryn's apartment, was packed for brunch. The rustic decor, complete with checkered fabrics, communal tables and an exposed beam ceiling, created a lively, homey atmosphere that belied the food forward menu. Fortunately, Karim had made a reservation, securing them a prime spot of their own near the window. He and Rhonda were already seated, Bloody Mary's in hand, when she arrived.

"Howdy, stranger," Rhonda gushed, standing to hug Taryn. She wore a pearl white cardigan over a peach summer frock. "We've missed you."

"Brightify is just not the same without you," Karim added, dressed as usual in cargo shorts and hoodie. He tipped his glass in a toast.

"What he means is our boss, Marco, is still an asshole," Rhonda confided as she waved to attract the attention of their waiter. "What do you want to drink?"

"Stella," Taryn ordered.

"How are you holding up? You were really close to Professor Bierman, weren't you?" Karim asked as soon as the waiter departed.

"Yes. He was a more than just my mentor. Much more." Taryn ducked her head and fidgeted with her purse, a diamond patterned Zara tote, her Beretta safely stowed inside.

"When's the funeral?" Rhonda chipped in.

"On Wednesday. I'm planning to go up for the day. There's going to be a memorial next month too."

She would miss the Professor. He had inspired her to become a soldier in his cyber war, a role that she accepted willingly despite the personal risks it entailed.

When the waiter returned with her beer, they ordered an array of dim sum - grilled lamb shooters, wasabi shrimp and mushroom spring rolls - and caught up on each other's personal lives. Rhonda enthusiastically detailed her new beau, another J-Date match. Karim had started playing on a beach volleyball team in Brooklyn Bridge Park with several college classmates.

"Speaking of Yale, have you heard from Fiona Peterson at all?" Taryn asked Karim, purposely moving onto shaky ground. She knew that the Israelis had quietly detained Fiona as an accessory to Priscilla Cabot's murder, but she wanted to discover what information, if any, had leaked to her friends.

"Nobody's heard anything from Fiona in a long while. I thought that she might be at the Cabot funeral last month but she didn't show. It was a small affair anyway. Just a few friends and family."

"How's Mr. Cabot holding up?" Taryn inquired.

"He looked battered, but he's got that patrician air, so it's hard to know what he's really thinking. I did speak to him privately after the service. He seemed relieved that he was able to keep the details of JJ's death out of the papers," Karim replied.

The food arrived, and they all unwrapped their chopsticks. Taryn reached for a shrimp.

"How's Jim?" Rhonda piped up, wiping a speck of green Wasabi from her lip.

"Improving," Taryn answered. "I was at the hospital on Wednesday."

"With Marcy?"

"No. She was working." Taryn took a swallow of her beer, then pointed the bottle at her girlfriend. "Look, Marcy and I get along fine. I'm looking forward to her wedding."

"No regrets?" Rhonda pressed.

"Not really. Jim and I were friends, always will be. But he wants to have kids. Like soon."

"No interest in little rug rats biting your ankles, huh?" Karim teased, dipping his spring roll in the plum sauce.

"I'm footloose and fancy-free," Taryn replied.

Rhonda laughed. "What about your friend Eli?" She wasn't giving up on Taryn's love life that quickly. "Last time we talked, I detected a romantic entanglement there."

"Well, he's been recalled to active duty," Taryn deflected.

"Tough to entangle much then, huh?" Karim smirked.

Before Taryn could reply, Blake Shelton started crooning again. Taryn glanced at her phone. Allison Gold. "Hold on a sec," she answered, standing up.

"I have to take this," she apologized to her brunch mates.

Taryn walked out into the street to continue the conversation with Allison. "What's up?" she asked, searching for a quieter place to talk.

"You're the girl who hacked the Russians? And the police let you go, right?" Allison asked.

"Something like that." Taryn pressed against the brick facade of a four-story apartment building, shielding her phone from the noise of the street.

"And now you're on the Mayor's cybersecurity task force?"

"Correct." Two young men wearing matching hoop earrings and tight jeans strolled by, arm in arm.

"Well," Allison dragged out her response. "I might need your help"

"Go on."

"Mayar designed a RAT for me," Allison blurted out. "I popped it into my friend, Merry's, computer last month when she was at lunch. It was just a prank. I swear it."

"Slow down," Taryn replied. "A RAT? A Remote Access Trojan?"

"Yes."

"Tell me exactly what happened." Taryn watched an elderly woman lean over to scoop her poodle's poop into a blue plastic bag.

"I didn't know that Mayar supported ISIS. I swear it."

Taryn waited until the woman was out of earshot. "Supported ISIS? What the hell are you talking about?" *I knew it.*

"Sarah and Amy told you about the black flag in Mayar's room, right? I didn't know about that until it was too late. Way too late. I'm sorry. I'm really sorry." Allison started to sob.

"Look, your little prank probably enabled Mayar Tabak to penetrate the network of the entire city government. Who knows what she's going to do with the data that she steals. You could be in trouble, serious fucking trouble." Taryn paused to let Allison recognize the depth of the crevasse that had swallowed her. "You need to tell me everything. Now."

"Will you help me? I don't want to go to jail," Allison pleaded.

"Meet me at my apartment in thirty minutes."

***

Mayar walked north on Riverside, struggling to keep the slithering reptile in her stomach at bay. She focused on the leaves of the trees weaving a dense green tapestry over the park. A small boat meandered down the Hudson River, its white sail billowing in the breeze. A father tossed a wiffle ball with his young son. *How much does Taryn Booker know? Is the FBI involved? Why haven't they arrested me already?*

The last question calmed her. If the FBI knew about her plans, she would be in jail by now. In two more days, it would be too late. Once Viktor's virus was injected into the grid, it couldn't be called back. Her fledgling country would celebrate a great triumph over the infidels and she would be in route to Raqqa. *Praise Allah!*

Mayar sat down on a bench looking out over the park to check her email accounts. Nothing from the police, or the university, or Taryn Booker. Good news. A private message alert from Pizza Boy surprised her. *He probably wants more money.*

She swiveled her head to make sure that no one was watching as she logged into the dark forum. Even worse, Pizza Boy's message contained a blackmail threat. He would notify the authorities, anonymously of course, if Sully did not come up with fifty thousand dollars by Monday evening.

Mayar spun sharply as a horn honked behind her. A yellow taxi pulled up to the curb. She was about to wave it away when she recognized Graeme behind the wheel. "Get in," he ordered as the rear door popped open. Nimr was already sitting in the back behind the vacant shotgun seat. As soon as Mayar closed the door, the cab glided uptown.

"What is troubling you?" Nimr asked. He listened intently as Mayar explained Taryn Booker's visit to her dorm. When she finished, he turned his head and stared out his window for several seconds.

"We are so close. We cannot take any chances now."

"I understand. May Allah grant us victory," Mayar replied.

Nimr issued a terse command to Graeme in Arabic. He headed crosstown on 135th Street to Amsterdam Avenue before turning uptown again.

"You will stay with us until the danger has passed," Nimr said. He reached over to Mayar, resting his fingers on her wrist. "We cannot risk any more of your jaunts around the city. You are too valuable to our cause."

"Thank you."

The taxi turned left on 149th Street in the heart of a largely Latino neighborhood and parked in front of a three-story brownstone.

"The headquarters for the Islamic State in America," Nimr announced. "We have a room prepared for you."

Mayar nodded, impressed by Nimr's level of readiness. "One more issue," she said, explaining Pizza Boy's threat.

"Let me see your mobile," Nimr requested. He read the message on Mayar's screen and slipped her phone into his jacket pocket. "Your friend, the Pizza Boy, wants to serve our cause. I believe that we have a final role for him to play."

Mayar didn't notice Graeme exit the driver's seat. He opened the rear door, ushering her out onto the sidewalk. As soon as Mayar was out of the vehicle, Nimr opened his door, stepped into the street and strode around the back of the taxi.

She found herself flanked by Nimr on the left and Graeme on her right. A set of stone steps led up to the main door of the brownstone, but Graeme pointed to a gate at street level. "You'll stay downstairs. It's better for you," he said softly, clasping her elbow. He steered her around a grime blackened bicycle chained inside the postage stamp courtyard.

Nimr reached roughly for the hood on Mayar's sweatshirt, pulling it up to cover her head. "There are men in the house. You must act like a proper Muslim woman."

Mayar looked up and down the block as she shuffled to her new home. The street, a mix of low rise apartment buildings and brownstones, was not particularly prosperous, but clean. A scatter of trees softened the urban landscape. The commercial bustle of Amsterdam Avenue beckoned from the corner. She inhaled a deep breath of fresh air before Graeme opened the door and steered her inside.

"Make yourself comfortable. We will visit with you shortly," Nimr said as he left her new abode. Mayar could hear a bolt lock into place. Through the iron grill guarding the window, she watched the taxi pull away.

***

"I've got the goods for you to arrest Mayar Tabak. Tonight," Taryn announced over the phone.

"Whoa, slow down," Lou replied, shifting his one-year-old son to his left hip. "What are you talking about?"

"I just finished a two-hour session with Allison Gold, a classmate of Tabak at Columbia. She's sitting right here in my apartment. You need to interview her yourself."

Taryn heard a wail in the background, then Lou calling for Kendra to take the baby. "OK, that's better," he said a few seconds later. "Give me a quick summary."

"I'm not her lawyer, but I'm pretty sure that Allison is going to want immunity from prosecution," Taryn said, looking over at the agitated young woman sitting on her couch, chewing on a fingernail. Allison nodded her assent, the eagerness apparent in her walnut brown eyes.

"I can't promise that," Lou replied. "But I can make sure that the proper authorities are aware of Ms. Gold's cooperation. I need to know her story first."

"Allison's an intern in the mayor's office. A fellow intern was having an improper relationship with a senior staffer that Allison felt might affect her own chances at a promotion. So, she enlisted the help of Mayar Tabak to create a RAT that would spy on the other intern."

"Your friend Allison's in deep shit," Lou declared, "Unauthorized access to a protected computer is a felony."

"She knows. That's why you need to hear the rest of her story."

"It better be good."

"The bottom line is Mayar Tabak is a genius hacker and a devout Muslim who keeps an ISIS flag in her room. And she had a much closer relationship with her brother, the ISIS commander, than she ever acknowledged to you and Jim."

"You know we can't prosecute anyone for their religious beliefs," Lou said. "But, if Tabak coded the RAT knowing that it was going to be illegally implanted at City Hall, we certainly have enough to arrest her. I'm not sure it's a federal case though."

"There's more. Much more," Taryn said, quickly bringing Lou up to date on her research about the potential threat to the New York City electrical system.

"Do you think that Tabak could be involved in the attack?" He asked.

"Allison sneaked a peek at Tabak's thesis when she ran into her in the library one night. It's entitled, "Architectural Vulnerabilities of Smart Infrastructure at the Municipal Level.""

"Holy shit," Lou replied. "Don't move. I'm on my way."

***

Mayar surveyed the ground floor apartment. It was a studio, spartanly furnished, with a threadbare rug providing modest cover to a pockmarked hardwood floor. A solitary bulb overhead and a rickety floor lamp provided the only interior light to the exposed brick walls.

In the far corner, freshly laundered sheets spruced up a single bed positioned underneath a faded travel poster advertising a seaside scene in Beirut. The Quran rested on the nightstand. A garage sale armchair upholstered in a hideous lime green squatted next to the bed, while a compact kitchen set-up, two burners and a half-height refrigerator, occupied the near wall. A teapot rested on the stove with two cracked cups on the counter nearby.

She opened the door in the rear of the apartment. It led to the bathroom, toilet seat up, specks of faded yellow stains circling the rim. Mayar wiped it clean with a few sheets of toilet paper, dropped the seat, and washed her hands. She dried them with the lone towel hanging on the rack.

There was no telephone, television or computer. *Shit!* She realized that her laptop was back in her dorm. Someone had to retrieve it. She would tell Nimr.

Mayar tried to open the front door, but it wouldn't budge. She forced the front window open a few inches, but the grill insured its security. Craning her neck, she watched a pillowy cloud drift across the sky disappearing at last behind the buildings across the street.

Nimr had said that there were men, fighters most likely, in the house. Men with unholy urges. The apartment defended her privacy and virtue. Nimr had planned well. She called out for him several times, then flopped down on the chair to wait.

The creak of the door jolted Mayar awake. Nimr and Graeme entered, the twilight sky providing only a dim backlight. She wiped the sleep from her eyes and jumped up.

"It's good that you are resting," Nimr said. "You have contributed much for our cause, but there is still much for us to do."

"Praise Allah, we will reap the fruits of our labor shortly," Mayar replied.

"Here is dinner," Nimr said, pointing to a tray that Graeme had just placed on the stove. The aroma of freshly grilled chicken stoked pangs of hunger in Mayar's belly, but she willed herself to stay focused.

"What is my next assignment?" she asked.

"I am waiting to hear from Viktor. He wants to inject the virus in forty-eight hours."

"I can help, but I need my computer." Mayar detailed its location. "And my phone," she added.

"I will send one of the others for the computer immediately," Nimr answered. "Graeme has spent too much time around Columbia already."

"Can he bring some clean clothes for me too?"

"I will arrange it."

"When will I meet the fighters?" Graeme coughed in response.

"Soon enough," Nimr answered. "We must go now."

"Wait." Mayar swept her hand around the room. "What am I supposed to do here?"

Nimr scowled in response. He lifted the Quran from the table. "Pray."

"And Pizza Boy? How are we going to respond to his demand?"

"Sajida, a good soldier does not ask so many questions," Nimr scolded. "Graeme will handle the Pizza Boy from now on."

Graeme lagged Nimr to cast a supportive smile in Mayar's direction as the two men left the basement.

CHAPTER 47

Just before dawn on Sunday, Lou Totti, body armor snug under his gray suit jacket, led the SWAT team into the dormitory. A half dozen agents in full riot gear trotted up the steps in two neat lines, trailed by three officers from Homeland Security in navy blue windbreakers. Mayar's hallway was deserted except for a half full bottle of Pinot Grigio lying on its side by the exit. Shields up, pistols drawn, the agents fanned out on both sides of her doorway.

Lou banged on the door. "FBI! Open up!"

Silence. He rapped again, repeating his command. Still no reply. He tried the handle. Locked. Lou stepped back. The lead SWAT agents assumed ready positions in front of the door. The one on the right nodded for his partner to proceed. The agent lowered his shield and rammed into the door. It splintered with a sharp crack and fell open. The SWAT team flowed around Lou to swarm inside.

"All clear," the lead agent declared.

Wearing a t-shirt and shorts, her hair spiking at odd angles, Amy opened her door across the hall. "Oh, my God!" she exclaimed.

"Back inside, ma'am," Lou ordered, tugging her door shut. He waited five more seconds for his team to complete their survey of Mayar's room before entering.

The room looked as if a tornado had just ripped through. The bed was overturned, drawers were askew, and the desk was flipped on its side.

"Someone beat us here," the lead agent said, holstering his weapon.

Lou spun around and knocked on the door across the hall. Amy, now wearing a bathrobe, opened it slowly.

"Do you know where Mayar Tabak is?" he asked, displaying his shield.

Amy shook her head. "She left around dinner time last night. We haven't seen her since."

"Did anyone come by her room after she left?"

Sarah joined her suitemate. "Her cousin stopped by last night. Late. Like midnight," she volunteered.

"Her cousin?" Lou asked.

"An Arab looking guy. Dark skin, big beard."

"Did he tell you his name?"

Sarah shook her head.

"And a friend of her brother's came by on Friday night. A redhead. Her name was Taryn Booker," Amy volunteered.

"She's on our side," Lou said.

***

After scarfing down a bowl of yogurt and blueberries, Taryn sat down with a cup of black coffee in front of the computer in her apartment at 8:30. Allison's parents and their family lawyer had driven down from Westchester the night before to support their daughter in her confession to Lou. Everyone had left around midnight.

Allison and a to-be-hired criminal attorney were due downtown at ten tomorrow for her official arrest and arraignment. Taryn was supposed to be reviewing the social media leads provided by Allison, but, as she replayed Allison's confession in her mind, a thunderhead of anger swelled. *How could I have missed it?*

"Allison's little RAT may have gotten Professor Bierman killed," she blurted over the phone before Lou could even say hello.

"What? Calm down."

"What if his report to Washington circulated at City Hall and CyberBanda hacked it via Allison's RAT?"

"You're going off like a machine gun," Lou soothed. "First, we don't know that Bierman's report made it to the mayor's office. Even if it did, we'd have difficulty proving that the Russians got it or acted on it. And don't forget, Ms. Gold is voluntarily providing significant assistance to our investigation of a possible major terrorist attack in New York."

"You're saying I'm too late?"

"Do you really believe that Allison Gold knew that her actions would facilitate a murder?"

Taryn took a deep breath. "No, I don't."

"Me neither. Without proving her intent, or at least prior knowledge, we wouldn't even be able to file an accessory charge."

"But…"

"Taryn, you're grieving for a close friend and stressed out from this investigation. I wish I could tell you to take a vacation, but I can't. We need you."

"Thanks."

"Look, Ms. Gold committed multiple federal offenses which she'll have to answer for. Aiding a terrorist is about as serious a crime as there is. I'm not sure what deal she'll be able to cut."

"I understand."

"I'll alert the prosecutor to your concerns and tell our forensic techs what to look for when they comb through Allison's files. But, remember, my priority right now is stopping a possible cyberattack, not investigating Professor Bierman's murder. I'm sorry."

***

Brian Valentine woke at ten to the sound of a heavy object scraping across the floor outside his bedroom. His head throbbed from the shots of Jack he had downed at a party in Bed-Stuy the night before. Almost got laid, too.

"Where the fuck are you going?" he called out while opening his door. His roommate was halfway into the hall pushing an overstuffed Patagonia Black Hole bag with his computer balanced precariously on top.

"Moving out bro. Today is payday," Dennis replied, hardly looking up.

"What?"

"I told you. My man Sully ain't no terrorist. I hit him up for some more dough and he's coming through big time."

"You're shitting me."

"Fuck you. You had your chance but you pussied out." Dennis worked his way around to the front of the bag to maneuver it through the doorway.

"Where are you going?"

"My old man lent me his van. I'm loading it up and hitting the road." Satisfied that his duffel had cleared, Dennis walked back into the apartment.

"You have a new place lined up?" Brian asked.

"Nope. But I hear Chicago's a pretty good town. Lots of nice, honest Midwesterners."

"Your kind of people, huh?

"They will be, soon enough. I left you the rent money for next month on the table," Dennis said, pointing to an envelope. "You should be able to get someone to take my room by then."

"You're leaving for real then?"

"For real, man. I've just got to make a quick stop at Fairway to pick up my money. Then I'm gone."

"You sure Sully's on the up and up? He's not scamming you?" Brian picked up the envelope.

"Open it up, man. His cash has been good so far. Don't see why the last fifty K won't be just as green."

"Fifty large? That's a shitload of dough."

"I told you, man, this job pays well."

Brian dropped the envelope back on the table - unopened. "Something's not right, Dennis. What did you do for Sully? You must have helped him out big-time to justify all that money. What's he getting out of it? Something's going to blow up and someone's going to get hurt. Maybe lots of people."

"Don't go waving that red, white, and blue flag at me. I don't owe this country nothing."

"You're an asshole, you know."

"Fuck you too," Dennis kicked the bottom of his suitcase and slammed the door closed, leaving Brian alone in the musty apartment.

***

Taryn's ringtone sounded at ten-thirty. Blake Shelton was starting to wear thin. She was surprised to see Rhonda's ID flash across the screen.

"Hey, I'm sorry for bugging out so fast yesterday, but something came up at work," Taryn apologized.

"Mayar Tabak and the electrical grid, right?"

"Shit, how did you know?"

"We were brought in this morning. Considering the imminent threat, the company's going to comply immediately with the FBI's subpoena to access Tabak's Brightify account. Marco woke Karim and me up with the good news."

"That's great. I don't know how much time we have, so the more hands-on deck the better." Taryn peered outside. A light drizzle pecked against the windowpane.

"The FBI raided Tabak's dorm at dawn, but she wasn't there. Neither was her computer, so we don't have much to work with. I'm reviewing her account for any ties to her half-brother or anyone else in the Middle East, but that's going to take some time. Looks like she's been pretty careful not to leave a trail."

"No surprise. She's a smart girl. What's Karim up to?" Taryn asked.

"He's looking for clues to any secondary accounts that might be under different names."

"Good move."

"I've got to go. We'll be in touch," Rhonda almost signed off.

"Wait a sec," Taryn snapped, standing up in front of her desk.

"Just before I came back home from Tel Aviv, Jim called to update me on the Con Ed hacker. He and his team tracked the security breach to a guy named Dennis Walecka. And, the police recently sighted Walecka outside the Sherman Creek power plant."

"You think that he could be working with Mayar Tabak? Rhonda asked.

"I'm not sure, but it's another name to check."

Taryn stood up from her desk, stretched, and headed to the kitchen to refill her coffee. Blake Shelton crooned again, prompting a vow to find a new tune, as an unknown number flashed on her phone.

"Hello," she answered tentatively.

"Taryn Booker?" a male voice.

"Yes. Who's this?"

A long pause. "You don't know me. But I know you pretty well. I'm going to send you an email with a little video. Take a look at it and call me back. You've got the number."

"Why would I want to call you back?"

"Bingos Pizza." Brian Valentine hung up before Taryn could reply.

By the time Taryn reached her desk an email from a domain server in Romania was waiting. She opened it and gasped. A GIF video of her, stark naked, prancing through her living room, began to play. She dropped her coffee cup in shock, the brown liquid splashing all over the floor. Quick-stepping backward to avoid the steaming spray, she grasped the sofa for support as the video looped again.

She was probably answering the phone, but the footage had been edited to look like the opening scene of a sex tape. *It had to be filmed by the assholes who had hacked her old computer. And her webcam, apparently. And had used her Brightify account to spear-fish the Con Ed employees.* She jammed her finger down on the call back button on her phone. "Who the fuck are you?" she screamed.

"Hey, slow down, I'm a concerned citizen and you're a hot shot computer whiz," Brian replied calmly, as if he had been expecting the outburst. "I think we can work together."

"You're a fucking pervert. Why would I ever work with you?"

"Calm down, and listen to me, Taryn. I've got the info on a plot to hack Con Edison and take down the electrical grid."

Taryn sat down on the sofa. "Go on. You've got my attention."

Brian recounted the details of his hacking escapades starting with the pizza website, keeping both his name and Dennis' clear of the conversation.

"You monitored my computer for months, didn't you?" she asked, calculating all the damage he had caused her.

"Yeah, but it wasn't my idea," Brian mumbled.

"Let me guess," Taryn said at last. "Your business associate is Dennis Walecka."

"Maybe," Brian sounded shocked. "Maybe."

"Where is Walecka now?"

"He just left. He's meeting some guy named Sully. That's the guy that hired him to run that Wi-Fi interceptor around the power stations."

"Where's the meeting?"

"I don't know."

"Think hard. You guys are scumbags. Sounds to me like you've also been participants in a terrorist plot against the United States. The FBI's going to lock you both up and throw away the key."

"That's bullshit, man. I'm stepping forward right now to serve my country. You've got to explain that to the FBI."

"I'm not Wonder Woman," she replied, struggling to maintain her composure. "Where is Walecka?"

"Look, I did a little hacking of names and addresses, low level shit, but I didn't have anything to do with that Wi-Fi device. Never even saw it."

"Right now, I don't care what you did or what you saw. I need to know where your buddy is. We have to stop him."

"If I destroy that video, will you help me out?"

"I won't promise you shit," Taryn said, sensing that Brian was ready to fold. "But, if you don't tell me where Walecka is, I'll make sure that you rot in prison for the rest of your miserable, fucking life."

"The meeting's at Fairway. That's all he told me. I swear it on my mother's grave."

"Fairway? Which one? Where?"

"I don't know. I mean it. I don't fucking know."

"OK. Where are *you* now?" After Brian provided his address, Taryn added, "Stay put. You can expect a call from the FBI any minute. Your best bet is to tell them everything."

CHAPTER 48

"Fairway?" Lou shouted into the phone. "There must be a dozen Fairway Markets in the city. Maybe more."

"Can you cover them all?" Taryn had recounted the details of her conversation with Brian, including his location in Brooklyn, but decided to squash any mention of the video. She'd climb that mountain another time.

"Yeah, probably. But, with this short notice, we'll be spread thin. I'll need to get the ball rolling right away."

"I'll get out of your way then."

"Sully sounds like a guy's name, doesn't it?" Lou asked.

"Yeah, I know. Maybe it's Mayar's partner. Or her boss. Or maybe it's just a clever screen name. Only one way to find out."

"I need to make a few calls. We can touch base in a few hours."

"Sounds like a plan."

"What are *you* planning to do this afternoon?" Lou asked.

"I'm going to take the subway up to Columbia to visit Mayar's thesis professor. He has Sunday office hours. I may be able to get some information that can help me track her coding work."

"OK, that's fine." Lou paused, then added, "Taryn, remember, you're in New York City now. You need to stay away from Walecka and let the pros handle him. Got it?"

"Got it."

Taryn showered quickly, dressing in jeans and a blue checked button down. She pulled up Walecka's General Assembly ID photo, the one that Jim had sent over, and studied it for several seconds. The rain had ended, so she jauntily perched a white fedora on her head and grabbed her tote.

*****

Her meeting with the professor lasted less than thirty minutes. The FBI had already interviewed him at length and there were two other students waiting outside his office. He did note that Mayar had demonstrated a surprising depth of knowledge on the architecture of A&B switches, but he was clueless as to her coding style, recommending that Taryn visit with one of Mayar's computer science profs instead. That could wait.

If Mayar was associated with Sully, she bet the meeting would take place at the Fairway near the Columbia campus. *Lou said the FBI would be hard-pressed to cover all locations. One more set of eyes can't hurt.*

Marked by a Starburst display of red, green, purple and yellow produce, the Fairway entrance was located on West 132nd Street underneath the elevated West Side Highway, a convenient location for automobile traffic both entering and leaving Manhattan. On the east side, traffic headed north along Twelfth Avenue and could easily access the highway. On the west side, traffic exited the highway onto Marginal Street, flowing south past the store and its parking lot before reaching the downtown ramp to reenter the highway. Marginal Street also bordered the city's Greenway, a sliver of a park that ran the entire West Side, encompassing a bike path and a neatly landscaped pedestrian promenade overlooking the Hudson River.

With her tote slung over her left shoulder, Taryn circumnavigated the half empty parking lot. Dennis Walecka was nowhere in sight. Two young children sat astride a shopping cart pushed by what looked like their grandfather; a middle-aged woman in tennis whites loaded a bag of groceries into the trunk of her Mercedes; a lanky, muscled young man in revealing black spandex shorts and skin tight jersey, unzipped to reveal a bushy swath of chest hair, locked his bike against the chain link fence. A yellow cab pulled in, veering into a spot in the far corner.

Taryn crossed the street and the bike path, sidestepping a cyclist spinning downtown, and wandered towards the river. The sun had poked through the clouds, painting the Greenway with a golden light while the market and its parking lot were still shrouded in shadows from the highway rumbling overhead. A black dude, resembling a villain in Star Wars, with spiked hair and frazzled goatee sat on a bench sipping coffee and reading the paper. Two women in running attire strolled by. A pair of uniformed NYPD cops patrolled the waterfront.

Taryn leaned against the railing, her back to the river, and surveyed the tranquil scene. *Maybe I was wrong about this location.* After fifteen minutes, she headed back towards Fairway, stopping next to two Little Leaguers in full uniform and their dads to wait for a break in the traffic.

A beaten up black van approached, rolling through the stop sign to turn left onto Marginal Street. As the driver pivoted with the arc of the turn, Taryn caught a glimpse of his profile.

The van swung left again, pausing to let a shopper pass, then glided into the Fairway parking lot. The driver seemed indecisive, stopping midstream, before finally selecting a spot against the chain link fence facing the river. Taryn quickened her pace reaching the entrance to the lot as he climbed out of the van.

An elderly man wearing a yarmulke struggled with an overstuffed shopping cart. "Let me help you, sir," Taryn volunteered, taking command and rolling the cart slowly towards the van, keeping her eyes focused downward. The grateful shopper followed a step behind. "My car is the blue Prius right over there," he pointed out.

Taryn pulled the brim of her fedora low as they shuffled within a few feet of her target, broad shoulders, a thick bronze beard and ponytail. The fire-breathing dragon tattoo on his right bicep confirmed her intuition.

Walecka was preoccupied, obviously searching for someone. Before Taryn could react, he started towards the supermarket entrance. She pivoted as well, wheeling the shopping cart in a 180-degree arc. *I just can't stand here and watch.*

"We've got to stop him," she shouted at the old man. Confused, he shuffled in her path, blocking her way for a second. "I'm sorry," she repeated twice as she burst by.

Walecka was now ten paces ahead. Hearing Taryn's footsteps, he spun around as she approached, his eyes popping wide open in recognition. "Fucking bitch," he muttered frantically searching for an escape route.

Taryn used the delay to gain ground, chugging forward, pushing the cart ahead of her like a bobsled at the top of the Olympic run. A container of milk, three apples and two tins of sardines bounced out, rattling on the asphalt. When Walecka turned towards the parking lot exit, Taryn launched the cart at him.

The hurtling wagon clanged into Walecka's backside, sending him stumbling. He steadied himself with both hands, then took off again.

A gunshot rang out behind Taryn. *Donal Brogan?* She dropped to one knee, spinning her tote in front of her. Before she could draw her pistol, chaos erupted. Shoppers scattered pell mell, diving to the ground, crawling behind cars.

"Get down!"

"She's got a gun!"

"What the fuck are you doing?" The woman in the tennis dress screamed as she tackled Taryn, knocking her flat on her stomach.

"We had him cornered," she howled, pointing to her partner, a walrus of a man, complete with thick mustache, who had emerged from behind the produce counter, ripped off his apron and was now chasing Walecka down Marginal. The two NYPD cops from the promenade trailed behind.

Taryn didn't have time to explain. The yellow cab peeled out of its parking spot in the back of the lot and accelerated past them. An arm, extended from an open rear window, fired another pistol shot into the air. Any shoppers who had ventured back to an upright position dove for cover once again. With groceries, shopping carts, assorted personal items, and crawling bodies scattered about, the parking lot looked like a yard sale gone badly awry.

The taxi screeched hard left out, almost up on two wheels. It raced past the two cops chugging down Marginal Street before slowing to veer in front of the FBI agent leading the charge, sending him sprawling to the pavement. It finally stopped ten yards ahead of Walecka, still running madly, arms pumping like twin pistons, ponytail flopping over his shoulders. The rear door opened; Walecka dove inside the taxi. It blasted through the red light on 125th and sped up the ramp onto the West Side Highway.

***

The driver quickly braked, settling the taxi into the rhythm of the light traffic on the highway. Dennis sat upright and brushed off his jeans. He searched the rear window for any signs of pursuit, breathing an audible sigh of relief when none materialized. "Thanks for the ride,

Sully," he wheezed to Graeme, who was sitting next to him, a compact Smith and Wesson nine-millimeter pistol in his lap.

Graeme nodded curtly in reply before issuing a command in Arabic to the driver, a short, wiry man with bronzed complexion and full, neatly trimmed beard. The cab slipped into the right-hand lane and exited the highway a minute later at West 96th Street. The ramp circled downward, running underneath the highway, before rising again to a traffic signal on Riverside Drive. The cab sat behind three cars until the light turned green. It turned left onto the narrow, tree-lined Drive, heading back uptown.

When the cab stopped at another red light, Dennis turned to Graeme. "Look, man, I can hop out right here," he offered. "Just give me my dough. No need to take me back uptown."

A thin smile crossed Graeme's lips as he pointed his pistol at Walecka's chest. "You're not going anywhere, man. You're now a guest of the Islamic State in America."

***

"You're lucky you're not in jail tonight," Lou said angrily over the phone. "We had to call in all our chits to get the NYPD to release you."

"Look, I'm telling you, I never even drew my gun," Taryn replied, back in her apartment after the tumultuous day, Stella in hand.

"Why were you at Fairway in the first place? I specifically asked you not to go," Lou carried on. "Both the police and the FBI at the scene blamed your meddling. We got you a license to carry a weapon for your own safety. In case Donal Brogan comes around. Not for you to gallivant around the city and interfere with a stakeout."

"I'm sorry. OK?"

"Look, whether you want to admit it or not, you're worried about Donal Brogan. I am too. It was my name behind the wheel in the newspaper."

"I don't need a bodyguard following me around 24/7."

"I've got a partner with me whenever I'm out on the street."

"No."

"Fine, it's your life. But you can't take rash actions that put other civilians in danger. Wanna bet on how long it will take for some shopper in that parking lot to sue the city?"

"Okay, I get it," Taryn relented. "I made a bad call. But I was just trying to help." *I nailed Ahmed Hazboun and two Brogans, didn't I? Not bad for a computer scientist.*

"Next time just listen to me," Lou said. "And stay put until I say otherwise."

"Got it," Taryn paused. "Were you able to find the cab? The one with the shooter?"

"Do you know how many yellow taxis are in Manhattan? We got the last two digits of the license plate, 3S, but that's not going to be enough."

"Back to square one?" Taryn asked.

"We're better off than that. Brian Valentine is already singing like Lin-Manuel Miranda. We'll get some good leads there."

"I'm going to check in with Rhonda and Karim. They've been chasing down Mayar Tabak's social media feeds all day," Taryn said. She drained the last of her Stella and slammed the bottle into the trash.

***

The beating began at nightfall. Mayar jumped at the first bloodcurdling scream that erupted from the rooms upstairs. The bulb in her ceiling rattled as the thumps, wails, and Arabic curses continued unabated for a good hour.

Kess ikhtak!

Kess ommak!

Telhas teeze!

At last, the victim, obviously an American, was dragged away. *Is he still alive?* She picked up her Quran and started reading to keep her thoughts at bay.

A few minutes later, Nimr knocked, then opened her door. Mayar shivered in her seat, but brightened when she noticed that he was carrying her gym bag overstuffed with clothes.

"I apologize for the ruckus," he said. "The infidel needed to be taught a lesson."

"Pizza Boy?"

"Yes."

"Is he dead?"

"No. We need him alive to serve our cause."

Nimr nudged the gym bag forward with his foot. "Here are your things."

Mayar dropped to her knees, opening the bag and sorting through it. "Where's my computer? My phone?" *My photo of Fatima?*

"Be thankful to Allah for what is there," Nimr replied. "I will see you in the morning." He spun around and left, locking the door from the outside.

Mayar pulled a black boot from her bag and flung it at the door. *Where is Graeme? Am I in a safe house or a prison cell?*

CHAPTER 49

Taryn and Montel walked across 14th Street to their meeting at Con Edison's corporate headquarters on the east side of Manhattan. She wore her only suit, a navy jacket and skirt with a high-necked parchment blouse, hair tied tightly back, for the big meeting. The sky was a canvas of Impressionist blue; the sun warmer than anticipated. A clammy dampness had invaded both armpits by the time they arrived at Irving Place.

"Nervous?" Montel asked as they rode up in the elevator.

"What makes you think that?" she replied, surreptitiously checking her blouse.

"It's your first time leading a dog and pony show for a Lightning Strike client."

"I've been in tougher situations. I'll be OK." Taryn tugged on the tote bag slung over her shoulder.

An administrative assistant was waiting at the fifth floor to lead them to the conference room. "You're the first to arrive," he said.

"Not too shabby for a public utility," Taryn commented, admiring the burnished wood table, leather chairs and mahogany panels on the walls.

"Leary said he was going to set us up with the brass."

"How long has he been Chief Security Officer here?"

"Ten years now, I think."

Taryn checked her watch. Almost two. The meeting should be starting in five minutes, but the room was still empty. She pulled out her laptop and five copies of her presentation.

"Why don't you give me a quick outline of your presentation before the Con Ed team arrives?" Montel asked.

"I'm going to start by showing a clip of the Kiev substation blowing up. That should get their attention. Then I'll review the particulars of the virus."

"Try not to be too technical here. Play to the audience."

"Got it. And I'll wrap up with the news from the weekend. The FBI has arrest warrants out for two highly competent hackers, Walecka and Tabak, who we strongly believe are targeting the Con Ed system."

"Do you really think ISIS would use a small-timer like Walecka?" Montel asked.

Before Taryn could answer, the door swung open and a trio of business-attired Con Ed executives marched in.

"Joe," Montel stood, reaching out to shake hands with his Army buddy, spindly tall with the baked complexion of an Irishman who had spent the weekend on the beach. A flurry of introductions circled the conference table. Leary's top deputy was Deborah Swenson, a trim blond, high cheekbones, light freckles, military bearing, pushing forty. Her assistant, Cheryl Montague, was not as blessed by the gods. A hulking woman with boyishly short dark hair and a flat snout that spread from cheek to cheek, she carried a bulky briefcase with apparent ease.

"Who else are we expecting?" Montel asked.

"This is it, I'm afraid," Leary said. "Tom Murphy can't make it. And, I'm not going to be able to stay. The CIO wants me in his office at two fifteen. Sorry."

"Really? Lightning Strike's put a lot of effort into this presentation. We wanted to give you a heads-up before the mayor's task force meeting on Friday," Montel replied, running a hand over his graying crew cut.

"Well, Deb sent out a memo to our senior staff this morning summarizing the situation," Leary offered weakly. "She'll brief me on anything new." His deputy's lips pursed into a victory smile.

Taryn's ego deflated as Leary closed the door.

"Now, I don't know about your relationship with Mayor Rosen," Swenson began, thrusting her head and shoulders forward, aiming directly at Taryn. "But, between us girls, if I'm going to get fucked, I want to get fucked - not run around and cock-teased for an entire weekend." She leaned back and interlocked her fingers on the table. "I trust that you'll pardon my language, Mr. Rice."

"Excuse me?" Taryn stammered. "I don't have *any* relationship with…"

"Well, my team at the SOC spent forty-eight hours straight humping away looking for your virus code," Swenson cut her off, nodding towards Montague who retrieved a copy of Taryn's original report and slid it across the table. "We went through all our Splunk data at the center and checked every device in the field and couldn't find shit. Our systems are clean and operating at one hundred percent efficiency."

"That's good news," Taryn replied, recovering. "But that doesn't mean an attack on Con Edison isn't imminent. You have to stay vigilant."

"Please don't tell me how to run my shop," Swenson snapped. "I was managing programmers before you were in high school."

"What Taryn means," Montel interrupted, "is that Lightning Strike can help you guard your systems from attack."

"Isn't that sweet. Lightning Strike will build us a custom virus shield. That's typical vendor talk. Create a problem then propose an expensive solution to solve it," Swenson retorted.

"You need protection," Taryn said.

"Con Edison is under attack every day, and we defend ourselves just fine. Now, you may be the kind of prissy bitch that makes her boyfriend wear a rubber just to fondle her titties, but I can't be bogged down by prophylactics. I have a business to run."

"Wow. That's a mouthful," Taryn replied. "I just hope you don't have to swallow those words - for all our sakes."

"I think we should be going," Montel said, standing. "I'm sure City Hall will be reassured when they hear about all the cyber security precautions you've taken here at Con Edison."

***

It was Monday, the day they were going to inject the virus. Mayar rose early, had a cup of tea and a leftover biscuit for breakfast, and read her Quran. Nimr would need her help, but the morning passed without a knock on the door.

At 12:30, Mayar heard the key in the latch. Nimr entered, followed by Graeme.

"Please come upstairs with us," he commanded.

Mayar tied a gray scarf tightly over her hair and stepped forward. Nimr looked her up and down, like he was inspecting a carcass of beef. "I'm pleased to see that you are attired as a proper Muslim woman," he said at last.

"I would prefer a burqa and niqab, like a true fighter," Mayar replied.

"The Al Khansaa brigade. Yes, that would be appropriate - in Raqqa. But here in New York, it would stand out. And I do not want you to stand out today."

In her brief moment outside of the apartment, Mayar reveled in the fresh air and sunlight. A small voice in the back of her mind urged her to run away, but she knew it was too late now. The trio quickly ascended the stairs to the main entrance of the brownstone. Nimr closed the door behind her and locked the bolt.

The living room looked like the fraternity house that she had visited once during her freshman year at Columbia. The furniture consisted of a worn sofa, scattered folding chairs, and a garage sale coffee table with a broken leg that was propped up on a stack of books. Brown socks and a tee shirt lay crumpled underneath it. A television hung precariously from the far wall.

Nimr led her into a barren space, probably designed as the dining room, and through a swinging door into the kitchen. A fighter, tall and surprisingly clean shaven, lounged by the sink, sipping from a mug. He wore a lightweight camo jacket with a pistol grip protruding from a side pocket.

"This is Mayar. Our comrade Ahmed's sister." Nimr provided the brief introduction. Ibrahim hardly looked up, his disdain palpable. Fortunately, Mayar's discomfort was overwhelmed by the excitement of seeing her laptop open on the kitchen table, an empty chair in front of it. The Jawbreaker interceptor device lay next to the laptop.

"We don't have much time," Nimr announced as he motioned for Mayar to sit. "Ibrahim, go upstairs and finish cleaning. The room needs to be perfect for tomorrow."

"Sweeping, mopping, painting. Woman's work," Ibrahim spit out.

"When you are finished, you can relieve Osama. He will be hungry," Nimr ordered, pretending not to hear.

"Has our guest behaved himself today?" Graeme asked after

Ibrahim had trudged past him.

"We gave him something to help him rest. When he wakes, he will need to rehearse his lines. He may need your assistance then," Nimr replied as he filled the tea kettle with water. He placed it on the stove and turned on the burner. "Did you purchase the camera?" he added.

Graeme nodded. "All set. We should rehearse tonight."

"Viktor is up on Telegram now," Mayar interjected, fingers flying over her keyboard. "I'm going to chat with him. OK?" she asked Nimr.

"Fully encrypted?

"Yes," Mayar replied.

"Then go ahead."

V: We are all set
M: Praise Allah!
V: You will load the Jawbreaker. It will inject the virus into the network. The virus will report back to your laptop every time it infects an A&B switch at a Con Ed power station.
M: An excellent plan
V: We also discovered another entry point
M: ???
V: An administrator disabled the security protocols to send a message to her lover last night
M: Fornicating infidels
V: Allah smiles on us
M: It could be a trap. A honeypot that diverts our attack off into a harmless sandbox.
V: We have two approaches. One will work.
M: Redundancy is always best.

After logging off with Viktor, Mayar tried to tap into Allison's computer to check on any new moves at City Hall, but the connection failed. She tried again – same result. *A network problem? Not likely.*

Mayar swiveled her head around the kitchen. Graeme had left, she heard the television newscast from the living room, and Nimr was reading the Times. She quickly logged on to her Amazon account, searched for *Goodnight Moon* and one-clicked it to Fatima, praying that her daughter's address hadn't changed since Ahmed's death. Hopefully, she would be able to deliver her next gift in person, but, if not....

No one noticed her little shopping spree. Mayar connected a USB cable to her laptop and loaded the virus on to the Jawbreaker. She stood, holding up the device. "Ready to launch."

"Let's go then. Osama will bring the car around. We don't have any time to waste today," Nimr commanded.

They dawdled in front of the television for a few minutes until a car horn bleated in the street. On Nimr's nod, Mayar walked towards the door, tightening her hijab on the way.

"You have scouted an injection point in Brooklyn?" Nimr asked as soon as they settled in the back seat.

"Yes," she replied, providing the address.

Nimr tapped the details into Google Maps on his phone. "Allah will guide us as well," he said, a trace of a smile crossing his lips for the first time that Mayar could remember.

***

Drained after her beat down at Con Edison, Taryn decided to take the night off. She went for a run along the river and picked up a salad and a six pack of Stella at the Korean grocer on the way home. Netflix would be her companion for the evening. Only halfway through the first season of *House of Cards*, she had some catching up to do.

Her phone rang before she was ten minutes into the second episode. Reluctantly, she uncurled from her sofa to answer it.

"Got a minute?" Karim James asked.

"Sure. My dance card is pretty empty tonight."

"I've been working with the FBI and the NSA cyber guys. They've got some neat toys."

"I should hope so." Taryn sipped her beer, wondering where the conversation was headed.

"We hacked into the dark forums where the credit card cheats hang out. Sure enough, we found some messages between Pizza Boy and Sully. They've been working together since last fall."

"No surprise. The government guys really are good if they can run a trace through that labyrinth."

"Agreed. But here is the surprise. We traced the Sully communications back to an IP address on the Columbia campus."

"Mayar Tabak?" Taryn hit the remote to turn off her television.

"Right on. Turns out that IP logs in regularly to a bank account in Somalia and requests a funds transfer to a Chase branch near campus."

"Mayar's operational funds."

"Sure looks like it. Probably paid Walecka in Bitcoins. She also connected several times to an IP at a residential address in Ramallah."

"Her brother's house?" Taryn sat on the side of her desk, gazing out the window at a Mercedes S550 trying to wedge into a parking spot on Bank Street.

"Not as far as we know. But, Mayar's been sending gifts from Amazon to that address on a regular basis for the past two years. We reviewed her account. Looks like they're for a very young girl. She just ordered a children's book a few hours ago," Karim replied.

"A niece? A cousin?"

"Nope."

"Does Ahmed have a girlfriend? Or maybe a wife?"

"The Israelis don't have any records of Ahmed's marriage. And, ISIS frowns on its fighters fathering children out of wedlock."

"So, who is the little girl?" Taryn asked.

***

After returning from Brooklyn, Mayar sat glued to her laptop in the kitchen, the aroma of roasting chicken and spices filling the room. Osama stirred a cauldron on the stove, his free hand nesting in his thick beard. She could feel his stare bore through her back like a knife. Nimr and Graeme wandered in, casting quick glances at Mayar's screen.

"Nothing yet," she said, answering the unspoken question.

"It's still early," Nimr replied. "The virus needs time to find its targets and launch."

Graeme started setting out silverware, glasses and plates on the table. Nimr reached into the refrigerator for a pitcher of juice.

"This is bullshit," Osama blurted. "All this for nothing." He swept his arm in a wide arc.

"Shut up," Nimr ordered, placing the pitcher on the table.

"We should never have relied on a woman. Her place is here at the stove. Or flat on her back in the bedroom," Osama continued to rant.

Nimr's hand slapped the table hard enough to rattle the pitcher and threaten a cascade of spilled juice. "You fool. This woman's place is right here - at her computer. Now, serve our meal."

Osama recoiled, a spoon clutched in his fist, but obeyed. The three men ate in silence. Mayar's stomach tossed, she could barely swallow. Graeme carried two plates of food upstairs when they were finished.

Mayar stood to clear the table, reaching for Osama's barren plate first. Nimr nodded his approval. Head bowed, she shuttled back to the sink three times, scraping the plates, rinsing them off, and loading the dishwasher. After the last trip, she peeked at her screen.

"Praise Allah!" Mayar shouted. The first infected switch had just reported in.

CHAPTER 50

After binge-watching until two AM, Taryn slept in on Tuesday morning. It was going to be a slow day anyway. Tossing on her robe, she made a pot of coffee and fired up her computer to scan the news. The first block of headlines was benign. Graft in Albany; airstrikes in Syria; construction delays on the Second Avenue subway project.

She paged down and nearly choked on her coffee.

Failed Israeli Raid in West Bank
Four Commandos Dead

Her vision blurred, but she forced herself to read on. Hamas had moved the captured Israeli soldier hours before the Israelis had attacked. The commandos walked into an ambush, bullets raining down from the rooftops of the apartment block in Ramallah. No other details were available now. *Eli??*

She logged into her Lightning Strike account. No emails or company news. Her telephone was a blank too. No texts or calls. *Keep calm. No news is good news.*

Taryn showered and dressed in a fog. Might as well go into the office. Eli was still a Lightning Strike employee. Bad news would reach there first.

***

The money only deepened his grief. Donal Brogan tapped his foot as he pretended to stare into the window of the D'Agostino's grocery on Greenwich Street. Within twenty-four hours of Professor Bierman's death, one million dollars had appeared in his offshore account, sender unknown. Michael and Timmy had earned it. Gerard too. *Not me. I was laying low.* His brothers should have waited for my call. But they were hot-heads. Always had been.

Where is the bitch that ran them down in Ithaca? She should have walked by here an hour ago. The papers had run a bullshit story about some FBI suit driving the murder car, but an IRA sympathizer on the force had told him the truth. *It's my fault. I should have been there.*

Now, all his brothers were dead, God bless their souls. Professor Bierman too - the Brogans always got their man.

There she was, walking out of Bank Street with her head down, tote bag bouncing on her shoulder. Ambling by without a glance at the traffic, she narrowly avoided a cruising taxi. Pulling his Yankee cap down, he followed ten paces behind, a pig-tailed middle school girl with a Taylor Swift backpack between them. *An eye for an eye.*

Donal unzipped the messenger pack swinging over his shoulder and slipped his hand inside feeling for the familiar grip of his Sig. Greenwich Street was much less crowded than he had expected; Booker's delay meant that she'd missed the morning rush hour crush.

He had scouted a cut-through a half block ahead that would serve as his escape route. Two shots with his silenced pistol, and he would disappear before anyone could identify him.

He checked his six one more time. A young woman pushing a stroller, a businessman sipping from a Starbucks cup, a biker speeding uptown. No problems there. Booker was just passing the cut-through, head still bowed, hands bunched in her pockets, oblivious to the world. He would be in position in a few more steps.

Donal veered to the side to set up the angle for his shots. The opening to the cut-through yawned in front of him.

"John O'Reilly! What a pleasant surprise to see you!" A familiar female voice sang out in a County Tyrone brogue. He spun around.

A wisp of a woman, barely five feet tall, Siobhan Callaghan sprinted the final steps to his side. Before he could react, she wrapped her arms around him in a fierce embrace, pinning the messenger bag to his hip.

"Or should I call you Donal Brogan?" she whispered, looking up into his eyes. The soft features of her densely-freckled face scrunched in anguish.

"How in the name of Christ?" he replied, his trigger finger slipping off the pistol.

"Do you think I'm daft? You know my family has relations in County Down. I've done my homework on the man I plan to marry." She released her grip, taking a half step back, but still clung to his right arm. "I called the warehouse this morning. When they said you hadn't shown up for work, I knew you were up to no good."

Siobhan's plan pummeled Donal's brain, cracking the fortress of concentration needed to complete his mission. They'd met in a pub the night after he'd arrived in the States. She moved in a month later. Good times. More love and laughter than he deserved. Siobhan obviously thought they had a future together.

A week ago, I probably believed the fairytale too. One more job, then settle down. Raise a family. Live out my life as John O'Reilly.

"Get out of my way! Go home," he commanded, desperately trying to get back on track. *The ghosts of my kin are calling for revenge.*

Siobhan swiped away a tear. "I just thank the Lord I got here in time."

Donal raised the back of his hand, as if to slap her.

"Go ahead. Hit me," she challenged. "Get your anger out. It might save your life. And hers." Siobhan's gaze drifted up Greenwich Street as Taryn faded into the distance. A uniformed cop emerged from a bodega, hesitated for a second, and then started to stroll in their direction.

Donal dropped his hand. "I have obligations. Debts to repay."

"We'll have a family of our own. All boys. We can name them Michael, Gerard and Tim."

"I can't…"

"Let's go home," she said, tugging him towards the subway.

Donal glanced at the heavens before shuffling underground. *I won't forget you.*

***

Lightning Strike's office was humming as usual. Breaking out of her bubble, Taryn realized that only a handful of people in the New York office even knew Eli Stern, and even fewer knew that he was now back on duty, an undercover Duvdevan operative in the West Bank. She plopped down at her desk, checking email, the *Times*, and the *Jerusalem Post*. Still no names or news. She skimmed the Kiev and Con Ed files one more time, searching for any clues that she might have missed. Or maybe Swenson was right. There was no attack in the works – at least right now.

Montel wandered over, knocking on the outside of her cubicle. "Look at this," he said, handing over a thin file. "Citibank discovered another intrusion in Long Island City. Has the same signature as several others. I just sent you an attachment with all the details."

"Trying to keep me away from Con Edison, huh?" Taryn asked.

Montel laughed. "You and Ms. Swenson didn't exactly see eye to eye."

"She certainly let me know it too."

"Typical Army brat. A woman's got to be pretty tough to survive in that jungle."

"I'll get started on this today," Taryn replied, scanning the Citibank paperwork. *Right after I check on Eli.* She dialed Shahar in Tel Aviv, letting the phone ring ten times. No news is good news, she told herself one more time.

***

Mayar sat at the kitchen table all morning, her optimism growing as infected switches continued to log in. The other members of the ISIA cell shuttled in and out as they prepared for the big day.

"Where are we?" Nimr asked, unloading a carton of groceries on the counter.

"Thirty-two," Mayar beamed. "Halfway home."

"We know from the public docs that Con Ed has sixty-one substations, but do we know how many switches are in the network?"

"Not exactly. But Viktor programmed the virus to check that a switch was directly connected to a substation before infecting it," she replied, spinning around in her seat. "We may get a few extras, but we think that sixty-one is our winning number."

Nimr grunted his approval as he stacked packages of chicken breasts in the fridge. He pointed Ibrahim, lugging two cases of bottled water, to a corner location. Even the surly fighter sneaked a peek at Mayar's screen as he waddled by.

"What if we don't get all sixty-one?" Ibrahim asked, once the water was set into place.

"We will," Mayar replied confidently.

"It really doesn't matter," Nimr explained. "We just need to strike fear into the Americans that we have the capacity and the will to black out their largest city."

"We will demonstrate our will this afternoon," Ibrahim spit out as he headed back to the front of the house.

Mayar ducked her head back towards her screen. She wasn't privy to the entire plan, at least not yet, but she was sure that it involved Pizza Boy.

Ibrahim returned shortly with another load of bottled water. "Two more to go," he intoned as he turned to leave.

"When you are finished, go upstairs and finish the preparations," Nimr commanded.

"Where's Graeme?" Mayar got up the courage to ask as soon as Ibrahim had departed.

"Helping the infidel prepare his confession. He's just a common thug after all."

"We should ship him to Raqqa then. He would fit in well with our fighters there," she quipped.

"Watch your words, woman," Nimr shot back.

"Motherfucker!" A scream, emanating from upstairs, pierced the air. Nimr pretended not to notice.

"When he is finished, Graeme will read his Quran and pray. He must steel himself for his task this afternoon."

"We will be doing the infidels a favor," Mayar backed down.

Nimr stared hard at her for several seconds. "You are a good soldier," he replied at last. He pointed to the closet that served as their pantry. "Please review our supplies and let me know if we're short on any staples. The grocery stores will be out of stock of everything by morning."

***

Taryn plugged away at the Citibank file well into the afternoon, munching on an apple at her desk for lunch. She didn't notice the incoming call on her office line until the third ring. Her hand palpitated as she reached for the phone.

"Eli's got a few bruises, but he's OK," Shahar skipped right to the point.

"Thank god," Taryn exclaimed, exhaling deeply. "Where is he?" No reply. "Sorry, I know I shouldn't have asked," she added hastily.

"You know we'll never leave one of our soldiers in enemy hands."

"I understand. Thank you for calling."

"I'll get a message to Eli that you're thinking of him."

Taryn hadn't realized how much she cared for Eli until that moment. The Citibank code waltzed on her screen for the next thirty minutes. Finally, she gave up trying to concentrate and took a stroll around the office.

She had progressed about ten steps when a low rumble began to swell, like a wave far out in the ocean. It quickly gathered force as Lightning Strikers jumped up from their desks, reaching tidal wave proportions as they poured into the main conference room to stare at the screen overhead, now showing a video feed from an unknown source.

"Holy shit!"

"Fucking ISIS - right here in New York City!"

Snapped out of her happy place, Taryn was swept along by the crush of her associates. She stared at the giant television monitor in shock.

A hooded man dressed in black jeans and sweatshirt, only his eyes visible, stood alone apparently reading from a prompter in front of the black ISIS flag taped to an exposed brick wall:

"I repeat, the cyber warriors of the Islamic State in America have successfully penetrated the command and control system of the New York City electrical grid, operated by Consolidated Edison. We are prepared to shut down all electrical service in the five boroughs at five PM tomorrow Eastern Daylight Time unless our demand for a ten-billion-dollar payment is met."

Wire instructions to a bank in Somalia scrolled across the bottom of the video like ESPN reporting scores from distant games. The video shifted to footage of Kiev, first panning over a well-lit city at night, then zeroing in on the downtown district as the lights sputtered then flared out. It concluded with a shot of a smoking mammoth power transformer. Two Lightning Strikers stared at Taryn, obviously aware of her work at Con Ed.

"We tried to warn them," she mouthed, but her reply was lost in the confusion as the ISIS leader continued:

"If you doubt our capabilities, talk to the people of Kiev. The cyber sword of Islam cut their power three weeks ago and they are still in the dark. Our sword is now in place in every corner of New York City, ready to slice your lifeline if the ransom is not delivered to our account tomorrow. This payment pales compared to the cost of a complete and total blackout in the largest city in the United States."

"How did we infiltrate your defenses? One of your own – Dennis Walecka, a money-hungry infidel - opened the gates for us."

On cue, four hooded militants marched into the room, dragging a bound prisoner in an orange jumpsuit. A purpling welt sprouted across Walecka's right cheek; his left eye was swollen shut. No one could tear away from the screen. A clip of Walecka sitting unfettered in front of the ISIS flag now ran. Over the next five minutes, he stumbled through an explanation of how he hacked Con Edison, ultimately manning the Jawbreaker that launched the virus.

Montel waded quickly through the crowd to reach Taryn. "This is not your fault," he whispered.

"Unfortunately, this whore could not contain his greed. He tried to extort even more money from our people and will now pay the price. Our justice is quick and unmerciful," the leader exclaimed as two of his fighters forced the captive to his knees and pinned him there. The fourth fighter slipped out of view, while the fifth, her profile revealing the hips of a woman, seemed to shrink back against the far wall.

The leader stepped out of the picture as the camera zoomed in on Walecka, a goofy grin plastered to his face. "The sword of The Prophet strikes down the infidel," the leader commanded.

The missing fighter stepped back into the picture and displayed his scimitar. He gripped Walecka by his hair, forcing his head up towards the camera. Taryn's eyes remained fixed on the screen, staring at Walecka's face for what she knew would be the last time. *No one deserves to die like this.* A woman in front of her cried out, burying her face in her hands. A man turned and sprinted towards the bathroom as the blade hacked downward.

·

CHAPTER 51

"The camera is off now," Nimr said stepping out from behind the tripod, and removing his hood. His four soldiers stood motionless, staring at the carnage splashed over the rubber sheet and hardwood floor. "We must clean up," he commanded. "There are mops and trash bags in the closet."

With her adrenaline dissipated, Mayar's arms felt as if they were weighted down with lead. She forced herself to shuffle her right foot forward. *Too late to question now. We must move ahead.* Stepping around the severed head, she led the way. Graeme dropped his sword and followed. The others fell in line as well.

The sunlight had faded by the time they finished. Nimr rolled out a frizzled rug. "It is time for evening prayers," he said. All five fighters prostrated themselves and recited the familiar words. Osama and Ibrahim rose first. They carted the black bags down the stairs, while Graeme retreated to his room.

Alone with Nimr, Mayar couldn't stop herself from asking, "Will the execution help our cause? Will it encourage the infidels to meet our ransom demand?"

When he ignored her, she pressed, "Or was it just for show? To prove our manhood to the world?"

"You performed admirably today, but don't press your luck," Nimr snapped.

"Our state will never succeed unless our women can play an equal role. We can use the ransom money to build schools and…"

"Lose your schoolgirl fantasies," he hissed. "The Americans will never pay a ransom. They will hunt us down like rabid dogs."

"What? Then why…"

"We needed to strike fear into the hearts of the infidels. They now feel the power of the Prophet and know that the apocalypse can destroy their corrupt civilization."

"And that is all? There must be…"

Nimr whipped Mayar across the cheek with the back of his hand. "Wake up woman. The deed is done. There is no turning back now."

Mayar reeled from the blow. She balled her fingers into fists at her side, but willed herself to remain silent. *I will not abandon Fatima to a life of broken dreams and misery.*

"I'm hungry," Nimr said, his anger vanishing. He started down the stairs. "Let's eat something. And check the count."

"Forty-eight," she mumbled when they reached the kitchen.

***

"What the fuck?" Bernie Rosen shouted into his speakerphone as soon as the ISIS video signed off. In that instant, he understood that his city had changed forever. He forced himself to formulate an action checklist, dragging his horror at the gruesome decapitation to the back of his brain. "Can ISIS do that?"

"Blackmail us?" Serena Thomas replied.

"No. Blackout New York City. The NSA said that only the Chinese and the Russians had that kind of cyber capability. Not the fucking Arabs." *Unless they were working together. Maybe Professor Bierman wasn't so crazy after all.*

"I'm on the other line with Murphy from Con Ed right now. I think you should talk to him yourself."

"Not yet. I need you to set up a meeting with all our first responders. We need to lock down the city. Then I want you to draft a press release. Let the people know that we mourn the loss of Mr. Walecka and are doing everything in our power to track down the perpetrators."

"What about the ransom demand?"

"No fucking way."

"Got it."

"Now, put Murphy through." Rosen stood up and stared out the window, the streets already churning with anxiety. "Tom, tell me this threat to the grid is all bullshit," he said when the call from the Con Ed exec came through.

"Mayor Rosen, the Con Edison power grid is safe and secure. We took our entire network apart this past weekend and couldn't find a single trace of the malware that the terrorist was talking about."

Rosen shoulders sagged in relief. "You're sure?"

"I just had a face to face with Joe Leary, our chief security officer. He personally organized the review. His top deputy was in the ops center 24/7 on Saturday and Sunday. I have her report right here in front of me."

"You're saying that terrorist in the video was full of shit?"

"I don't know what he's full of, sir."

Rosen paced back towards the window. "I'd like to believe you, but I need another opinion. Do you know Lightning Strike? Taryn Booker?" *She was close to Bierman.*

"Yes, sir. I believe she had a meeting with our IT people yesterday."

"And?"

"She thought Con Ed might be under attack."

"But your people disagreed?"

"Like I said, our IT staff took the entire network apart and couldn't find any trace of the malware that Booker presented."

"Let's get Lightning Strike on a call then," Rosen ordered. "Immediately."

Before the telephone line was even cold, Katherine Whitworth appeared at the door, her stoic composure unfazed by the brewing storm. "I have the Governor *and* the Secretary of Homeland Security on hold. Who would you like to talk to first?" Rosen just rolled his eyes in reply. "The commissioner of police and a general with the US Cyber Command also called," she added, maintaining her voice on an even keel.

***

"Into my office. Now," Montel finished his command before his feet were planted inside Taryn's cubicle. He pivoted sharply, jerking his thumb in a signal for Taryn to follow. Taryn ripped her eyes from the Kiev virus gnawing her screen and leapt to her feet.

Montel assumed a parade position behind his desk while motioning for Taryn to take a seat on the other side. He banged down on the speakerphone button, announcing, "We're both here sir. I can also conference in our staff in Tel Aviv if you want."

"Ms. Booker, this is Mayor Rosen. We've crossed paths, but I don't believe we've ever met."

"No, sir," Taryn replied.

"Tom Murphy and Joe Leary from Con Ed are on the line. Representatives from the NSA, the Army Cyber Command and the FBI too."

"Got it."

"The Con Ed team is telling me that they scrubbed their systems this past weekend and that they are secure. Do you agree with that assessment?"

"I believe that statement is accurate as of Sunday night, sir," Taryn said.

"But, it is now Tuesday evening. Could the situation have changed significantly?" the mayor questioned. Montel nodded his head, signaling Taryn to give her honest opinion.

"It is a definite possibility," she replied, fidgeting in her seat.

"We suggested that Con Ed maintain ongoing vigilance, but Mr. Leary's deputy believed that effort would harm the performance of their systems," Montel interjected.

"Murphy here. Con Ed fights hackers every day. We never let our guard down."

"You don't run across hackers this good every day. They've been preparing this attack for years. We believe that they adapted the Stuxnet virus that was originally designed by the US and Israeli military to sabotage Iran's nuclear plant - which was also heavily defended," Taryn said.

"Who's they? Do you believe the ISIS terrorists had technical assistance?" Rosen asked.

"Yes." Taryn replied. "The ISIS terrorists in the video probably injected the virus into the grid, but we believe that the virus itself was actually designed by the Russians who used the attack on Kiev as a test drive."

"Russia? That's bullshit," Murphy exploded. "What proof do you have?"

"Cyber Command here. The true source of a cyberattack is almost impossible to prove. There's no videotape or fingerprints for evidence. Soldiers aren't storming the beaches; planes aren't flying overhead. All we know is an attack on a complex system, like the New York electrical grid, requires an incredible level of sophistication, coordination and pure manpower that only a handful of nation-states can provide."

"Unless we can follow the money," the FBI guy interjected. "That's the only way to get hard proof."

"That's what my mentor, Professor Bierman, was trying to do before his assassination," Taryn added, the steel in her voice apparent.

"But this is Manhattan, not Kiev. Our systems were perfectly clean on Sunday night," Murphy persisted.

"Why don't you check your systems again?" NSA asked. "Let's see if the Kiev code is present or not."

"How long would that take?" Rosen's turn.

"We can't review every line of code in every switch by the deadline, but we've already started sampling," Leary replied.

"Let's say this Stux-monster has penetrated New York, what kind of damage could we expect?" the mayor again.

"Worst case?" NSA asked.

"Worst case."

"New York City could be without any power for at least six months, maybe longer," NSA said solemnly.

"That's a real longshot," Murphy declared, but the quiver in his voice betrayed him. "Let's not panic. Leary's people should have the results back from their tests in a few hours."

"But, even if they find the virus, we may need weeks to disarm it completely," Taryn piped in. "We've only seen the tip of the iceberg. We're going to have to dig to find where the virus buried its payload, exactly what processes it's attacking, and if it has set up any alternative penetration vectors."

"What if the FBI catches the bastards tonight?" Murphy searched for the winning lottery ticket.

"I'm not sure that changes anything. I doubt the ISIS team here in New York could shut down the virus even if they wanted to," Taryn replied.

"We can't leave any stone unturned or the transformers will be at risk. If they blow up, like in Kiev, it could take a year to replace them," the FBI concluded.

***

Osama was the bomb maker. He stacked the five vests on the kitchen table alongside electrical wires, nine volt batteries and a hatbox of metal pellets. The combustible ingredients, including bleach and nail polish remover, were organized on the counter next to the sink. He donned rubber gloves and began to mix the death brew.

Mayar sat alone at the table; everyone else had left the room as soon as Osama set up shop. A message from Viktor interrupted her morbid fascination.

V: Allison Gold is in police custody
Viktor knows everything.
M: I feared as much.
V: I have destroyed your RAT so there will be no connection to us
M: Praise Allah
V: You have done well. Your mission is almost complete
M: The ransom?
V: Money is not important. We fight for the glory of Allah
Easy for you to say. Whoever you are. I'm fighting for the girls of Allah. And they need money to build schools.
M: Praise Allah
V: Do not waver now
Don't worry. I won't.

She unplugged her laptop, lifted it into her arms, and carried it through the vacant dining room.

"Where do you think you're going?" Nimr asked. He was sitting on the couch in the living room, poring over a map of Manhattan with Graeme.

"To my room. I can't work with Osama in the kitchen."

Nimr scratched his chin. "OK," he decided at last. "I'll send Graeme down in a few minutes to see if you need any assistance."

Her plan was a long shot, but it was her only hope. She rushed into the basement studio and fumbled through the bag of clothes that Nimr had delivered from her room at Columbia. Whenever she went to the Columbia library, she stashed a zip drive in a pocket somewhere just in case. She had worn her jeans the other day.

Mayar tossed two shirts out on the floor before she grasped the denim fabric. Her fingers dug into one front pocket, then the other. Empty. The rear pocket held the prize. She yanked it out and flopped down on the floor to open her laptop. Footfalls shuffled upstairs. *Please Allah, give me five minutes.*

Mayar copied the file with the current list of infected substations. Still no one at the door. She added the blueprint of the virus design that Viktor had shared with her, as well her own notes. At this late stage, nothing could save New York City from a blackout; but, her little gift could significantly shorten the time needed to recover.

Now Mayar had to get word to the one person who could help to implement her plan. Viktor and Nimr would undoubtedly monitor all emails so she had to improvise a more roundabout approach. She called up the virus code on her screen and inserted an Easter egg. The next time an infected sub-station logged in, her computer would slip her message into the return traffic. The NSA, the FBI, the CIA, DHS - someone somewhere would discover the virus code in the next few hours - and could play the postman. It was her only chance.

An urgent knock interrupted her.

"Come in," she called, ejecting the drive and pocketing it.

"Osama is finished," Graeme said as he entered, closing the door.

"Good. I need to go back upstairs," Mayar replied popping to her feet. She looked past Graeme, pleased to see that he was alone. "But I was hoping that we could talk for a little while first," she added, reaching for his hand.

He interlocked their fingers and closed his eyes. "I'd like that."

"This afternoon. You did what had to be done."

"Yes. Thank you. It was Allah's will." Graeme squeezed his eyes shut; his shoulders wobbled like a volcano bubbled beneath them. "I've never…"

"You don't have to explain," Mayar soothed, drawing him into her embrace.

"Allah saved my life. I'd be nothing without Him." Graeme pulled back to search Mayar's eyes, keeping her hands securely in his grasp. "I grew up in Gloucester, just north of Boston. My dad was a fisherman, chasing cod in the North Banks. He went overboard in a storm when I was five. They never found his body. My mom couldn't handle it. She started drinking more. And popping pills. Oxy. One night she boiled water, trying to cook dinner. I was pushing a truck on the kitchen floor. The water spilled…" Graeme touched the strawberry mark on his cheek.

"She called an ambulance. They knew the way. It wasn't the first accident in our house. My grandparents took me in, but they both passed on when I was twelve. I shuttled around foster homes till I was eighteen. Learned to defend myself. Didn't have much choice sometimes. I've been on my own now for four years."

"Where is your mother now?"

Graeme shrugged. "Somewhere out West, I think. She wanted to start a new life. Without me."

"I haven't spoken to my mother in years either," Mayar commiserated. "How did you find Allah?" she asked.

"Online. Through Faisal."

"Who?"

"I was searching for clues as to why all this shit happened to me. There had to be a reason. Faisal reached out on Twitter at first, then Skype. He talked to me for hours, explaining the ways of Islam. It was hard for me to believe in God, any God, for a long time, but something about Allah just felt right. Faisal asked me to download the Islamic Hub app, so I could receive a hadith message every day."

"The words of The Prophet are very comforting," Mayar soothed.

"Faisal helped me learn the Quran. He instructed me in my daily prayers and sent me a DVD and several books so I could learn Arabic too."

"Where does Faisal live?"

"In Syria, I think. He introduced me to more of his friends online. They were fighters, revolutionaries building a new country. They talked to me every night. They wanted *me* to help them."

"Where does Nimr come in?"

"Two years ago, I asked Faisal about a mosque in Boston where I could convert to Islam and worship. He said that there was no need to go to a local mosque. I could post my Shahada online. He would be my first witness. Abu Mosa is my Muslim name."

"Abu Mosa. That is a beautiful name. And how did you meet Nimr?"

"Nimr reached out to me. He would only communicate online for the first year. Until he could trust me."

"Now you are his most trusted lieutenant. We are jihadists together, but I must go upstairs now. I still have work to do." Mayar stood on her toes and kissed Graeme's cheek, then quickly stepped away.

Graeme followed her. Nimr was still sitting in the living room when they walked in.

"You were downstairs a long time," he commented to Graeme.

"We read the Quran together," Graeme replied.

"And you? Why are you up here so late?" Nimr stood, pointing to Mayar, ready to whisk her back downstairs.

"I want to check the count again. And the Wi-Fi sucks in the basement," she said.

Nimr sniffed at her choice of language, but didn't argue. He followed Mayar into the kitchen. Osama had cleaned up meticulously. No sign of his labor was evident.

She opened the laptop, pointing to the Wi-Fi icon, now fully engaged. Nimr nodded his approval to proceed.

"Fifty-four," Mayar proclaimed, praying silently that her missive was on its way.

***

Mayor Rosen addressed his constituents at ten that evening. The networks carried the speech nationwide, interrupting all regular programming. Taryn watched from the Lightning Strike conference room with Montel and the entire staff. She noticed two blue sleeping bags and a red cooler tucked into the corner. Some of her co-workers were preparing to hunker down and work as long as needed.

Sitting behind his desk at City Hall, crisply suited and jut jawed, Rosen focused straight ahead: "My fellow New Yorkers, an hour ago, with great regret, I asked the Governor of our state to request the President of the United States to declare a state of emergency in New York City under the Stafford Disaster Relief and Emergency Assistance Act. The President just informed me that he has granted this request, effective immediately.

Con Edison, the distributor of electricity to much of our city, has uncovered multiple traces of the computer virus that the terrorist representing the Islamic State alluded to in his video message this afternoon. The security forces of the city, state and federal government will be working around the clock to disarm this cyber weapon, but, we are not certain that we will be able to do so by the deadline set at five PM tomorrow.

At this time, we do not know what, if any, damage the cyber weapon may cause, how widespread any damage might be, or how long any disruption of service might last. We do know that our great city will never pay a penny of ransom to anyone at any time. We will devote every law enforcement resource at our command to hunt down these terrorists and bring them to justice.

I am confident that New York's finest, our police and fire department, will protect our safety, and the safety of our property, during this difficult time. My administration has secured commitments from our neighbors and corporate partners to deliver food, water and sanitation to those who may be in need. Nevertheless, because of the significant uncertainties resulting from any disruption of electrical service, I ask all New Yorkers to stay close to home tomorrow and prepare to evacuate if necessary. We will provide more details as soon as they become available.   Although we now find ourselves in a new era of cyber warfare, our traditional values of freedom and liberty for all shall prevail. New Yorkers must unite to help one another and defeat our common foes. God bless America. God bless New York City. Thank you."

The network commentator immediately cut in, dissecting the mayor's speech. He highlighted all that the municipal officials did not know about the threat as well as the potential for enormous damages both to physical plant and to the morale and global reputation of New York. What would happen to the airports? Bridges? Tunnels? Banks? Subways? Water supply? Stock exchanges? Cities around the globe had invested heavily in smart infrastructure but were now just learning their vulnerability to cyber-attacks.

A photo of Mayar Tabak flashed. A Columbia engineering student and a possible suspect. A hotline number scrolled by. The commentator intoned that a new era of cyber-terrorism had begun.

"The mayor didn't even mention that poor guy who got his head chopped off," a Lightning Striker behind Taryn tossed out.

"He probably confirmed that Walecka was a crook," she retorted.

The network segued to footage of the blackout in New York City in 1977: buildings on fire, looters wheeling shopping carts of stolen goods through the streets, shop owners standing guard with guns at the ready.

"Not a pretty sight," Taryn said.

"This blackout's not going to be a surprise though. I bet the mayor will have the national guard on standby to protect the city," Montel replied. He banged on the conference room table to get his staff's attention. "Alright, everyone back to work. We're going to go through our threat database and see if we can find any successful antidotes for the malware. Taryn will coordinate with our team in Tel Aviv."

***

Mayar watched the mayor's speech from the couch along with her four fellow jihadists, smiles all around until her photograph filled the screen. She gasped and shot forward from her seat.

Nimr reached out to steady her. "It is the price of our success," he soothed. "One day the Americans will know all our names."

"What if her computer virus doesn't even work?" Ibrahim sulked, not even trying to conceal his jealousy of his compatriot's moment of infamy.

"It doesn't matter. We've already achieved our objective," Nimr replied pointing to the television. "The infidels are afraid."

The cameras swept around the city, showing New Yorkers crowding grocery stores, boarding shop windows, and lining up their cars outside gas stations.

"Tomorrow, panic will set in. Guns and generators will only be available on the black market. Vigilante groups will form. Soldiers will patrol the streets. The airports and train stations will be mobbed. It will be a glorious day," Nimr added.

"When do we implement the next phase of our attack?" Osama asked. Nimr shot him a shut your mouth glance.

"I'll go check the count," Mayar said, hopping off the sofa. Graeme followed her into the kitchen.

"Still fifty-four," she glummed, scrolling quickly through the code as Graeme looked over her shoulder. *Even more disappointing - no reply to my message.*

CHAPTER 52

The caravan of black Escalades pulled into Gracie Mansion at 2:14 AM. Every government cyberspook was chasing down the virus. Every cop had Mayar Tabak's photograph on their tablet and was searching for a yellow taxi with a license plate ending in 3S. The fire department was calling in all hands. Social services officials were preparing their fallback plans for life without electricity. Mayor Rosen had participated in a whirlwind of meetings but needed to crash for a few hours. The day ahead would be even worse.

He was surprised to see the light on upstairs in the master bedroom. Dressed in bathrobe and slippers, Jackie was on the phone, splicing a smattering of French into her conversation. She smiled wanly and held up one finger. With pride, he watched her for five minutes before retiring to the guest room.

Jackie padded in just as he climbed into the four-poster bed. "That was the assistant to the chairman of Nestle in Switzerland," she explained.

"Chocolate?" Bernie asked, stifling a yawn.

"No. Water. They'll truck in one million extra bottles if the blackout lasts more than four days."

"Good work. The details are mind-boggling, aren't they?"

"You're doing the best you can," Jackie replied, pacing over to the window.

"Wish the terrorists had waited two more days," he gallows-chuckled. "We would have at least had the first meeting of the task force. We could have hashed out some of the issues."

"How did Taryn Booker get on the task force?" Jackie asked, turning around to face him.

"I invited her," Bernie replied as he plumped up his pillow. "I knew you wouldn't be thrilled, but I wanted the best cyberminds in the city. Turns out she warned Con Ed about the attack last week, but they couldn't find the virus."

"Are you sure you can trust her?"

"Booker's working as hard as anyone to save our city." He tucked the comforter around his hips. "Her patriotism trumps any personal grudges – at least right now," he added.

Jackie nodded, sitting down on the bed as Bernie rolled to his side. "I've spoken with food banks in Boston, Philadelphia and Washington. They're going to organize drives to help us out for as long as necessary," she said.

"How are our sons holding up?" Bernie asked, his voice slurring in exhaustion.

"They're coming home tomorrow. They want to help too," she replied, lifting the comforter and slipping between the sheets. "We'll ride this out together. Now get some rest." She curled her arm over her husband's shoulders.

***

The ring of her office phone lured Taryn back to consciousness. She shook off the cobwebs and pushed up from her desk, spilling the last drops from a can of Red Bull on her lap. *Shit! How could I fall asleep?* She hurriedly righted the now empty can and looked out the window. Still dark outside. The lines of code were marching across her screen like soldiers on an endless parade.

The ring of the phone was relentless. The caller ID read Fort Meade, Maryland.

"This is Taryn," she answered.

"Taryn Booker? Lightning Strike?" A starched female voice inquired. Impressively authoritative at three in the morning.

"Yeah, that's me."

"This is US Cyber Command. We just found a message for you. From Mayar Tabak. She wants to meet you at three o'clock this afternoon on a bench on Riverside Drive. Alone."

Taryn's farewell to Professor Bierman would have to wait until the memorial next month. She was sure he would understand.

***

"I thought you'd want some breakfast," Katherine Whitworth said, placing a tray with a mug of black coffee and a pumpernickel bagel plastered with cream cheese on the mayor's desk.

"Thanks," Rosen replied, taking a hearty bite as he swiveled his chair to look out the window. The sepia half-light of dawn bathed the downtown skyline. Media trucks huddled like a herd of nervous cattle in the plaza poised to stampede at any shred of news.

"I think you need to see this," Serena Thomas huffed, barging into the office, her suit crumpled as if she had slept in it. She handed him the morning edition of the *Daily News*. "You're not going to like it."

CITY HALL HACKED
MAYOR'S INTERN AIDS TERRORISTS

"What the fuck?" Rosen blurted, skimming quickly past the headline to the body of the story.

"Allison Gold," Thomas replied.

"I thought we had that under wraps."

"Someone must have leaked the story. We're going to have to brief the press this morning."

"The District Attorney's on the line," Whitworth announced, poking her head back into the office.

Rosen immediately stabbed the button on his speakerphone. "We don't need this finger-pointing shit right now."

"I know," the DA replied. "The Allison Gold leak didn't come from my office. We're working with the FBI on another angle right now. I thought you'd want to hear about it first."

"Shoot."

"Deborah Swenson. She's a top dog in Con Ed's IT department. The FBI discovered that she took the security down on her computer to send some private messages on Sunday night. They're pretty sure that's how the virus entered the network."

"Messages to ISIS?" Rosen asked, pushing the remainder of his breakfast away.

"No. The FBI traced the messages to another Con Ed exec. A married guy. Some photos too. They were pretty explicit."

"Naked photos?"

"You got it. It appears she wanted to show off her new Brazilian wax."

"Un-fucking-believable."

"We're going to bring her in for questioning today. Any suggestions?"

"Parade her ass in front of the TV cameras - while they're still working," Rosen replied.

***

"We're up to fifty-eight," Mayar announced, sitting at the kitchen table.

"Only three more to go," Graeme added. "With eight hours until the deadline. Cheers!"

She nodded her appreciation but kept her eyes locked onto the screen, scanning the virus code as it scrolled by. *The meeting is on!* As she had specified, the response to her message was buried in a seemingly meaningless string of text.

"Is everything OK?" Nimr asked, stepping away from the sink. "You look surprised."

"No. I mean yes. Mayar spun her head around. "Our attack appears all set to strike the power stations as planned."

"Excellent. You should eat something then and rest. We will be busy tonight."

She forced herself to down a cup of tea and a half bowl of oatmeal, although it settled like cement in the pit of her stomach.

"I'm going downstairs. To pray," she said, pushing back.

Nimr nodded his consent. He smiled as he spread the morning papers on the table and scanned the headlines.

***

Michael. Gerard. Tim. Each slipped in turn into the burning fires of hell. While he stood, back turned, attention focused on a football match on a giant television screen.

Donal snapped awake, sweat lathered across his torso. He tossed off the thin sheet and sat up. Siobhan was sleeping soundly,

289

lassoed around a pillow, an opaque pink night shirt swamping her slender body. He stood, padding noiselessly to the bathroom.

"Donal?" Siobhan called out before he could finish dressing.

"Forget that name," he commanded. "And go back to sleep."

"Where are you going? It's early."

He could hear her rustling to her feet. He zipped his jeans and stepped out of the bathroom, still bare-chested.

"Go back to sleep," he repeated, pushing past her to reach his dresser.

"I'm not going anywhere until I know what you're up to."

"You don't want to know what I'm up to," Donal replied, pulling a black t-shirt over his head.

"You can't go back there." Siobhan reached for his arm. "Please."

Donal slapped her face, sending her sprawling across the bed. "I can and I will. Don't try to stop me again, woman."

Anger flared in Siobhan's freckled cheeks as she turned towards him. "You're going to throw your life away? For what?"

"What life is there for a man who cowered at home while his brothers died?"

"Our life. We can start over. Build a future together."

"We have no future," he hissed. "I'm Donal Brogan, not John O'Reilly. I turned from my brothers once. I won't do it again."

Siobhan stabbed her finger at his face. "You're a fool then. You're going to follow your brothers to hell."

"Then hell is where I'm going." She was right. He would kill Taryn Booker today to avenge Michael and Tim. Jim Mangano would be next, if he ever got out of the hospital.

Her eyes turned cold. "I won't let you do it. I'll call the police." Siobhan reached for the phone on her night stand.

Donal leapt over their bed, locking her wrist in his grip, slapping her again and again. The phone slid across the floor. Blood oozed from Siobhan's lip. He tossed her backwards, but she bounced right to her knees.

"You're a cold-blooded murderer! A thug! A common criminal!" She spat a scarlet trail onto the white sheets.

Donal clenched Siobhan's shoulders and wrestled her down into a nest of pillows. He reached for a plump one, her initials embroidered on the flap, clamping it down over her face. Siobhan twisted, coughed, kicked, but Donal wouldn't relent. He was a Brogan again, an unstoppable force. The humble farmhouse in County Down flashed in his vision, his family gathered around the dinner table. He heard a final gag before Siobhan's body went limp.

Donal's shoulders sagged. His fingers relaxed. His breathing slowed. *I'm dead now too.*

***

Taryn returned to her apartment and crashed for two hours, but she was too wound up to sleep. She showered and dressed as instructed: loose, comfortable, casual clothes - jeans, cherry red polo, running shoes.

She sat down at her desk, gazing at the greenery fluttering in the breeze outside the window. It was already a sunny, warm spring day. Perfect weather to meet with a jihadist.

Ten minutes after she had hung up with Fort Meade, the FBI had called. A face-to-face meeting between Taryn and Mayar would be the only way to discover if there was a simple antidote to the malware that clearly had infected the Con Ed grid. The alternative would be days, weeks, months - who knows how long - grinding through every line of code embedded in every switch in every substation, while large tracts of New York City lay in darkness.

The FBI had considered substituting one of their own agents, but couldn't take the chance that Mayar had seen photographs of Taryn in the press when the Rosen affair blew up. They would work with NYPD and DHS to ensure Taryn's safety. Snipers on rooftops, undercover cops on the streets, bomb disposal units close at hand - everything humanly possible to protect her.

Could she convince Mayar to rat out her fellow jihadists? It would be Mayar's last chance to save her own life, the FBI emphasized. Clearly embarrassed by their failure to identify the sleeper cell before it struck, the law enforcement officials seemed more than willing to offer Mayar a deal to learn its whereabouts.

The ringtone on her mobile sounded, she hadn't ditched Blake Shelton yet, but the caller was a welcome surprise.

"Jimmy! Wow! Hi! Where are you?"

"Just getting ready to leave the hospital."

"You sound great."

"I still warble a bit, but I was really lucky. My speech came back much faster than my docs expected."

"That's fantastic. It's a crazy day in the city." She wandered into the kitchen to refill her coffee.

"Yeah, I can see out the window. It looks like a ghost town," Jim replied.

"Everyone's staying home before the blackout deadline."

"That's what I wanted to talk to you about. Lou filled me in on some of the details of the investigation."

"Good." Taryn wasn't sure what she could reveal.

"We blew up the photograph of the executioner. We couldn't see much because of the mask, but the scar below his eye matches with a guy who was withdrawing cash from a hawala uptown that we were watching, thanks to input from Israel. We've identified him as Graeme Flanagan. Unfortunately, the FBI interviewed Mr. Flanagan two years ago because of his militant contacts, but didn't follow up. He seemed harmless at the time."

"That was a mistake." She sat down at her kitchen table, sipping her coffee.

"Anyway, we have photos of Flanagan and Tabak in circulation. We're going to catch them and the rest of their gang soon."

"I know we will."

"You don't have to go to the meeting with Tabak today. It's much more dangerous than those suits from headquarters have told you. She could be a walking kamikaze."

"We talked about that." She stood, leaving her cup on the table, and paced back into her living room. "But, I'm in too far to quit now." *And I owe it to Professor Bierman.*

"If Mayar learned that you were the one who killed her brother, she might be setting a trap," Jim said.

"I have to trust my gut. If Tabak and her ISIS friends wanted revenge, why wait almost two months? Something went wrong and Mayar Tabak wants out."

"That's what I thought you'd say. Just be careful. Remember Donal Brogan may still be out there too."

"We haven't had a Donal Brogan sighting in months. And my name was never in the paper anyway. It's Lou, and you, that he'd be going after, not me." Taryn donned an orange windbreaker emblazoned with the Broncos Super Bowl championship logo, her good luck charm.

"I would feel much better if you let us provide some protection for you, particularly if the lights go out," Jim said.

"You're worrying too much. Brogan may be back in Ireland for all we know."

"I'm going to request an extra detail to patrol your street. Just to be safe."

"OK. As long as no one is pacing back and forth in my living room."

"Understood."

"I'll be standing proud at your wedding, don't you worry." Taryn checked her watch. Time to go.

"We're counting on you. Marcy and me." Jim clicked off.

Taryn placed her Beretta in her right-hand pocket and looped a small midnight blue purse across her torso. An NYPD cruiser waited outside her front door to whisk her uptown.

CHAPTER 53

"We're on our own now," Bernie Rosen declared as he hung up the phone He sat behind his desk at City Hall alone with Jackie who had come in at seven to coordinate relief efforts. Only five hours until the terrorists' deadline.

"What did the President say?" she asked.

"The short answer? We're going to make New York great again. The truth is - it's the best he can really do right now." He stood, reaching for his jacket. "Come on, we need to address the troops. They're waiting in the conference room." Bernie reached for his wife's hand. "Maybe we'll print up some hats and tee-shirts with the President's slogan."

"Over my dead body."

***

Mayor Rosen coughed into the microphone to get everyone's attention. "I just got off the phone with the President of the United States. The nation fully stands behind New York, but…" he noticed several sets of eyes rolling upward. "But, America will never pay a ransom. And Washington will not order electrical power diverted from other regions. New York City is just too large. Any re-routing runs the risk of seriously overloading power lines and bringing the whole country down."

"Washington is just going to let New York go dark?" Serena Thomas asked.

"Not quite," the Mayor replied. "The federal government will supply temporary generators for law enforcement, fire department and hospitals. The National Guard will help patrol the streets if we need them. We'll have unlimited federal funds to rebuild our infrastructure."

"Can't our cyberspooks find the virus and eliminate it?" a female voice piped up from the back of the room.

"They're working around the clock, Beverly, but it's not that easy. We have to find every location of the virus and every process that it may attack before we can neutralize it. Otherwise it might just spawn again," Rosen replied, struggling to maintain his patience. "I understand that we may have one last chance to find a silver bullet. We should know by three."

"Otherwise?" Crock asked.

"Otherwise I'm going to order Con Edison to shut off the transmission of electricity. It's the only way to save our grid." He held his breath to let the pronouncement sink in. It didn't take long. The chorus of objections exploded like Fourth of July fireworks.

"Shut off the power?"

"To the entire city?"

"For how long? "

"How much is it going to cost?"

"How am I going to get to work?"

Rosen waited for his staff to calm. "A blackout of New York City will be a catastrophe of enormous proportions," he said, pausing for effect. "But, our city is resilient. We've bounced back from disaster before and we will bounce back again. However, if we allow the terrorists to call the shots, we risk total destruction. The city might never recover from that."

***

No one noticed that Mayar had changed her footwear downstairs, swapping out flats for black ankle boots, the wrap-around strap and buckle securing her secret zip drive in its hiding place. Mumbling grudgingly, Ibrahim scraped over a few inches on the frayed couch in the living room to allow her to squeeze in between him and Osama.

"Shhh," Nimr hushed. "It's starting now."

"A pompous, little Jew," Graeme smirked as the television camera centered on Mayor Rosen stepping up to the podium at City Hall.

"My fellow New Yorkers," Rosen began, but then paused to check his notes. "Despite the herculean efforts of our cyber defense teams both here and in Washington over the past twenty hours, we have yet not been able to eliminate the computer virus that has infected our power transmission grid. Unless I am confident that our grid is secure by four thirty this afternoon, I will have no choice but to order Consolidated Edison to shut off the supply of all electricity to the city at that time. I have complete faith that our military and law enforcement teams will thwart this malicious attack and bring the perpetrators to justice. Unfortunately, the timetable for their success is uncertain. Accordingly, to protect the safety of all citizens, I must order the evacuation …."

Osama and Ibrahim jumped up in jubilation, sandwiching Mayar in their victory dance.

"We've won!"

"The infidels have capitulated!"

"They will sing our names in Raqqa!"

"You fools!" Mayar expectorated, wriggling away from the embrace. Nimr leapt towards her but she pushed him away. "Don't you see. We've lost. The Americans will not pay a ransom. Our country will have no schools, no libraries, no industry. In a few weeks, their electrical grid will be operational again, their defenses will be stronger, and we will be…"

"Dead!" Nimr finished the sentence for her. "We are jihadists, not bureaucrats. We accept our martyrdom for our faith." He grabbed Mayar's wrists and whipped her back on to the couch. Osama and Ibrahim pinned her arms to her side. "Are you afraid to die?"

"We are lackeys for Viktor and his Russian friends. That is all we are," she hissed.

"Fuck!" Graeme exclaimed, pointing to the television and interrupting the inquisition. His photo had now joined Mayar's on the most wanted parade.

"You are a stupid woman," Osama spouted.

"A weak, stupid woman," Ibrahim piled on.

"I am a *mujahid*. And I will die like one. But I will not take orders from you or Viktor any longer," Mayar screeched, twisting her shoulders to loosen her captors' grasps.

"Let her go," Nimr commanded.

The cold calculus of her situation sucked the air from her lungs like a dive into the waves at Brighton Beach in January, but she willed herself to stand upright. *There is only one way I will ever leave this house on my own volition. There is only one way I will complete my jihad.*

"What are you saying?" Nimr asked.

She squared her shoulders and raised her chin. "I will take the battle to the infidel."

***

"Where will you strike?" Nimr asked, surrounded by his cadre in the kitchen.

"My school," Mayar replied.

"The main lawn?"

"Yes," she lied.

"An excellent choice. It will be full of students. I will send Ibrahim with you to insure that you arrive there safely."

"No." *Why? Think fast.* "Ibrahim does not have a student ID. Security will stop him at the gate. I will go alone."

"Are you sure you will be up to the challenge?"

"It is my jihad. Allah will guide me." *Nimr may not trust me but my offer is too good for him to haggle over. The publicity will be priceless to Raqqa.*

"*Alhamdulillah,*" Nimr replied. He nodded crisply as he pointed to Osama, "We must help our brave comrade get dressed."

Osama emerged from the pantry closet with a suicide vest, now weighted with a full load of ball bearings and shrapnel. Mayar raised both arms as he cinched it around her waist. Her shoulders drooped under its heft. She couldn't feel, or see, the cellphone-sized box containing a GPS tracking device and back-up detonator attached to the rear panel.

"Shouldn't you wait at least one more day? To make sure that the virus is working properly?" Graeme asked, hovering behind her.

Nimr shook his head vigorously. "Viktor has assured me that all is in order."

"Yes. It is in Allah's hands now," Mayar concurred.

"The police may be on the look-out for gloves, particularly on a warm day," Osama said, kneeling now with a white wire in hand. "I can run the detonator cord down your leg and into your boot. You will just need to reach down as if you are adjusting your buckle."

"No!" Mayar jerked her leg back and grabbed the snap of her jeans. She had almost forgotten the zip drive. "I am still a Muslim woman. I do not want you touching my legs."

"As you wish," Osama retreated, reaching for an oversized, black burqa from his kit. He helped Mayar ease it over her shoulders, but allowed her to smooth it over her hips by herself. He threaded the twisting cord down her right sleeve and into her palm. "I will tape the switch to your forearm for now."

When Osama had finished, Mayar took a tentative step, then another, stumbling slightly before she regained her composure. Osama handed her a niqab to cover her head. She hesitated for a second, but Nimr again nodded. "Your face is known," he said.

"How will you get to Columbia?" he asked.

"The bicycle in the courtyard would be best."

"I'll get the key for you," Graeme volunteered. He led the way to the front door. "I wish we had more time together," he whispered before she left.

"Me too." Mayar reached for Graeme's hand. "I am in Allah's hands now. *Ila-liqqa.*" It was two o'clock. Her time was running short.

"Yes, we will meet again in Paradise," Graeme leaned over and kissed her lips. "*Allahu Akbar.*"

"*Allahu Akbar,*" she answered, slowly drawing away.

Mayar bent over the once-red bike, fumbling with the lock. Graeme stepped outside to help, then retreated with the chain back into the house. She straddled the bike, arranging the folds of her burqa and balancing her load. Satisfied, she eased onto the seat and pedaled off without a backward glance.

***

Graeme set four AR-15 rifles and four Glocks on the living room floor, stacking extra magazines of ammunition nearby. Osama solemnly placed a suicide vest and black nylon jacket at each place. Staring at the vests for a long second, Graeme prayed that he, that all of them, would have the strength to complete their mission.

A rattle from the basement interrupted his prayers. Nimr and Ibrahim emerged, hoisting a second bike, a black one, between them.

"Allah has delivered a golden opportunity to us today. We must not fail to capitalize on it," Nimr said displaying his phone. A beacon flashed, displaying Mayar's progress west along 149th Street. He reached into his pocket for a second device, handing it to Ibrahim. "Ibrahim will follow our brave comrade to ensure that she does not waver on her route to Paradise."

"You doubt Mayar?" Graeme asked.

"Mayar has wandered off on her own before. You did not think that I would let her stray today, did you?" Nimr replied.

"Mayar is our sister-in-arms. Her faith in Allah is pure," Graeme said, his voice rising in anger.

Ibrahim aimed the remote control out the window, pulling an imaginary trigger. "The *alkulba* will be in Paradise shortly. By her own hand – or mine," he said, displaying a wicked grin.

"No!" Graeme shouted, seizing Ibrahim's wrist.

"Stop fighting, you fools," Nimr commanded as Ibrahim twisted away, setting his feet for combat. "Graeme, we cannot take the chance that Mayar's faith weakens when she is alone among the infidels."

"Then, I will be the one to accompany her," Graeme volunteered.

"Everyone has seen your photograph by now. As Mayar said, there is security on the Columbia campus," Nimr explained. "Ibrahim must be the one for this task. You'll ride with me and Osama."

Graeme twisted to lunge for a pistol, spinning to point it at Ibrahim. "I will not leave Mayar's martyrdom to *him*." It was the first time he had ever defied Nimr.

"You love her, don't you?" Nimr asked softly, stepping between his soldiers, guiding Graeme's gun hand down.

"Yes," Graeme replied, grinding his teeth.

"But, you love Allah even more, don't you?"

"Yes."

"Then you will obey my orders."

"No," Graeme repeated, steel in his voice. "I will not let Ibrahim murder Mayar for his own pleasure."

Nimr's phone beeped, distracting him. "She stopped. Something's wrong." He looked at Graeme.

"I executed the infidel, didn't I?" Graeme challenged.

"You will wear a hat. Low on your forehead," Nimr said as Graeme nodded in agreement. "Stay out of Mayar's sight. Don't spook her, but do not hesitate…"

"How can you question my commitment to Allah?" Graeme sealed the deal.

"Give him the detonator," Nimr commanded Ibrahim.

"But…" Ibrahim protested.

"I said give him the detonator. Now. Mayar may be in trouble."

Graeme tucked the Glock into his belt and the detonator into his pocket. He pushed the bicycle towards the door.

"There is no time to put on the vest," Nimr cautioned, stuffing the pockets of one of the black jackets with extra ammo before handing it to Graeme along with a Mets' cap. "May Allah ride with you."

***

The FBI and NYPD set up shop outside Morningside Park, overrunning the plaza with squad cars, communications vans, ambulances, bomb squad trucks, and SWAT team carriers. It looked like the backlot of a Hollywood movie set, only all the gear was loaded with live ammo.

After her final briefing, Taryn strode away from the HQ trailer, returning nods of good luck from the cops and assault teamers prepping for their assignments. She had white, iPhone-like buds plugged into each ear to relay messages from central command. A dime-sized microphone nestled between her breasts would broadcast her conversation with Tabak back to the support teams.

She hiked along 120th Street, heading west. The block between Amsterdam and Broadway, the north side of the Columbia campus, was a long one. Joe's Coffee Bar overlooking the street from the second floor was packed. Taryn crossed Broadway along with several students.

Uniformed police in full combat gear patrolled the next corner, Claremont Avenue, quietly turning away any casual passers-by. They waved Taryn through with barely a nod. The young couple holding hands ahead of her and the homeless man poking through the garbage can had to be undercover.

Taryn paused as she approached Riverside Park, an oasis of green in a concrete jungle. The gothic spires of the mammoth Riverside Church soared overhead. A jogger emerged from a side door and set off uptown. She scanned the windows but didn't see any bristling rifle barrels, although her earbuds informed her that her support teams were settling into position.

Her phone, tucked into her small purse, buzzed. Command central? No. A text from an unknown overseas number.

Shoot first. Fight dirty. Run fast. L'chaim

Eli was alive and well. Not the most romantic message, she chuckled, but practical advice from a pro. She reached into her pocket to check her pistol, switching off the safety. *L'chaim.*

Taryn swiveled her head in both directions. A white van with a dry cleaner's logo double-parked halfway down the street. A boxy orange and gray U-Haul truck slowed to a stop a block uptown. A hot dog vendor wheeled his cart into place and busied himself rearranging the condiments. But, no sign of Mayar, or anyone else. Riverside Drive, four lanes wide here, was completely devoid of pedestrians or automobile traffic.

She walked across the street, continuing past empty benches and the banked strip of grass that separated the Drive from a well-shaded asphalt path set aside for walkers and bikers. The designated meeting spot was a circular promontory, maybe five paces in diameter, framed by a low stone wall jutting out from the path. Like a castle turret, it commanded the high ground, overlooking a pastoral landscape that dropped off precipitously before tumbling into the Hudson River. Peering through the foliage, she marked a Coast Guard patrol boat tethered close to shore. A helicopter churned overhead.

"Testing, testing," she said to no one in particular as she sat down on the wall to wait.

***

The residents of the Sugar Hill neighborhood on the upper, upper west side, Latino and Caribbean working class, had no place to go, so they congregated in the street to wait for the blackout. Chicken grilled on charcoal; baseballs flew from hands to mitts; the competing aromas of weed and incense wafted skyward.

The sight of a cyclist, completely swathed in black, a narrow slit in her hood revealing only her eyes, was not a welcome one on most days, but it was particularly agitating today with the threat hanging over the city.

A ball, hard and white, glanced off Mayar's shoulder. She flinched, but kept pedaling.

"Perra! Cono! Go back to your own country."

"Fucking Arab!"

Two teenage boys jogged alongside her bike, tossing more insults. One, rasta dreaded hair flopping over his shoulders, reached for her handlebars. The other, acne popping out all over his face, grabbed the rear of her seat. She couldn't risk falling over, so she dropped both of her feet to the pavement.

"Let me go, please," she implored.

"Going to cut someone else's head off?"

"Got a bomb hidden under there?" Zit-face laughed as he reached for the sleeve of her burqa.

"Don't touch me." She brushed his hand away, her eyes wide open in fear. A trio of older men lounging on a nearby stoop sipping from paper-bagged cans turned their heads, but resumed their conversation as if they saw nothing.

"Let go of my bike," she tried again.

"Fuck you," Rasta boy replied, his beer breath assaulting Mayar's senses.

She struggled to maintain her balance. The detonator switch loosened, threatening to pop out of her sleeve. *I should blow these infidels up right now, but I'm not ready to go to Paradise yet. Help me Allah!*

"Hey boys! Leave her alone!" A bespectacled priest in his black frock yelled. He placed a bag of groceries down on the sidewalk and jogged down the street.

"Father Rodriguez! *Mierda!*" The youths shouted in unison as they raced off. Mayar wrestled the handlebars, her knuckles white, to keep the bike upright, while praying the switch stayed hidden.

"Here, let me help," the priest offered, steadying the rear wheel. "I'm sorry. I try to teach the boys to respect members of all religions. But it is hard, particularly today, you understand."

"It is a difficult time for all of us. Thank you. Thank you so much." Mayar lifted her right hand to her eye as though she might cry. *A miracle! Allah had sent his messenger in disguise.*

"Where are you going?" Father Rodriguez asked. He looked Mayar over from head to toe. *Can he see through my clothing?*

"To meet a friend," she replied, re-gripping the handlebars and steadying her nerves.

"Please be careful."

***

Graeme braked as Mayar came into view, talking to a black-frocked priest while two youths sprinted away and ducked into an apartment building. *Is Mayar in trouble? Does she need my help?* Scrunching down, he hesitated, unsure whether to reach for the detonator or the Glock as Mayar's conversation continued. *There are not enough infidels on the street to justify Mayar's martyrdom here anyway.*

He had envisioned a glorious exit from this world. Mayar would send tens, if not hundreds, of infidels to the fires of *Jahannam* as she blasted herself to Paradise. He would mow down the survivors with his pistol offering no mercy to the non-believers. *I welcome my own death. I will spend eternity with Mayar in Jannah.*

Mayar's hand went to her niqab. *Is she taking it off? Was I wrong about her faith?* Hands shaking, he retrieved the detonator from his pocket and sighted it towards Mayar. *Allah is my salvation. Nimr is my leader. They mean more to me than my own mother. I can't let them down now.*

Graeme uncoiled in relief as Mayar stepped up onto her pedal and eased away. She turned left on Riverside Drive and headed downtown. He trailed fifty yards behind.

***

"Drive slowly," Nimr directed from the backseat as Osama steered the yellow taxi down Broadway. Osama didn't need to be told twice. He had packed the trunk of the taxi with explosives the night before. The detonator switch sat in Nimr's lap.

The ride would be short, only thirty blocks or so. Their vehicle was comfortably lost amid the armada of cabs that sailed towards midtown to offer a last chance ride to stragglers escaping the city before the imminent blackout.

Ibrahim rode shotgun, scanning the street for trouble. "Where's Mayar? And Graeme?" he asked as they approached their destination. "We should have passed them by now."

"She's riding down Riverside Drive. Much less traffic there," Nimr replied, checking his phone one more time. "Park over here," he pointed to a vacant spot across from the Columbia campus. "Ibrahim and I will set up outside the main gate. We'll open fire when the students come running away from Mayar's blast. Osama, you wait until the first responders arrive. Then ram them."

303

"And Graeme?" Osama asked.

"He will be in position on the quad. Or in paradise."

"I don't like it," Ibrahim persisted, craning his head to check up and down the boulevard. "Too many cops around. And they're heavily armed. The NYPD Strategic Response Group. What the fuck is that?"

"You sound like a woman now," Osama ribbed.

"We'll see how they respond to this," Ibrahim boasted, fondling the automatic weapon under his jacket.

Nimr scanned his phone again. "Be still. Mayar's almost here."

CHAPTER 54

"Tango approaching southbound in the park."

"She's riding a bike."

"Dressed in black. Head-to-toe."

Taryn bolted upright as she picked up the chatter from command central on her earbuds. She peered along the path but it curved quickly out of sight.

"Passing the Grant Memorial. Two hundred meters to the Turret."

"I don't like it," a woman's voice now. "Tango's struggling to stay balanced."

"Zoom in on her face."

"It's dark under all those trees."

A pause. Taryn trotted uptown to the bend as the bells of Riverside Church tolled.

"One hundred fifty meters to the Turret."

"Someone use their fucking night vision gear."

"Can only see her eyes."

"One hundred twenty-five meters."

"She's either sweating or crying. Neither one is good."

"Stop her! Now!" the woman ordered.

The U Haul roared to life, careening down the embankment. It slammed to a stop, blocking the path fifty meters ahead of Taryn. The rear door opened as two bomb disposal techs, swaddled in space suits, guided a robotic wheelbarrow straight out of Star Wars down the ramp. It sported tank-like treads and a long, hinged arm tipped with yellow pincers. Two more heavily padded cops crouched into shooter's positions on either side of the truck. Another held a muzzled German Shepherd on a tight leash.

Taryn could see Mayar now, pedaling slowly towards them.

"Mayar Tabak. Stop immediately and dismount!" The woman's voice again, now amplified by a bullhorn.

Mayar braked, dropping both her feet to the ground, clearly surprised by the greeting party awaiting her. The bullhorn repeated the command, this time in Arabic. Mayar swiveled her head. A police siren wailed, as another fortified van screeched into view behind her, cutting off any hope of retreat. She swung her right leg over the bike, flinging it to the pavement with a clatter.

"Stay right there!" Back to English.

Mayar raised both hands as if surrendering.

"That's good. Now remain completely still. Keep your hands where we can see them!"

Mayar looked towards the river as if she were contemplating a leap. Her niqab concealed any expression on her face.

"Are you armed?"

"I want to talk to Taryn Booker. I have information that can help," Mayar called out. Hands still aloft, she turned ninety degrees, stepping boldly towards the black wrought iron fence that protected the drop into the park, seemingly unafraid of the consequences. When she reached the fence, she spread her arms, gripping a stanchion with each hand, facing out towards the river.

Taryn approached the cab of the U Haul. "I'm right here," she announced.

"What the fuck do you think you're doing?" The commanding officer, Lauren Rizzo, demanded, wisps of auburn hair straggling from beneath her helmet.

"Trying to help," Taryn replied.

"Stay out of our way then."

"Do you want to be the one responsible for the blackout of New York City?"

"What are you going to do?"

"Talk to her. Sounds like she's coming over to our side."

Mayar stood stock still, an apparition in black, crucified on the fence. Two more pregnant seconds passed in silence.

"It's your life," Rizzo said. "Let's stay frosty," she added for the ears of her troops.

"Thanks." Taryn strode around the truck, stepping into the blast zone.

"Mayar, it's me. Taryn Booker."

Mayar turned slowly, keeping all ten fingers in full view. She pulled the niqab over her head, shaking out her hair. "I thought you'd come."

"Holy shit! There's another Tango on a bicycle! Back there under the tree," a familiar voice barked into Taryn's earbud.

"Who the fuck is this?" Rizzo questioned.

"Special Agent James Mangano. I'm downtown watching the video feeds."

Taryn forced herself to tune out the chatter. "What do you want?" she asked Mayar.

"A trade."

"Is there a kill switch for the virus?"

"No."

"I didn't think so. What do you have to offer then?"

"Are you sure Tango 2's not a friendly bystander?" Rizzo broke back in.

"We're zooming right now," Jimmy said. "There's the scar on his right cheek. That's Graeme Flanagan, ISIS executioner. Identification confirmed."

Taryn slipped her right hand into her jacket pocket to grip her pistol.

"I have the blueprint. It will help you disarm the virus," Mayar answered.

"That could be useful. Where is it?" Taryn asked.

"On a zip drive tucked into my right boot." Mayar raised both hands upward, displaying her empty palms. "I think it's better if you retrieve it."

"Are you wearing a suicide vest?"

"Yes."

"Why?" Taryn took a useless step backwards.

"Why? Because I want a better world for the Islamic State. I want America to stop bombing our cities and killing our children. I want schools - for girls."

"We can make that happen."

"Make what happen?"

"A school for girls. But you have to take off your vest." Taryn reached out with her left hand. "Let me help you."

"No. It is the will of the Prophet."

"No. It's the will of a bunch of frustrated, middle aged men in Raqqa and Moscow who want to play king. Please – don't let them use you anymore."

"How did you know about Viktor?"

"Where is he? Viktor?"

"I don't know." Mayar remained still as stone.

"Mayar, blowing yourself up furthers his cause - not yours." Taryn took a half-step forward. "There has to be a better way."

Mayar hesitated, looking skyward. "It's too late now."

"Foxtrot Oscar do you have eyes on Tango 2?" Rizzo demanded.

"Tango 2 is in my glass," the Forward Observer replied.

"Do I have another confirmation of Tango 2's identity?" Rizzo again.

"Why? What else have you planned?" Taryn gripped the trigger of the Berretta.

"Nothing. I haven't planned anything," Mayar replied, shrinking for the first time.

"Who else is working with you?"

Mayar shook her head.

"Think of Fatima. She's a beautiful little girl. You love her, don't you?

"Yes," Mayar whispered, tears dampening her eyes.

"Tango 2 is confirmed. Graeme Flanagan." A new voice on the wire.

Taryn flinched, but Mayar didn't appear to notice. "Don't you want to see Fatima grow up? Into a world of light not a world of darkness?" She asked.

Mayar remained silent, wavering perhaps. Taryn pressed. "Please tell me more about Viktor. Let Fatima see that her mother has the courage to live and make the world a better place."

"Foxtrot Oscar, go to Red Con One," Rizzo ordered.

"Red Con One confirmed."

"Flanagan's pulling something out of his pocket," Jim Mangano screamed.

"Foxtrot Oscar, you are now cleared hot. Eliminate Mr. Flanagan. Immediately," Rizzo again.

"Please confirm target elimination order," Foxtrot Oscar

demanded.

"Elimination order confirmed."

"Roger."

"Take the zip drive and leave me here." Mayar's countenance hardened even as she displayed her empty hands. "I won't harm you."

Taryn wasn't going to press her luck any longer. She released her grip on the pistol and stepped forward, both hands now in full view. Kneeling, she rolled up the hem of Mayar's burqa, loosened the boot buckle and retrieved the drive. "Come with me. We can work together." *One last try.*

"You should go now, sister," Mayar said.

"I'm not your sister," Taryn replied as she backed off, her gaze never wavering from Mayar's eyes.

"Tango 2 eliminated," Foxtrot Oscar stated calmly.

Mayar broke away first, returning to her perch overlooking the river. She lifted her face up to the sun. A zephyr ruffled her curls.

Taryn darted back to safety behind the bomb disposal truck, her shoulders knotted in anticipation of Mayar's suicide blast. Lauren Rizzo huddled next to her, offering a handshake. "Well done," she said.

***

"Mayar's chickened out," Ibrahim squirmed in the shotgun seat. "I knew she would."

"The infidels could have captured her," Nimr came to Mayar's defense, and his own.

"Where's Graeme then? Has he gone soft on us too?" Ibrahim pressed.

"Something's definitely wrong," Osama added. "We need to get out of here."

"It's too late now," Nimr declared, staring out the rear window of the taxi.

Two blue and white NYPD vans barricaded Broadway. A picket line of SWAT teamers in full riot gear formed a Spartan wall of shields on both sides. The barrels of automatic rifles protruded from the menacing cordon.

Osama started the ignition and shifted into drive. Ibrahim placed a restraining hand on the steering wheel. "There's nowhere to go," he said, flicking his eyes forward to watch a bright red fire truck wheel into position. Another team of tactical response troops sprinted to its flanks.

"You are surrounded. Come out with your hands up!" A loudspeaker commanded first in English, then in Arabic.

"We will fight here," Nimr ordered, checking the magazine on his rifle. "On my count…"

Osama couldn't wait. He jammed open the car door and rolled out, spraying a blossom of bullets down Broadway. Returning volleys ripped from both sides, exploding his head like a candy-stuffed piñata. The barrage shattered both windshields of the taxi. Ibrahim's body danced into the now vacant driver's seat while his brains splashed over the dashboard.

Hot lead burned a gaping wound in Nimr's shoulder, but he was still alive. *What happened to Mayar and Graeme? Did they desert the cause?* He would never believe that. Slumping down to the floor, he struggled to clasp the detonator in his good hand. He forced his brain to envision nubile virgins romping through a flowering desert. The cacophony of gunfire receded. One last deep breath. "Allahu Akbar!"

***

Wearing a headset to communicate with central command, Bernie Rosen watched the video feeds on separate screens in his office at City Hall. He pumped his fist and cheered as Taryn scampered to safety.

"Maybe I was wrong about her," Jackie commented, standing beside her husband, while a cadre of top staffers milled about.

The office erupted in shock as a fireball exploded on the second screen. Broadway lay in ruins when the smoke subsided: a tree trunk impaled in what had been a shop window; the burnt-out shell of a taxi flipped upside down, leaving an arm lying unattached on the asphalt.

"Any casualties on our side?" the mayor asked. "Unknown," he repeated the response. Bernie watched for another five minutes, the video feed switching to a view from a helicopter overhead, before tossing his headset on his desk. "I'm going to need the room now," he announced.

After his staff departed, Rosen sat down behind his desk as his wife paced behind him. He made a final round of calls: NSA, Homeland Security, NYPD, fire department, sanitation, health services. Brief updates, terse commands, words of encouragement.

He rose and walked over to the window. 4:25PM. A smattering of offices in the building across the plaza were still lit.

Jackie slipped her hand into his. "It's time," she said.

Mayor Bernie Rosen lifted his phone off its cradle. Katherine Whitworth completed the connection. Tom Murphy answered in his office at Con Ed.

"Turn out the lights," Rosen commanded.

CHAPTER 55

Far downtown, Bank Street also rumbled from the explosion on upper Broadway as the news spread on television and social media. A stay-at-home mom in pink sweats, a same sex couple, both artists wearing paint-smeared smocks, schoolchildren giddily looking forward to an extended vacation, and a Broadway headliner congregated in the street trying to assess the meaning of the blast.

"The terrorists are dead!"

"Is the blackout over?"

"Does that mean we have to go to school tomorrow?"

"Fucking Muslims, pardon my language kids."

With a battered leather messenger bag slung across his shoulder, Donal Brogan lingered on the outskirts of the gathering. He had been in position outside of Booker's apartment since early morning, watching in bewilderment as a police cruiser dropped his target off and then picked her up again a few hours later, frustrating any opportunity for a shot. *Booker didn't have police protection yesterday.*

Two police officers on horseback approached, a new addition to the street's security detail. *Were they in place to protect Booker too?* No matter, he was prepared as well. Donal slipped his right hand into his bag to grip the comforting weight of his Sig. The faces of his three brothers danced in his head.

"No change to the mayor's plan to turn off the lights, at least as far as we know," Simone Williams, an African-American with straightened, shoulder length black hair sneaking out from under her riding helmet, announced from the saddle.

Her partner, Sean O'Rourke, a scarlet-cheeked young Irishman, appeared to be listening to a command in his earbud. "She's five minutes away," he commented quietly. "We should take our positions."

The cops separated, walking their horses towards opposite ends of the block. The throng slowly dispersed, heading back inside to await further news. Donal trotted on foot beside his fellow Irishman.

"Another big VIP moving in on Bank Street, eh lad?" he asked, adding an extra dose of brogue to his inflection.

"I don't know about that. We just got a rush order are to add a bit of protection for a young woman who lives here," O'Rourke replied helpfully. "Might be someone famous, I guess." He added with a conspiratorial nod.

Donal quickly checked out the street. Almost deserted now. No moving vehicles in sight.

He made a great show of pumping his arms to catch up to the mounted cop. Drawing even, he stuttered, gagged wildly, and fell, making sure to land between two parked cars.

"What the hell?" O'Rourke exclaimed. "Are you OK man?"

Donal lay still in the shadows, a few feet from the horses' hoofs. He reached for the switchblade in his boot.

O'Rourke dismounted, holding the reins with one hand as he leaned over to help. Donal clasped his forearm and yanked him downward. With assassin's speed, he slashed his knife across the cop's throat, blood splattering the blue uniform.

"My apologies," Donal muttered as he rolled the dying policeman over, eyes fluttering as he passed on to a better place. He unbuckled the powder blue helmet and tugged it off in one motion. Donal squeezed the helmet on to his own head, a tight fit but manageable. O'Rourke's shirt, now stained crimson, would be useless. But there was an NYPD windbreaker lashed to the saddle of the horse, waiting patiently three feet away.

Donal stroked the horse's mane as he donned the jacket. He shifted his Sig to the pocket and tossed his messenger bag to the curb. The Brogan family farm in County Down had a stable of three horses which the brothers took turns riding as they grew up. He surveyed the street again. No signs of alarm. He jammed a foot into the stirrup and swung into the saddle. Keeping the reins in his left hand, he walked the horse slowly back down Bank Street. The fingers of his right hand stayed buried out of sight, curled around the trigger of his pistol.

Donal flinched as a horn beeped behind him. A police cruiser glided alongside, the driver giving a friendly salute to a fellow officer. Donal could see Taryn Booker sitting alone in the back seat. After the cruiser passed, he nudged his horse to pick up the pace.

The cruiser pulled to a stop at the curb in front of Booker's apartment building. Her escort popped out of the shotgun seat to open the rear door.

Williams, approaching from the far side of the block, quickly recognized trouble. "What the hell? Where's O'Rourke?" she shouted, spurring her horse towards Donal.

Donal yanked the reins hard, stopping his horse in its tracks. His right hand emerged from hiding, firing off a quick burst from the Sig. Williams toppled off her horse, crashing onto the street.

Features contorted in shock, the cop holding the back door of the cruiser reached for his gun. Donal's second burst ripped his face apart before he could unholster it. At the first sound of gunfire, Taryn dove face down on the back seat and out of sight.

"Officer down! Officer down!" the driver shouted into his radio. He stomped on the gas pedal and swerved hard left to pull away from the curb into the middle of the street. A mistake. It opened the driver up to Donal's pistol. He emptied the magazine into the cruiser's door and window. The driver slumped over the steering wheel, its horn blaring his death song.

Donal scanned the carnage for his true target, his view blocked by the fractured windows of the bullet-riddled cruiser. His horse whinnied, trying to turn away, but he kept the steed moving forward. He reached into his pocket for another magazine and jammed it into the Sig.

Taryn didn't wait for the next volley. She plunged out the door and barrel-rolled towards the curb, the clink of her Beretta falling on asphalt registering briefly in her racing mind. She tucked behind a parked gray minivan, peeking around the bumper to see her pistol lying on the ground underneath the patrol car, well out of her reach.

"Booker!" Donal roared, as he leaned down to peer into the rear seat.

Williams' horse lingered only a few feet away, bravely standing guard over the patrolwoman's lifeless body. Launching from her hiding place, Taryn sprinted to its side, vaulting into the saddle as

Donal and his mount stepped around the wreckage.

Klaxons sounded in the distance. Taryn kicked her horse's flanks and galloped towards the wail. Leaning forward, she clung to the horse's neck as she heard a volley of bullets whistle by. Her blue purse flapped against her hip.

She ripped the reins hard right at the corner onto Greenwich, a narrow tree-lined residential street. "Come on, baby. Step on it," she urged, prodding her horse to speed against the one-way. A black Toyota, driver's eyes wide open in surprise, veered out of her path and smashed into a parked yellow taxi. No other moving vehicles were in sight.

Donal made the turn as well, the hoofs of his horse clattering against the pavement. He fired wildly, cursing as his bullets shattered a ground floor window.

Taryn galloped across West 11th, also devoid of traffic on blackout day. Donal gained ground as they passed the Spotted Pig pub. A couple, sitting outside on the ivy-covered patio, dove under their table as the chase swept by.

Donal fired again. Taryn's horse lurched, sagging to its front knees, tossing her forward. She fought to keep her feet in the stirrups as her momentum came to a sudden halt. A spray of blood washed over her back. The animal toppled to its side, pinning Taryn's right leg under its dying body.

Taryn screamed in pain. She tried to twist free but her leg was trapped. Donal braked ten feet away and jumped down from his mount, a gloat of triumph creasing his face. The police sirens were closer now, but they would not arrive in time.

Shoot first. Fight dirty. Run fast. Eli's text flashed through Taryn's mind. She fought through the pain to shift her torso. The purse hanging around her neck now dangled within reach.

"Booker! It's your turn to die!" Donal planted both feet, pistol in hand. He stared at his quarry, spittle leaking from his lips.

Taryn slid her right hand into the purse, the compact Derringer pistol fit neatly in her palm. Holding two bullets, accurate only at close range, it was her weapon of last resort. But Donal was still too far away. If he pulled the trigger now, she was dead.

She slowly propped herself up with her left arm, a searing pain erupting from her lower body with every twitch. Her brain screamed to stop and lie down. Taryn shook the hair from her eyes and focused on Donal. She needed to lure him three steps closer.

"Please, please. Don't shoot me." He would want to hear her beg.

"What did you say, woman?" Donal's right foot approached.

"I'm trapped. My leg is broken. Please don't shoot." A wave of agony swept over her. She fought to stay conscious.

"You're asking me for mercy? After you murdered Michael and Timmy?" He took another step closer.

"I'm sorry. I'm sorry." Taryn ducked her head in mock shame, her hair tumbling over her right hand, camouflaging its movement. Her finger closed on the Derringer's trigger.

"Look at me. I want to see your face when you die." Donal's boots crunched louder.

Taryn pitched forward, peeking up. She locked her left elbow for support forcing through the pain. Donal lowered his pistol as he approached. It was now or never.

She lifted her head, tossing her hair out of her vision, and extended her right hand, firing off both shots in rapid succession. Donal didn't see her weapon until it was too late. The first bullet sliced through his chest; the second one blasted his skull.

Sirens blaring, three police cruisers and an ambulance wheeled into view. Taryn dropped her head to the asphalt and passed out.

EPILOGUE

"If I had known how deep was the sea, I never would have swum;
If I had known my end, I never would have begun."

Nizar Qabbani
Letter from Under the Sea

CHAPTER 56

Jim Mangano picked his way through the throng of spectators milling in anticipation on the roadway leading down from the Brooklyn Bridge on to Center Street in Manhattan. The sun had just dipped below the taller buildings, casting a gray cloak of twilight over the east side. The skyline looked like a punch-drunk prizefighter, lights out but still standing.

For the past three weeks, sunset had marked the time for New Yorkers to shutter their windows, bolt their doors and patrol their neighborhood streets - colonial times revisited. The Great Blackout had thinned the city's population by half but New York had survived.

Tonight, the bright lights of Broadway would shine again. People had staked out spots on the bridge hours ago when the news began to percolate. They spread beach towels, fired up charcoal grills, and prepared to open that special bottle saved for the big occasion. The tent city lining the shore of the East River, nicknamed Jackieville in recognition of the daily food deliveries orchestrated by the mayor's wife, already bristled with campfires.

A cheer erupted when a stripe of windows illuminated high up on the Freedom Tower. Just testing, the National Guardsmen on patrol informed the crowd. The big show would start at dark.

"Slow down, Jimmy," Marcy huffed as she caught up to her fiancé. "You'll hurt yourself."

"I bet it's a zoo down there already," he replied without dropping his pace.

"Are you sure there's a spot for us? We can just watch from

here." Marcy linked her hand on Jim's elbow.

"Taryn reserved two seats for us right on the City Hall plaza. Lou brought the tickets by the apartment yesterday."

"Where's she going to be?" Marcy's grip tightened as she asked the question.

"Up on the podium with all the big shots."

***

John Cabot pushed off from the dock in the Rodney Bay Marina in St. Lucia, the spires of the Piton Mountains looming over the lush foliage. He had taken a sabbatical from Credit Lafayette, setting sail from Greenwich Harbor the day before the blackout. He planned to journey around the world. Solo. No rush. Plenty to think about.

His friends said he was crazy. Tormented by the deaths of his wife and son. They were right on the last counts.

***

Allison Gold packed her tote for the third time, the realization that she would need little taking a long time to sink in. She would be leaving in the morning with her parents for the drive to the minimum security federal women's prison camp near Alderson, West Virginia, to serve a one year sentence for computer tampering. Her lawyer had hoped she could avoid jail time completely, but this was the best deal the prosecutors would offer. The penalties for espionage and treason were much more severe.

Hayden Bierman had been more forgiving, replying gracefully to Allison's letter of apology. No one would ever know the true motive for the Professor's assassination, but Allison would live the rest of her life with the knowledge that her actions might have contributed to his untimely death.

***

"You're gonna miss it," Constance Booker yelled from the den of the ranch house in Carbondale.

"I'm coming. I'm coming," Mark strode in from the kitchen, wooden spoon still in hand. He dropped down on the couch next to

320

his daughter. "Dinner'll keep."

"Wish we could airmail a plate to Sis. She looks like she hasn't eaten in a month," Constance quipped as the television announcer pointed out the mayor's guests standing on the top step of City Hall. "She could've put on some make-up at least."

"Give your sister a break, Con," Mark replied. "Taryn's worked her butt off."

"When's the mayor going to turn the lights on?"

"He's a politician. He's got to make a speech first, right?" Mark zinged. "But seriously, that Rosen has been a real leader. When I first saw him on TV, I didn't think he'd last a month as mayor. Now, people are talking about him running for President one day."

***

Mayar Tabak sat alone in her cell in the maximum-security penitentiary in Florence, Colorado, reading the Quran. She wore the standard prisoner's uniform, khaki slacks and work shirt. A simple white hijab covered her hair. She could have watched the lighting ceremony on television, but she didn't care about New York City anymore.

The information on Mayar's zip drive had saved the city months of time in finding and eliminating the virus in the electrical grid. Despite endless hours of interrogation, she had nothing else to offer. Everyone she knew in ISIS was dead, except Viktor who was untraceable and likely unprosecutable as well. *Did Viktor even exist at all? Or was he just a false front for a larger organization that manipulated her little sleeper cell to attack New York City?*

Mayar had pleaded guilty to assorted counts of terrorism and sabotage, so that she could start her prison term as quickly as possible. The judge had factored her cooperation into her sentence. She expected to be released in time for Fatima's college graduation.

I may be in prison, but my jihad is not over. As far as she could understand, the Quran defined jihad as the struggle for the sake of God. It didn't say jihadists had to embark on a holy war or murder innocent people. The women of Palestine and Raqqa still needed schools, libraries, hospitals, and, most of all, opportunity. Her jihad could have taken a different path, but it was too late now. She would keep striving to serve Allah even from here.

Goodnight Moon, lying open on Mayar's bed, reminded her of happier days. Her fingers quivered as she thought about how close she had come to detonating her suicide vest, but, she reminded herself again, she had made a conscious decision to live. *Graeme didn't push the button either, Praise Allah. A small triumph for love over death. Maybe they would meet in Paradise. Someday.*

Mayar determined to make the rest of her life worthwhile. Taryn Booker had vowed to uphold the bargain that they had struck on Riverside Drive. That was the best that she could ask for right now.

***

Russian tanks retreated from the Ukrainian border, reversing a week-long, military build-up that had threatened to escalate into a full-scale invasion. Kremlinologists believed that America's overwhelming response to the New York City black-out discouraged Moscow from pursuing its dreams of reunification.

Armed with Professor Bierman's financial investigation, Mayar's confession, Allison's RAT and Taryn's research into the virus code, Washington publicly accused Moscow of playing a major role in the cyberattack on Con Edison. Moscow vigorously disputed the charge, calling the evidence "circumstantial at best." In response, our President pushed for the reallocation of funds from the construction of a physical barrier along the Mexican border to the construction of a cyberwall protecting our country's critical infrastructure from hack attacks.

***

Leaning on her crutches, Taryn stood on the top row of the City Hall steps along with twenty policemen, firemen, sanitation workers, doctors and nurses who had been singled out for their exceptional performance during the blackout. She wore a classic blue FDNY tee and gray sweatpants to cover the cast that ran from her right ankle up to mid-thigh, while the others wore their service uniforms in various state of grime and disrepair.

Leadership of these respective organizations sat in white folding chairs in the front row below the steps on the plaza. Their uniforms, suspiciously starched, must have been helicoptered in for the occasion.

She waved to Jim and Marcy when they sat down next to Rhonda and Karim.

The bank of television lights was the brightest that Taryn had seen since her stay in the hospital the first night of the blackout. Although hobbled, she still sat side by side with the techs from the NSA, the FBI, and Con Edison in a dimly lit trailer parked downtown at the base of Whitehall Street near the Staten Island Ferry terminal. With fresh fruit and vegetables delivered by boat, a corner spot for her sleeping bag in the tent that served as the women's dorm, harbor breezes to rustle the body odors and port-a-johns that were flushed out daily, her blackout accommodations were far better than most New Yorkers'.

Taryn watched a plume of white smoke trail across the twilight sky. *Professor Bierman is still watching over me.* Commercial air traffic would resume from JFK in a few hours, albeit on a limited basis. She had just learned the day before that a first-class ticket on tonight's red-eye to Tel Aviv bore her name. The Israeli Defense Force had granted Eli two weeks' leave starting tomorrow. She would be there to welcome him home.

Taryn also had another mission in Israel. She would be meeting with Palestinian officials in Ramallah to lay the groundwork for the creation of the Riverside School for Girls. Mayar had suggested the name during Taryn's one brief visit to Riker's Island before Mayar was shipped out. Through the bulletproof partition, they had shared their passion for education and opportunity for women. Not quite a sisterly bond, but maybe the start of a partnership.

The crowd stood to applaud when the fire department's band began to play "New York, New York." The noise notched up another decibel level when Bernard and Jacqueline Rosen, holding hands, stepped out of the City Hall rotunda and onto center stage. The mayor wore crisp khakis and a denim work shirt open at the neck, while his wife wore jeans and a black jersey newly minted for the occasion. On the front was the city seal with the headline, SURVIVOR - NYC 2018. When she turned to greet the honorees on the steps, the assemblage got raucous. The back of her shirt read "DARKNESS CAN NOT DEFEAT US."

As the cheering swelled, Taryn could see a victory smile break across Jackie's face and a tear well in her eye. The First Couple worked their way slowly down the line, stopping to say a few words with each guest.

Taryn fidgeted in her place, wishing she could scratch the sweaty, itchy skin under her cast. She was apprehensive about her first face-to-face meeting with the Rosen's.

The mayor took the lead, shaking Taryn's hand and inquiring about her leg. *A typical "kiss the baby" greeting.*

Jackie, however, reached out for a motherly embrace. "I hear you have a nice Jewish guy waiting for you," the first lady whispered, a twinkle in her eye.

"I'm not sure about …"

"Good men are hard to find, you know."

"I'll try to remember that," Taryn laughed, shaking her head in surprise, her ticket to Tel Aviv no longer a mystery.

With the last greeting complete, the mayor stepped up to the podium. He asked for a moment of silence for those who had lost their lives during the blackout. Then, he pivoted ninety degrees to face the American flag billowing over City Hall. Everyone on the plaza rose to stand at attention as the band launched into *God Bless America.* After the music faded, the mayor waited patiently for the crowd to hush.

Taryn adjusted her crutches and surveyed the plaza. The clock stopped. The breeze died. People froze in place. The portrait of this moment would sit alongside Washington crossing the Delaware, Lincoln at Gettysburg, the marines on Iwo Jima, and President Bush at Ground Zero, preserved for eternity on museum walls, tee shirts and beer mugs.

Taking his place in history, Mayor Bernie Rosen tugged an imaginary switch with his right hand. "Let there be light!" he pronounced.

And there was light.

ABOUT THE AUTHOR

SM Smith has longed to write fiction since high school, but needed to "detour" through a career in the investment world first. As one of the first Wall Street analysts to specialize in the information industry, and then as the co-founder of a successful hedge fund, Smith has researched and invested in the technology sector for the past thirty years. *Darkness is Coming* is Smith's second novel, but he is already at work on the next. If you are interested in receiving updates, please email brooklyn25518@gmail.com.

Made in the USA
Middletown, DE
13 July 2022

69267483R00186